GALEN SWORD
MUST HIDE SOON .. !

"Saul Calder is shifting shape," Martin said.

Startled, Sword looked quickly from Calder's rocking human form to Martin and back again. He felt the hairs on his arms stiffen as he stared at Calder. The shape shifter's hands weren't clutched to his chest anymore. They were now clenched about the small leather pouch that hung around his neck. From within that leather pouch, a familiar red glow began to pulse.

At that instant, as Sword felt himself once again rushing toward the mad violence of the First World, Calder's head snapped up, jarringly underlit by the red energy pouring out beneath him. It was no longer a human face, but a beast's, which stared out at them.

D1386544

Exploring New Realms
in Science Fiction/Fantasy Adventure

Titles already published or in preparation:

Echoes of the Fourth Magic by R. A. Salvatore

When a U.S. submarine set out from Miami and was drawn off-course by the murderous magic of the Devil's Triangle, Officer Jeff DelGiudice survived the terrifying plunge through the realms. But his good fortune had a shocking consequence. He found himself stranded in a strange world awaiting its redeemer. Here four survivors ruled the corner of the once-great Earth with the ways of white magic ... until one of them tasted the ecstasy of evil. Thalasi, Warlock of Darkness, had amassed an army to let loose death and chaos, and only the hero promised in the guardians' legends can defeat such power. Now Jeff must face his destiny — in a dangerous, wondrous quest to lead humankind's children back to the realms of Light.

The Earthsea Trilogy by Ursula Le Guin
Wizard of Earthsea • The Tombs of Atuan
The Farthest Shore

As long ago as forever and as far away as Selidor, there lived the dragonlord and Archmage, Sparrowhawk, the greatest of the great wizards — he who, when still a youth, met with the evil shadow-beast; he who later brought back the Ring of Erreth-Akbe from the Tombs of Atuan; and he who, as an old man, rode the mighty dragon Kalessin back from the land of the dead. And then, the legends say, Sparrowhawk entered his boat, *Lookfar*, turned his back on land, and without wind or sail or oar moved westward over sea and out of sight.

THE CHRONICLES OF GALEN SWORD

BOOK 2
NIGHTFEEDER

JUDITH AND GARFIELD
REEVES-STEVENS

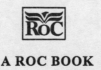

A ROC BOOK

For Denyse, Don, Gary, Dave, and all at T. D. Royal
Orchard for letting us bank on their support and
encouragement time after time.

ROC

Published by the Penguin Group
Penguin Books Ltd, 27 Wrights Lane, London W8 5TZ, England
Penguin Books USA Inc., 375 Hudson Street, New York, New York 10014, USA
Penguin Books Australia Ltd, Ringwood, Victoria, Australia
Penguin Books Canada Ltd, 10 Alcorn Avenue, Toronto, Ontario, Canada M4V 3B2
Penguin Books (NZ) Ltd, 182–190 Wairau Road, Auckland 10, New Zealand

Penguin Books Ltd, Registered Offices: Harmondsworth, Middlesex, England

First published in the USA 1991
First published in Great Britain 1992
10 9 8 7 6 5 4 3 2 1

Copyright © Judith and Garfield Reeves-Stevens, 1991
All rights reserved

The moral right of the authors has been asserted

 Roc is a trademark of Penguin Books Ltd

Printed in England by Clays Ltd, St Ives plc

ONE

Alone and unprotected on the deserted beach, the vampire waited for the sun to rise.

It was his ritual; its origin lost in the mist of too many centuries of memories—his own and those whose lives had nourished him, now bound within his heart and soul forever. Because he was a vampire, he knew what forever truly was.

There on the beach, the surf calm in the still air before dawn, the slate sky to the east slowly brightening as the far western stars glimmered in the last deep blue of night, the vampire felt his body resonate with the conflicting echoes of lives consumed beyond his ability to count. Each lost name called out to him, struggling to be his own. Each hidden voice cried to tell its story. But the vampire knew there were only three truths within the chaos. Three truths above all.

His name *was* Orion.

The sun was his enemy.

And he would survive again.

A lance of white fire erupted from the rounded crest of the coastal mountains before him and Orion clenched his fists at his sides as he bore the first brunt of the sun's assault. His olive eyes narrowed in the brilliant glare but he did not, would not look away.

The sun rose and Orion called out his challenge to it.

A full third of the sun's disk blazed above the mountains now and the vampire's shadow stretched out behind him to the rising waves of the Pacific. Gusts of wind rose up to blow his long brown hair away from the hard and handsome planes of his face, and flap his loose white shirt and pants against his straining muscles.

His war was not just with the sun.

It was with nature.

Orion's hoarse cry of defiance became a bellow of torment as the searing rays of sunlight enveloped him. His bare toes dug into the moist sand like talons. Dark scarlet blood dripped from the wounds his own nails dug within the palms of his clenched fists. Instinctively, his razor-sharp feeding incisors slid from their hidden sockets behind his human teeth and extended to their full fighting length. His vision clouded with overwhelming rage.

Then, in his challenge to the sun, in his cry to nature, suddenly one word was clear above all else.

"*Iiiiisis!*"

This was his agony worse than any the sun could inflict, for his Clan was Isis, and he was the last adept to carry its name.

Now, half the killing disk bulged above the mountains and Orion knew he had won enough of his battle for today. He wrenched his stinging, tearing eyes from the fierce face of his enemy and ran forward from the beach to the small white clapboard house that waited silently for him, set back from the Malibu beach, his refuge from the day and those who would destroy him.

Even with the force of the light still burning on his skin and in his flesh, he ran faster than the sun could rise to stop him, swifter than the scorching wind that poured forth from the morning's approach, more silently than the smallest drops of water that fell from frothing waves upon the beach's sand. He *had* survived again and, as he did from all that gave him life, he once again had taken from nature those powers with which she had tried to crush him.

Within moments, Orion was safe within the shade of the beach house's old and sandscarred porch. He paused then, one hand braced against a thick wooden pillar, filling his lungs with cool air, feeling the hideous flush still fading from his golden skin, watching the sun's glimmer spread on the rising waves as a general watches the enemy's troops regroup to attack again. Someday, he knew he would see the sun's full disk rise into the terrible blue sky and he would stand beneath its glare at noon. On that day, he would be invincible, and those who had destroyed Clan Isis would at last be repaid for their treachery.

But until that day, Orion had other, more compelling concerns, and if those vampires who had passed successfully through the centuries had learned anything from their immortality, it was that patience was always rewarded. Always.

Secure within the shadows, Orion's eyes slowly cleared and the full range of his hypersensitive vision was restored. He focused on the tangle of scrub and twisted trees that surrounded the isolated beach house, probing for the flowing black forms of those who guarded him during the day. Perhaps alone of all the creatures of the First and Second Worlds, only the Seyshen could match a vampire's prowess—though it was not a battle Orion would seek out. For now, by the terms of the treaty, their presence around his refuge gave him sanctuary from the assassins of Tepesh and the constant threat of black hunters.

But nothing moved within the scrub, no shadows flowed.

Orion's lips parted as he began his search again, eyes tracking through the landscape with the precision of a hawk's, his mouth gently drawing in the air to taste for the presence of his guards.

Nothing.

He had been abandoned. Protection lifted. After thirty-eight cycles, the treaty had been abrogated without warning.

Orion's hand gripped the porch pillar he rested against and, without his awareness, the solid timber splintered beneath his fingers. Burning now with swift anger instead of pain, he turned his back on the day and pushed into the shuttered depths of the beach house. There was a telephone inside, a human toy which required no wires or connections. He had been given a number he could call—if there were any left who would answer. The telephone had been part of the treaty that had brought him here.

The door to the porch slammed shut behind him, encasing him in lifegiving blackness. He halted abruptly, commanding his heart to stop its pounding, willing himself to calmness. He was in danger.

Something moved to his side. He heard the ripple of wooden louvers covering a window just as a dozen parallel shafts of sunlight sprang into the room, striping the wooden floor at his feet.

The vampire remained still, inches from the threatening light, and squinted through the swaths it sliced through the dust-filled air. A backlit figure sat in an armchair by the window, swinging the louver cord idly in its hand.

"A thousand apologies, vampire." The figure's voice was soft and whispery with a distinct British accent, bred in the highest circles. "I did not expect you to be out of your pod so late in the morning." The louvers remained open and Orion had no doubt who he faced, *what* he faced past the cloaking glare of the sun.

The vampire reached out without looking to the light switch on the wall behind him, knowing exactly where it would be. An overhead fixture came on and lessened the contrast between daylight and darkness with a dull tungsten glow.

For an instant in that added light, it seemed as if in the chair by the window a shadow twisted like oil on water, but by the time Orion's eyes had adjusted to the new light level in the room, the Seyshen had reformed in its open aspect—a perfect human male. Orion recognized the creature. It was Gérard.

"Where are the sentinels?" Orion asked. It was a simple matter to keep his voice even, but keeping his fangs retracted required great effort.

Gérard smiled. In his open aspect, the Seyshen's teeth were shockingly white, precisely even, framed by lips full and soft. His face was narrow, but exquisitely balanced. His eyes dark, intelligent, quick. His black hair slicked back tight against his skull.

"Have they been withdrawn so soon?" the Seyshen replied. He reached within his white linen jacket and withdrew a black enameled cigarette case, snapping it open without taking his eyes from Orion. He slid a thin white cigarette from the case.

"We have an arrangement," Orion said. "The sentinels are to be present always during daylight."

"The period of your greatest vulnerability," Gérard agreed consolingly, drawing out the final word. He dabbed the end of the cigarette's tip against his tongue and the slender white cylinder came away glowing red and smoking. The Seyshen turned the cigarette elegantly in his fingers and took a long draw from it.

Orion flicked his eyes around the parts of the beach house he could see, listening intently for sounds from those other parts he could not, trying to determine if he and the Seyshen were alone. "Am I to assume that the conditions of our arrangements have been changed somehow? Without discussion?'' The small house seemed empty to Orion's heightened senses, though if other Seyshen were present in their closed aspect, he knew it would be difficult for even a vampire to be certain.

Gérard sensually rolled the smoke from his mouth. ''What could there possibly be to discuss, vampire?''

At least a vampire was direct, Orion thought bitterly. At least a vampire, having chosen a nourisher, took that nourisher cleanly and quickly. But the Seyshen were like cats with mice. They lived for the hunt and not its culmination.

''The war with the Clan Arkady, for one,'' Orion said. He knew that conflict had been brewing for years, ever since the elemental adept, Tomas Roth, Regent to the Clan Pendragon, had become consort to Morgana LaVey, Arkady's Victor. The Seyshen were determined to prevent the shapeshifters of Arkady from amassing any more power within the First World, and Clan Arkady had clearly known that the Seyshen would be assembled against it. An open war between the two clans had been inevitable for years, for thirty-eight cycles.

But Gérard raised his eyebrows, ''War with . . . Arkady?''

Orion felt a chill of uncertainty. Could Arkady have been defeated so quickly? Before the war had even begun? ''That *is* why Clan Seyshen concluded its treaty with Clan Isis,'' Orion said. He was to have been a living weapon in the Seyshen arsenal. They would keep him safe during daylight, holding him in reserve until the war was declared. In the First World, no shifter dared take on a vampire by choice. With his presence alone enough to change the tide of battle, Orion was as close as the Seyshen could come to a guaranteed victory over Arkady.

''Times change, vampire,'' Gérard said lightly. ''What is true one day, is . . . open . . . the next.'' A perfect ring of smoke rolled from his rounded lips, appearing to pulsate as it flared and dimmed and flared again, moving through the bands of light streaming through the shutters.

Orion knew then that he truly had been abandoned. Once more he was alone. But how had it happened? And why?

Orion fought to keep the icy shock he felt from his voice.

''Last night was to have been Arkady's Ceremony of the Change. Your strategists had expected the entire clan would go to shifterform in preparation for the war.'' Gérard maintained his expression of bland amusement. Orion pressed on. "I do not believe that even the Seyshen could have defeated the entire Clan Arkady in one night, by themselves."

"Perhaps . . . we had help," Gérard suggested, taking a final draw from his cigarette. The smoke from it swept away from the Seyshen as if being repulsed by an electric charge in the air surrounding him.

"*I* was to have been your help, Gérard. And even with my help, you could not have defeated an entire clan of shifters in one night. Nothing in the First World is that powerful."

Gérard rolled the stub of his cigarette between his palms. When he took his hands apart, the stub was gone. "Perhaps . . . our help was not First World."

Orion frowned. He had no knowledge of any within the Shadow World with substance enough to alter the balance of power between the clans. "A *halfling* gave you the advantage you needed?" But the idea was absurd. Since only one of a halfling's parents was an adept, a halfling's substance could only be less, not more than what would be found in the First World.

"A halfling?" Gérard repeated. Then he smiled silkily again. "Whatever made you think our help came from the *Shadow* World?"

For an instant, Orion stopped breathing, so great was his surprise. "The *Second* World?" he asked.

Gérard's smile grew.

"A *human* helped you *defeat* Arkady during the Ceremony of the Change?"

The Seyshen could not resist and let a bit of its true self slip out into its open aspect. The smile Gérard wore grew even broader, stretching across the full width of his face, angling up to his ears, gleaming teeth appearing in even rows behind the splitting skin of the Seyshen's human disguise.

"Impossible," Orion said flatly, ignoring how the Seyshen's head was bisected by its gaping grin. He had seen far worse sights in his centuries.

"Then where are your sentinels, vampire?" Gérard's mouth melted back into something more human. "Arkady is no longer a threat." He twirled the louver cord around one long finger. "And Orion is no longer protected by Seyshen."

"How did it happen?" Orion persisted, still disbelieving the creature's story. "What kind of human could face an Arkady shifter and live? What kind of human could face the massed clan?" The very concept was madness. "Who was it?"

Gérard tugged aimlessly on the louver cord. "Galen Sword," he said, angling his eyes to stare at Orion, checking for the vampire's reaction.

But Orion had none. He had expected the name of a general, or a politician, or a mad killer. "The name means nothing to me."

"Even a vampire must have heard of the Swords," Gérard said mockingly. "The Swords of Pendragon?"

Orion was thoroughly disconcerted. Pendragon was a Greater Clan of elementals. One of the oldest. In that context, the name Sword belonged to the history of First World. "But you said this . . . Galen Sword . . . was a human."

With his free hand, Gérard adjusted his white jacket. "Alas, to the great and lasting shame of his illustrious line . . . he *is* human. Only human." The Seyshen laughed without humor.

Then Orion remembered. *"That* Sword?"

The Seyshen stared at Orion, not bothering to answer such a senseless question.

"But," Orion protested, "that . . . that's just a Softwind tale. That Sword is only a legend."

Gérard's finger tightened on the cord one final time. "Ah, but then you must remember, clanless one, that in the Second World in which the legendary Galen Sword now lives, so are . . . vampires."

The shutters instantly clacked shut and the overhead fixture sparked and was extinguished, plunging the room into darkness.

Orion whirled as he glimpsed the dark form of the Seyshen's closed aspect reform out of its disguise and heard the clatter of its undulating claws move swiftly to the front door. Then the bottom of the door burst outward into shards as the Seyshen passed through without slowing.

Unprepared for the sudden entry of so much daylight, Orion leaped backward, squinting as his eyes adjusted once again. But by the time he had gathered himself to face the renewed threat of the sun, the Seyshen was gone and all was silent, except for the rhythmic pulse of the distant surf on the deserted beach.

Orion stayed motionless in the shadows as he rapidly calculated the most probable next step to be taken by the Clan Seyshen. For thirty-eight cycles he had been under its protection. Now, he was a marked target again. But since none of his enemies would have risked tracking him when he was surrounded by Seyshen, there was a good chance that for the moment his whereabouts were unknown. The Seyshen, of course, would trade that information within days, if not hours. Not for any gain the information might bring them, but simply to start a black hunt in motion, to keep the worlds in the disarray the Seyshen thrived upon.

But for now, Orion concluded, he was safe. Through all his long lifetime it had always been this way—despite immortality, his survival could only be measured from one instant to the next. Thus, treaty or no treaty, Seyshen ally or foe, nothing had changed. Orion was alone again, the last of his clan, without friend or future, with only his vow of revenge to keep him alive one night to the next.

The situation was nothing he had not faced before, and thinking that he smiled grimly at what the Seyshen itself had said. His life *was* the stuff from which legends were made, in the First World of adepts as well as in the Second World of humans. Even in the shifting Shadow World that lay between, where humans and adepts made business and sport and, sometimes, halfling progeny cursed to belong to neither world, the fear of the vampire held sway.

But vampires belonged to the First World and Orion was sworn to regain full status there. Though without the Seyshen to aid him, he knew that his chances for victory were as ephemeral as moonlight.

Unless, he decided, he could find another to take the Seyshen's place.

Moving as soundlessly as the darkness that was his home, Orion stepped into the bedroom of the beach house where he kept his pod. The dim sheen of the hibernaculum's brushed stainless steel finish was comforting to him and he yawned, so ingrained was the association of his pod's presence and the promise of undisturbed sleep.

Another to help him, he mused, as he tapped his fingers over the pod's number pad, inputting the proper code. Then he stood back as the pod's armored lid puffed up on its pneumatic hinges. Someone fearless enough to join with a vampire. A fighter powerful enough to face an entire clan of shifters. And win.

Perhaps there was a warrior worthy of a legend, Orion thought as he lay back within his pod, arming its detectors and defenses, watching as the lid descended and its seals engaged and locked.

If what the treacherous Seyshen had said were true, there might be one more chance for him. As quickly as possible he must find the warrior who was both a human in the Second World, and a legend in the First. The warrior who, if the Softwind tales were true, held the fates of all the worlds in his hands. The warrior a vampire could turn to for help, even if he were only human.

The warrior named Galen Sword.

TWO

"**D**amn, Galen, what's your problem? Think you're Superman or what?"

Galen Sword winced as Dr. Leah Bernstein peeled back the blood-caked bandage that was stuck to the deep gash on his left cheek. The doctor shook her head each time he involuntarily twitched away, ripping more of the thick scab from his flesh. Sword concentrated on the way the overhead fluorescent lights caught the silver strands in Bernstein's thick gray hair as he tried to keep from moving, to keep from feeling. But it wasn't working.

When Sword's wound was at last completely exposed, Bernstein whistled silently and Sword could smell the stale cigarette smoke on her breath. In all the years he had known her, the doctor's only concession to the health lobby was to no longer smoke in her office's examination room, during an actual examination. "You should have gone for stitches in this right away, kiddo."

"Only happened last night," Sword said through clenched teeth. Now that the bandage was off, the pain of the wound flooded back as if to make up for the past twelve hours he had ignored it. He could feel his left eye starting to swell shut. His whole face throbbed in time to his pulse, feeling as though Dmitri's talon still tore at him with each heartbeat. But that was impossible of course. Dmitri was dead. Worse than dead.

"Yeah, yeah, you already told me that," Bernstein muttered as she snapped open a plastic pouch and impatiently shook out a hypodermic needle. "The mugging." She said the words with an exaggerated sigh.

"The mugging," Sword agreed. He took a deep breath, slouching as he sat on the crinkly paper covering Bernstein's examination table. He felt as if he hadn't slept for weeks, even though he knew it had been barely thirty hours. At least the doctor had stopped grouching about her own loss of sleep caused by Sword's early morning telephone request to meet immediately at her office.

Bernstein peered over the clear plastic rims of her bifocals and jabbed the hypo through the rubber membrane capping a small glass bottle, all her attention on withdrawing the precise amount of clear fluid from within. After she had slipped the bottle off the needle, she looked again at her patient. "Why don't I believe you?"

Before Sword could think of a reply, Bernstein swabbed a patch of skin above his wound and slipped the hypo in. She repeated the process in three other spots on his face. "I'll tell you why I don't believe you," Bernstein said, taking no notice of the way her patient ground his teeth together each time her needle struck home. "Because I've been listening to your bull for the past fifteen years and I've never believed you yet." She tapped the left side of Sword's face with the tip of a rubber-gloved finger and studied his reaction like a painter putting the final brushstrokes on a masterpiece. "That helping?"

Sword nodded. The freezing was spreading into his lips, making him unsure of how well he could speak. But even that silent nod pulled on the older wounds in both his shoulders, changing the location of the pain that pounded through his body. He wondered where all this agony had been less than three hours ago, when he and Ko and Martin had been surrounded by the howling, bloodcrazed shifters of the Clan Arkady, watching in disbelief as humans became werewolves, and werebears, and *tagonii,* and—

"Your mugging story is bull, too. No way that's a knife wound." Bernstein brusquely cleaned his numbed cheek with swabs. She lifted a small mirror from a tray of instruments on the cabinet beside her, then paused for a moment as she held it up for Sword and saw how startled he was when he finally glimpsed his reflection.

It was the combined effect of two separate images that struck Sword. The first image that disturbed him was the appearance of his face. When Sword had last looked at his reflection—he had a sudden flash of Ko helping him with his tie the night before, and of standing with her in front of his dressing mirror, feeling odd in a rented tuxedo—he had seemed strong and confident to himself. His black eyes had appeared to gleam with an inner light and his lean face looked open and ready to meet any challenge. He had felt that last night was to be the glorious end of three years of searching. But, instead, it had become the bloody beginning of a new mission, with no easy end in sight. As if to underscore how his search had changed, so too had his face. It was open no longer. There were secret things hidden in it now, and the fire that fuelled his eyes was a shadowed reflection of the horrors he had witnessed last night, and those he knew were still to come.

For an instant before the doctor's mirror, Sword thought he heard Ja'Nette's last thin cry for her mother as the werewolf, Seth, brought his jaws down to the child's tender young neck and—Sword forced the sound and the image from his mind, dragging himself back to the present.

The wound, he focused on the wound, the second image to shock him. Before Bernstein's injections had begun to deaden his inflamed nerves, Sword had thought that fully half his face must have been carved away by Dmitri's talon. He shuddered at the memory of the creature—a living skeleton, held together by taut, dead white skin, eyes of translucent blue filled with swirling silver specks, but only as long as he wore an oddly twisted silver crucifix. Dmitri had been a Ronin in the First World, a warrior without clan or honor, and not even his masters had known what he truly was. But Sword had known. Dmitri had been an assassin. Dmitri had used his blue power to incinerate Marcus Askwith, the man who had started Sword in his quest to discover his true heritage, and who had died because of it.

Twelve hours earlier, Dmitri had dangled Sword against the wall of a small reception room in the American Museum of Natural History, while his masters, Tomas Roth and Morgana LaVey, carried out their interrogation. Because of a single hesitation in Sword's tortured responses, Dmitri had used a gleaming hooked claw to give his captive a taste of what it meant to defy the adepts of the First World.

"Knives tend to cut, know how it is?" Bernstein said, still frowning at the wound. "A clean incision. This has been ripped. A triangular tear." She stepped back, pursing her lips. "People who're mauled by bears get this kind of wound, kiddo. Want to tell me about this so-called mugging of yours again?"

Sword shook his head, almost imperceptibly. He tried to smile. "You should see the other guy." But he was certain no one would ever see Dmitri again. Sword had forced the Ronin to enter a fardoor—a First World teleportation portal connecting two distant places as one—and then had collapsed the fardoor's perimeter, turning it into a one-sided doorway into nothingness. Dmitri had been the first adept to pay the price for challenging Galen Sword that night. Seth had been the second. With a grim satisfaction he would not have believed he could possess only days ago, Sword knew that there would be others who would share Dmitri's fate.

"The other guy . . .," Bernstein grumbled in disgust. She stared at Sword for a few moments longer, then peeled off her pale gloves. "So, tell me, what's the story on your friend out there?" She nodded in the direction of her waiting room. "Same . . . 'mugging'?"

"I wouldn't be here if it weren't for Martin," Sword said simply.

"That so?" Bernstein's expression became uncertain for a moment, as if in that one statement she at last detected some ring of truth. "You go sit tight on that chair and let the freezing really take hold. I'll get . . . Martin . . . in here." She left for the waiting room and Sword slipped awkwardly from the table to collapse on a vinyl-padded metal chair, hoping that Martin would remember the story he had been coached to tell.

Martin shambled into the examination room as Bernstein held open the door. The halfling was hunched over, obviously as exhausted as Sword felt. But when he saw Sword's eyes upon him, he drew himself up to his full height of five and a half feet to keep the backs of his hands from brushing the floor.

"Hello, Martin," Sword said softly to the teenager. He saw that the raw wounds across Martin's massive chest were still wet with blood. The hooks of the Snare of the Silver Death which had bound Martin to Arkady's sacrificial stone had gone deeper than Sword had realized and than Martin had let on.

Martin glared at Sword for an instant, his dark eyes flashing like those of a captured animal's beneath his heavy brow. Martin's mother had been human, he had told Sword, but his father was Astar, a powerful Arkady shifter according to the terms used in the First World. A werewolf according to those terms used by humans. That parentage made Martin a halfling, a hostage to the conflicting fortunes of both worlds, belonging to neither, trapped somewhere in between, in the Shadow World.

Martin swept his gaze around the examination room, instinctively looking for a way out. He did not like being indoors. Three hours ago, he had told Melody Ko that he didn't like Sword either and that he didn't want to stay with the man.

Bernstein bunched up the paper Sword had sat on, discarded it, and pulled out a fresh sheet for Martin. "Hop up on the table and I'll take a look at those scrapes," she said. Sword could see her eyes quickly assess Martin, taking in his densely muscled form, oddly attired in ripped sweatpants, the tattered remains of a sweatshirt, and a sturdy black canvas equipment vest similar to the one Sword wore. Sword knew that, detail by detail, there was really nothing anyone could point to and say that Martin was not wholly human, but taken all together there was something recognizably wrong about him. It wasn't that his ears tended to sweep up almost to points, nor that his nails were black, nor that his body hair had almost—but not quite—the same texture as coarse fur. But in the way he moved, swinging arms a bit too long, shifting heavy legs a bit too short, there was something unchained in him. It was not a sense of the unnatural held at bay, but that of nature raw within him. He did not like being indoors because he did not belong indoors.

Martin cocked his head at the doctor, his version of a question.

"Up here, Martin," Bernstein said, patting the table and speaking with the emphasized pronunciation she might use to encourage a dog to perform a trick.

"Why?" Martin's broad nostrils flared as his eyes fixed on Bernstein in alert suspicion.

"So I can see to those cuts on your chest." Bernstein tapped the table again to reinforce her request.

Martin shifted his eyes to Sword.

"It's all right, Martin. She's doing the same for me." He gestured to his own face.

Martin turned back to the empty table and grunted heavily. He placed an oversized hand upon it, as if checking its relative strength, and then he was sitting on it. There had been no preparation for his jump, no change in stance or flexing of muscles. Martin had simply *moved* and was instantly and without effort in position. The paper beneath him rustled softly once, scarcely disturbed. The halfling sighed.

Bernstein shot a glance at Sword as she drew on a second pair of latex gloves, then went to work on Martin, carefully pulling away the strips of cloth that clung to his wounds. "So, are you still in school, Martin?" However difficult his appearance was to interpret, his youth was still apparent.

Martin frowned. "Martin not in school. Martin in doctor office."

Bernstein acted as if he had given her a completely normal response. She lifted a pair of long-handled scissors. "I'm going to have to cut away some of your sweatshirt," she warned.

"Not Martin sweatshirt," Martin said, watching closely everything Bernstein did near his chest. "Adrian sweatshirt. Melody say so."

Bernstein nodded calmly as she dropped blood-soaked strips of canvas and sweatshirt on a tray. She looked over her shoulder at Sword. "I see. Were *they* involved in this mugging, too?"

Sword didn't attempt to move his head. "No."

"But Melody Ko and Adrian Forsyte still do work for you?"

"The Sword Foundation."

Bernstein rolled her eyes to the ceiling. "Oh, well, that *is* a completely different situation, isn't it."

Sword didn't reply. After what Ko had said to him this morning, after they had stepped out from the hidden passageways beneath the city onto the rainslicked sidewalks of Central Park West, he didn't know if she and Forsyte really were still on the payroll. Investigating claims of paranormal phenomena for an eccentric millionaire was one thing. Facing the inhuman creatures of the First World with him was another.

"What's the deal with Martin?" Bernstein asked Sword as she efficiently laid out an assortment of wide gauze strips.

Martin abruptly leaned forward. "Say what?"

Bernstein blinked at his use of the expression, then readdressed the question directly to him. "Do you work for Sword—excuse me—the Sword Foundation?"

Martin peered at Sword again.

"Just signed him on," Sword said quickly. He dropped

his voice as if passing on a secret. "English isn't his first language."

"Ah," Bernstein said, "I'd never have picked that up." She walked over to a small refrigerator sitting on another cabinet. "So, where are you from then, Martin?"

Martin sat upright, looking as if he were about to tap his fist forcefully against his chest. Then he glanced down at his open wounds and thought better of the gesture. "Martin Clan Arkady."

Bernstein considered his answer as she prepared another hypodermic. "Ah, then *perestroika* brings you to my office at this ungodly hour."

"Yellow taxi cab bring Martin Galen Sword to office," Martin said in one breath, as though suspecting the doctor was trying to trick him.

"I see." Bernstein gave Sword a thoughtful smile. "Would you know if your literal-minded friend here has any allergies to penicillin?"

"I don't know."

"And I don't suppose he has a copy of his inoculation record? You know, that form that Immigration likes to see before they let most foreign nationals into the country."

Sword's answer was in his eyes.

Bernstein studied the hypo in her hand for long moments. "I'm guessing that you're in some kind of trouble here. Again."

"It was just a mugging, Leah." Sword knew he sounded unconvincing. "That's all."

"*Were* Melody and Adrian involved?"

"Yes."

Bernstein looked at Sword. "Then I'd like to know why they're not here also."

Sword saw what she was thinking. "They're not here because there's nothing wrong with them. Martin and I are here because we're the ones who were . . . jumped."

"Do you know how positively lame this all sounds, Galen, and how familiar?" Bernstein frowned and chewed on her bottom lip a moment. "How about that child you and Melody were looking after? Janet Connery? Where was she last night?"

The pain in Sword's face and shoulders was suddenly nonexistent, replaced by the ice cold twisting in his guts at the mention of Ja'Nette's name. "Ja'Nette," he said as he looked down at his hands. "Her name . . . is Ja'Nette Conroy."

Behind the doctor, Martin made a soft moaning sound in his throat.

"She went home." Sword continued to look down at the hands that had been unable to save Ja'Nette. "To her mother. She went back home." He saw Ja'Nette's limp body as she lay on the wet dark grass outside the museum, her throat torn out by the fangs of a werewolf. He felt certain that if he looked up now, the doctor would see the child's fate in his eyes.

"Are you drinking again, Galen?" Now the doctor's tone was crisp, distant, and professional. She had been his physician for fifteen years. She knew what he had been like.

"No," Sword whispered. And it was true. No matter what stories were still being told in New York, the Algarve, Costa Smeralda, and who knew where else, Sword hadn't had a drink for three years. *Not since the accident in which I faced my own death and was brought back to life by my brother, Brin.*

"If I take blood samples . . . am I going to find that you're on anything else . . . ?"

"No." And that was also true. No matter what was still said about the old Galen Sword, the old crowd, the old ways, he hadn't been like that for three years. *Not since I walked out of the hospital with a small cast on my wrist ten hours after being admitted with my chest torn open and my skull crushed in a fiery crash. Not since I awakened with the blocked memories of my childhood restored to me and the knowledge that my birthright within the First World had been stolen.*

Remember, Brin had told him in the emergency ward that night, speaking without words, his healing blue power arcing from his hand. *You have a destiny.*

That blue fire had coursed through Sword's body, knitting flesh and bone.

And mind.

You must fight, Brin had told him.

I cannot fight, Sword had answered.

No one else can fight for you.

I will not fight.

No one else can fight for us.

I . . . must not fight.

I know. But that will change.

"Okay . . . okay . . .," Bernstein finally said. "I'm going to see what I can do for Martin here, short of admitting him. Then I'll see how much of your cheek is going to be permanently scarred. And *then* we're going to have a long talk. I must insist on that much. You know why."

Sword gave an almost imperceptible nod of his head. Bernstein accepted it as an answer, then turned back to attend to Martin.

Just don't ask me to tell you the truth, Sword thought as he closed his eyes for a moment's peace, trying to forget the nightmare of last night. He twisted the heavy gold ring that Brin had given him—their mother's ring gleaming with the entwined sword and dragon of the Pendragon crest. *Because I don't know what the truth is, anymore.*

The driver from the car service ran toward the lobby doors with an umbrella to meet Sword and Martin as they left the doctor's building. At the curb, a dark blue Continental idled with its headlights on, windshield wipers slapping back and forth against the autumn rain, windblown exhaust curling out from around its tires.

Sword knew that having a car stand motionless for longer than three minutes with all systems running was now illegal in New York, but he was thankful for the blast of hot dry air from the car's warmed-up heater just the same.

The driver shut the back passenger door on Sword and Martin, then hurried around to the car's other side. Sword heard another car's horn blare as the driver opened his own door. Water drops ran from the clear plastic cover the driver had pulled over his uniform cap. Watching the drops fall, so slowly it seemed, Sword realized just how tired and how full of painkillers he was. Everything seemed soft and slow around him. The talk could wait till later in the day, Leah Bernstein had told him. Right now, he was supposed to go home and rest.

The driver asked where Mr. Sword would care to go and Sword gave him the address of the Loft in SoHo.

"Very good, sir," the driver said. The service had taken Sword there many times before. As far as anyone knew, it was where he lived now.

"Aren't you cold?" Sword asked Martin, settling into the comforting softness of the padded seat. Beside him, the halfling wore only his borrowed sweatpants, his elaborate chest bandages, and an old brown cardigan Dr. Bernstein had volunteered from her collection of lost clothes left in her waiting room.

Martin stuck out his lower lip as the Continental pulled out into Manhattan's morning rush hour. "Not cold outside. Why Martin be cold inside?"

Sword had no answer. In the brief walk from the lobby to the car, he hadn't seen his breath cloud the air. But Martin's breath had. Forsyte and Ko were right. The halfling's metabolism was completely different from human norms. He wondered how different Martin was from shifter norms as well.

Seth had tormented Martin last night by saying that the halfling had become friends with Ja'Nette because all shifters knew the flesh of human children was sweeter to the taste.

And Martin, in tears, had not denied it.

Never forget, Sword had warned himself. Half-human, half-*shifter.*

The car stopped at a red light and the driver spoke over his shoulder. "There's coffee in the door trays, sir."

Sword glanced down and saw two large white cardboard cups nestled in an indentation on his door's side pocket. He picked up one and peeled back the tab on its cover, enjoying the smell of the hot liquid within. It was much easier to focus on the here and now since Bernstein had given him those shots. Much easier to forget. . . .

"Would you like some?" Sword offered the cup to Martin.

"What?"

"Coffee."

Martin sniffed the air. "Ground-up burned-up bean things. Make Martin gug like carrots apples green things." He turned to stare out the rain-streaked window. A bus was idling beside them, so there was nothing to look at.

"Oh." Sword settled back again and sipped at the cup, suspecting he was burning his numbed lower lip but not caring.

Beside him, Martin picked at his chest bandages.

"Those feeling okay?" Sword asked. He wanted to sleep. Then he could think about what was going to come next.

And how he could convince Ko to come back with Forsyte. But that would be for later.

"Thought Doctor Leah Bernstein supposed to make bloodrips better."

"Don't they feel better?" Sword had lost all sensation of pain on the left side of his face, and in his shoulders where Dmitri had impaled him and lifted him at Softwind.

"Still there," Martin said, frowning as he peeked beneath a swath of white gauze. "Leah Bernstein not good wizard. Flower breath smell dead. No crystals. No sweet things on sticks for after."

Sword glanced at the driver, who was trying to act as if he weren't eavesdropping. Sword lowered his voice. "Leah isn't a wizard, Martin. She's a doctor. She's the person humans go to when they're sick or hurt."

"No crystals. No sweet things. Why go?"

"To make things better."

"What things?"

Sword took a deep breath and let it out slowly. Martin had been raised in a hidden enclave of shapeshifters, apart from human company, and Forsyte estimated he had an emotional age of twelve. *And he saved my life,* Sword thought. *At least twice. Be patient.*

Sword leaned closer to Martin. "Those wounds on your chest, from the Snare, remember how much they hurt?" Martin nodded. "But they don't hurt as much now as they did when we were back in that . . . cave or whatever it was where the ceremony was held—"

"Layer," Martin interrupted. "Ceremony of the Change Arkady held in layer. Shifters pass through layer to be there."

"Okay, the layer, then. The point is, though, that the wounds don't hurt as much now. Right? Do they?"

"Not hurt as much now," Martin agreed.

Sword settled back into position, happy to have gotten his point across. "And that's because Dr. Bernstein helped fix them."

"No," Martin said.

Sword looked at Martin without turning his head. "What do you mean, 'no'?"

Martin pulled down on the top of his chest bandage, breaking through the gauze with the edges of his nails.

Sword held out his hand to stop him. "Don't. You have to keep them covered so they don't get infect—"

The wounds were closed. Instead of open, weepy rips in the halfling's flesh, all Sword could see were bright red streaks of shiny skin, bare against Martin's dark chest hair.

"—Martin, how . . . why are they like that?" But Sword knew the answer even as he asked it. Half-human, half-adept. His metabolism was different. All the rules were different.

"Martin know take long time," the halfling said, poking at the freshly formed scars on his skin. "Bloodrips made by silver hooks. Silver kill shifter. Martin only half shifter. Silver only hurt Martin. Silver bloodrips take longer time to go away. See?"

Martin made a wide circle of his lips and pointed at the corners of his mouth. For a moment, Sword wasn't sure what he was supposed to be looking at, then he remembered. At some point before the Ceremony, Martin had been roughly gagged by thick rope. The corners of his mouth had been abraded and crusted with blood. But now, there was no mark upon them.

"Don't you ever get sick, Martin?" There was so much to understand. Ko and Forsyte *had* to come back to him.

Martin closed his mouth and rubbed at his chest. "Sometimes Martin sick here." He tapped at his chest and, even in the short time they had been uncovered, the scars were not as inflamed. "Bad things Martin thinks." The halfling's voice was low, almost a whisper.

"What bad things?"

Martin sighed and turned away again. "Martin mother. Martin father. Martin little halfling sister Ja'Nette. Make Martin sad."

Ah, Sword thought. *That kind of sickness.* And whether it was the painkillers, or his fatigue, or some new level of understanding, Sword reached out across the seat and placed his hand over Martin's.

"I know what that feels like, Martin." Sword saw the images from his own restored childhood memories. He saw his mother as she had been when he had been sent away, her stomach full with the promise of his younger brother. He saw his father. All lost to him, all stolen from him by the wizard with the breath of flowers and the frothing vial of liquid. "It makes me sad, too."

For a moment, Martin let his hand rest beneath Sword's, but then he drew it away and wrapped both arms around his chest. Sword brought his own hand back to his side, wondering what he had done to deserve all that had happened to him. Whatever events had resulted in his expulsion from his First World heritage at the age of five had been, he was sure, beyond his ability to influence or even understand at the time. But the rejection he now suffered in his present life—from Forsyte's brittle co-existence with him, and Ko's rarely disguised hostility, to their complete abandonment of him now when he needed them most—somehow he felt he *was* responsible for that. Or that he should be.

But how he could acknowledge that responsibility, how he could win his colleagues back, he didn't know. He didn't even know how he could begin to try.

Sword sat deep in silence for the rest of the ride to the Loft, feeling as abandoned in the Second World as he was in the First.

THREE

Melody Ko's hands shook as she poured the dry cat food into 'Bub's bowl. She stopped for a moment to refocus her concentration. Her hands *never* shook. She would not allow it.

All around her, the Loft was uncustomarily still. Faintly, she could hear the slow, irregular ticking of the van's engine as it cooled where she had parked it in the street-level garage below. But this time, there was no background hum from Forsyte's electric-powered chair as its treads drove over the textured black rubber of the Perelli floors. The scientist was resting in Ko's apartment now, blocks away in Greenwich Village, and his Loft computers and monitors were switched off. Only the vainly flashing lights of the phone message system were lit up on the walls of equipment that lined the high walls of Sword's main lab. Someone was trying to reach Sword or his team, but Ko no longer cared.

Even more unusual, even worse, the sound of Ja'Nette's television, thudding with the music of MTV, no longer filtered down from the Loft's fourth-level living quarters. Neither did her eager footsteps echo on the metal stairs as she ran from one open floor to the next. Ja'Nette was dead. Killed by a werewolf. And as Ko replayed that grotesque moment of the child's savage murder over and over again in her mind, she slowly came to understand that what had happened to Ja'Nette was not just Galen Sword's fault. It was hers as well. Neither she nor Sword, as team leaders, had truly realized what they would face in their ambitious attempt to infiltrate the gathering of a First World Clan of shapeshifters. But the mistake wouldn't happen again. Couldn't happen again. Sword's quest was finished, at least for her and Forsyte. They had quit.

There, she thought as she watched her hands steady with the force of her will. A slight smile formed on her lips, seemingly out of place on her spare, Oriental features. She knelt down by the bowl on the floor and rubbed one hand over her bristle-cut black hair, bringing her fingers down to massage her temple. Thirty-six hours without sleep, but it was almost time to rest. All that was left for her now were a few loose ends: Getting Forsyte's backup chair from her workshop. Making sure 'Bub was all right, because Sword certainly couldn't be counted on to feed her. And Ja'Nette— Ja'Nette's body. Still in the van, wrapped tenderly in a blanket. Something must be done about dealing with the child's body, Ko knew. Even if it meant that she would have to wait at the Loft to talk with Sword. Something she never wanted to do again.

Ko's hands began to betray her again and she put the box of food down beside the cat bowl. The bowl was made of heavy white plastic, with Mickey Mouse and Goofy stenciled on its side. Ja'Nette had brought it back for 'Bub from her trip with Ko to Disney World. Ja'Nette had said she wanted to go back to the theme park with Martin because he might feel at home there. Ko's hands trembled with the bittersweet memories.

"C'mon, 'Bub." Ko rose to her feet and called out, her voice small in the waiting silence of the Loft. "Breakfast time." No response.

Ko leaned down and picked up the bowl again, shaking it to make the mounded hard pellets of food rattle in what she hoped was an appetizing manner. 'Bub ate about five times what an ordinary, eighteen-pound cat could be expected to need; more evidence that no matter what 'Bub looked like when she wore her collar, she definitely wasn't an ordinary, eighteen-pound cat. With 'Bub's ravenous appetite, Ko knew the animal couldn't resist the sound of food for long.

Ko stopped shaking the cat bowl for a moment, listening for the sound of 'Bub's feet. She heard nothing. Then she saw there was no use in looking for the animal because 'Bub's collar—a worn green leather strap holding a clear crystal pendant—lay empty in the middle of the lab's floor. Without that collar, for reasons about which Ko and Forsyte had almost given up developing theories, 'Bub was transparent to electromagnetic radiation at wavelengths of between 380 and 720 nanometers. As far as Ko was concerned, that was much more preferable to saying that the damned cat was invisible.

"C'mon, 'Bub. Chow time. Let's move it."

Still nothing. Ko tried to think if there was any way that 'Bub could have escaped from the Loft in the absence of the team. But the Loft was virtually impenetrable without one of the electronic code keys which controlled the garage door or the interlocks on one of the ground-floor entrances. The only entry points that the security-minded Sword had not originally armored in the entire Loft were the fourth-floor living quarter windows—and once he had seen how easily Martin had scaled the building's sheer outer wall to enter Ja'Nette's room, Sword had decided to have those barred as soon as he could get workers to come.

'C'mon, 'Bubster. I can't go looking for you."

Ko stood up and gave the bowl another determined shake. Could the cat be trapped somewhere? Or hurt? Or—

"Bloody hell." Ko's sudden intake of breath made her chest and sides ache all over again from where the werewolf had, she suspected, cracked one or two of her ribs. She had forgotten the one other loose end that still remained in the Loft, down in the basement holding cell: Saul Calder, the Arkady humanform shifter Sword and Martin and she had captured four days earlier. The shifter whose mate Ko had killed. The shifter who would stop at nothing to do the same to Sword and her.

Moving silently and swiftly, ignoring the pain of her stiff muscles and tender ribs, Ko placed 'Bub's bowl on a slanted control console and moved to an equipment locker. Gingerly, she lifted the latch on the metal door and swung it open. Inside, most of the racks and pockets for the specially designed devices she had built for Sword were empty. The night's excursion into the "other streets," as Martin called them, snaking through unsuspected tunnels deep beneath the city, had cost the team most of its weaponry as well as Ja'Nette's life. But there was a single gas pistol remaining, and tranquilizer darts, because when they had set out last night, they had not intended to take captives. Their weapons had been chosen to kill.

Ko slipped the harsh-angled pistol from its mount and snapped a clip of three darts into its side breech. As long as Calder was still in humanform, the darts should stop him just as they had stopped Martin that first night. Assuming, of course, that Calder had somehow broken out of the holding cell and needed stopping.

Ko paused for a moment, staring at the pistol in her hand, daring it to waver in her grip. But her familiar self-control was back. Carefully, she began to close the locker door just as a sudden crash echoed behind her.

In a heartbeat, Ko spun, dropped to one knee, and brought her pistol out before her with both hands, firmly locked in a stiff-armed firing position. She swung the gun back and forth across her field of fire, looking for the slightest movement, the smallest target. Then she saw what had made the sound—'Bub's bowl had slipped from the control console and spilled its contents across the floor. She studied those contents, she knew who the intruder was.

One by one, the tiny pellets of cat food were jumping up into the air a few inches, and then disappearing. 'Bub was back and, as always, she was hungry.

Ko rose slowly, once again feeling the protest of her driven body. She inclined her head in the general direction of the Loft's unseen house pet. "Good girl, 'Bub. You just keep eating." Ko slid the gas pistol into a loop on her equipment vest, then crossed quickly over to the collar with its crystal pendant, still lying on the floor. She scooped it up and held it behind her back.

"Where have you been, old girl?" Ko asked as she knelt down near where the pellets disappeared most rapidly. She held out her hand like a blind woman feeling for a wall. "Gooood girl, 'Bub. What a good girl." The pellets stopped disappearing. One skittered a few inches away as if it had been swatted. Then Ko felt the familiar, though still slightly unsettling sensation of a faceful of invisible fur pressing against her fingers and heard the odd, musical purr of 'Bub saying hello. As always, the deep resonance of the sound, and the size and position of the unseen face, seemed to make the transparent form of 'Bub appear to be about four times the size she was when her collar was on. But Ko had no inclination to consider that other perversion of the laws of physics at the moment.

Ko continued her praising of the animal, scratching at whiskers, rubbing amply covered ribs beneath extravagant fur, all unobservable, until 'Bub's purr sounded as loud as a kettle about to come to a boil. Then Ko closed her eyes so her visual sense would not confuse her, swung the collar out from behind her back, and expertly ringed 'Bub's neck with it. She opened her eyes just in time to see the silvery shimmer of 'Bub—now at her usual size, whatever the word *usual* meant in her case—as she coalesced back into a solid white form. She didn't stop purring. Ko was a favorite.

Ko double-checked the collar's buckle, surprised once again that 'Bub had managed to undo herself, then gave the fat Persian a final chuck under her chin. "Now, help me out by cleaning up this mess," Ko said as she stood again, smiling as 'Bub obliged by vacuuming up the scattered food. Then Ko drew her pistol and moved stealthily toward the staircase leading down to the garage, and to the basement's holding cells.

And for a moment, with the invisible feline now back under the influence of an unidentifiable crystal, as she headed down to check on the captive shapeshifter, Melody Ko couldn't shake the feeling that somehow, in some way, things at the Loft of Galen Sword were finally back to normal.

The car-service driver waited in the Continental while Sword punched in the entry code on the keypad beside the Loft's main door. Except for a few men discussing a window display in a store on the corner, the rest of the SoHo street was a deserted row of truck-loading platforms and steel-shuttered, graffiti-covered store fronts.

The keypad telltale flickered from red to green and the door's lock clicked. Sword turned back to the car and waved. At his side, Martin watched Sword's movements, then repeated them exactly, also ending with a wave. The long dark blue car drove off through the rain.

Inside, after closing the door, Sword hit the entry way lightswitch, then jerked back reflexively as he saw what waited for him at the end of the short hall. Melody Ko. Her pistol was aimed squarely at him.

Unsurprised by Ko's presence, Martin studied Sword with open curiosity.

"What are you staring at?" Sword asked Martin with annoyance. "I didn't expect to see her, okay?"

"But Melody there when door open," Martin said. "Galen Sword not see Melody when door open?"

"*I* can't see in the dark," Sword snapped in spite of himself, then turned away from the halfling to frown at Ko. "I thought you'd quit."

Waiting a moment too long, Ko finally dropped the barrel of her pistol. "Unfinished business."

"I know," Sword said. "Saul Calder. Is he still in the—"

"Haven't looked yet." Ko stepped out of the way as Sword led Martin out of the entry hall into the garage. As soon as Sword saw the black van with "THE SWORD FOUNDATION" painted discreetly on its door, he knew what Ko was going to say next. "We have to do something about Ja'Nette." Her voice broke slightly on the child's name.

Beside Sword, Martin made a low oooing sound. "Ja'Nette not go home yet? Ja'Nette not go home?"

Ko spoke softly, misunderstanding Martin's concern. "This was her home, Martin."

But the halfling waved his hands as if driving off flies. "No, no. Ja'Nette halfling. Ja'Nette mother Clan Marratin. Ja'Nette go home to Marratin."

Sword placed his hand on Martin's shoulder and the halfling twisted away. "It's okay, Martin. We'll deal with that later," Sword said, looking at his hand in empty air. "First we have to check on Calder."

Martin sniffed the air, his wide nostrils flaring. "Why check? Saul Calder still here."

"How can you be sure?" Sword asked.

Martin shook his head. "How can you not be sure, Pendragon?" He growled as he said Sword's clan's name.

Ko's mouth tightened in a smile. She offered Sword her pistol in challenge. "You want to go down first?"

Sword took the pistol without hesitation. After what he had faced at the Ceremony of the Change Arkady, one humanform shifter held no terror for him. He checked the safety and the clip, estimating that three darts should be enough to kill a humanform. From experience, he knew that disposing of a shifter's body would not present any trouble. If Calder was as old as his mate had been, his corpse would dissolve into dust within minutes of his death. Sword hefted the pistol in his hand. He turned from Ko without a word and headed past the van and the other vehicles parked beside it—his Porsche, the Checker cab, and the Harleys, going for the stairwell that led to the Loft's basement levels.

But as he stepped across the threshold of the first stair, Martin called out to him. "Why go there?"

"I have to check on Saul Calder," Sword said.

"Martin know that. But why Galen Sword go downstairs to check Saul Calder?"

Sword turned abruptly on the staircase as he realized what Martin was trying to tell him.

But Ko beat him to his next question. "Why shouldn't Sword go downstairs to check on Calder?"

Martin sniffed the air again. "Because Saul Calder upstairs." He raised a thick, black-nailed finger upward, pointing to the open grillwork of the metal stairs and overhanging levels of the Loft's interior, soaring into the shadows above the garage's hanging light fixtures.

"Sword . . .," Ko began.

"I know," Sword said, jogging back from the stairwell. "Can you tell what level he's on, Mar—"

A dark shape fell through the air from the steel beams of the ceiling, hitting Sword on the back. A scream like an enraged ape's split the air, echoing among the vehicles and the brick walls. It overwhelmed Sword's cry of pain and surprise.

Sword knew it was Calder who had jumped him even before he had been smashed to the hard concrete. His wounds and muscles twitched in agony and the sound he made in protest was done without his conscious control. All he could think of was his anger at not being prepared for this possibility. He watched, furious, an observer in his own body, as he saw his outstretched hand slam against the oil-stained floor of the garage so that the gas pistol was thrown from his grip.

He felt Calder's iron hands lift him from the floor with incredible strength. *How fitting,* he thought, *first Ja'Nette, and now me.*

Calder was still humanform, but Sword had expected that. Shifters, as far as Sword had learned, had no regard for the full-moon legends of humans. Their change came only at the specific times when their ceremonies were held, when some unknown energy from a giant red crystal triggered the release of their inner self. *So many questions,* Sword thought in despair as Calder held his face inches from Sword's, *never to be answered.*

"You killed my mate!" Calder raged at Sword, and

though he appeared human, there was much of the beast within him. Even more now that his thick features were distorted by the overwhelming madness of his grief. Calder lifted Sword as if he were no more than a child, as Seth had lifted Ja'Nette.

Then Sword saw Ko's knuckles drive into the side of Calder's head with the force of a bullet. Calder grunted with a foul explosion of rotting meat breath and tumbled off to the side, releasing Sword from his killing grip.

Sword backstepped quickly to keep his balance, then moved forward again to help Ko to her feet. She was kneeling on the floor, rubbing at the arm with which she had hit Calder.

But before Sword could pull her up, he heard Calder growl as the shifter charged again. Sword wheeled to take the impact of the blow. ''Get the gun!'' he cried to Ko, leaning forward to meet Calder's assault. Ko rolled backward. Calder screamed, long arms outthrust. His short and heavily furred, stocky body was naked except for a small leather pouch he wore around his neck. His mouth bubbled with yellow froth. *What must his shifterform be like?* Sword thought, prepared to sacrifice himself not for Ko, but for Ko's better chance at victory. Then two strong hands shoved Sword to the side as Martin leaped through the air and met Calder feet first, a yard from where Sword had stood.

The collision of the hurtling bodies cracked like thunder. Calder fell over backward and Martin ricocheted off him gracefully, righting himself with a neat tuck and spin in midair to land beside the van.

Calder snapped himself onto his stomach, then bounced up like a charging beast, crouching on both feet and both hands. His glaring eyes fixed on Martin. He lunged at the halfling, snarling.

Martin threw both hands above his head and seemed to fly upward, spinning his legs over his head as he vaulted to a perfect upright landing on the roof of the van. Unable to stop his rush, Calder slammed into the van at full speed, crushing the metal wall like a wrecking ball. Martin jumped off the van roof at the instant of impact, somersaulting in a blur to land solidly on both feet, two yards behind Calder.

The humanform shifter pushed himself out from the indentation he had made in the van. Dark blood streamed from a long gash on his low forehead. Gasping audibly, he bared his teeth at Martin and the blood made them glisten.

"*Stasus krell tak, Myrch'ntin. Stasus t'krell Arkadych,*" Calder wheezed at Martin.

Martin stamped his feet on the concrete. He pounded his fists together before his chest. "*Arkadych krella taz!*" the halfling growled in answer. "*Arkadych leel! Tagonii leel! Myrch'ntin Pendragych!*"

At the word *tagonii,* Calder's body stiffened as if an electric current arced through him. Sword knew that *'tagonii'* was Martin's word for the bizarre four-armed creature Calder's mate had been in shifterform. But what he didn't know was what Martin had apparently retorted about Clan Pendragon.

Then there was no more time for thought. Calder pounded his own fists together. He bellowed deafeningly. A red-flagged tranquilizer dart struck the middle of his chest yet he didn't lose the rhythm of the invective he spat at Martin. But when the second dart connected, he stopped, looked down, and shuddered.

Martin bayed, his lips forming a thick, outthrust circle of glee. Calder grasped one of the darts, ignoring its tearing barbs as he ripped it from his flesh. He crushed the plastic cylinder in his massive hand. Then he tore free the second dart.

Ko moved to Sword's side, her pistol still held ready.

"Fire the third," Sword said tensely. Three would kill.

The pistol hissed as the dart flew home. Calder stumbled back against the buckled van wall. He flailed wildly at the new projectile, missing it.

Martin stamped his feet. "*Arkadych leel! Sulcaldr'tin leel ka!*" He yowled wordlessly in triumph.

Blood dripped from Calder's mouth as he wrenched the last dart from his torn chest. More blood streamed from his jagged wounds. "Not yet, halfling," he gasped, then lurched away from the side of the van, and staggered behind it as if searching for a place to hide.

Martin was after him in an instant. Ko shouted at the halfling. "No, Martin. Stay back. Let the drug go to work."

Martin hesitated, glancing back at Ko and Sword. "But drug not work on Saul Calder."

"It worked on you in the pet store," Sword said, holding

his position and waving Martin to join him and Ko as they blocked the garage entrance.

But Martin ignored Sword's words and spoke to Ko instead. "Drug work on Martin because Martin halfling. Saul Calder shifter. Full shifter."

Sword glanced at Ko. "Any more darts?"

Ko shook her head. Her eyes snapped back and forth around the now silent garage as she maintained her ready stance in case the shifter again tried the unexpected. "Might have a couple of tasers in my workshop. I know there're a few more spray cans of the silver emulsion. Anything in the Porsche?"

In answer, Sword started past the van toward his sleek black 928 s4. He halted suddenly as he caught sight of Martin now squatting on the yellow hood of the Checker cab, obviously watching Calder in the far corner of the garage. "What's he doing, Martin?" Sword said softly to the halfling.

"Shifter praying," Martin said without turning.

Sword spoke quietly to Ko, who had now reached his side. "Get whatever you can from the workshop. I'll get the prod from the car."

"Praying?" Ko asked, not moving.

Sword shrugged and resumed his cautious approach to his Porsche, parked just beyond the cab. He had a small case in the back seat stocked with the items he had needed for the werewolf hunt that had brought him Martin. The long-handled electroprod would keep the sedated Saul Calder at bay until Ko returned with the photographic emulsion spray. As Calder's mate had been the first to find out, the fine silver mist the aerosol cans produced sent shifters into fatal anaphylactic shock.

Sword snapped the two ends of the prod together as he came up beside Martin, still perched on the front of the cab. Ko was no longer there. Calder was on his knees by Ko's tool-covered workbench, next to a set of metal shelves that held two gas cans and several pouches of motor oil. He was hunched over, hands clutched to his chest, rocking slowly back and forth.

"Still praying?" Sword asked.

Martin shook his head. "Praying over."

Sword twisted the handle of the prod, arming the circuit. He pressed the discharge stud and a blue spark crackled between the sharpened metal poles on the three-foot-long prod's opposite end. "Then what's he doing now?" Sword really didn't care. From what he'd seen and experienced, the shifters were an abomination, eaters of human flesh, killers of children. In a few moments, he thought grimly, the world would be less one monster, praying or not.

"Martin Melody Galen Sword must hide soon. Saul Calder shifting," Martin said.

Alarmed, Sword looked quickly from Calder's rocking form to Martin and back again. "But . . . how can he?"

Martin turned to stare at Sword, heavy brows furrowed. "Saul Calder shifter."

"I know that, Martin. But I thought you said shifters can only change during the ceremony. And the ceremony was last night. Calder wasn't there."

"Best shift with Crystal of the Change Arkady," Martin said. "But other crystals, other shifts."

Sword felt the hairs on his arms stiffen as he stared at Calder, fifteen feet away. The shifter's hands weren't clutched to his chest anymore. They were now clenched about the small leather pouch that hung around his neck. From within that leather pouch, a familiar red glow began to pulse.

At that instant, as Sword felt himself once again rushing toward the mad violence of the First World, Calder's head snapped up, jarringly underlit by the red energy pouring out beneath him.

And it was no longer Saul Calder's face that stared out at them.

FOUR

In the shadows of the Loft's garage, the shifter *changed*.

"What other shifts are there, Martin?" Sword swung the electroprod in front of him, holding it like a rifle with bayonet. "What other shifts?"

The halfling hopped down from the cab. "Ceremony best shift. Body changes. Mind doesn't." He reached out to take Sword's arm. "Small shift like this, body changes, mind changes, too. Like old times, Galen Sword. Bad old times."

"What is he becoming, Martin?" Sword's voice was tight and low.

"Bad," Martin said. He tugged sharply on Sword's arm. "Time to hide. Almost done."

Now Calder's hands were no longer fixed to the glowing pouch on his chest. Each touched the ground where it splayed out into three hooked talons. Sword could hear the claws scrape against the concrete floor as they burst from the flesh that encased them.

"Melody!" Sword shouted but his voice was drowned out by Calder's sudden cry of . . . pain . . . release . . . Sword couldn't tell. The sound was louder than anything Calder the human might have made. The being that produced it was no longer human.

The new beast rose on two thick legs, each bent backward with an extra joint, the muscles and the tendons of them obscured by a thick covering of black fur, still rippling as it formed. Its head moved unsteadily back and forth as brilliant yellow eyes streaked with oblong pupils twitched unceasingly. It snarled again, like no sound Sword had ever heard, and three thin black tongues slithered out from the foot-long, outthrust jaw, still growing from the pointed head. The gaping jaw bristled with triangular teeth, the two foremost ones lengthening to become fangs, then tusks.

At least eight feet tall now, the creature lurched forward,

massive arms swinging ponderously at its sides. It ducked its head, then arched it up again, stretching and straining until the curling growing tusks twisted apart and the bottom jaw split in two with a spray of blood, rotating and opening like insect mandibles, dripping with glistening ropes of thick gray saliva.

Then the quivering flesh around the creature's vertical nostrils suddenly flared open and the burning yellow eyes at last ceased their frantic movement, clearly focusing on Sword and Martin.

"All done," Martin said.

Sword opened his mouth to call for Ko again. But she was already there.

"Here, Sword," she said calmly behind him.

The beast was struggling upright now, caught between the workbench and the rack of metal shelves. It dragged its claws across the workbench, scattering metal tools noisily to the floor. Sword heard the creature's thick muscular tail whipping back and forth behind the beast, jarring the metal shelves.

"The spray's too risky," Sword said as he and Martin and Ko edged carefully backward along the length of the Checker cab. "Can't get close enough. The arms are too long. Claws too sharp."

"Agreed," Ko said. "Martin, does that type of creature have a name?"

"Saul Calder." Martin's eyes were wide and alert to their danger.

"I mean, like *'tagonii,' "* Ko clarified. The three had reached the open area of the garage. With slow, heavy strides, the creature began moving away from the workbench. The air whistled from the force of its thrashing tail. The creature's eyes were still shut tight as it swung its head back and forth, scenting the air.

"Might be many things. Each time different," Martin said, eyes darting to the exposed iron beams in the ceiling, almost twenty feet above him. "Solo shift. No control."

Ko shot a glance at Sword. "That would explain why the shifters gather together for the ceremonies. To control the phenomenon."

"Can we discuss this later?" Sword asked as he moved protectively in front of Ko and Martin.

"Assuming there is a later." Ko stepped out to stand

beside him. All she held was a small canvas bag. Sword could hear spray cans clanking inside it.

Behind them, Martin pulled hard on Sword's arm to catch his attention as the creature raised itself up on its hind legs and shook its head, as if it were still dizzy from the rapid transformation. "Saul Calder form not good for climbing. Melody Galen Sword go upstairs. Use rope go roof. That form not follow."

Sword nodded to Ko. Going with Martin's experience was fine with him. The halfling had lived in an enclave of Arkady shifters.

"But what about you?" Ko asked Martin without taking her steady gaze from the beast who loomed before them.

"Open big door," Martin said, glancing at the wide metal panels of the double-width garage door.

The creature that had been Saul Calder now stepped forward jerkily. It might still be getting used to its new configuration and center of gravity, but it knew how to use its lungs. The deformed wall of the van vibrated with the force of the howling the creature made.

"We can't let that thing out on the street," Ko told Martin.

Martin blinked. "Yes Martin can. Open big door. Saul Calder go."

They had now backed into the middle of the garage area, equidistant from the parked vehicles, the main doors, and the staircase. The creature moved slowly forward between the van and the cab, scratching at their paint as it used them to keep its balance.

"Martin," Ko said quickly, her glance fixing on something that lay behind the beast, "if you let that thing out onto the street, it could kill people."

"If shifter stay here," Martin retorted, still studying the bars and lights that ran beneath the floor above, "shifter kill us." He made a move as if to go toward the garage door.

Sword acted instinctively, surprising himself, wondering where those instincts had come from. He reached out and put his hand on Martin's shoulder, twisting his fingers in the halfling's sweater as Martin tried to pull away from the unwanted contact. Martin snarled and bared his teeth at Sword.

But Sword didn't turn away or relinquish his grip. "No, Martin. Saul Calder stays in here. With us. He has to."

As if gaining strength and confidence, the creature stepped past the cab and the van and raised both taloned arms above its grotesquely stretched head. *"Swoooorddd!"* it howled, fang-studded mandibles slicing back and forth like scythes.

Ko made a sudden break for the garage door.

The creature ignored her, keeping its eyes locked on Sword.

"Ko!" Sword shouted, hanging on to the struggling Martin with one hand while he held the long electroprod before him, knowing it wouldn't slow the huge beast for an instant. "Where are you going?"

Ko didn't answer. She disappeared behind a thick concrete support pillar. The creature began to pace toward them, its movements gaining in sureness and speed.

"Go upstairs," Martin pleaded, tapping the back of his hand against Sword's side.

But the staircase was near where Ko had run.

"Kiiilll maaate!" the creature roared.

Martin made a soft oooing sound in his throat. Sword didn't move. He couldn't see Ko. The creature's muscles were bunching for a final spring.

"Run now! Run now!" Martin shrieked, then tore himself from Sword's grip and barreled at the creature, flipping over in midair at the last moment to change his course.

The creature's rush was aborted as it swung a huge arm after Martin, missing by inches. Martin bounced once, scrambled up onto the roof of the Porsche, then leaped for the ceiling beam above it. The creature bellowed as it watched Martin spin around the iron beam by his hands and disappear into the ceiling's shadows. Then it started to turn its back on Sword.

Ko was at the workbench past the van and the cab.

"Hey!" Sword cried loudly. "Calder! I killed your mate! Remember?" He couldn't believe what he was doing, but somehow, he had to divert the beast's attention from Ko.

The thing that had been Calder swung slowly back to Sword. Its three black tongues snaked from its gaping mouth with a deep hiss. But whatever Ko was doing behind its back resulted in a loud clang of metal. The creature turned back to her.

"Sword!" Ko called out. "I need more time! Do something."

But there was nothing more to be done. Except the obvious. And the insane.

Sword swore. He had no choice. He pressed the stud on the prod and the contacts on its tip crackled to life. Then he ran shouting at the creature and thrust the prod deep into its back.

The beast's roar was thunderous. But it was a cry of anger and not pain. Sword wondered if there were anything he could do which *could* cause it to feel pain.

The creature turned and Sword released the prod without a struggle. From the corner of his eye he saw a monstrous set of claws swinging for him. He ducked, doubting he was fast enough for the creature not to compensate, but he heard the talons slice the air above him.

He's too big, Sword thought suddenly. *Uncoordinated. He isn't used to being this size or shape.* He saw his chance for victory and took it. He slammed his fist into the creature's black-furred side, then jumped back as it brought its arm and leathery elbow down on him—and missed again.

Whatever else this First World creature is, Sword thought, *it still has to fit within some version of the natural laws. Its musculature can't dampen the momentum of its arms too quickly. Its legs aren't efficiently constructed for fast changes in direction.*

Sword raised his fists to the beast again, daring it to attack.

Then something grabbed his ankle.

Before he could look down, his leg was snapped out from beneath him and he landed flat on his back against the concrete floor. His breath exploded from him with a ragged grunt and he couldn't breathe.

Then his leg jerked up into the air. He saw what was holding it. The tip of the creature's tail had slipped around his foot and ankle like a tentacle. Now it didn't matter that the creature came at him so slowly. He couldn't move.

Sword opened his mouth to call for help, but his lungs were empty. All he could do was feel the disgusting heat of the thick liquid streaming from the creature's mouth to cover his own chest and face. All he could smell was the cutting stench of its breath—acid like vinegar. All he could think was that there were no natural laws. They were only a false veneer of optimism over the true chaos and horror of the one real world—the First World.

The beast's mandibles spread out before Sword. The three tongues lashed out, as much tentacles as the tail. They wrapped around his head and neck and shoulders like whips. They pulled Sword toward the gaping mouth. He saw three more layers of triangular teeth slide back within, preparing for the kill. And still he couldn't breathe.

But he dug his hands into the black cords of the grasping tongues and pulled. He kicked with his free leg. He screamed soundlessly into the creature's face, refusing to concede. Not after what had already been done to him.

The creature roared. It sounded like laughter. Then suddenly it squeezed its bulging yellow eyes closed and snapped its mandibles shut. The fur surrounding its nose and eyes sprang forward and then appeared to be dragged down. The beast shook its head, ignoring Sword.

Sword tried to make sense of what he was seeing. Some invisible force was attacking the creature's head. Was Ja'Nette using her translocation ability? But Ja'Nette was dead. She couldn't be at the Loft. She . . .

Two of the tongues ripped away from Sword's neck and shoulders and grasped at the creature's own head. Sword wheezed with his first breath as he saw the black ropes coil around an invisible shape. He heard the roar of an enraged jungle cat.

" 'Bub!" he gasped.

The creature's third tongue joined the others, holding the writhing, unseen shape above Sword as he fell back to the floor.

'Bub roared again, nothing like the sound a housecat should make. The creature opened its mouth once more to finish off its new attacker. But then a dark shape cannon-balled through the air and the black tongues were wrenched from the beast's mouth, their thick severed roots sending forth three gouts of blood as the shifter shrieked at last in what could only be unbearable pain.

Sword felt the grip of the tail on his leg weaken and he kicked away, desperate for air, rolling out of reach. Ten feet away he saw Martin, crouched in concentration, carefully unwinding the lifeless tongues he had torn away from the empty space that was 'Bub.

Something flickered in the corner of Sword's eye. He turned back to the beast as its voice echoed through the garage. One monstrous hand clutched at the pouch that still hung around its massive neck. Sword saw the telltale crimson glow of a working crystal gleam through the grasping claws. Two huge mounds began to pulse at the creature's sides.

It can't shift twice, Sword thought simply. *That's just not fair.* But then he realized that the first flicker he had just seen had not been the light of the working crystal. It had come from something on fire. He peered past the transforming creature. Something in Melody Ko's hand was in flames.

Sword struggled to his feet and stumbled to join Martin, keeping his eyes on Ko. She held what looked to be a Molotov cocktail, disinterestedly assessing the strength of the flames that flared from it. Then she tossed it straight at the creature's back and whatever it was exploded on contact.

The beast tried to reach behind itself but fell forward, writhing and shrieking. Sword saw Ko wrap another cloth around a small spray cylinder of silver emulsion. The cloth dripped with gasoline from the cans behind her. She held a butane lighter ready.

The screeching creature rolled onto its side, curling into a monstrous fetal position in a spreading pool of noxious liquid that oozed from its fiery back. Ko lit the rag, waited till it flared blindingly, then threw it at the beast.

The flaming cylinder hit the creature's shoulder, rolled down past its chest, then exploded in a spray of fatal silver mist.

Sword heard the beast suck in a huge breath to scream again, but the silver seared its lungs and it could make no sound, only shudder in excruciating agony as the fine particles of metal ate at it inside and out.

Martin came to stand by Sword, his thick arms wrapped gently around 'Bub's unseen form. Ko ducked around the van to join Sword as well.

"Do you have a video camera in the car?" she asked.

Sword shook his head, wondering how she could think of that now. "It's upstairs in the workshop."

Ko frowned. She turned to Martin. "Is that thing going to last much longer?"

The beast was no more than a gelatinous red worm writhing without skin in a black and rippling liquid pool.

"Not long," Martin said.

"Where in the workshop, Sword?" Ko asked.

"How should I know? Ja'nette had it. She—" How could

Ko think of *anything* right now? After all that had happened.

The worm stopped moving. All around it, the liquid it had exuded bubbled up into white mist, evaporating without residue.

"Too bad," Ko said. "Adrian would have liked to have seen this."

Sword couldn't take his eyes off the transformation before him. "You can come back anytime, you know. Adrian can see whatever he wants."

Ko watched the transformation as well, not looking at Sword. "We've already been through this. It's over. There's too much going on that we don't understand. It's not safe to continue." A black ridge began to grow along the topmost portion of the pulsating shape in the center of the mist.

Sword disagreed. "I know what's important, Melody. These things are murderers. They're monsters and—"

"Bloody hell, Sword. There *are* no monsters!"

"No?" Sword pointed at the slug-shaped remnant of the shifter as the black ridge suddenly puckered inside out and the shape began to roll up into itself like film footage of rising dough running in reverse. "Then what the hell do you call that?"

"An anomalous incident," Ko said firmly. "An unexplained phenomenon."

"Anomalous incident? . . . Melody, the only thing anomalous about *that* is that we're not going after the rest of them." Slowly the shape was reducing itself to the size and mass of Saul Calder.

"Sword, last night we took on *one* of these . . . things . . . and it cost us Ja'Nette. Today, this one almost killed the rest of us. It's not worth it. We don't know enough about them."

"Then stay and *learn,* damn it! Don't give up. Last night we also took on more than a hundred of these and won! In the cave!"

Ko shook her head. "Only because you threatened their sacred crystal or whatever it was. If that hadn't been around, Sword, we'd have been so much hamburger in twenty seconds. Besides, you're not interested in stopping them."

Sword glared at her, ignoring the remains of the beast.

Ko held his gaze, unwavering. "You're only interested in

finding out where you fit in. You don't care about anything else but that.''

''You can't really believe that. You—''

Martin made his soft murmur of concern and held 'Bub closer to him. Sword turned away from Ko. A pinpoint red glow appeared in the center of the dark shape half-hidden in the mist rising from the concrete floor.

''Oh, for . . . not *again,* '' Sword said.

Ko tapped Martin's shoulder. ''What's happening, Martin?''

''Not enough silver,'' the halfling said.

The red glow suddenly flared like a silent explosion, and when the light dimmed again, Saul Calder stood in the mist, one hand clutched to the pouch that hung around his neck.

''Is he going to shift again, Martin?'' Sword asked incredulously.

Ko answered instead. ''Look at him, Sword. You can see his ribs now. He's lost about thirty pounds. I'm betting he doesn't have the energy to do it again. Right, Martin?''

''Didn't feed, can't shift soon,'' Martin said.

Warily, Sword studied Calder's form more closely. Ko was right. The naked figure was hunched over, breathing hard, and clearly leaner than he had been when he had attacked in humanform before. But that would mean that shapeshifting did follow some set of rules. Perhaps not natural laws, but something that resembled logic.

Sword looked around to see where his electroprod had fallen.

Martin stood upright. He handed 'Bub to Ko, who sagged under the burden of the invisible cat. ''Martin tag *Sulcaldr-'tin.* He die now.''

''No, Martin,'' Ko said. ''You musn't—''

A piercing explosion of shrieking metal blasted through the garage. Sword wheeled to face the garage door, both hands covering his ears. A long low hole had been ripped through the bottommost metal panel as if artillery shells had burst against it. Something black like smoke swirled around the hole, something Sword couldn't quite focus on. Then Saul Calder rushed past Sword, threw himself to the garage floor and rolled through the ragged opening.

Ko flew to a control panel at the side of the garage door and slammed her fist against the door switch. The metal panels began to rumble open. Sword and Martin ducked beneath the bottom of the door and stopped on the sidewalk outside the Loft, looking down both ends of the deserted street. But Calder was gone—the naked running man had disappeared far too quickly and easily in the misty rain-swept streets of SoHo.

Martin shook his head and scattered raindrops like a soaking dog. Sword stepped back inside the garage. Ko had stopped the door halfway up and was studying the hole made in it.

"An explosion?" Sword asked.

Ko shook her head. "Something mechanical pushed through. No residue from a chemical detonation."

"So Calder had friends to break in and save him," Sword said. Suddenly, the aches and pains of his old and new injuries hit him all at once. Leah Bernstein's painkilling needles no longer had any effect.

"Not exactly, Sword." Ko ran her finger along the jagged slivers at the edge of the hole in the door. "Look at the way the metal's deformed. Whatever went through this was already in the Loft. It burst *out*, not in."

Sword glanced around the garage. "They were waiting for me," he said softly.

"Who was?" Ko asked irritably. "And why you?"

"Calder's friends. Other shifters. Because I killed Calder's mate, they were coming for me." Sword wrapped his arms around himself, trying to quiet the throbbing of his wounds.

Ko stomped her foot on the floor. "Damn you, Sword, this is exactly what I mean." She stared angrily into his uncomprehending eyes. "You didn't kill Saul Calder's mate. I did! None of this is just about *you*. It's about all of us." Her face flushed. "Including Ja'Nette." She covered her face with her hands. "Bloody hell," she whispered.

Martin went to Ko and lightly tapped the back of his hand to her shoulder. His dark eyes blazed at Sword.

Sword knew he should try to offer some comfort to Ko as well, but he couldn't. He didn't know how. He could feel only anger. The same anger he saw in Martin's eyes. The same anger he had heard in Ko's words. The anger of betrayal.

Maybe that's what it will take to make us a team again, Sword thought. *Not a common pursuit, not a sense of higher purpose. But the betrayal we all feel. The anger and the frustration and the loss . . . the only things we can understand. The only things we can share.*

Sword turned his back on Ko and Martin and walked deeper into the garage. He stopped at the metal stairs leading to the upper levels.

"You're wrong, Melody. Right now, *everything* is about me. Because I'm the only one still here. Still going forward. You can take Adrian away if you want to, and Martin and 'Bub, but it won't work. Calder and the others, they'll come for me first, but then they'll come for you. You can only postpone what's going to happen. You can't stop it by running away."

Sword wanted to go to Ko, to place his hands on her to comfort her as Martin did, yet knew without a doubt that if he did, she would leave immediately. With his dispassionate dismissal of her, she uncovered her face and stared at him, eyes flashing, mouth tight, but listening to, and considering what he said.

He continued. "If you really want this to be about *all* of us, if you want to survive, if you want Adrian to be whole again, then come back and help me to help us all."

"Damn you, Sword," Ko said. "Damn you to hell."

"I'm not asking you to like me, Ko." Sword thought back on what Brin had told him about his destiny. "All I'm asking you to do is help me fight. Because any of us who don't fight are going to have to run and hide for the rest of our lives.

"Together, *we* can hunt *them* down, we can . . . understand them, and we can beat them. Everyone. Everything in the whole First World. And if you do that with me, then you can damn me to whatever hell you want."

He held up his fist to her. "Just help me fight."

"I don't want to help *you*, Sword."

Sword smiled bleakly at her. He hoped it would enrage her more. *The anger and the frustration and the loss.* "I don't care why you come back, Ko. I just want you *to* come back." He turned from her and started up the stairs.

Her voice called after him. "What about what I want, Sword? What about what *I* want?"

He paused without looking back. "If I thought you knew what you wanted, I'd ask you that, too." And then Sword continued upstairs to the workshop, leaving Ko at the half-open door, telling himself he couldn't hear her start to cry.

FIVE

O rion walked the streets of the city an hour before sunset, cloaked by the shadows of the towering buildings, the darkly overcast sky, and the long black coat and wide-brimmed hat he wore, ostensibly for protection against the cold and drizzling rain.

It was two days since Gérard's visit and the flight from Los Angeles to New York had been uneventful—it was only the simple shipment of a casket in a crate, heavier than most, but nothing PanAm didn't deal with a dozen times a day. As for the funeral homes that had delivered and received the crate, Orion had utilized two establishments with strong First World ties. The humans of the Second World would be surprised, and no doubt appalled, by the living and unliving cargo that regularly traveled their lands safely hidden in the coffins of the dead. The New Jersey-based mortuary that had claimed Orion's disguised hibernaculum at Kennedy had even allowed their client to pay by American Express.

Orion paused at an intersection, waiting for the signal light to change, though he knew that he would have no trouble moving through the speeding traffic before him as nothing more than a blur to human senses. There would be time for that freedom later, after his business had been conducted, when it was truly night and the hunt would. . . . Orion wrenched his thoughts from the frenzied images that suddenly sprang before his eyes. It was not yet time to think of the hunt or of feeding. To function undetected in the humans' world he had trained himself to keep his desires hidden and contained until the proper moment. But what had broken through his concentration? What had triggered this sudden collapse of his defenses?

Other pedestrians, humans who were homeward bound after a day of work, clustered at the corner where Orion waited. Some huddled beneath the bright yellow umbrella of a pretzel vendor's metal cart. Some slouched behind up-turned collars. A large black woman wearing small yellow earphones sang tunelessly to herself, ignoring the rain that soaked her and the courier package she carried. An impa-tient young man in a stylish trenchcoat awkwardly held an opened newspaper over his head, though his long dark hair already made damp feathers against his neck.

Orion's intent gaze stayed on the young man. It was his scent that Orion had caught—a sudden blaring note of prom-ise that drowned out the city's mélange of bus fumes and charring chestnuts and restaurant exhaust. Instinctively, the vampire's nostrils flared to better separate out the man's scent from the others. He felt the teasing tickle of his feed-ing fangs slowly shifting in their hidden sockets. Unbidden, his mouth began to water.

To compose himself, Orion glanced away to study the others near him. In spite of the congestion of the sidewalk and the lengthy wait for the light, the vampire noted that the humans had left a clear space around him of more than a foot, as if their unconscious instincts, too, were working and had recognized him for the predator he was.

Then, just as the signal changed, Orion caught the young man's eye. As the other pedestrians streamed forward onto the rainslicked street, the vampire and his prey remained motionless.

No, Orion thought. *The time is not right.* He shuddered as he felt the growing pressure of his fangs against his tongue. Despite himself, he opened his mouth just enough for the tip of his tongue to emerge and moisten his dry lips. The man's scent exploded in him with the sudden inrush of air. *No,* Orion raged, knowing it was too late, aware that the imprinting of hunter and prey had already begun and the young man, unknowing, was already within the vampire's power.

Hesitantly, the human pushed through the moving wall of pedestrians to be by Orion's side. The puzzled expression in his eyes showed that he had no idea what he was doing.

''Are . . . are you all right?'' the young man asked, seek-ing some reason for his action, the soaked newspaper for-gotten at his side.

Orion's fangs burst forth within his mouth, gouging his tongue, straining for release. He reached out a black-gloved hand and clutched the young man's upper arm. The human did not protest. He stared directly into Orion's eyes.

He imprinted.

In an instant, all that the young man was became known to Orion. The vampire's eyes fluttered with the suddenness of the knowledge that overwhelmed him, all carried within the molecules and compounds of the young human's scent.

The human was twenty-four, Orion sensed, his metabolism just in the first shifting from the delicious growth of youth to the downward descent into impaired function and death. He ate too many eggs for his health. He had had red wine—a Cabernet—with lunch. His gabardine suit beneath the coat he wore was new—the cloth manufacturer's sizing not yet obscured by the dry cleaner's chemicals. The damp linen scent of Second World money clung to his hands, mixed with the harsh perfume of an inexpensive soap. He was a teller in a bank, Orion knew, and judging from the rush of blood beneath the young man's skin and the pheromones he produced, he was on his way to a meeting with someone important—his lover.

Orion closed his eyes as the sense memories of the young man's passion transferred to him. He saw a woman, long hair rippling against cool sheets. She worked in the bank with him. Her perfume smelled of sandalwood and musk. Then the final deep connection was made and Orion felt his body resonate with the power and the passion of the hunt.

The vampire's eyes flashed open. His hand dug cruelly into the young man's arm. But the youth still said nothing, did nothing, transfixed as a deer by the headlight of an onrushing train.

"Her name is Paula," Orion gasped, struggling against the need for knowledge of the taste of the young man's blood.

His statement was unexpected. The young man shook his head as if awakening. For a moment, he seemed confused by the crush of the other people who moved around him, eyes ahead, ignoring what they did not want to see.

"Paula? Do you know her . . . ?" the young man asked.

"Your name is Keith," Orion said roughly, hearing the pounding tides of the young man's heart. Knowing again all that was contained within himself—the old blood that still flowed, the old thoughts that still reeled, the lost histories of a thousand forgotten lives contained within him crying for yet another to join them.

Keith's eyes opened wide as he heard his name pass from Orion's lips. "Do I know you?" he asked, dazed by the complementary need that grew within him. The need to submit to whatever this stranger might choose to do with him.

"Oh, yes," Orion said, trembling with the savagery of the conflict that raged within him. "You know me now." He pulled his hand away from the young man and drove it deep within his coat pocket. "You will *always* know me, now."

"I . . . I don't understand," the young man said. He began to reach out his own hand to reestablish contact. To surrender.

But Orion stepped back, shaken. How could he have let his control falter so badly? Had he really forgotten a thousand years of discipline during his time with the Seyshen?

"Then understand this, Keith." Orion lifted his head beneath the shadows of his hat brim. He opened his mouth. "Run. For the love of your god, run now while you can."

Keith's eyes were riveted on what he saw gleaming in Orion's mouth.

"Run!" the vampire commanded.

Keith jerked back a step. Then another. He stumbled against the courier with the earphones standing by the pretzel cart, looked at her, turned back to Orion, then turned again and ran, slipping on the damp sidewalk, but gaining speed, obeying his master.

Orion forced himself to turn away. Despite what its inhabitants might think, New York wasn't Beirut. There a hunt could be run in the open and any atrocities the humans might see could easily be blamed on other humans. But in New York there were established protocols to be followed and precautions to be taken. Otherwise . . .

The light was red once more and Orion placed his hand across his eyes to rub at his brow. His fangs still throbbed against his tongue. He wondered again how he had allowed himself to come so close to exposure. There was something about this city, he decided wearily, something about being so close to the layer.

It *had* been a long time since he had been to the north shore. That must be the reason.

He drew a breath and tasted the customary polluting ox-
ides of a human city, relieved that his momentary lapse had
not cost him more. It had been a mistake, he knew, and he
was not used to making them.

The light changed back to green and with a crowd of
unwitting humanity accompanying him, Orion stepped off
the curb and crossed the street. The danger had caught him
unprepared but once again he had survived. And now, more
than ever, he needed the respite and safe haven he sought.

Now, more than ever, he needed Softwind.

This time, the door was inside a narrow and ancient
building on Tenth Street in the Forties. At street level, a
small grocery store spread out its bins of produce beneath
a tattered green-and-white-striped awning. Next to a stack
of lettuce crates, a partially opened doorway with no number led to a rickety wooden staircase.

Orion stood beneath the shelter of the awning, the last of
the rain dripping from his hat. He saw the grocer watching
him from the cash register behind the greasy windows of
the shop, and he wondered who else the woman had seen
pass through the door this day, *what* else the woman had
seen. But the grocer nodded once, then turned away. Perhaps she was used to the visit of the door. Perhaps she
served a nearby enclave.

Orion put his hand on the door and pushed it fully open.
The stairs beyond were empty, sagging with decades of
wear. The vampire concentrated and ascended without
causing the stairs to make the slightest creak. He smiled.
Not all of his skills had been lost in the safe cycles of the
Seyshen's protection.

The long second-floor corridor led past thickly painted
and flaking wooden doors. Orion tasted the air and listened
carefully, but he sensed nothing on the other sides of any
of them. Then his eyes caught the faint, almost imperceptible flicker of a fardoor perimeter, set against the cracked
corridor wall between two ordinary doors on his near right.
He went to it, no more than a large rectangle drawn with
what might be the fine silk of a spider's web, disappearing
beneath an intent gaze, reappearing only when attention
shifted from it.

Orion placed the fingers of his left hand against the wall
contained by the fardoor's boundary. With a whisper, he

uttered his name and made his greeting in an ancient shadow tongue, then tapped his fingers once against the wall. The wall seemed to swing open with a strobing flicker.

He stepped through—

—into the welcome air of Softwind.

It hadn't changed. He hadn't expected it to. It never did. For centuries it had served as a tavern, a meeting place, a lodging hall for travelers who moved between the worlds, and always in its same safe location, sheltered deep within the north shore.

The walls of Softwind never moved, only the doors that led through them.

Pausing before a free-standing wooden partition that cut off the view of the fardoor from within, Orion removed his hat and opened his soaked coat as he took in the familiar scents and sounds of the place. The rich air was heavy with the smell of blood-cured tobaccos, sour beer, and exotic First World spices. The poignant chords of Kerobi sea pipes danced in and out of the drone of a hundred conversations. For an odd and unexpected moment, Orion felt that he had come home.

"Guten Abend, Herr . . . ?" One of the tavern keepers approached Orion from the edge of the partition. He was no more than four feet tall, with a thick white moustache elegantly curved to frame his intricately lined face. He dried his hands on a lace apron the color of robins' eggs and looked at Orion expectantly, without recognizing him.

"Herr Isis," Orion said softly, amused to see the tavern keeper's clumsily concealed reaction to his clan name. Wizard adepts were always responders, which was why they were so trusted and dependable. They were incapable of hiding the truth. The tavern keeper reached up for Orion's coat and hat and the vampire passed them over. Beneath his coat, he wore a black silk shirt tucked into black jeans—innocuous clothes chosen because their description would not give human authorities useful information should any of his activities be witnessed.

"It has been a long time, Herr . . . Isis." The tavern keeper smiled up at Orion as he effortlessly folded and re-folded the vampire's hat and coat until they were no larger than a small book. Then he ringed the compact form once with a quick gesture of his finger, leaving a glowing blue trail in the air. Just as the trail dissolved, the moisture that had been folded up along with the coat splashed out to the floor. The tavern keeper shook a few last drops from the bluebound shape and handed it back to Orion. "Do you wish a room?" His breath smelled of flowers—the metabolism of magic.

Orion shook his head. "A visit only."

The tavern keeper bowed deeply and gestured past the partition to Softwind's main hall. Orion entered.

He was disappointed to recognize no one at any of the more than one hundred round wooden tables crowded into one section of the huge, warehouselike room. And he was surprised at the number of humans who were present—a rarity in his earlier days on the north shore. Most of the humans present were Japanese and they crowded along the zinc-covered bar at the far end. Two of them, women, appeared to be deep in conversation with the treaty beast tethered at the end of the bar. It was a horse—a night-black thunder rider with the silver lightning bolt of Clan Greenstalk emblazoned on its side, and Orion was intrigued by its presence. He had not been aware that Greenstalk was apart in Council. But he had been away a long time, he reminded himself. Conditions had probably changed again among many of the clans, not just between Arkady and the Goychen.

After observing the crowd for a few moments, Orion made his way to the side of the room and walked past the massive, metal-wrapped wooden pillars that supported the wooden roof twenty feet above him. He glanced up and once again was surprised by yet another unexpected sight. The light fixtures were not the graceful floating crystal facets he remembered. They were electric—Second World hanging metal shades sending down cones of artificial light through the smoke-filled air. Orion shook his head at the loss of tradition the new lights represented. What were the worlds coming to?

He arrived at the bar. Two fliers glanced at him, then moved to the side to make room, chittering nervously to themselves, their coppery hair bristling on their heads as if they were about to take flight that instant.

Orion leaned against the bar and ignored them. He was a vampire. He was used to that reaction, even from other adepts. He tapped the bar top and another wizard approached him from behind it.

"Welcome back, Herr Isis," the small adept said. As Orion had expected, the wizards had shared their knowledge instantly. This one was bald, with a closely trimmed white goatee through which his baby pink skin showed clearly. He crinkled his tiny blue eyes in a smile. "Will it be the usual?"

Beside Orion, the two fliers stopped talking and stared intently at him, fearful of the answer he might give. Orion was tempted not to disappoint them, but he still had work to do before feeding.

"No," the vampire said. "Just water. Deep Well."

The barkeeper nodded and left. The two fliers began to breathe again, feeling safe once more. Orion continued to ignore them and gazed down the length of the bar to try to make out what the Japanese humans had to say to the treaty horse. Concentrating on the movements of their lips, he was able to filter out the women's voices from all the other noise of the hall, but then found they spoke not in Japanese but in a language he did not know. Annoyed, he turned his eyes from the humans, thinking that, the way Softwind was degenerating, he wouldn't be surprised if management began to admit gills.

Suddenly, one of the fliers beside him did take off with a high-pitched squeal, her copper hair and cloak spraying out with a crackling charge of static electricity. She only lifted a few feet from the sawdust-covered wooden floor before recovering from her shock and settling lightly to the ground again, but whatever had startled her was something that stood behind Orion. The vampire calmly turned to see what the flier had seen.

"So the Seyshen have finally tired of their pet."

To first appearance, the speaker was a human woman, no older than thirty, six feet tall with an athlete's powerful build. She wore dark leather trousers and a long leather jacket, open to bone-yellow flesh. And she carried the ceremonial, inch-long twin brands of a keeper on the side of her long neck. Orion did not know her name, but he recognized the clan ring she wore—a golden web encasing a blood-black stone as if to squeeze the life from it. An apt representation of the minds and ambitions of those who wore it, Orion had always thought.

He raised his clenched fist to her, knuckles forward in the greeting of the First World.

"Tepesh," Orion said, hissing her clan name like a curse.

She stared at Orion's fist, her full lips twisting into a leer as if she found his gesture amusing. Her dark eyes met his, catching the overhead lights to shine out from the pale perfect smoothness of her face and the brittle black lacquer of her drawn-back hair. Her smile grew until she exposed her own feeding fangs, fully extended.

The vampire of Clan Tepesh held her own fist out to Orion, rigid knuckles only an inch from his.

"Seyshen," she said mockingly, insulting his clan.

Orion pushed his fist to hers and she responded, knuckles grinding knuckles. Their arms trembled with the awesome strength they exerted against each other. "Isis," he corrected, instructing her as he would an apprentice.

Still they pushed against each other, neither conceding to be the first to yield in greeting. Orion became aware of conversations dying around them as all eyes turned to the vampires at the bar.

Then the female was joined by others of her clan. Two males, dressed as she was, took their places flanking her. They also exposed their fangs to Orion.

"Why waste your strength, Seyshen?" the closer of the two taunted. "Especially when the clan you salute has more than one member."

Orion refused to give himself to the bloodrage the Tepesh hoped to provoke. He channeled all his strength and anger to the fist of the keeper.

"My clan is *Isis.*" His voice was low and menacing.

The keeper laughed recklessly. "The moon *pulls* Isis." It was the ultimate insult.

Orion began to lift his other arm. The two males of Tepesh moved closer to their keeper. Only the sea pipes could be heard in the hall, pulsing with the long slow rhythms of the tide.

Then a crackling red glow enwrapped the joined fist of Orion and the keeper and Orion felt the muscles of his arm go slack.

"Hey, hey, Softwind here. *Soffft*wind." A small, thin figure in a rumpled white suit suddenly stood beside the vampires. Her head was cleanshaven and her long nose and thick black eyebrows made her sharp features appear to stretch out like a half-shifted rodent's. In her hand she carried a blazing red crystal—the source of the sapper charge encasing the vampires' fists and arms.

The bald woman's eyes darted back and forth between Orion and the Tepesh keeper. The corner of her thin-lipped mouth twitched. "If you want to give each other grief, then take it out to the beach, all right? But if you want to Deep Well yourselves that badly, then remember where you are."

The woman tapped a finger against the glowing crystal and Orion felt his arm move by itself to his side. The keeper's arm made the identical movement.

But the keeper wasn't as accepting of the small woman's red power as was Orion. "Who are you to interfere with me?" she charged.

The bald woman frowned and stared up at the ceiling. "Hey, Tepesh, don't be starting anything in here. I'm with the management, okay? I'm supposed to keep things soft. And you, I tell ya, are not helping. Y'know what I mean or y'know what I mean?"

"You?" the keeper said with scorn. She glanced around the silent room. "Where's Dmitri?"

The woman in the white suit briskly scratched the tip of her nose. "Sort of on the wrong side of a one-way fardoor, if you catch my meaning. Now, you going to behave or do I turn up the glitter?" She narrowed her eyes in warning as she lifted her glowing crystal. "I'm on an open tab here, babe."

The Tepesh keeper glanced once at the two others of her clan who shook their heads, then glared at the bald woman. After an impolite number of seconds, the keeper's fangs retracted. "I was greeting Herr Isis in the manner of our clans," the vampire said. "No harm done. No disrespect."

The bald woman adjusted her collar and the sapper charges faded. "So let's just keep it that way. Like maybe back at your table."

The keeper turned away from Orion without another glance. Her two companions followed dutifully.

Orion worked his hand back and forth, letting sensation return. Whoever this crystal user was, she was brave.

"Thank you," he said to her as she watched the Tepesh vampires return to their table by the other end of the bar. Three Close trolls were waiting at the Tepesh table, their long-lashed eyes watching Orion and his new companion with interest. The trolls were dressed in human clothes, rumpled and unkempt on their squat and muscular bodies.

Orion thought it odd to see them in anything but their battle garb, and wondered what brought them here.

The bald woman turned abruptly to Orion, then looked over both her shoulders. "Is this a trick?"

"A trick?" Orion asked.

The woman pocketed her extinguished crystal. "I sapped you, bloodboy. Nobody be thanking Tantoo for a sap." She raised her thick eyebrows in qualification. "Except for some humans who really seem to like it. There was this guy once . . ." She snapped her attention to Orion again. "So what's the deal? I haven't seen you here before."

The barkeeper placed a foot-tall flute of clear liquid on the bar by Orion.

"I haven't seen you here before, either," Orion said. At the bottom of the glass was a quarter-inch layer of something dark. The vampire picked up the glass and tilted it back and forth, making the darkness swirl up like a tiny cyclone until an unbroken black tendril stretched through the center of the liquid. He downed half the flute in one swallow.

The bald woman sidled up to Orion and spoke to him from the corner of her mouth, her eyes constantly surveying the rest of the hall. "Don't mind me saying, bloodboy, but I'd go easy on that stuff with three Tepesh ready to rap fists again."

Orion closed his eyes as the achingly cold Deep Well water coursed through him. It didn't travel well past the layer and he had missed it. When he looked again, the bald woman was leaning back with her elbows against the bar, jacket riding up, completely ignoring him.

"What *is* a Tepesh keeper doing on the north shore?" Orion asked her, swirling the silt snake back into life in his drink.

She didn't look at him as she replied. "Hey, why not, bloodboy? They got an enclave on the other side. Movin' uptown, you know what I mean?"

Orion swallowed the rest of the living water and placed the glass gently on the bartop, controlling his surprise. He hadn't expected *that* much to have changed in his absence. He turned his back on the bar and rested his elbows against it, matching the bald woman's position.

"How could a vampire enclave take hold in a city like

New York?'' he asked. "There are police, hospitals, reporters. Not even the Tepesh could hide from them all.''

"What can I say? They got good keepers. Spread some glitter to keep the shirleys confused and they're in like the good old days.'' She turned her head to wink at Orion. "Can't tell me you don't miss the good old days, hey, bloodboy?''

Orion stared straight ahead. By tradition, there was no room in Softwind for individual names. 'For in identity lies conflict,' the governing rings of the First Clan said, though none except the Clan of the Deep Forest followed their teachings exclusively. Still, that did not mean that Orion must remain silent to colloquial insults.

"My clan is Isis,'' he said. "You may call me that.''

The woman glanced up at him from the corner of her eyes. "No disrespect. Isis, hmm? But I didn't think any of you guys were left. Not after Wormwood.''

"No,'' Orion agreed bitterly. "Not after Wormwood. Not after the Tepesh betrayal.'' He took a moment to calm himself. The Deep Well water had affected him more than he had anticipated. "I am the last of my clan.''

The woman turned to him, staring up at the composed face he wore in public. She reached into an inner jacket pocket and brought out a small yellow crystal, cloudy but unblemished, the size of a child's fingertip. She held it out to Orion.

He hesitated, then took it, puzzled. A vampire had no use for waiting crystals. They had no elemental powers.

But the yellow crystal shimmered in his hand and, for an instant, the light that filled Softwind came not from electric fixtures, but from the floating facets of the past.

"A light to better days,'' the woman said softly. "Only a few spans left in it, so I wouldn't be wasting it on Softwind, y'know?''

As soon as Orion realized what the woman had given him, he clenched his fist tightly around it—a memory window, already charged so that anyone could use it.

He tried to thank her, but he could not find the words. Did she have any idea what her gift meant to him? Could she know?

He kept the crystal in the safe darkness of his fist and stared down at the woman, trying to see if any trickery lay behind her motives. "This . . . it is a fairy custom, is it not? A turn of the Light Clans . . . ?"

The woman rubbed a finger beneath her nose. "So, I get around, okay?" She leaned back against the bar, straightening her jacket without success. "It's not good to be the last of a clan."

Orion held out a loosely closed fist to her, offering her the honor of greeting him with a hand less bound. But the woman refused the gesture and honored Orion instead. She made her hand a tight fist as she brushed her knuckles against his, showing herself to be a fighter in his cause. Orion found it to be a gallant gesture.

"You used a name earlier . . . ?" he prompted.

"Tantoo," the woman said.

Orion frowned. It wasn't a clan name, as if she had none. "My name is—"

Tantoo held up a thin hand to cut him off. She cocked a finger at him. "Softwind, Isis. No names. Not here." She pursed her lips to the side, making a rueful smile. "Last one to use his name here was Dmitri, know what I mean?"

Orion didn't recognize Dmitri's name, though he guessed it was a Ronin who had worked here before Tantoo. "Dmitri being the previous . . . soft keeper whom you pushed through a one-sided fardoor?" Orion asked lightly. He knew how jobs were obtained in Softwind.

But Tantoo waved her hand in disagreement. "No false glitter for me, Isis. I had nothing to do with it. Got this job on the up and up because I'm the best counter on the whole north shore." She winked at him again. "You ever need a chant lifted, hard or soft or in between, you come to Tantoo." She turned back to the Softwind crowd, doing a bad job of trying to bob her head in time to the music.

Orion was suddenly concerned. No one liked the idea of a fardoor malfunction. "This Dmitri didn't have his accident with any of the Softwind fardoors, did he?"

Tantoo rolled her eyes in disbelief. "Softwind doors are triple charmed, Isis. Dmitri weren't no accident. Wasn't even here."

"Someone *pushed* him through a one-way fardoor?" Even to a being such as Orion, that kind of nondeath was outrageous. No one deserved it.

"Shoved him through *and* broke the boundary," Tantoo confirmed. "The poor skull's halfway to everywhere by now." She pushed herself up on tiptoes to see what was going on in a far corner of the hall. Another tripe contest was threatening to get rowdy.

"Ahh," Orion said. If Dmitri had been a skull, then perhaps he had deserved his fate after all. But now he was faced with a new mystery. "Tell me, Tantoo, what kind of adept would risk getting close enough to a skull to push him through a fardoor?"

"Weren't no adept," Tantoo said. She stuck two fingers into the collar of her shirt and tugged it away from her scrawny neck. "A coldblasted shirley did it during the Arkady Change a few days back."

Orion stepped back from the bar rail to face Tantoo. "A *human?* Attacked a *skull?* During the Arkady Change?" *It can't be,* he thought. *Can it?*

"Probably didn't even know what he was doing, neither. Meddlesome little thorns, I say." She looked down the bar at the humans clustered around the treaty horse at the end of the bar. "Feed 'em to the shifters, I say."

"Was it Sword?" Orion asked suddenly, remembering what the Seyshen, Gérard, had told him of the Ceremony of the Change Arkady. "Sword of Pendragon?"

Tantoo turned back to regard Orion. Her face was serious.

"That's not a name to be saying around here, Isis. No matter how long you've been away."

"Galen Sword of Clan Pendragon," Orion muttered, lost anew in his own thoughts. A human mad enough to take on Arkady shifters. Mad enough to attack a skull.

"Like I said, Isis, don't be saying that name around here. Legends or no legends, he's not long for any of the worlds. That's what I hear."

Orion looked at her, then held up his hand and snapped his finger for the barkeeper. He bowed to Tantoo, fangs carefully hidden. "Tantoo," he said gravely, "permit me to offer you a drink from the Deepest Wells." He glanced sideways at the table where the Tepesh sat, but they now ignored him as if he didn't exist, caught up in some discussion with the Close trolls.

"Why do you want to know about Sword?" Tantoo asked. Though she licked her lips in anticipation of the living waters Orion had offered, she knew their price was information.

Orion glanced once more at the table where the Tepesh sat, then looked back to Tantoo before the other vampires could sense his gaze. Somehow, he must also find out how his enemies had learned to survive within the Second World. Perhaps there was a way to deal with both his concerns at once.

"I've been away too long," Orion said. "There are many things I must make up for."

Six

It was a young girl's room. A stereo and television set were crammed into a bookshelf overflowing with comic books, fashion magazines, and an untouched set of Grolier's encyclopedia. A small and tattered stuffed dog with matted blue fur took a place of prominence on the top shelf. Beside it, a cardboard box with a picture of Garfield the cat overflowed with small treasures. A string of tiny friendship beads hung over the side.

The desk was a mound of loose papers and spiral-bound notebooks. One corner was cleared off so a portable computer could rest on a level surface. It was a Mitsubishi Wayfarer, not a child's computer—the only jarring note amongst such normality. Above the desk was a large poster of Catherine and Vincent; a photograph of Arsenio Hall cut carefully from a magazine; others of Paula Abdul, The Princess, Nelson Mandela, and They Came from Jersey. It was a young girl's room with all the contradictions and scattershot interests and confusion and disorder and passion for life that childhood meant.

Except there was no life here. Not anymore.

It was Ja'Nette Conroy's room in Galen Sword's Loft, and she would never be returning to it.

On her bed, wrapped tightly in the rainbow-covered duvet, the halfling Martin rocked slowly back and forth, staring straight ahead without seeing anything, not even the bedroom door as it slowly opened and closed.

'Bub's unfastened collar floated into the room, dangling a foot from the ground as it approached the bed. Then the bed sagged and squeaked as if a hundred-pound weight had landed upon it. Martin looked at where the imprints of four invisible fist-sized feet pressed into the bedclothes. He loosened his grip on the duvet that covered him and reached out to empty air, finding 'Bub's unseen head to scratch it. A loud, rasping vibration filled the room, most uncatlike.

"I know," Martin said sadly. " 'Bub hurt, too."

The halfling changed his position and the duvet fell from his shoulders. His bandages were gone, no longer needed, and he wore a large gray sweatshirt that was stretched tightly over his solid muscles.

Martin took the collar from the air and fastened it around nothing. His thick fingers were surprisingly quick and deft.

As the collar buckled shut, the clear crystal pendant that hung from it chimed once like fine metal, then a small ball of brilliant sparkles coalesced into 'Bub's visible form. Her usually snowy fur was soiled and dingy. The fight with Saul Calder had been a strain for her as well. Two days later she still had not recovered.

" 'Bub not worry," Martin said, then patted his duvet-covered lap in invitation. "Ja'Nette go home tonight. To Marratin." 'Bub stepped into the softness and began to delicately groom her coat with her bright pink tongue as Martin lightly scratched at her ears. "Little halfling sister go home," he said quietly.

Martin fell silent then, too confused by events to think in words. It had been almost two weeks, one half of a cycle, since he had met Galen Sword, and he had not yet understood the full consequences of that meeting.

Most importantly, he knew, he was no longer a plaything of the Clan Arkady. Those shifters would have to find a new target to tag for their sport. He was glad of that change, even if it meant he could never again return to his own room in the Arkady enclave. He looked around Ja'Nette's room one more time and decided he wouldn't miss his mattress and the meager pile of pretty rocks and picture books that comprised his possessions. The Loft was a nicer place to stay, he thought. Then he remembered: He couldn't stay here.

" 'Bub go, too," Martin said to the cat. 'Bub stopped grooming for a moment and looked up at him. "Martin know 'Bub sad to leave Loft. Warm here. Good food. Melody sometimes. But Galen Sword bad man. Want all leave. But 'Bub not worry. Martin stay to help. 'Bub Melody Adrian not be sad alone anymore. Martin be with you." He stopped to catch his breath. It had been a long speech for him to make.

'Bub rubbed her head against Martin's hand, sealing his promise. Martin felt his eyes fill with tears. With Ja'Nette gone, he felt that no matter how well he was able to help the *others,* there was nothing that could stop *him* from feeling sad alone for the rest of his life.

'Bub's ears suddenly flattened against her head. She twisted to look at the bedroom door. Martin cocked his head. Someone was on the stairs leading to the fourth level. From the rhythm of the footfalls, it was Sword.

Uncharacteristically, Sword knocked on the door before entering. He even asked permission to come in. Martin decided it was a trick. Sword wasn't to be trusted. Martin didn't answer.

Sure enough, after a few moments the door swung open, anyway. There was no exclusion enchantment anywhere within the Loft that Martin had been able to detect. Sword hadn't needed permission after all and Martin couldn't understand why he had asked in the first place.

"Hello, Martin." Sword walked stiffly into the room, looking around it as if he too were pretending to feel sad alone. But Martin wasn't fooled. He knew that Galen Sword felt nothing.

" 'Bub here too," Martin said, defending his friend.

Sword stared at the white-furred creature in Martin's lap. Martin could see the momentary frown on Sword's face, before it was hidden. "Hello, 'Bub," Sword added. He walked to the bookshelf, angling his head to read the names of the books there.

"Galen Sword not worry," Martin told him. "Bloodrips gone. Martin leave soon."

Sword turned. "You don't have to, Martin." Martin didn't understand what Sword meant. "I would like you to stay."

"Melody go," Martin said. After the fight with Saul Calder, Ko had followed Sword upstairs where they had talked with Martin about sending Ja'Nette home. Martin had tried hard to tell them that there were only certain times to go home. Certain places. They had asked so many questions, said so many words, that Martin had had to cover his ears and run away to be in the van with Ja'Nette's body.

Melody had finally come to tell Martin that she and Sword would do whatever he said about sending Ja'Nette home. Then Melody had left, still telling Martin that he couldn't go with her, that it was best for him to stay in the Loft. But

Martin didn't want to stay anywhere alone with Sword. "Martin go too," he had pleaded. But because of the blood-rips, he had had to stay.

Martin could hear Sword start to take a breath, then cough. Doctor Leah Bernstein hadn't been able to fix him either, Martin decided. She had been one of the worst wizards he had ever seen. She had had no candy for after.

Sword went to Ja'Nette's desk, carefully moved the small computer to the side, then leaned against the cleared-off corner. "I'm going to try to explain this to you again, Martin. Please listen carefully."

"Martin always listen carefully." He tapped an almost pointed ear. "Father's ears. Astar. Powerful shifter."

Sword seemed not to pay attention. Instead, he asked a question. "Who looks after you, Martin?"

"No one sees Martin. Martin fast. Martin careful."

Sword looked at the floor for a moment. "No, I mean, who takes care of you? How did you get food to eat? Clothes to wear? Who gave you a room at the Arkady enclave?"

Sword had finally said something that Martin could understand. But Martin didn't know how Sword could not know the answer to such an obvious question.

"John and Brenda get food clothes. John and Brenda Arkady keepers."

"Ah," Sword said, as if just remembering something. "Keepers. You've mentioned them before. Humanform shifters who take care of the enclave's business in the Second World."

Martin didn't know about any of that. "Keep Arkady safe." That's what keepers did. Sword was saying senseless words again.

"Who will keep you safe now, Martin?"

Martin looked down at 'Bub. He cupped both giant hands around the purring cat. "Martin keep 'Bub safe. Poor chanted Light."

"I know," Sword said. "I know you'll keep 'Bub safe. But who will keep *you* safe, Martin? If you leave here, where will you go? Melody said she can't take you in."

Martin hugged the cat fiercely and 'Bub didn't protest. "Martin go Shadow World. Martin halfling." He looked over at Sword. "Ja'Nette say halfling special. Martin be special in Shadow World."

Sword stood away from the desk. "Is the Shadow World safe for you, Martin?"

Martin shook his head. No place was safe for him, neither human nor adept.

"The Loft is safe for you. This place. Here." Sword patted the desk behind him. "I want you to be safe, Martin. I want you to stay in the Loft."

"Why?"

Sword looked over to the window. Fast gray clouds dashed between the distant towers in the downtown financial district. After two solid weeks the rain still wasn't letting up. "Because you have no other place to go, Martin. Because I know what that's like."

"Galen Sword have Loft."

"I haven't always had this place." He came over to sit on the bed, and 'Bub stopped purring to fix him with her unwinking gaze. "I was like you, Martin. I had a home in the First World. I had a family there. But everything was taken from me." He looked into Martin's eyes and Martin didn't understand if there was another question there to be asked or another explanation to be offered. "Why that happened, I don't know. Maybe because I'm a freak. An adept born without powers. A human in a world where none should be. I don't know.

"But I suspect . . . I think . . . that whatever happened that made them—made Roth—exile me, make me forget my past, whatever that was has something to do with what's going on now."

Martin forced himself to continue listening to Sword, but the frustration of trying to understand so many words, one after another, was making his head hurt. "What's going on now?" he asked, repeating Sword's last words because he could think of nothing else to say.

Sword leaned forward, resting his elbows on his legs, hands held together, fingers rubbing at the heavy gold clan ring he wore. "I'm not sure. I was hoping you'd know more. But I think it has to do with that war going on in the First World. Arkady and the . . . Seyshen I think you called them?"

Martin nodded. "Arkady Seyshen apart in Council." As far as Martin knew, the Seyshen were apart with just about everyone in Council.

Sword stared down at his ring. Martin had heard Sword's

brother call it their mother's ring. "From the way Roth and
Morgana were acting, in the museum, then in the Pit of the
Change, I got the feeling that I was interfering in their plans.
As if they'd always known that I might and had tried to keep
me away." He glanced at Martin, dark eyes wide with a
new idea. "They sent me away more than twenty years ago,
Martin. How long have the Seyshen and Arkady been apart
in Council?"

Martin squinted in concentration. "Half a change. Four,
maybe six cycles shorter."

Sword looked again at his gold ring. "Adrian said a
change was about seven years . . . how many cycles to a
change?"

Martin carefully lifted his hands from 'Bub and spread
out his fingers. But the number of cycles in a change was
more than the fingers on his hands. He shrugged. "Lots."

"Cycles of what?" Sword asked.

Martin pointed up. *"Leel,"* he said. "Two face in sky."

Sword was silent for a few moments. "The moon?" he
asked at last.

"That what Martin say." The halfling returned to strok-
ing the soft cat in his lap. 'Bub finally turned away from
her study of Sword to roll over on her back, rapturously
kneading the air.

"Okay," Sword said, speaking quickly to himself. "So
there're about thirteen lunar cycles to a year. A half-change
would be three and a half years, less four or six cycles is
about three years." He sat up straight, stretching his arms
against his legs. "I was sort of hoping that I'd find out that
their war started when I was exiled. But if it's only been
three years . . ." His eyes seemed to see something far
beyond the room. "That's when I had my accident and
started to remember all this." He shook his head and turned
to face Martin. "Anyway, war or no war, I feel responsible
for you having nowhere else to go. I *want* you to stay here.
To live here. With me."

Martin was relieved that Sword had finally stopped talking.

Sword held out his hand, abruptly changing it into a fist
as if he were greeting Martin. Martin stared at the fist, not
knowing what Sword meant by it. Sword hesitated, then
seemed to change his mind. He opened his hand again and
brought his fingers down on 'Bub's downy stomach. In-

stantly, the cat's paw stopped moving, and her claws extended, one by one. Sword quickly pulled his hand away.

"Please stay," Sword said. "That's the best I can do. Please, Martin."

Martin rolled down his lower lip in thought. "Melody stay, too?"

"I want her to stay, but I can't speak for her. Let's see how things go tonight with . . . with Ja'Nette." Again Sword looked at Martin as if he were trying to speak with more than words. "Melody's just upset with me right now. She's been upset with me before and she's gotten over it. Maybe . . . maybe she'll get over it again."

"Where Martin stay in Loft?" The Loft's garage was too big. Too smelly. But Martin hadn't wanted to go upstairs. That would be too close to Sword.

Sword looked around the room. "Why not stay here? This can be your room now."

"This Ja'Nette room."

Sword nodded his head. "I think she would have liked it if she thought it was going to be yours."

Martin watched Sword carefully, tuning in to the sound of his breathing, the smell of his sweat. The halfling could tell it was important to Sword that he accept his offer. He wondered how far Sword was willing to go to ensure that he would.

" 'Bub stay?" Martin asked warily.

Sword seemed surprised by the question. "Of course she can stay. She can stay in here with you if you promise not to leave the window open."

"You lift 'Bub chant?"

"By all means, if you think Tantoo will talk with me again after what happened last time. But remember the questions that Tantoo was asking. There's a chance that 'Bub isn't from a Light Clan, enchanted or not."

Martin turned away from Sword's stare. That wasn't a possibility he wanted to consider. 'Bub *had* to be a Light. The alternative was . . . Martin shuddered.

"Are you all right?" Sword asked.

Martin ran a hand through his coarse black hair, making it stand up on end. "Galen Sword be keeper for Martin?"

Sword rubbed at his chin. "I tell you what, Martin. I'll be your keeper in the Second World, and you can be *my* keeper in the First. We'll help each other, okay?"

Martin was at a complete loss. He didn't know where Sword got his ideas about the way the worlds worked. "No keepers in First World, Galen Sword. Martin be keeper in Shadow World. As far as Galen Sword can go and stay alive." He could tell from Sword's sudden tensing that he wanted to say something more, but after a moment, Sword held out his hand, knuckles forward, half-closed.

"Deal?" Sword asked. "Arkady?"

Martin shook his head. "Martin no Arkady. Arkady *leel.*" But to Sword's surprise, he held out his own fist as if to agree. "Martin *Pendragych,* now." He brushed his knuckles against Sword's, his own fist opened to match Sword's exactly. He looked up at Sword measuringly. "Same as Galen Sword." They were equals now.

Sword stared at the halfling. He seemed poised to say another thousand words. Instead, he nodded slowly and spoke only four.

"Yes. Just the same."

His eyes held all the rest unspoken.

SEVEN

The teak-lined elevator hummed smoothly around Galen Sword, carrying him thirty stories above the city, carrying him deeper into one small part of his past, one small secret.

At times, he felt beyond making sense of any of his three lives. There were the brief, dreamlike memories of his childhood, hidden by an elusive conspiracy of wizards and potions and politics so far removed from common reality that he sometimes woke at night fearing that it was all a nightmare—a split second of almost coherent thought which might have blossomed full within him as he passed from sleep to consciousness. But always, he would waken in his spartan quarters in the Loft and take some small comfort from the ever-present sounds of his computers and workshops—every tool of rational science brought to bear on the investigation of the irrationality of myths and superstitions. All to prove the point that his dreams *were* real.

Then there were the years spent as trust fund orphan, guided through life by well-meaning but distant advisors and guardians who were always quick to write a check to keep him happy, and to remedy the consequences of his temper and his appetites—appetites which had no need to be constrained by lack of financial resources and which had led to his legendary reputation as a sensation-seeking hedonist.

But that life had also been a lie, a placeholder between his expulsion as a child from the First World and the accident three years ago that had brought his memories back.

Now there was his new life, as a searcher, an investigator, compelled by his disturbing memories to travel in unknown directions toward a destination he could not yet visualize, let alone truly believe in. At times it seemed to him that the past three years of near-useless effort were no more than dreams themselves. For all the frustrations and confusion he felt, for all that he had struggled to keep his bitterness and still maddening shortcomings hidden from those who helped him, he felt he might just as well be trapped in yet another suffocating nightmare, with him running in slow-time through its thickness, always coming closer, always approaching, but never ever arriving.

Sword brought his hands to his head seeking the solace of darkness. He wanted to go home and he didn't know where home could be found. He wanted to regain his life and he didn't know what that life was. He wanted to fulfill his destiny, and he was afraid to discover what the cost of that destiny would be.

He felt the elevator slow around him, bringing him to the one destination he *could* imagine, a destination he had managed to keep secret from Ko and Forsyte and almost all the others who had worked with him through these years. Here, the place to which he always retreated waited for him once again, undemanding, unquestioning, all-enveloping.

The elevator doors opened before him. He stepped out onto the cool marble floor. He was in the private entrance foyer of his apartment in what had once been called the Trump Tower. He was stepping back—for a few hours or days at least—into the old life of Galen Sword. A life without questions, without demands. A life only of instant distraction, of escape, and of mindless peace.

Sword pressed the switch on the wall panel which would lock the private elevator in place until he decided to leave. Then he stood in the foyer, savoring the silence and the stillness of his secret home.

Ko and Forsyte thought he had sold this place when he had purchased the Loft in SoHo, and in truth he had transferred the apartment's title from the Sword Foundation through intricate maneuvers to a numbered corporation. At the time, he hadn't known exactly why he had gone through such a complicated process. He had guessed that it was simply a reaction to his years of being in the public eye, when strangers and reporters alike had felt no compunction about intruding on his privacy. He had decided that retaining the apartment would provide him with somewhere to withdraw in case those he happened to recruit turned out to be like most of the others he had met in his life—demanding too much from him, in time, emotion, or money.

But that had been three years ago when he had been full of the promise and excitement of finding a new purpose to his life. Now, with that new purpose slowly being poisoned by the same relentless routine and lack of success that had invaded his previous life, Sword was finally able to admit that he kept his luxurious home because he enjoyed its solitary comforts.

His quarters in the Loft were severe and ascetic in another way, a way he knew Ko approved, and that grudging approval, Sword had found, was necessary for keeping her with him as long as she had been. He knew she merely tolerated him, even actively detested him from time to time, but by the evidence she saw at the Loft, she at least believed that Sword was truly dedicated to his quest and she respected that. Combined with her insatiable curiosity about those things they investigated, such respect was enough to keep her with him.

At least, it had been.

Sword sighed and experimentally pushed against the tightness of the almost healed wound on his cheek. He had labored in the Loft for three long days, repairing damage and replenishing supplies, preparing for what Martin called Ja'Nette's "going home," finally scheduled for tonight. Now that that work was done, he estimated that he would have only a few hours before his headache struck—his body's usual reaction to the sudden release of tension and stress. But the few hours of peace that being back in this apartment would bring would be worth a day spent in a darkened room, feeling the throbbing of his head through the muffled layers of painkillers.

Serenity, most of all, was what he craved now. But when he opened the foyer door leading to his apartment, he knew at once he would not have it tonight.

There was someone waiting for him.

Sword couldn't tell who it was for he could see nothing. But there was a difference in the air of his home. It was not the bland dry scent of undisturbed air conditioning he had expected. There was too much humidity, as if the shower had run too long, and a scent almost of perfume, almost of . . .

A dark figure stepped into the hallway twenty feet away. Sword froze. The scent, almost floral. The silhouette, so familiar. He was confused. Fear rose in him. There had been a shadow in the Loft when Saul Calder had escaped.

"Galen? Is that you?"

In the instant he heard and recognized the voice, Sword's sudden alarm evaporated, but the rush of adrenalin it had brought made him feel as if he resonated to an inaudible, high-pitched tone. His breath left him in another sigh.

"Kennie. What are you doing here?"

Kendall Marsh strode down the hallway to Sword. She was barefoot, in faded blue jeans, one knee torn and tufted with white. A billowing white shirt floated loosely around her. A man's shirt, Sword realized. His own. As she came closer, he saw that her shoulder-length, loosely waving hair was flatter than usual, damp against her, making small wet stains on the shoulders of the shirt. That explained the humidity. The shower had been on.

His hand reached out to a lightswitch and a series of shell-shaped sconces came to life, softly illuminating the hallway. He watched without understanding as the look of concern on Marsh's dark face became a look of shock.

Only when she stood before him and raised one hand to touch the bandage on his face did he realize why her expression had changed.

"Jesus, Galen . . ." Her hand on his face was as soft as her whisper. "I've been leaving messages at the Loft for days. I *knew* you were in trouble, but . . ."

Sword took her hand to draw it away from his face.

"No trouble. I was mugged. That's all."

A trace of the old anger flickered in Marsh's deep brown eyes. It reminded Sword of the arguments they had had. The ones that had come with more and more regularity until the only way they could be stopped was by breaking up. Eventually, that was the way the arguments *had* ceased entirely.

"You're full of it, Galen."

Sword let go of her hand. It fell from his reluctantly.

"You're breaking and entering, Kennie. You shouldn't be here."

She stuck out her tongue at him. "The concierge watches my newscast and you never changed the locks."

Sword shrugged and looked away. She was right. He hadn't. Maybe he had hoped that someday she'd come back. But as always, her timing was off.

"I've got to sit down." Sword turned from her, leaving her in the hallway.

He slouched wearily in his study's soft leather couch, staring at the empty glass of the aquarium that had been built into the antique oak paneling of the walls. When he had moved to the Loft, he had given the aquarium's rare saltwater denizens to the couple who ran the service that had cared for them all the years Sword could not be bothered. He kept thinking he should do something with the empty space but could never decide what. Even empty, it still seemed too much work.

Marsh sat on the opposite end of the couch, legs pulled up under her, staring at him.

"I'm angry at you, Galen."

Sword nodded at that, but didn't look at her. "When haven't you been?" *Just as everyone else is,* he thought. *That has to change. That will change.*

She ignored his question. "Three nights ago I see you for the first time in . . . well, since you ran off to Greece. You're back in a tux, for God's sake. You look great. You seem glad to see me. You talk about having lunch. Giving me a story. And then . . . boom. The old Galen. You disappear."

Sword gave up pretending to study the empty aquarium and closed his eyes. "The old Galen," he agreed. He wasn't up to this. Not now.

"Damn it, Galen. Look at me when I'm angry at you."

Sword leaned back against the down-filled leather cushions and looked at her, really looked at her. She was different from the time they had first met in the kitchen of Marcus Askwith—a victim of Dmitri's power to cause spontaneous human combustion. Sword had been only days out of the hospital from his accident, filled with the rush of new information and purpose. Marsh had been an up-and-coming reporter for *LiveEye News.* They had seen each other off and on after that, trading information whenever their paths crossed, sharing stories about Detective Trank. One night, almost a year later, they had met for dinner and Sword hadn't gone back to the Loft for four days afterward. Another year had followed. *Almost* another year.

"Damn you, Galen. I'm worried about you."

"I thought you were angry at me."

She crossed her arms and narrowed her eyes at him.

"Worried *and* angry. Same old Galen, same old Kennie. All right?"

Sword said nothing, did nothing. His unreadable gaze remained on her.

"The police don't know what the hell happened at the museum that night. Said the explosives were pretty sophisticated to have caused as little damage as they did. They're guessing it was a diversion for something else, but they don't know what." Marsh uncrossed her arms and rubbed at the loose mass of damp hair at the back of her head. "Museum's staff is running an inventory, but I don't think they're going to find anything missing. Do you?"

"Couldn't say."

Marsh studied his lean form for long moments. "Police wanted to know how I managed to get my crew there so quickly."

She stopped and Sword could tell that she was trying to provoke him. But he knew her better than she thought he did. There was no way she would have told the police that she had received her tip from Forsyte. He knew what she had told them.

"I told them it was an anonymous tip." She frowned because her ploy hadn't worked. "It was good enough for them. But it's not good enough for *me.*"

Sword knew what was coming next. He tried to head her off. "Look, Kennie, I've had a rough couple of days. I'm tired. That mugger—"

"Out your ass, Galen. Remember who you're talking to. There was no mugger."

Sword shifted as if to stand. "I won't argue with you."

"I'm not arguing with you. I'm *telling* you." Marsh moved forward, rolling her legs under her until she was kneeling in the middle of the couch, looking as if she were ready to attack if Sword dared leave the room before she was finished talking with him. "You show up at that party, looking gorgeous, and wearing a James Bond lie detector. You tell me you're onto something that's not illegal because no one's thought to write laws against it. And you tell me I might get into trouble if I hang around you and that creepy bitch in the green dress. Next thing I know, the museum's a bomb site and you show up looking like you went five rounds with Godzilla. I'm not going to settle for you being

tired this time, darlin'. I want to know what you're up to
and I want to know now.''

Their eyes met and held and passed no secrets, only
memories.

Sword looked away first. ''What if I said I don't know
what I'm up to?'' He glanced back at her to judge her reaction.

She made a playful fist at him. ''I'd say you were about
to go into round six.''

That made him smile. So much about her did that for
him. Too much about her, he had decided. That realization
had somehow made the arguments come more easily.

''But I truly don't,'' he said. ''I don't know what's happening. I don't know what's going to happen next.''

Marsh's broad shoulders sagged then and she made a
sound like a moan of exasperation. She took Sword's closer
hand in hers. ''Jesus, Galen, listen to yourself. Haven't you
learned anything?''

He stared at her, making no move to take his hand away,
not knowing what she meant.

''I know I kid you about . . . ghostbusting and all that,
and I'm sorry. I know I shouldn't. But even if I don't take
it *all* seriously, I've never doubted that you care about what
you're doing.'' She squeezed his hand tightly in hers. ''I
know you know something, Galen. Something that maybe
nobody else knows. And I know it has something to do with
that time you walked away from that car crash with nothing
but a sprained wrist.''

Sword bit his lip. Had he been that obvious? Had he managed to hide nothing from her? Had she cared enough then
never to try to get him to say more?

''And whatever it is you know,'' she continued, ''that's
what's making you . . . go on, doing the stuff that you do
down in SoHo with Forsyte and . . . whatever her name is.''

''Melody Ko.'' Sword's voice cracked as he said the
name. He coughed to clear his suddenly dry throat.

Marsh's eyes darkened. ''Yeah, her. But anyway, there
you are, knowing something, wanting to find out more, and
you're probably the one person on the globe who *can* find
out anything that can be found out.'' She looked into his
eyes, holding his hand even more tightly. ''Really, Galen.
You've got more money than you know what to do with.

You've got the mind for it. And . . ." She shook her head and dropped his hand.

"And what?" Galen's hand still felt warmed by her touch.

Marsh held out both hands to him. "And you're still just sitting there like a damned bump on a log waiting for something else to happen to you."

Sword could hear the frustration in her voice.

"Don't you get it, Galen? That's not the way it's done. *You've* got to do something. *You've* got to take control for once. No, don't turn away."

Sword felt the wounds on his face and shoulders flare with pain as Marsh took hold of his arms to force him to look into her intent face. She leaned forward from where she knelt, leaned over him. The fragrance he had detected came from her and he was surprised by the power her perfume still had over him, the memories it brought back.

She brought her face closer to his. *"You're* the one who has got to make things happen. If you're ever going to find out . . . whatever it is you want to find out . . . whatever it is you *have* to find out . . . you're the one who has to take action."

Sword looked from her eyes to her lips to her eyes again. He felt dazed with the oncoming migraine, the pain of his recent wounds, the heat of her body, her scent. She was too close, she wasn't close enough.

"Of all the things I could do," he confessed hoarsely. "I'm not sure which is right, which is wrong."

Marsh's hands became gentle on his arms as if she suddenly recollected the pain he must feel. "That's not important. The point is that you have to do something . . . anything . . . so that you will be the one controlling what happens. If you find out you've made the wrong choice, well, then, change your mind, do something else." Her hands were a caress. "The important thing is that you at least take charge. That you at least choose your own direction. Right or wrong, you have to act."

Her lips were full. Her eyes hypnotic. Sword found it difficult to talk. He thought it must still be the effects of the doctor's painkillers or the strain of the battle with Saul Calder. Or was it only her?

I know. But I don't know how, he thought despairingly. In his life, with his constantly changing advisors and guardians, and his money and his isolated existence, he had never learned those lessons. He had never had to.

Marsh moved even closer. "It's simple, Galen. As simple as this."

With a kiss, she showed him how it was done.

EIGHT

Adrian Forsyte closed his eyes as the van Ko drove to Central Park bounced around him. The movement reminded him of the horseback riding he had done years earlier. It reminded him of having his arms and legs and hands in his control, guiding his horse with a complex interplay of muscles—knees gripping, reins pulling, the rhythmic breathing and posting—back in the days when he had been whole. Back in the days before he had known Galen Sword.

Now, only the jarring of his head against the high back of his computer-controlled wheelchair told him he was moving. Except for his left index finger, the rest of his body was dead to him, unfeeling and unmoving, except in his dreams.

The large black Sword Foundation van slowed as Ko took it around a corner, swearing as a tire caught the edge of a deep pothole. Her words were the only ones spoken in the van. Beside her, in the passenger seat, Sword remained silent as usual. Behind them, even Martin sat without comment, glumly holding 'Bub's carrier cage on his lap. On the floor between Martin and the rails to which the treads of Forsyte's chair were locked, the pitiful white bundle which contained Ja'Nette's body lay in a silence even more profound than the tension and animosity which filled the van.

Forsyte opened his eyes to see the outside streetlights flash through the van's tinted windows in strobing bars of yellow and orange. He saw a small red ready light glow on the display screen on the left arm of his chair. The onboard computer had detected the motion of his eyes through the change in the reflectance pattern from the small lasers mounted in his glasses. The machinery that attempted to replace his body's capabilities stood ready to respond to any of the signals he could send it through switches that responded to his eyeblinks, his exhalations, and his one useful finger. But he had no orders to give. Tonight, he was just a passenger, at the mercy of whatever Ko and Sword had decided should happen next.

The vehicle lurched to a sudden stop and Forsyte heard his chair creak against the lockdown levers that held it in place.

"You all right, Adrian?"

Forsyte glanced up to the front of the van to see Ko looking over her shoulder at him. He could see a red traffic light through the windshield. For once in the past few weeks, the wipers weren't on. The autumn rain had finally stopped.

"Okay," Forsyte's voice synthesizer said in response to the command code his finger tapped out on his keypad.

Ko held his gaze as if she didn't believe him. She held his gaze so long that even Sword turned in his seat to look back.

Damn you both, Forsyte thought. *Why won't you talk to each other? Why won't you say the things you damn well know have to be said between you?* But none of those phrases was programmed into convenient keystrokes in his synthesizer. He turned his eyes away, unable to tell Ko or Sword anything, thinking that the brutes who had done this to him might just as well have banished him to the edge of the solar system where there could never again be any chance of spontaneous communication. Anything important he had to say these days took long minutes, even hours to assemble in his computer before he could express his thoughts. He could make small talk and have technical discussions using preprogrammed phrases and words, but to speak what was in his heart was next to impossible. By the time he had prepared his synthesized statements, the moment of interaction had long fled along with any chance of being understood within context. More than ever, he was realizing, it was better to ignore and forget that part of himself. He must become the machine that his chair and computers made him resemble. Until the day he could take his revenge.

A horn blared behind the van, echoing in its interior, and Forsyte was jerked against the straps which held him upright as Ko began driving again. The physicist still wasn't sure where they were going. In fact, only Martin seemed to have any clear idea—though the teenager had distinct problems when it came to understanding the layout of New York and had ultimately told them that he would know the place when he saw it and not before.

Martin's inability with maps was another question that gnawed at Forsyte. The halfling had managed to evade Sword and Ko and Forsyte for three months before he had been taken by surprise and captured. During that time, Martin had surely demonstrated an incredibly detailed knowledge of the city's back alleys, forgotten streets, and empty buildings. But he couldn't relate any of the routes he had taken to any of the maps that Forsyte had displayed to him on the Loft's computers. Forsyte almost got the impression that the city Martin moved through was not the same city that the maps showed. Some streets were the same . . . but most were different. Forsyte's mind spun with the outrageous solutions that might solve that problem.

"There, there," Martin suddenly growled. "Stop now."

Ko slowed the van. Through the windshield, Forsyte could see the vehicle's headlights illuminate high and blackened stone retaining walls. They were driving across Central Park. Even with the defensive equipment this new van carried—though no match for the fully equipped one that had been damaged by Saul Calder—this was not a good spot to stop.

"Where, exactly?" Ko asked.

"By bridge," Martin said, swiveling in his seat as the van passed a break in the wall where a dark staircase led up to a park path.

Forsyte watched as Sword peered out his window. "You mean that staircase, Martin?"

"Back there," was all that Martin replied.

Ko stopped the van and she and Sword discussed what to do. Forsyte could hear the tightness in both their voices. It had been in Ko's since earlier that night when Sword had been late to return to the Loft. When he had finally appeared two hours after he had said he would, with no hint of an apology or explanation, Ko had become even angrier.

At last, after a conversation in which most sentences were only a few words long, Ko turned the van around in the narrow roadway and headed back the way she had come, ignoring Martin's protests as she passed the staircase—or the bridge—once more.

"We have to find a place to park the van," Sword explained to Martin.

"Go too far, might not find again," Martin warned.

A few hundred feet past the spot Martin had identified, Ko pulled the van into a small turnaround intended for park vehicles. It was just after two A.M. and, since turning onto the park road, Forsyte had not seen the glare of any other headlights. There were better ways to travel from one side of the city to the other late at night than by going through Central Park. At least other people were sane enough to know that.

"Do you think it's safe to leave it here?" Ko asked as she pressed down on the parking brake pedal.

Sword turned back to Martin. "How long will this take?"

Martin looked out the window beside him. Forsyte saw him sniff the air as if forgetting the glass cut him off from the outside world. "Hard to know. During dark. Before light." Martin peered into 'Bub's carrier. " 'Bub not know either."

"Before dawn could be up to four, four and a half hours," Ko said.

Sword put his hand on the door latch. "Doesn't matter. We've got to do this." He opened the door and the overhead lights came on. "Just throw all the alarms and carry the beeper."

Ko began flipping a series of switches to the right of the steering column and the van's back door clicked and began to swing slowly open beside Forsyte.

Forsyte was surprised. He tapped out a command sequence and his voder voiced his question. "Am I coming?"

"Sword insists," Ko said grimly.

I'll be damned, Forsyte thought. *Good for Sword.* But then he reconsidered. In his association with the unpredictable and reticent millionaire, he had learned that whenever Sword did something unexpectedly generous, it was only because he was about to ask to be repaid with interest. Just like the first time they had met. Just like the very first time.

In those days, Forsyte had been a handsome man and he had known it. He was seventy pounds heavier, most of it muscle since he found that he could ponder the complexities of quantum physics just as easily during workouts and running as he could sitting and staring at his desk. And as often as not, those complexities were remade into simplicity itself within the brilliance of his intellectual exploration of them.

His doctorate had come at an early age from the University of Toronto, where he had toiled deep in the dripping basement of the old Physics building, coaxing realworld, observable events from the unobservable phenomena of quantum physics. His thesis—*Naked-Eye Quantum Effects in Delta Saturations of Halide Emulsions*—had garnered him three job offers before he had even been called upon to defend it: an associate professorship at Cambridge, where he knew he and everyone else couldn't help but remain in Hawking's shadow till at least the end of the century; a research fellowship at Kodak in Rochester, where the money would be good but too much of his research would be unpublishable in order to hide it from the company's competition; and a straightforward contract teaching position at MIT, where he would be given his own lab facility in lieu of being placed on the tenure track—subject to review when budgetary conditions took a turn for the better.

The offer of his own lab facility had been the key and at the age of thirty, Forsyte had been contentedly ensconced in a creative and invigorating academic environment. He taught the brightest undergrads, worked with the best graduates, and made excellent progress on developing a startling application of his previous research—a transformable tunneling electron waveguide which, he had calculated, would let him extend the quantum effect by which electrons traveled from point A to point C without passing through point B, over a distance limited only by the installed length of the waveguide itself. Hardwired communications could become virtually instantaneous. Computers could be made as large as necessary to overcome heating and maintenance problems yet still operate as fast as the speed of light in a vacuum. The world would be transformed by Adrian Forsyte's work—made better, safer, and more efficient while he became rich and famous for all time.

His life was perfect, not only in what existed, but in what was promised.

And then the exchange students came.

According to the records at the time—and he had studied them exhaustively after the fact—the admissions office claimed that the two young women were from the University of London, where they were working toward their doctorates in astronomy and physics. Their advisors had decided that their work in anomalous rapid signal propagation in novae detonations could be aided by an examination of Dr. Forsyte's work in transformable electron tunneling. There was a chance, the women had explained upon their first meeting with Forsyte, that the physical effect he was trying to create through engineering might already exist—however briefly—in the almost inconceivable energies born in the instants following the detonation of a supernova.

Forsyte's first reaction had been one of intense disappointment. If the transformable tunneling effect did exist in nature, then he knew he couldn't patent the concept, though the equipment which reproduced it would be fair game. However, the students' intense enthusiasm, and their apparent understanding of the problems involved, which seemed to surpass even Forsyte's accomplishments, soon led him to welcome their interest and their help.

Within two days of their first meeting with Forsyte, the excited physicist had introduced the two to his finest undergrad—the young woman who singlehandedly kept his lab functioning and supplied with prototype equipment—Melody Ko. At that time, Forsyte had less than four weeks of normal life remaining.

Forsyte was shaken from his memories by the sudden stop and crunch of gravel as the platform of his chair lift hit the ground behind the van. Martin stood before him, clutching 'Bub—now out of her carrier—tightly to his broad chest. Tonight, the halfling wore a bright red sweatshirt. *My last new one,* Forsyte thought resignedly. He hoped Sword would take Martin shopping soon.

"You going to take it from here?" Ko asked as she came around the side of the van. She wore a black canvas equipment vest over her sleeveless black tank top, and her loose, dark green pants were tucked into the tops of her high black sneakers. Forsyte noticed that more than half the loops and pockets on the vest were empty. The assault on the Clan Arkady had cost them almost all of the customized materiel Ko had created for them over the past two years.

"Okay," Forsyte made his voder say, then tapped out the commands that disconnected his chair from the lifting plate.

As he rolled forward, he heard the plate grind back up to the level of the van's floor, then slip inside on double worm screws, pulling the door shut behind it.

When the doors locked themselves, Ko held up a small

black box and pressed a button on it. An electronic chirp sounded from the van and Forsyte saw against the dark windows the reflections from a series of small red lights flashing inside.

"Fully armed," she said as Sword appeared beside her, gently carrying the small white bundle that had been on the van's floor.

"Including gas?" Sword asked.

Ko glared at him and Forsyte could see the struggle in her as she tried not to look at the shape hidden beneath the white cloth. "Fully armed," she repeated. Then she turned to Martin. "Can you find it again?"

Martin snorted. Forsyte took it to be an affirmative answer.

Ko looked at Sword, then at Forsyte. "Martin and I are going ahead until we see where we can continue off the road. You and Sword are waiting here until I come back."

Forsyte blinked once in shorthand for yes. Ko nodded then tapped Martin on his shoulder. "Go," she said.

Martin dropped down like a linebacker, one arm clutching 'Bub like a football, then rushed away on two legs and his free hand. Ko jogged easily after him, disappearing past the van. Forsyte listened carefully, but he could only hear Ko's feet on the pavement of the dark road. Martin might just as well have been the wind.

Sword stood silently beside Forsyte. He shifted his burden in his arms. He looked down at Forsyte.

"Are you all right?"

Forsyte's finger tapped the keys. "Are you?"

Sword shook his head. "Adrian, I don't know anymore."

Never did, Forsyte thought, but he tapped a different message on the keypad. "Thank you for letting me come. Tonight."

"I wasn't sure if you'd want to." Sword took a step forward and craned his head around the van. Forsyte no longer heard Ko's footsteps. "I didn't even know if Melody really wanted to."

"Cared about Ja'Nette," the voder said.

Sword nodded, but Forsyte knew that Sword would never make such an admission himself. It just wasn't in him.

"So did I, Adrian."

Forsyte stared at Sword in surprise, but Sword didn't notice. *I can't believe he said that,* Forsyte thought. But then again, so much had happened to them, how could any of them stay the same?

"Adrian, I don't want you to go. To leave the Loft. The team." Sword continued without giving Forsyte a chance to respond. "Martin's staying. For the time being, at least. We've come to an . . . arrangement. I've asked Melody to stay, too." He shifted the little body in his arms again. "I . . . I have no apology for what's happened. How things have escalated . . . so much more than whatever it was I was expecting . . . but I can't stop now. I don't think any of us can, or should." He ducked his head to look intently at Forsyte and the physicist did have to admit that for all of Sword's faults—and there were many—he never had treated Forsyte like a cripple or as anything other than a competent human being. "I'm not saying that you have to like me. Melody doesn't. I know Martin doesn't. I . . . I suspect that you don't. But that's not the point. It doesn't have to be, at least."

"You are right," Forsyte's computer voice said.

Sword waited for a moment. "About what?" he finally asked.

"Everything."

Sword tried to shrug. "Will you stay?"

Forsyte stabbed at his keys, trying to remember the sequence of phonemes for those words not stored, and the codes for those words which were. "Look at me. It's not up to me. I must go with Melody."

"I can get you ten assistants."

The word is "attendants," Forsyte thought bitterly. *And just having one is insult and embarrassment enough.* "Not the point," the voder said.

Sword looked away. "If it *were* up to you, *would* you stay?"

I'm a scientist, you fool. You are the key to a world of creatures who change shape against every law of biology, to a world of glowing crystals and magic independent of anything I can call science. How could I knowingly turn my back on that? How could I not stay? But Forsyte tapped no keys, gave no answer. It might only be in a small way, but he was still determined to make Sword feel as he did—cut off and abandoned.

Sword turned back, expecting a reply, and the two men held each other's gaze for long moments. "As I told you,"

Sword finally said, "you don't have to like me. I don't expect it. I don't need it."

Ah, but you do, Forsyte thought, glad for once that his near immobile face could show so little of what he thought or felt. *Especially now that you have admitted your feelings for the child. Whatever happened to you in the fight at the museum, whatever else happened to you in the days since that I don't know about, what people think about you, how people feel about you, is starting to matter to you. I can see it, Sword, I can hear it. I even know what's causing it. For once, you're beginning to understand what it means to be alone. Welcome to the club.*

But almost before he realized what he was doing, Forsyte's finger typed out a simple sequence of numbers.

"If it were up to me," the voder spoke, "I would stay."

This time, Sword remained silent. They both knew there was nothing more to be said.

Ko jogged back to them a few moments later. Forsyte was surprised to hear her so out of breath after such mild exertion. Perhaps the ribs she had told him she had bruised were causing more trouble than she wanted to admit.

"That staircase is the place," she told them. "Martin calls it a bridge, but whatever it is it leads up to the park."

"Can the chair handle it?" Sword asked. The rubber treads on Forsyte's chair could carry him up and down most modern flights of stairs, but an old, narrow-stepped stone staircase might be too steep for the mechanism.

"Probably," Ko said. "But Martin says he'll carry the chair up to save time. I think we're on some sort of schedule here."

"Schedule?" Sword asked.

Ko knelt down to check the battery cable connections on Forsyte's chair. "Martin wants us to hurry. Won't give a reason."

"Then we'll hurry," Sword said as he moved away from the van.

Ko stood. "Adrian and I should go first."

"We'll go together."

"Right," Ko protested. "And if a car drives by and sees the parade . . . ?"

"Hasn't been a car along here the whole time we were waiting for you," Sword said.

Both Sword and Ko turned to Forsyte as they heard clicks from his keypad. "No cars. Unusual," the voder said.

Ko disagreed. "It's late. People don't like the park after dark. Nothing unusual about that."

"Good," Sword said. "Then we *will* all go together."

Ko frowned as she realized how Sword had twisted her words. But then she stepped behind Forsyte and he heard her swing up the chair's manual control bar and snap it into place. "Slip it into neutral and I'll push," she told him. Forsyte tapped the gear control and he was off. Ko's rhythmic breaths sounded behind him in time to her running. The road was rougher than he had expected and, as they moved from the pale pool of light from one dim overhead streetlamp, Forsyte was almost convinced that the asphalt of the road slowly changed over to old-style paving bricks.

A second pale streetlamp glowed over the stone stairway leading up from the road. Martin crouched at the top as Ko and Forsyte arrived. His arms were empty. Ko saw it, too.

"Martin," she called up in a half-whisper, half-shout. "Where's 'Bub?"

"Waiting," Martin said simply as he bounded down the stairs.

Sword arrived then, breathing more heavily than Ko, Ja'Nette's white-wrapped body firmly held in his arms.

Forsyte felt himself rise suddenly into the air as Martin lifted his chair as easily as if it had been a barstool. "Hurry Galen Sword," the halfling said, then ran up the stairs.

When Martin lowered Forsyte to the ground again, the halfling wasn't even winded. He watched impatiently as Ko and Sword ran up the stairs behind him.

"Very strong," Forsyte tapped out on the voder.

"Like father," Martin said. Then the halfling looked up past the black, leafless branches of the trees above, as if expecting to see something. "Martin father Astar. Powerful shifter."

Ko and Sword reached the top of the stairs. Sword was close to wheezing.

Martin held out his arms. "Martin take Ja'Nette."

But Sword made no move to relinquish his burden. "I brought her here. I'll help her . . . go home."

Martin accepted that. He lowered his arms.

Ko had something else on her mind. "Where exactly is 'Bub waiting, Martin?"

Sword's eyes narrowed. " 'Bub's not here?"

"Martin call for Lights from Marratin. 'Bub wait where Martin call. Hurry, hurry." He loped off down the path leading from the top of the stairway.

Sword stepped off the last stone step, tentatively moving his foot back and forth. "You'd think with all the rain we've been having that this would—"

But Ko interrupted him. "We're going to lose him, Sword. You go ahead. We'll follow."

Forsyte remained a passenger as Ko pushed him along the path. Sword had been right in what he had been about to say, he decided. The path was little more than packed earth and it *was* far too dry for the amount of rain that had been falling on the city. Forsyte kept trying to glance up to catch a glimpse of the sky where the low clouds glowed with the reflected light of the city, but it only showed through in small strips and slices, too quickly for him to observe its condition. *Perhaps the tree branches are thick enough to protect the earth from the rain here,* Forsyte thought. But he wasn't convinced.

After a few hundred feet and four or five gentle turns, the covering trees became denser and Ko asked Forsyte to switch on the chair's lights. "We should be far enough from the road that no one will see," she explained. Twin headlights molded into the plastic coverings of the chair arms just beside the taser barrel pods stabbed into life at Forsyte's command.

"Bloody hell," Ko whispered in shock. Forsyte had to agree.

The vegetation that surrounded the pathway was unlike anything Forsyte had ever suspected could grow in New York City. Rough and heavily textured vines like impossibly long and twisted tree branches formed a rolling barricade on either side of the path, looking like barbed wire as much as anything organic. None of the coiled and looping vines carried leaves either, only a sparse and random assortment of smaller branches which stuck out like needles on a cactus. Up ahead, Sword stopped as his shadow stretched out before him, trapped in the lights from Adrian's chair.

Ko caught up to him in seconds and when Sword turned, Forsyte could see that he didn't recognize the vegetation either.

"This is like when we went into the cave that night,"

Sword said. "About the same place, but underground. We thought we were under Central Park but . . . everything changed."

Ko stepped out in front of the chair, blindingly lit by the headlight she stood before. Shadows stretched up her, hiding her eyes in dark pools. "We went through a fardoor in the tunnels, Sword. We haven't passed through anything up here."

"Pass through layer," a voice said from the darkness and both Sword and Ko started. But Forsyte, whose body could no longer react to such hair-trigger stimuli, remained calm for the half-second necessary to recognize Martin's presence.

"What's the layer?" Sword asked as Martin stepped into view. Forsyte saw he had removed his sweatshirt, and vest and pants as well. Only his heavy furlike body hair hid his nakedness this night.

"Layer what we pass through to be here," Martin explained. "Must hurry hurry," he added before anyone could ask another question. Then he stepped back and returned to the darkness.

"First World?" Sword asked the air. "Some sort of dimensional shift?"

"Martin said that the First World isn't a separate place. It's just a name the adepts use for themselves and for the parts of the world they keep hidden from us."

Sword turned to stare at Ko. "Melody, do you honestly believe we're still in Central Park?"

Ko stepped back behind Forsyte's chair. "I don't *believe* anything. I either know, or I don't know. And for now, I don't know and that's all I'm willing to say."

Forsyte saw Sword try to conceal a smile just before he turned to follow Martin once again.

After only a few more minutes, the headlights showed that the path suddenly widened and dropped. Ko stopped pushing Forsyte's chair. "Adrian, kill the lights."

Forsyte toggled the lights off and saw that they were no longer needed. The path had led them to some sort of wide dark clearing and, free from the cover of the towering trees, enough moonlight managed to filter through the overcast sky to enable Forsyte to see. Here at least the ground looked wet, he noted with relief. But then he saw from the way the light rippled as it was reflected that it wasn't ground he looked at—it was water. And wherever they were in the park, they were far from the reservoir.

"Over here. Come come hurry," Martin called from the side of the path.

As Ko turned his chair, Forsyte saw that Martin squatted near a scattering of wide flat rocks near the water's edge. It wasn't a large body of water—it was well within the scale of the park—and Forsyte could see the black silhouettes of trees a few hundred yards away on the other side. If he admitted that it was possible that he had gotten turned around in their drive here, then it was also possible that they were still in the park. Perhaps just farther south than he had anticipated.

Beside Martin, Forsyte could see 'Bub sitting motionlessly on her haunches. As Sword approached, the cat lifted one paw and began to groom herself.

Martin hopped back from the rock he was on and gestured to it. "Here here," he said, looking rapidly from the rock, to Sword, and to the sky.

Forsyte looked up, also. The moon was unexpectedly bright through the clouds. He decided that the clouds were thinner than they appeared to be, though if that were the case, he knew he should also see at least a handful of stars. He didn't.

Sword knelt carefully by the large flat rock Martin indicated and gently laid Ja'Nette's body upon it.

"Do we . . . have to . . . unwrap her?" Sword asked Martin.

Martin shook his head, then moved around the small white shape and took Sword's hand in his. "Back here, back here." Martin led Sword back to stand beside Ko and Forsyte.

For a few moments, all were silent. Only 'Bub moved, sitting a few feet from Ja'Nette, purposefully licking first one paw and then another.

"Is there anything we should be doing?" Ko asked.

"Too late," Martin said softly, still scanning the night sky. "Already done. Little halfling sister dead."

Forsyte noticed that Martin hadn't let go of Sword's hand and was holding it as a worried child might.

Sword seemed to sense the same thing in Martin, for when he asked his next question Forsyte was surprised at how gentle his voice had become. "What are we waiting for, Martin?"

At first, Martin acted as if he would say nothing. Then he lifted one powerful arm and pointed a single thick finger up to the clouds.

"Waiting for them," the halfling whispered.

Forsyte followed Martin's gaze and saw what had suddenly appeared in the sky. Perhaps they weren't in Central Park any longer. Perhaps they weren't even on the same planet.

"Bloody hell," Ko whispered beside him. "What are they, Martin?"

"The Lights," Martin said.

And they were coming closer.

NINE

Ko watched as a dense constellation of stars flared through the low-lying clouds, scattering sparkling reflections across the small dark pond before her.

In one small part of her mind, she knew that the phenomenon she was viewing was indescribably beautiful—the colors of the objects were so pure, their flight so graceful, the regular pulse of their flickering so satisfying that she feared that if she stared at them too long, she would cease to be aware of anything but their beauty.

But that realization was carefully compartmented in a place within herself she kept hidden and ignored. There was no room for beauty in her life, nor rapt appreciation of anything or anyone. That option had been cruelly taken from her and for now all that was left for her was to analyze, break down, and comprehend. Above all else, she *must* comprehend.

The hundreds of objects that Martin called *Lights* were closing slowly, darting back and forth across the surface of the pond as if reluctant to approach all at once. Their sudden shifts in direction—sometimes at random and sometimes in formation with a dozen or more moving in precise unison—led Ko to suspect that they were under conscious control, even if that consciousness were no more than that possessed by a firefly.

However, at the rate the objects were pumping out photons, Ko knew that whatever chemical process lay behind their bioluminescence, it had to be more energetic and efficient than that possessed by any firefly species she knew of, and since she knew so many, she suspected it was not yet known to modern biology.

"Where have they come—"

"Shhh!" Ko said sharply, interrupting Sword's question. Didn't the fool realize that she had to listen carefully for any sound that these things might make? Perhaps she might hear the sputter of ignition—they could be artifacts after all, small gliders with blazing thermite. Or perhaps she might hear the whine of small motors. They could be witnessing a clever illusion engendered by a flight of remotely controlled model aircraft.

"Aren't you at all curious about these things?" Sword whispered accusingly. "Look at them. They're magnificent. Whatever the hell they are."

"Not hell," Martin said quietly, rocking gently from foot to foot. "Lights, Galen Sword. Marratin Lights come for Ja'Nette."

But first they came for the others.

Ko ducked suddenly as one of the sparkling Lights dove straight for her. She felt the heat of its passage on her upraised hand and heard a small flutter as it passed, a flutter slower than wings should be—if they were organic—and quieter than any motor might make.

"Melody . . . look at Adrian." Ko heard in Sword's voice the awe she would not permit herself to feel. She knew there had to be an explanation.

But what explanation could there be for what she saw now? A hundred glowing sparks of light swirled madly around Forsyte in his chair, bathing him in liquid blue radiance.

Within his luminous cocoon of trailing light, the flickering shadows that played across his face almost made him look as if he were smiling, almost made him look as if he were no longer a sunken, hollow prisoner of his chair but a fuller, healthier version of himself. Ko gazed in wonder she refused to acknowledge as the streaming light that flowed around Forsyte made him look as if he were raising his immobile arms to embrace it, a smile on his useless, unchanging lips.

"No," Ko said, determined not to accept only the evidence of her eyes. She reached out her hand to the cords of shimmering light that encased Forsyte. She wanted to push them away and gaze on him with undistorted vision. One small quiet part of her mind pleaded with her to accept that the dream might have come true, just as she had seen humans change to beasts and a cat disappear from the normal spectrum. Perhaps such things were possible. Perhaps such things must be possible.

Her hands moved closer to the Lights.

"No Melody *no no no.*"

But Martin's warning was lost in the sudden scalding contact she made.

Ko choked back a cry of shock and pain and clasped her hand to her chest. Tears of surprise came instantly to her eyes as the place where she had touched the spirals of light surrounding Forsyte slowly pulsated like ripples in a pond.

She felt Sword beside her, his arm around her, and at first she thought he was trying to console her. But then she heard the laughter and she pulled roughly away from him, ignoring the searing agony in her hand. Too late, as the stream of circling flying Lights peeled off from their vortex around Forsyte and came for her, she realized that the laughter had not come from Sword but from *them.*

There were things in the Lights. In each Light. Small perfect figures in some. Naked, laughing, inches high, transparent as mist. And other things. Hideous things. Skulls and organs and slippery pulsing lengths of flesh which Ko had to squeeze her eyes closed against, despite the dictates of her logic and her quest for knowledge.

But closing her eyes didn't help. Whatever flew before her was seen with a sense other than vision. The Lights that ringed her, encasing her as they had Forsyte, were just as clear to her with her eyes closed as with her eyes open.

"No," she said to them and heard only their laughter in return.

"No," she pleaded, eyes open again to see Sword and Forsyte and Martin past the shimmering curtain the Lights had formed.

A single Light paused before her, a flutter as of a hummingbird's wings behind the perfect body. It was female, Ko saw, peering closer in fascination. Oriental? She was puzzled, looked more closely. Saw cropped black hair almost short as bristles. Saw a familiar smile and set of eyes. Recognized herself in the Light's glowing form. Felt her skin crawl with electricity, with astonishment, with fear, she couldn't tell what. She reached out again with her uninjured hand to try and touch the apparition, and as her hand grew closer, the perfect replica of herself shrivelled away, skin sagging, flesh drooping and drying till it puffed away as so much dust to leave a tiny perfect skeleton floating before her, hideously grimacing, raising long clawed skeletal arms, growing fangs, screeching over the deafening flutter of the other swarming Lights until, when Ko's trembling hand was only inches away, it darted at her outstretched fingers and bit and clawed savagely.

Ko twisted away with a scream she had no hope of controlling. She felt herself hit something writhing and warm and yielding, and then was through that barricade and falling again at normal speed until she hit the rocky earth beneath her.

When she looked up, she saw Sword holding out his hand to her. She glanced apprehensively at Forsyte but he was unchanged, unhurt, and had turned his head toward the Light's new location. Ko grasped Sword's hand and pulled herself to her feet, not fighting his grip as she stood unsteadily, one hand throbbing with a serious burn, the other with bloody cuts and gashes. The Lights now swarmed around Martin. At least, she thought it was Martin.

"What are they?" she asked Sword, inwardly appalled at the hoarse tremor of her voice. "What are they doing to us?"

Sword said nothing. His eyes were riveted on Martin—or the thing that Martin had become.

Behind the swirling mad wall of streaking light, Martin's outline had grown to almost double height and width with each muscle perfectly defined within the glow. And two pinpoints of light shone brighter than any of the others—not Lights that circled but lights that came from within the vortex. Lights that were Martin's *eyes*, blazing fiercely.

"What's happening to him? What are they doing?" Ko asked. She wanted answers. She *had* to have answers.

"It's like that night," Sword said. "When Ja'Nette died . . . Martin rose up . . . Martin rose up and his eyes were glowing. Just like that."

Ko looked back at Forsyte. The physicist was enthralled by the transformation they witnessed.

Ko tugged on Sword's arm. "What did I look like when they were around *me*, Sword? What did *I* look like?"

Sword turned to her and even in the unearthly glow of the Lights, Ko could see the discomfort in his eyes.

"There was . . . nothing," he said. "You weren't even there."

Ko tried to think of another question to ask. Any question to ask to make this all make sense. But she could think of nothing except her pain. Except seeing Forsyte's arms move, sure and muscular, reaching out . . .

"You'd better get back," Sword said. Ko felt him loosen his grip on her and step away from her.

A few yards over, Martin's silhouette had returned to normal size, his eyes no longer glowed, and like a swarm of electric bees the Lights lifted from him, gathering above him in a glowing, sparkling cloud.

"It's my turn now," Sword said. He stood alone on the rocks, his tall figure well back from the others. Ko wondered what he would experience within the Lights. She wondered what she would see.

Sword stood ready. The Lights swarmed ten feet above the ground. They moved slowly, like fog at sea, roiling toward Sword.

And they stopped.

Sword lifted his head to them, raised his arms to them. "What is it?" he called out. "What do you want?"

Like a squadron of bombers, the Lights abruptly swerved away, over the pond, forming a double moon of brilliance above the still water.

Sword's hands fell to his sides as he watched the Lights withdraw. He turned to Martin. "What did they want, Martin? Why didn't they swarm around me?"

But Martin said nothing. He crouched on the rocks, hands flattened before him, staring at Sword with eyes wider than Ko had ever seen him with before.

"Martin! What's wrong?" Sword demanded. "Why didn't they swarm?"

Martin's only reply was the low oooing sound he made when he was in distress.

Before Sword could say anything else, the twin glow over the pond changed position again, coming back.

"Now?" Sword asked. "Now are they coming for me?"

"No," Martin growled softly. "Lights coming for Ja'Nette."

The swarm swerved and twisted and compressed itself until Ko could no longer see separate sources of light, only a rippling sphere of incandescence rolling over the surface of the water, heading directly for the white-shrouded figure which lay on the flat rock.

Like an immense, glowing wave, the sphere hit the rock and broke over it, erupting in a slow spray of sparkles and silver dust. 'Bub sat motionlessly at the edge of the rock as the dazzling specks danced in her fur. She was unconcerned by what transpired, as if she had seen it all a thousand times before. The luminous surf hung in the air for long moments, then slowly fell upon the still shroud, sucked into it as if a powerful wind blew down on it, filling it with blinding light.

The very air around the child's enshrouded body began to shine now. Reflexively, Ko held her arms up to protect her eyes, ignoring the pain in both her injured hands. Beside her, she could see Sword hold one hand before his face and another before Forsyte's. To herself, she thanked him for that kindness.

Seen through the cracks between her fingers, the white cloth surrounding Ja'Nette took on the luster and sheen of molten silver. *Where is the heat from this radiance?* Ko asked herself, still trying futilely to make these events fit within what she knew of how the universe must work. *What is the energy source? Where are the waste products of the conversion process? How high a wavelength is needed to excite the retina even behind closed eyelids? And* what *is moving within the light?*

Something did move there, barely discernible in the glare. It was something humanform—how easily she had come to use Martin's term—something that stood beside the shroud and held out a hand . . .

. . . and another, small dark hand reached up through the shroud to take it.

Ko turned her head away just as she saw something—someone—Ja'Nette—sit up on the rock and she couldn't look any longer. She didn't want to know. She couldn't know. There was too much pain, too much confusion, too much that just didn't make any sense at all.

Ko pressed both agonized hands against her face, afraid to look, afraid to even understand the fear which filled her so powerfully, so unexpectedly. *This is wrong,* she found herself thinking, dazed. *All I am witnessing is visual information. There is nothing here to harm me. Nothing here to cause me to feel fear. Why am I reacting this way? Why can't I just open my eyes and look back at the rock and see whatever is there to see?*

Ko took a breath. She straightened up. She opened her eyes.

A tall black woman stood mere inches in front of her—a

cloud of long black hair spraying out from her head as if blown by a raging wind.

Ko gasped despite herself. The woman's face was human normal, but her eyes were twice any normal size and solid black, endlessly black, soul-swallowing end of all time and space and hope black.

The woman opened her mouth and Ko could see through it as if the woman were no more than a projection. Martin and Sword stood behind the apparition. Sword seemed to be calling something out to her, pointing at her to look at something . . . look at something.

Ko looked down.

The tall black woman was not alone. Beside her stood Ja'Nette, but not Ja'Nette. The transparent image of the child had Ja'Nette's size and shape, had the hideous wound across her throat where the werewolf had almost severed the child's neck with one bite, but this Ja'Nette had eyes like the woman's—twice as large as they should be and solid, fathomless black.

Ko stared without thought or feeling. The transparent child looked up at her. The transparent child said her name in a voice like a thousand raging winds.

Ko lost her fight. She screamed.

And the black woman looked away and the child looked away and both images of both people broke down like a computer graphic dissolving into low rez and then suddenly exploded into a blinding flurry of Lights.

The blazing sparks glittered over the rocks and Forsyte's chair, between Sword and Martin, around Ko, and she felt tugs on her vest and her clothing and saw Forsyte rock in his chair and watched as Sword and Martin waved their hands as if battling enraged mosquitos.

Then the Lights fell for the center of the pond and spun together and rose back up into the night and passed through the low clouds, glowing briefly within until the clouds were dark again and there was nothing left except for 'Bub, knuckled down by the torn open and empty white shroud which once had held a small body.

Ko was the first to speak. She wondered if she could be heard over the thunder of her heart. "Did we . . . did we all see that?"

Sword nodded his head.

Forsyte's keypad clicked beneath his finger. "What did we see?" the voder asked.

"Lights," Martin said. "Just Lights.'

"Who was the woman?" Forsyte's computer voice was reassuringly technical and sound to Ko. Some of the laws of logic and science were still working at least.

"Martin think Ja'Nette mother. Ja'Nette mother Clan Marratin. Woman Clan Marratin. Ja'Nette mother come take Ja'Nette home."

Sword went to Martin. Ko was surprised to see that both Sword and the halfling looked as unsettled as she felt. "Where is the Clan Marratin home?" Sword asked.

"Lights know. Martin not know. That's why Martin call Lights."

"Can you call the Lights again?" Sword asked.

Why, Ko thought, *why would anyone want to go through that again?* And she thought, *why didn't any of us think to bring a camera?*

"Martin call Lights when Martin have to," the halfling said. He straightened up and moved over to a small rock where Ko saw he had piled his clothing.

"When's that?" Sword asked.

Martin struggled to pull on his sweatpants. Ko heard the fabric rip as he forced one leg in the wrong place. "When someone die, Martin call Lights to take someone home."

Sword slipped his hands in his pocket and looked out over the pond. The light from the moon rippled across its surface. For a moment, Ko was puzzled by how bright the moon seemed. She looked up and saw it partially obscured by clouds, marring all detail. Or else it had none.

"Will you call the Lights for me, Martin?" Sword asked in an odd voice. "When I die?" He sounded as if he were trying to remember something long forgotten.

Ko watched as Martin shook his head. His pants were back on but he was staring at the sweatshirt in defeat.

"Lights not gather round Galen Sword tonight. That mean Lights not come for Galen Sword when time to go home." Martin made a ball out of the sweatshirt and heaved it away into the water.

Sword turned to look at Martin. His shoulders were slumped. He looked more tired than Ko had thought he could be and still stand.

"What do you mean by that, Martin? Do you mean that even when I die I won't be able to . . . go home?"

Ko had never seen Martin look at Sword the way he looked on him now. With pity, Ko decided. *Martin actually feels sorry for Sword.*

"Could be," the halfling said softly. He reached out to Sword and touched his arm with the back of his hand in a gesture of compassion.

"Even when I die . . . ?" Sword repeated, for himself more than for anyone else.

"Could be Galen Sword not die," Martin said, gently patting Sword's arm. "Could be Galen Sword never die."

And however chilled Ko felt by that simple statement, she could see in Sword's haunted eyes that *his* fear was more than she might even imagine.

TEN

Sword had found it difficult to speak as they had returned from the calling of the Lights. They all had found it difficult.

Martin had guided them back along the path to the stone stairway leading down to the road through Central Park, and this time there had been no urgency to his pace, no exhortations to hurry. Even 'Bub had not complained when Martin had slipped her back into her carrier.

The black van was untouched where they had left it on the turnaround. It was obvious to Sword that Ko's hands were too badly injured to drive, so he had taken the wheel without discussion.

Just as he had started the van's engine and was preparing to pull back out onto the road, another car had passed—the first they had seen that night. But no one commented on it. The presence or absence of cars was the least of the questions Sword contemplated then, and he had had no doubt that for once the others shared his priorities.

Ko had wanted to be taken to her apartment in the Village. Sword had asked to see her hands under the van's interior lights. The burn, though extensive, was red but not blistered and the scratches, though deep, were little more than what a cat might inflict in play, so Sword had not insisted she go to a hospital and agreed to drive her to her home.

Forsyte left the van with Ko. She had a room for him in her apartment, and the proper facilities. Sword hadn't argued. He hadn't even wondered if he might be losing his last chance to convince her to return to the Loft. Once again, they had shared something so remarkable, so divorced from their normal perceptions of reality, that when Ko had said that they should talk in the morning, Sword had known that she would keep her word and he *would* see her back at the Loft.

This time, none of them could ignore what they had experienced and, despite the growing complexity of the mystery threatening to consume his life, Sword felt the first glimmer of hope that he might at last be on the road to victory.

Ko had walked up the steps to her building as Forsyte's chair had climbed beside her, the center stalk of it angling to keep the physicist level at all times. Ko had not looked back to the street as she had held the door open for Forsyte. She had not said good night, and Sword knew she would be back not just for one meeting, but for good. He knew she no longer had a choice. All that remained was for her to realize that as well.

Martin was quiet as Sword drove the van back through the dark and empty streets to the Loft. Sword decided not to burden the halfling with any of the thousand questions he needed to ask. The morning would come soon enough. Martin would be there. Ko and Forsyte would return. The search would begin again, and this time in earnest, with no more surprises. Sword found it hard to believe that after tonight he could be surprised by anything more.

Sword stopped the van by the Loft's corrugated metal garage door. In the gleam of the headlights, he could see the mismatched metal plates that Ko had used to repair the hole which had been blasted through the door when Saul Calder had escaped. Each was still in place.

Sword folded down the dash keyboard of the van's computer and typed in the access code for the Loft's Cray-Hitachi Model II, securely installed in the renovated warehouse's second basement. Instantly, the computer informed him that the Loft's security system was intact and that it had not been challenged since he had armed it earlier that evening. He typed in the code to open the garage door. Slowly, the metal panels rolled upward. Sword put the van in gear. But Martin opened the door beside him before the van began to move.

As the halfling began to slip from the passenger seat to the street, Sword spoke. "Wait till we're inside, Martin."

Martin turned back to Sword, holding the van door open. "Martin not go inside."

"Why not?"

Martin looked behind him, looked up, rolled his lips out, and knitted his heavy brows together. "Just not."

"Is something wrong?"

Martin took on the appearance of a small child desperate for a restroom. He shook his head rapidly.

"Then why can't you come in?"

Martin bit his lip. "Night outside. Night. Martin night . . . Martin go . . ."

He looked at Sword, conveying with his eyes what he had no words for.

"Will you come back?" Sword asked, not knowing what Martin wanted, but recognizing the power of the drive within him.

"Martin live Loft now Ja'Nette room Martin 'Bub." He took a step away from the van, rocking back and forth edgily.

Comprehension at last came to Sword. Martin had to do what he had done for the past three months that Sword had hunted him through the streets and alleys of the city.

"You're going to go for . . . for a run, aren't you, Martin?" Sword smiled, tying to make it look friendly. Martin was a creature born for the outdoors, for the night.

But the word *run* wasn't exactly what Martin had in mind. "Martin just . . . go. Then come back." Sword realized that Martin had very few words in mind. Not that it was any sign of a lack of intelligence. It was just that he thought in different ways, with different patterns.

Sword understood. He wouldn't stop Martin. But there was one thing he required of the halfling's skills and abilities. He held out his hand to Martin. "Do one thing for me before you go? Please?" Sword had been known to use that word often, but what felt odd to him this time was that in some way he realized he meant it.

Martin widened his eyes to ask his question, almost as if the pull of the night was interfering with his ability to speak.

"Come into the garage with me and check it out. Sniff the air or whatever you do."

Martin tilted his head, no comprehension in his expression.

"To see if Saul Calder has come back," Sword explained. "Or . . . or anything else."

Martin bared his fangs at the mention of the shifter's

name. He nodded as if awakening. "Martin keeper for Galen Sword. Martin hunt shifter for Galen Sword."

Before Sword could voice his thanks, Martin had jumped back from the van's door and barreled into the open garage. When Sword had driven the van in and parked it beside the Checker cab he used for unobtrusive surveillance, Martin was dangling from an overhead iron beam by one foot and one hand.

Sword stepped out of the van and looked up at Martin as the halfling swung slowly back and forth. "Anything here?"

Martin didn't look down. "Saul Calder stink Loft but Saul Calder not here now. No one here now." His deep, rough voice echoed in the oversize garage.

"Thank you, Martin. That's all I wanted to know."

Martin continued to swing back and forth without looking at Sword. His eyes were half-lidded, unfocused.

"Martin! Thank you! You can go now!"

Sword's raised voice made Martin blink and look down as if coming out of a trance. Then he let go of the beam, flipping over twice as he dropped sixteen feet to land on the garage floor as silently as falling snow. For a moment, he froze in position, crouched over on fists and feet.

"Doesn't that hurt when you do that?" Sword asked, and he was serious.

But Martin only stared at him as if he had never seen Sword before.

"Martin? Are you . . . all right?"

Martin's nostrils flared. He rolled once, dropping to his shoulder, spinning over on his back, then righting himself once more. Sword said nothing. For a moment, he wondered if he should think about getting back in the van.

But before Sword could move, Martin slapped the concrete floor of the garage with the flat of his hand, making noise like a crack of thunder. Sword jerked at the sound of it. Martin slapped the floor again, louder and harder than before. He curled his lips and hooted, slapped twice more, rolled again, and then he was nothing more than a silent streak rushing out through the open garage door into the night.

Sword waited for a moment by the van, unsure of what he had just witnessed. *Half-human, half-shifter,* he reminded himself again. Then he walked out to the sidewalk of the SoHo street. It was empty, almost soundless. From far away, he heard something which might have been a distant siren, or the cry of a halfling. In this city, who would know the difference?

Sword turned to go back into the garage. He felt a wave of complete exhaustion come to claim him. He had not had the sleep he needed this morning. He walked over to the garage control panel, hoping that Ko and Forsyte would sleep in, saving their meeting for later in the day.

He heard footsteps on the sidewalk outside.

He stopped.

A long shadow moved across the sidewalk outside the garage, bouncing in time to the click of metal-shod heels against concrete. It took a moment for Sword to realize that the shadow was deformed by the angle of the street lights and not necessarily because it represented the true shape of the creature who cast it.

Careful, Sword warned himself. *Can't start thinking that everyone I see is a First-World shapeshifter.*

He held one hand over the garage door control. He kept the other hand next to the only weapon he had in his half-empty equipment vest—a small, twin-needled taser.

A form appeared at the edge of the doorway. A human form.

Sword watched the figure warily. It was a man, human, tall, muscular, in a long and open dark coat. He wore black jeans tucked into high black boots and a black shirt beneath his coat. His long brown hair was gathered loosely into a ponytail at the back of his neck, and his skin was reminiscent of the Middle East. But the man's angular features didn't match his skin color. They were . . . Sword didn't know what they were, other than different. Striking, certainly, but somehow unexpected.

The man stopped at the entranceway to the garage. He stared in at Sword.

"Can I help you?" Sword asked.

The man looked up at the outside of the Loft, then to either side as if searching for something, perhaps a street number.

"I am looking for a Galen Sword." The man's voice was smooth and sure, but Sword could detect no hint of any accent. Whatever the man's origins, they were well hidden.

Sword didn't move from the control panel. "Why?"

"Do you know him?" the man asked. He did something

odd then. He tilted his head back, parted his lips just a fraction of an inch, and inhaled gently. Sword had seen 'Bub do much the same thing whenever a particularly interesting scent caught her attention. He told himself to remember to take the cat from her carrier in the van before he shut down for the night.

The man suddenly looked at the parked van, as if Sword had spoken aloud instead of just thinking about it.

"Come back tomorrow," Sword said. *When the rest of my team is here. Then we can deal with anything.*

The man gave nothing away with his expression. "Tomorrow might be too late."

Sword refused to go for the bait. He didn't reply.

The man smiled and nodded, acknowledging Sword's assessment of his words. He still hadn't moved past the threshold of the garage. "Have you no curiosity?"

"Not tonight," Sword said.

The man eased his hands into the pockets of his coat but didn't seem to be reaching for anything. He was just adopting a more comfortable stance, apparently having no inclination to leave.

"I understand that Galen Sword is an investigator."

Sword said nothing, hand still on the door switch.

"I believe I am aware of events which Galen Sword might like to investigate."

Sword decided the man wouldn't leave until he had stated his case. "What events are those?"

The man stared intently at Sword. "Do you know where I can find him?"

Sword took a breath, more from exhaustion than anything else.

"I'm Sword."

The man's eyes widened as if in surprise. "I . . . had expected an older man," he said, then quickly recovered.

Sword ignored the comment. He felt old enough tonight. "What events?" he repeated.

The man looked down at the threshold of the garage for a moment. "It might sound unusual. Perhaps even . . . improbable."

"I'm used to that."

The man looked up again. "Then you *are* an investigator? Of the . . . improbable?"

The man made it sound as if Sword were engaged in a

quest for strange sexual practices. "Unusual *phenomena*," he clarified. "Short-lived, psychic, paranormal, inexplicable."

The man nodded. "And beings?"

"Such as?"

The man held Sword's gaze in silence before replying. Sword sensed that some decision was being made. An irrevocable decision.

"Vampires, Mr. Sword. In New York City."

Sword wanted to sigh again. He had heard the stories. From Dracula fanatics and borderline cases who wanted to drink blood themselves. Lots of people believed there were vampires in the city. Lots of people believed that *they* were vampires in the city. And Sword had spent too many months in his first year discovering that those who had come to him with their knowledge and their accusations of what really went on in the city streets at night were stricken not with vampirism, but with delusions and unfulfilled fantasies for which he had no time.

"Vampires," Sword repeated.

This time the man said nothing.

"In New York."

Still nothing.

"I've heard those stories before. Too many times. If you call me tomorrow, I can give you the names of some groups that get together around here. I think they'd be more interested in what you have to say than I would be right now." He pressed his fingers to the door switch.

But the man raised his own hand, as if to stop Sword's action, even though from where he stood he could not possibly see Sword's fingers moving against the control.

"Perhaps I have used the wrong term, Mr. Sword. Perhaps I should point out that the term 'vampire' is one which . . . humans use. Those I wish to talk to you about . . . they call themselves adepts."

Sword's hand slowly moved away from the garage control. He gestured to the garage. "Please, come in."

The man's face instantly blossomed into a wide smile, as if Sword had granted him an incredibly generous favor.

"Ah, thank you," the man said as he quickly stepped across the threshold, walking purposefully to Sword, hand extended in greeting. "My name is Ryan."

Sword shook Ryan's hand as the garage door finally rumbled shut for the night, thinking that he had never seen skin so golden. Or teeth so white and perfect.

Off the main lab on the second level was a small meeting room that also served as the Loft's main kitchen. Sword searched through the black laminate-covered cupboards lining one wall above a sleek black counter, trying to discover where Ko had decided would be the most efficient location to keep coffee. He hadn't been surprised to find that it wasn't directly over the coffeemaker. Her efficiency systems forever remained convoluted and obscure to him.

Behind him, Ryan sat patiently at the long conference table, his folded hands lying on their own reflection in the table's glossy black surface. A few feet away from him in the center of the table, 'Bub sat on a small stack of unread newspapers, knuckled down on all four paws, staring at Ryan intently.

Ryan answered Sword's most recent question, ignoring the repetitive banging of the cupboard doors as Sword continued his hunt.

"Like you, Mr. Sword, I am a searcher. An investigator. Though I do not believe that, up to now, I have enjoyed your success."

Sword pulled a green cardboard box of Irish Breakfast Tea from the cupboard farthest from the hotplate. What had Ko been thinking about when she organized this room?

"I haven't had any success." Sword held out the box of teabags to his guest. "How about tea instead of coffee?"

"Whatever you're having," Ryan said. He kept his eyes on 'Bub, appearing to be as interested in the cat as the cat was in him. "But did you not say that you have already investigated claims of vampires within the city and proven them to be false?"

Sword gave up trying to find a kettle. He filled two off-white Dean & DeLuca mugs with water at the stainless steel sink, then placed both mugs in the microwave oven. He had no idea how long the oven would take to boil water, so he set the timer for ten minutes as a guess. It had always seemed to take Ko or Ja'Nette at least ten minutes to come back with tea or coffee after he had asked for some. At least, those times that they had actually agreed to make some for him.

"I've proved a lot of different claims of the paranormal

to be false," Sword said as he moved back and forth along the counter, making his preparations. "But proving them false is not what interests me."

Ryan leaned back gracefully in his chair, keeping his hands clasped before him. Sword was mildly puzzled that he had yet to hear the old wooden chair creak beneath his guest's considerable mass. Ryan was at least six two, not counting his boots, and appeared to be solid muscle.

"Still," Ryan suggested, "with each such claim you discount, that narrows the range you have in which to continue your subsequent search, does it not? If you choose to investigate my tale of vampire adepts, your previous experiences will help you focus your efforts, do you not agree?"

Sword pulled back another chair and sat down by 'Bub's central position on the papers on the table. The cat shifted her eyes to him as if daring him to just try and pet her. Sword kept his hands well away. He found that the events of the past few days had made him much better at learning lessons of behavior.

"What about *your* investigations?" Sword asked. "Why come to me?"

Ryan shrugged, meeting Sword's eyes in apparent honesty. "I have, shall we say, pushed too hard in my most recent case. I have alerted my quarry to my presence and cannot approach any further without great risk." He nodded his head in deference to Sword. "It is time for—" he smiled "—new blood. I believe that would be the appropriate phrase."

Sword put an elbow on the table, ignoring 'Bub's glare. He rested his head on his hand. "You use the word 'case.' Did someone hire you to start this particular investigation?"

Ryan looked puzzled. "Do people hire you?"

Sword nodded against his hand. "Sometimes. Sometimes people ask me to look into things and pay me for it. Occasionally I help out a friend in the police—mostly breaking up psychic scams and that sort of thing. But up to now, my best work has come about because of leads that I or my associates have discovered on our own."

"Associates?"

Sword decided he had said enough. It was time he had the mysterious Mr. Ryan provide some information about himself. "I don't work alone. How about you?"

Ryan straightened in his chair. "Alone, Mr. Sword. Very much so."

"Except for now?"

"Except for now," Ryan agreed. "I know there are vampire adepts setting up an . . ." He hesitated, as if searching for the proper term.

"Enclave?" Sword suggested.

Ryan studied Sword for a moment. "That *is* a term I have heard used."

"And they're setting up this enclave in the city—you know where, but you can't go near it so you want me to take a look."

"I want to destroy it, Mr. Sword." Sword didn't have to ask the next question. Ryan offered an explanation immediately. "They destroyed my family a long time ago. I've spent many years tracking them down. And now that I have found them, I am quite powerless to act."

There was a long silence in the room, broken only by the hum of the microwave's exhaust fan.

Sword knew from dismal experience with those who claimed to have inside knowledge of unusual events that he could spend the next ten hours in fruitless debate concerning the validity of the answer to the question he knew he must ask next.

"What proof do you have?"

"For myself, enough. For you, I'm not sure what it will take." He held up an exceptionally long finger before Sword could interrupt. "What I propose is to give you a location and the descriptions of those beings and activities you should watch for. I am quite confident that what you observe under the conditions I describe will convince you as I have been convinced."

Sword didn't like it. Ryan was being too reasonable, a perfect client compared to the ranters and the obsessed who usually tried to track him down and tell him all they knew of otherworldly conspiracies. He decided to raise the stakes.

"What do you know about the First World?" Sword had to know how much Ryan was concealing.

But Ryan only raised his eyebrows questioningly. "I am not aware of that term."

"Yet you are familiar with the term *adept*?"

Ryan frowned, no hint of deception about him. "It is a word they use among themselves. Is it significant?"

Sword glanced over at the microwave, trying to collect his thoughts. The window of the oven was fogged with moisture. ''One of the problems with investigating the events and phenomena that I do is that I keep hearing the same stories.'' Sword stood up from the table and went over to the humming microwave. ''I suppose that could mean that the stories have a common basis in fact, but what it usually means is that the people who come to me have read the same lurid books or seen the same movies.''

''They lie to you?'' Ryan asked, turning in his chair to watch as Sword opened the microwave's door. He sounded shocked by the idea.

Sword peered into the oven. The bubbling of the water in the mugs stopped almost instantly. ''Most lie to me. Some know they are lying. Some honestly believe that what they tell me is true, not knowing it's a delusion.'' He reached in for the mugs but the water had transferred too much heat to their ceramic handles. Sword snapped his hand out of the oven, shaking his fingers and looked for a pot holder or dishtowel. Wherever Ko had decided *those* belonged.

''You can distinguish the difference then?'' Ryan asked as Sword started going through the drawers beneath the counter.

''You mean between those who believe their stories and those who know they're lying?'' Sword opened the drawer beneath the coffeemaker. There were five plastic foil pouches of ground coffee in it, along with a stack of coffee filters. Sword tightened his lips in a frown. Who in their right mind would keep coffee in a *drawer?*

Ryan rose in one fluid motion and moved to the microwave. ''No, my curiosity is more basic than that. I meant, can you distinguish the difference between those who lie to you and those who tell the truth?'' He reached into the oven with both hands and withdrew the mugs, placing them quickly on the counter.

Sword looked at Ryan's hands as the visitor let go of the mugs.

Ryan saw the puzzled look in Sword's eyes. ''The trick is to do it quickly,'' he explained. ''Before the heat can travel.''

Sword leaned against the counter, folding his arms as he watched Ryan drop a teabag in each mug. Then Ryan reached back to the microwave, shut the door, and changed the program function to time for two minutes. The oven beeped in response to each tap of Ryan's finger. Sword had yet to figure out the purpose of most of the oven's controls.

Ryan turned back to Sword and smiled, offering another explanation. "I enjoy cooking. A hobby of mine."

Sword nodded, still not quite understanding the apparent low-key nature of their conversation. Vampire adepts setting up an enclave in the city and here they both were, making tea in the middle of the night. *Could it be possible to get used to these things? To accept them as part of the normal world? Normal worlds?*

"To resume, can you tell the difference?" Ryan asked again, resting his hands behind him on the counter, his back to the microwave where the glowing green time display smoothly counted down.

"Between lies and truth?" Sword asked, to confirm they were both still talking about the same thing. "Some times. Most times."

"Do you believe that I am telling the truth?"

A fair question, Sword thought. *And one not usually asked by those who lie.* "Is it important?"

Ryan looked puzzled once again. "Surely it must be."

Sword shook his head. "I'll go where you tell me. I'll look for what you want me to see. If I find it, you're telling the truth and what I believe now is of no importance." Sword thought Ko would enjoy that statement. He wondered how she would react to the news that he had widened the scope of his search to include vampires.

But Ryan was confused by Sword's words. "Then that means you accept what I've told you enough to look into it further, but you suspect I might be lying to you just the same?"

"First of all, what reason would you have to lie to me? And second of all, you haven't told me anything yet. It's a bit too early to be arriving at any conclusions."

Ryan looked thoughtful again, then glanced at the tea mugs and reached for the small paper tag hanging down the side of one. Just as he touched it, the timer on the microwave beeped five times. Sword was impressed by Ryan's sense of time.

"You were implying that the term 'adept' had some significance to your decision to listen to me," Ryan said as he cupped the scalding teabags in his hand and carried them to the sink. "Something about hearing the same stories?"

Sword picked up a mug of tea, decided it just wasn't worth it to find out where Ko had hidden the sugar, and sat back at the table. He noticed that, throughout Ryan's movements in the kitchen, 'Bub hadn't taken her eyes from the man.

"Most of the stories are just that," Sword said as Ryan returned to his chair as well. "Stories. One person hears one, likes it, tells it to another. Maybe it gets printed in a specialty magazine, passed around in a newsletter. Pretty soon everyone is seeing the same monster in the woods, watching the same aliens come out of the same flying saucers. Whatever elements of the stories might have been true become tainted by the extra false layers of details."

"Ah," Ryan said. "So what you wait for is something which you have never heard before." He held his tea mug beneath his nose, appreciatively inhaling the vapor that rose from it.

"Or a detail I know hasn't been spread around. A detail that could only come from a common source other than word of mouth." Sword sipped his tea. There was little flavor to it which he could detect. About all he could say about it was that it was hot.

Ryan placed his mug on the table. "And the term *adept* is one of those details?"

Sword nodded, wondering when Ryan would give him the rest of the details he claimed to have.

"Tell me, Mr. Sword, have you dealt with any adepts before?"

Why not? Sword thought. Perhaps they could trade information. Perhaps some of it might be useful.

"Yes," he said. "I have."

Ryan took on a serious expression. "And were they vampires as well?"

"Shifters," Sword said. He cradled the slightly cooling mug in his hands now, enjoying its warmth.

Ryan shook his head, indicating his ignorance of the term Sword had used. "I'm sorry . . . ?"

"Shapeshifters," Sword explained. Ryan's face was completely blank. "Werewolves," Sword said bluntly.

"Ah, of course." Ryan held his hands to the mug in front of him.

"Have you heard any stories of werewolves?" Sword asked.

Ryan shook his head.

"Yet you accept them so easily?" Sword took another sip of his tea. "Tell me, do you believe in werewolves?"

Ryan looked up and smiled again. "Mr. Sword, I believe in vampires. I find it no great stretch to encompass werewolves as well."

Sword thought about that for a moment and then he smiled, too. "I suppose I could say the same thing about vampires."

"Yes," Ryan said quietly. "I suppose you could."

The silence lasted longer this time. With the microwave off, the only sound now was the faint murmur of the Loft's circulating fans.

Might as well get right down to it, Sword thought. He put his mug down on the table. "Where is this enclave being set up?"

Ryan didn't hesitate. "Are you familiar with the World Plaza?"

"In Hell's Kitchen?" Sword asked.

"Perhaps an appropriate term. The cover is a company called BioproEx. Within a block of the World Plaza."

Sword hadn't heard of the company. "Sounds medical."

"It is a commercial blood bank."

Ryan said it with a straight face but Sword laughed anyway. It felt good to have something to laugh at again.

"You have a problem with that, Mr. Sword?"

Sword looked at him frankly. "It seems far too obvious."

"Which is as it should be, do you not agree? Imagine the concern if inhabitants of this city were being discovered drained of their blood. How many law enforcement agencies might become involved in an investigation? To say nothing of news media.

"But, there is nothing amiss if inhabitants of this city choose to sell their blood at a clinic. Blood is still drained from them, but it is in the course of an accepted business transaction and no investigation is called for."

Sword studied Ryan carefully. "You're serious, aren't you?"

"These adepts are . . . exceptionally long-lived, Mr. Sword. They have had ample time to learn the ways of human customs and alter their behavior to fit them. In the past, perhaps it was enough to travel from village to village, taking their victims boldly and moving on, leaving only legends in their wake. But in these times, there are few places in the world where such unsubtle strategies are still productive. To survive, vampires have changed. Adapted.''

Sword started to laugh again, but something in Ryan's mood told him it would not be the appropriate response a second time. Perhaps Ko might see some sense in this: vampires behaving in a Darwinian fashion to retain whatever niche they occupied in the . . . worlds.

"You have an address for the clinic?'' Sword asked.

Ryan nodded.

"Open only after sunset, I presume?''

Ryan's deep green eyes clouded. "Again, Mr. Sword, such an unorthodox business practice would draw attention to their operation. The BioproEx clinic has a full staff of human technicians and operates as does any other commercial blood bank. Except, they do not sell the blood they harvest.''

"What *do* they do with it?''

Ryan narrowed his eyes at Sword. "Really, Mr. Sword, I believe the answer to that question is terribly obvious.''

Sword finished the last of his tea in a long swallow. 'Bub's ears twitched when the mug hit the table again but she didn't turn her eyes from Ryan.

"I expect that you have a plan to propose to my associates and me?'' Sword felt the fatigue he had been warding off finally begin to win. He'd try to wrap this up quickly.

Ryan half turned in his chair and withdrew a long and thick brown envelope from an inner pocket of his coat. "Not for your associates, Mr. Sword. Just for yourself.'' He slid the envelope across the table to Sword, but kept his hand on it. "The adepts are on alert. One person, perhaps, could escape their scrutiny. Two or more, I fear not. I must insist that to ensure my efforts are not lost through carelessness, you must be the only one who takes on this investigation.''

Sword glanced at the envelope but made no move to take it. "If the vampire adepts are anything like shifter adepts, I would be foolish to go against them alone.''

"I am not asking you to go against them, Mr. Sword. I merely ask that you confirm their presence, define the scope of their operation so they may be isolated, and then, if exposure is not enough to force them to relinquish their plans, *then* we shall talk about more physical means. Believe me, what I propose is quite safe . . . for *one* experienced investigator of such things.''

Sword thought it over. If Ryan's story were true, then he was offering Sword another doorway back to the First World. Perhaps a doorway that could replace the one he had lost in his confrontation with the shifters of Arkady. And it was just a reconnaissance assignment, after all. No risk, a lot to gain. He nodded, accepting Ryan's terms.

Ryan took his hand from the envelope. ''These are charts, floor plans, lists of names, invoices. Everything I have managed to gather. We should go over them together.''

Ryan stood and came around to the side of the table. Sword opened the unsealed flap of the envelope, withdrew a fat sheaf of folded-over papers, then also stood so he could spread them out over the table.

He jarred the table as he stood. 'Bub hissed but didn't move. Sword couldn't tell if she were hissing at Ryan or himself, but he didn't care. He wanted to see what was on the papers that Ryan now unfolded. Above all else, he wanted to find a way back to the First World.

For an instant, he saw a glistening ring around Ryan's tea mug, left at the table's end. *Must have spilled when I hit the table,* Sword thought, even though he knew he hadn't hit it hard enough to slosh the tea around. Unless the mug was still just as full as when he had served it. Unless his guest hadn't touched his tea at all.

But the intriguing diagrams on the unfolded papers before him distracted his attention, and despite his exhaustion, despite the still tender wounds of his face and shoulders, Sword turned all his awareness to what Ryan began to tell him. And despite what he had told his guest about it not mattering what he believed, Sword felt with utter conviction that he was at last being given a second chance to go home.

ELEVEN

Ko watched patiently as Forsyte laboriously typed in the phonemes of what was obviously going to be a long and important statement. With each feeble, plastic click of the keypad, her heart ached for what had been done to one of the world's most gifted scientists, for what had been done to a man she had hoped might someday . . . Ko broke out of her reverie and looked across the long black table of the Loft's meeting room at Sword. Though his face appeared drawn, he waited calmly as well, looking down at the table's reflective surface.

Whatever Sword did last night and this morning, Ko thought in annoyance, *he obviously didn't get any rest.* He had been too busy cluttering up the counter and cupboards in this room as far as she could tell. She had been appalled to see that he actually had left teabags in the sink. But she had refused to clean them up, which she could have done despite her bandaged hands. *Sword will have to start learning to take care of himself,* she thought, *now that he won't have Adrian and me around.*

Ko had been in bed a half-hour after Sword had dropped her and Forsyte off the night before and, uncharacteristically, she had slept through till almost noon, when she had been awakened by Forsyte's sudden cry of panic from the guest room. Another bad dream, he had told her. The nightmare of flying and movement and . . . as always, he wouldn't tell her the rest of it.

Forsyte sighed with the effort of his intense effort focused on just one finger and a sequence of eyeblinks, but he kept going. Both Ko and Sword had long ago learned to abandon any sense of urgency they might feel about the length of time it took Forsyte to communicate with them. What he had to say was always worth listening to. Ko just berated herself once more for not being able to devise some method that would let him speak with less effort.

As Ko waited, 'Bub jumped up on the counter by the sink and gave a small hoarse cry. Ko knew the cat's bowl of food was full—overflowing, actually, because Martin had been the last to feed her and had yet to understand that even 'Bub's appetite was not the equivalent of his.

Ko turned to 'Bub and the cat stared back at her expectantly. Sword had explained that 'Bub was developing a new habit—becoming skittish each time she was apart from Martin. Ko had been furious when she had arrived back at the Loft in the afternoon to find that Martin had left last night and not returned, but Sword was adamant that the halfling would come back. He had actually told Ko to remember that they were dealing with a personality that wasn't fully human and Ko still felt indignant that Sword, of all people, would think he could ever tell her anything she didn't already know.

Recalling that half-argument she had had with Sword, she found herself thinking that, if Martin indeed did not return to the Loft, she would miss him. She also found herself thinking that she would miss the Loft and her work here. And then a true moment of revelation occurred for Ko: It was not her work, her companions, or even the hazards that she faced that were driving her from the Loft—it was her employer, Sword. And if *he* could just be persuaded to leave, then Ko could still work for him. She'd stay here with Forsyte and Martin and 'Bub, and lead the Foundation's research and the investigations herself.

Ko felt her mind race with the clarity of her idea. She leaned forward in her chair, about to blurt out the decision she had arrived at, then remembered in the last instant that they were still waiting for Forsyte to make his address. She rocked back in her chair again, ignoring Sword's sudden, curious look. It was a perfect plan, she knew. Sword could move out and she would report to him regularly about her progress. He wasn't interested in doing the actual work, she told herself. He only wanted the answers to the mysteries of his origins as quickly and as simply as possible. If he could be convinced that Ko and Forsyte working together was his best bet, if he could be convinced to maintain the Sword Foundation's funding of the Loft, then *it would work*.

She suddenly was aware of complete silence. Forsyte had finished with his keypad. He was looking at her, a single tiny dot of red laser light reflected in each eye making sure that she was ready to give him her full attention. She nodded at him and saw his left finger gently press the playback key.

The voder spoke. "You fight like children. Too much energy is expended against each other when it should be expended against the enemy."

"Enemy?" Sword repeated.

The left side of Forsyte's mouth twitched up in what Ko recognized as the ghost of his former smile.

"Yes, Galen, enemy," the voder said. Forsyte had anticipated Sword's reaction and had programmed it into his speech. Ko smiled, too. Sword *was* so predictable. She was sure that Forsyte could see through him as easily as she could.

The voice synthesizer continued. "The shifters prey on humans. We are food to them. We are sport to them. They have done this for centuries. This must end."

"Any suggestions?" Sword asked, even as the voder told him.

"Two ways. First they must be understood. How are the adepts organized? Who are their leaders? Where are they based? Most important, why were you expelled from their ranks?"

"I have no powers," Sword said. "No adept abilities."

But the voder didn't wait for him. "Why weren't you killed? We have seen no compassion in them before. Why was it shown to you? All these things we must understand.

"Second, they must be stopped. They are the enemy. Wherever we find them, we must fight. We cannot allow them to prey on us any longer. We must fight a war.

"But to fight them, we cannot fight among ourselves. That is how they will win. That is how they have always won—hiding their true natures behind myth and legend, ensuring that any who stand against them and call others to the fight will be ridiculed and scorned.

"Two ways. First find their secrets so the world can be warned and truly believe. Then stop them. Wherever we find them. No other choice."

The background hiss of the speech synthesizer clicked off, returning the room to silence. Ko didn't want to acknowledge the implication of what Forsyte had said. At least she was sure that Sword wouldn't be able to see it right away. Perhaps she still had some time to change Forsyte's mind. She turned to him. But Sword spoke first.

"Adrian, you say that *we* must fight. Does that mean that you will stay?"

Damn, Ko thought. *My way is better. Why didn't Adrian talk to me about this before we came over?* "Look, Adrian," Ko began. "I agree with most of—"

But the voder came back on line with a single keystroke. The sentence had already been stored in memory. "Melody and I will both stay."

Ko felt her cheeks stain with ready anger. Facing physical danger was one thing. She could stay calm under those circumstances. But there was no way anyone was going to tell her what to do, not even Forsyte.

"Now wait one bloody minute, Adrian. You and I have to talk—"

This time, Sword interrupted her. "Hold on, Melody. I suspect that Adrian has a few more things programmed into the voder. Right, Adrian?"

Forsyte's mouth twitched again. He blinked his eyes once.

"Let's let him finish," Sword said. Then added, as if trying to soften the outrage he thought Ko might be feeling, "I'm as surprised as you are."

Forsyte touched the keypad again. "Two conditions for us to stay."

Sword gestured for Forsyte to continue. He was at least open to discussion.

"One. No more individual actions. We must all have full access to all information acquired. Next time you go to a shifter ball, Ko goes with you. Martin, too."

Sword looked unconvinced. "That could limit us, Adrian. Martin couldn't have gone to the—" he smiled at the term "—shifters' ball at the museum."

"Then you shouldn't have gone," the voder said. "Safer my way. Only way." Forsyte stared evenly at Sword. "Do you agree to the condition?"

Sword hesitated. Ko could see he didn't like it but that he also realized it was a small concession to make.

"I agree to the first condition," Sword said at last. "What's the second?"

Forsyte turned his head a few inches until he faced Ko directly. Ko understood what he wanted.

"I agree, too," she said reluctantly.

The voder came to life again. "Two. You are no longer in charge."

Sword got to his feet. His face revealed his shock, suspicion, and outright anger, all within three seconds. Ko loved it.

Sword started to say something with each change of expression, but when he finally composed himself, he simply sat down again, and asked a question. "Then who the hell is?"

Forsyte pressed a single key. Ko waited expectantly for the answer that would come forth.

"I am."

Ko was glad Sword wasn't looking at her to see the shock appear on her own face.

Sword's face hardened. "No way, Adrian. I'm paying the bills. I'm the one who got kicked out of the First World. I'm the one who wants to get back in. Sorry, but it's my show."

Forsyte hit a replay key. "Two. You are no longer in charge."

Sword gave a small bitter laugh. "No negotiation, is that it?" He waited for Forsyte to say something else, but nothing came. He spread his hands on the table, ready to stand again. "Then give me a reason, Adrian. Give me a damn good reason."

Forsyte gave it to him. "Why did you go to Greece?"

In the midst of her own mixed feelings, Ko smiled at the confusion that appeared on Sword's face. She could see him trying to decide what Greece had to do with anything. "Because of the stories, of course," Sword said. "About the werewolf."

"Who uncovered those stories?"

Sword blinked. "Well, Melody did the legwork. But only after I told her what those diggers had told me in Australia."

Forsyte ignored Sword's qualification. Ko could see that the physicist was proceeding through a series of questions he had already prepared in advance.

"Who analyzed those stories to isolate the werewolf's most probable migratory pattern?"

Ko could see Sword's face whiten, almost matching the color of the bandage he still wore. He didn't like the way Forsyte was directing the conversation. Ko did. "The three million dollar computer in the basement analyzed those stories, Adrian. The computer *I* paid for.''

But Forsyte had called him again. ''Who programmed your computer?''

Sword said nothing, lips tight.

''You went to Greece by yourself,'' the voder accused. ''What happened?''

Sword did not speak. All three of them knew the story well. Sword had at last caught up with the werewolf in the ruins of a temple near Delphi. He had closed in on the werewolf. And at the last second, an unidentified woman had appeared out of the rain and the night and had killed the creature, but not before it had looked up to Sword and with its dying breath called his name. The expedition to Greece had been the most notable of Sword's many disasters.

''You failed,'' the voder said. ''How did we track down Martin?''

Sword waved his hand angrily. ''Go ahead and play them all, Adrian. You don't need me for this.''

Forsyte's finger stabbed at his keypad and he let his stored sentences continue on by themselves.

''Who designed the motion detector system?'' Click. ''Who built it?'' Click. ''How many of us did it take to capture Martin?'' Click. ''We worked as a team, that's why. We followed my plan, that's why.'' Click. ''We were successful once. We can be successful again.''

Ko glanced at Sword's silent figure. He looked more enraged than she had ever seen him before. For a moment, she felt true apprehension. For all the time they had spent together, she suddenly realized that there were many things about this man that she still did not know. There were things about him it would be better perhaps not to know.

''Is that all, Adrian?'' There was an unfamiliar harshness in Sword's voice now.

''Two,'' the voder repeated. ''You are no longer in charge. I am.''

''Why not Melody?'' he snapped. He said her name like a curse.

''I am.'' The voder said nothing else.

Sword tapped the fingers of one lean hand against the table. Ko had to give him credit. He was managing to give the impression that he was thinking about what Forsyte had

said. But she knew that there was no way he would accept
that second condition. Sword was too full of himself, too
spoiled by inflated notions of his own self-worth. Maybe
that went with the territory, Ko conceded. Maybe it was the
unfortunate legacy of how Sword had been raised, without
direction, without continuity. But whatever had made him
the way he was had no bearing on what was bound to happen in the next few seconds. Sword was finally going to
break. He was going to throw Forsyte and Melody out. And
maybe even 'Bub.

Too bad Martin isn't here, Ko thought. *He could flatten
Sword again the way he did the first night we brought him
here.*

"I accept the second condition," Sword said in a measured voice.

Ko froze. She wanted to ask Sword to repeat what he had
said, but her surprise was so great she couldn't speak.

After a moment, she realized that Forsyte had turned to
her again. He was waiting for her to agree as well. But she
couldn't.

"Sword," Ko asked, "do you realize what you just
said?"

Sword's lips thinned as if he was holding back unimag-
inable anger. "I said I accept the condition, Melody." His
words were perfectly stated, hinting at the self-control he
must be exerting. "Is there something more you'd like me
to do?"

"But *why* are you agreeing to this?"

Sword got up slowly from the table and turned away from
her. "You talk to her, Adrian."

Ko jumped to her feet. "No, Sword. *You* talk to *me!*"
She stepped around the table to confront him. "I've spent
the past three years talking myself bloody blue in the face
just to try and get you to accept my advice, or even to just
listen to my opinions, and you've ignored me completely.
And now . . . now . . . you're backing down one hundred
percent! You're going to let Adrian make all the decisions!
And you're not even putting up a fight!"

Sword stopped and stared down at Ko. This close to him,
she couldn't understand what she was seeing on his face.
Anger was still there, certainly, but something more as
well. Disappointment? she wondered. Surely not . . . sorrow.

"Didn't you hear what Adrian said?" Sword asked, and

the unfamiliar sound of acceptance was evident in his voice as well as in his dark eyes. "If we fight among ourselves, we can't fight against . . . the enemy. So I'm not fighting with you."

"This isn't like you, Sword."

Sword looked away, as if unwilling to keep eye contact with Ko. "You expected me to say no, didn't you?" He glanced back at her. "But that's what I've always done, and what has it brought us? Maybe it's time for us all to try it a different way."

Ko sneered. "Oh, right, and the first time things don't go the way you want them to go, you change your mind and tell us all to go to bloody hell."

"I'm trying, Melody. Don't make this harder." Ko thought Sword probably intended his words to sound like a request, but she heard the threat that hid there.

"You're doing it again, Sword. You don't want it to be hard on *you*. Well, what about Adrian, and me? What about Ja'Nette?"

Sword held his hands up to Ko, stopping her. "Melody, that's enough."

Ko didn't turn from him. She knew that she was staying. She couldn't go without Forsyte. And she knew that Sword was committed to her rejoining him, for at least the next few days, until he changed his mind again. For once, she felt, she had power over him. She knew she would be able to make him suffer the way she had, so many times in the past.

"What are *you* going to do, Melody?" Sword asked again.

"Stay," Ko said, regretting her answer as soon as she had said it, yet knowing that she found solace in the astonishment that showed on Sword's face.

Sword turned to Forsyte. "I'm taking the rest of the day off. If that's all right with you." Then he pushed past Ko and left the room without waiting for an answer.

Ko stood by the door to the main lab, listening to Sword's footsteps clang down the metal staircase to the garage. She heard his Porsche start up and the garage door open. *Good,* she thought. *Maybe you'll hit another lamppost.*

"You didn't have to speak to him that way," Forsyte's voder said.

Ko wouldn't look at the physicist. "I know," she agreed.

But she had had to, driven by her need to hurt Sword as he had hurt her.

"He's trying to change," the voder said.

"He can't change."

She heard Forsyte's finger move over his keypad. "Do you really want to leave?"

Ko turned to him. His eyes were so alive, so intelligent. She thought of captives peering out from prison windows, trapped forever. "I want *Sword* to leave. I want it to be just us."

She couldn't tell what Forsyte was thinking as his finger hit the replay key.

"Do you really want to leave?" the voder asked again.

"No. I can't." Ko crossed her arms and held them tight to her chest, ignoring the pain of her bandaged hands. She looked down at the floor, unable to meet his eyes as she spoke the words she knew she must finally say to him.

"I love you, Adrian. I always have." She tried, but she couldn't look at him to see his reaction. She was afraid to see it, afraid to see rejection in his face. But then she remembered the way Forsyte had anticipated all of Sword's questions and arguments. She remembered the quality of the mind that was trapped in the useless body before her. What she had just said could not possibly be new to him. Not to Forsyte.

"But then," she said, voice thickening despite her efforts at control, "you probably know that already, don't you?" She tried to smile, convincing not even herself, and at last met his gaze. "You've always known, haven't you?"

Forsyte looked back at her, a prisoner in his own body, a victim of the war that had just begun, and he blinked his eyes once.

For yes.

TWELVE

The television newsroom was in a state of permanent chaos and Sword felt right at home in it. His mind still reeled over the maneuver Forsyte had pulled on him not two hours earlier, and he still wasn't sure that capitulating to the physicist's conditions was the best way to proceed. But the truth was that Sword didn't feel he had any other realistic options. More than anything else, the events of the past two weeks had brought home the understanding that something had to change. And since Sword didn't know what that something was, he had decided to give Forsyte the benefit of the doubt. As far as Sword was concerned, after the death of Ja'Nette Conroy things couldn't get worse, even though his personal chaos of half-remembered incidents from early childhood seemed to suggest that in some way things *could* get far worse. More than he could even dream of.

"Hey, bud, help you with somethin'?"

Sword glanced around at the man who had spoken. He was, Sword guessed, pushing sixty, with reddish-brown hair so thick and sticking up so high from his head that it had to be a wig. The man wore a blue-striped shirt with rolled-up sleeves, chewed gum with a reformed smoker's zeal, and carried two large black videocassette cases in one large hand.

"I'm looking for Kendall Marsh," Sword said. He held up the white paper bag he carried as if that was excuse enough.

The man eyed Sword suspiciously. All around them, the noise and commotion of the other thirty or so station employees continued without pause. Phones beeped, printers clacked, people swore and laughed to each other and on telephones. Almost everyone seemed to be on the telephone.

The man made up his mind. "Try reception." He used his thumb to show Sword the way back to the main doors.

Sword took a half-step away. "Thanks, but I know where her office is." At least, he knew where it had been two years ago.

The man stepped closer to Sword and Sword didn't understand why the man was going out of his way to be so unpleasant.

"I said, try reception. You can't go waltzin' through a newsroom without—"

Sword still couldn't abide anyone attempting to interfere in whatever he wanted to do. It was such a simple and straightforward proposition—Sword wanted something so Sword got it. As in the old days, a cruel thought came to Sword's mind: *Doesn't this underling know who I am? Doesn't he know I can have him fired?* But then Sword remembered that he no longer had that influence or power. He was no longer the Galen Sword the *Post* had so enjoyed writing about. Donald Trump, Leona Helmsley, and Dave Stern had pushed him from the front pages and the gossip columns long ago.

Sword tried another tack. He guessed it was his day for new strategies. "Look, I'm an old friend of Kennie's and I'm just trying to surprise her."

The man was unimpressed. He clamped a powerful hand to Sword's biceps and pulled. "Yeah, well, Marion E. doesn't like her top reporters surprised, okay? Now—"

Sword winced as the pressure on his arm traveled up to his wounded shoulder. He pulled back, shrugging the man off. But the man bellied up to Sword. He tossed his cassettes to a nearby desk, reaching out to grab at Sword's other arm, then glared up at his captive belligerently. "Now *what*, asshole?"

Sword's jaw tensed. He ignored the pain that shot through his arm as the man applied even more pressure. This man couldn't know that he had battled a living skeleton in a tavern filled with monsters. That he had fought a werewolf in hand-to-hand combat, stood up to hundreds of shape-shifters in the throes of their transformation. Now that Sword had faced death and he had caused death, he knew without doubt or hesitation that he had it within himself to kill this man before him.

But he wouldn't. This man was not the enemy.

"Nothing," Sword said mildly, stepping back until the man was forced to lessen his grip.

The man grinned and went back to noisily chewing his gum, misunderstanding the nature of his victory. "That's the attitude, bud. Now let's go see security." He pushed at Sword to get him to face the main doors.

Sword took note of the perplexed faces of the newsroom staffers who had begun to notice the altercation in their midst.

"Everything okay, Lee?" a young woman in a yellow baseball cap asked. She held a telephone receiver in each hand.

"Nothin' I can't handle," the man said, continuing to push Sword along. "I'll get those tapes down to editin' in a minute."

It's all right, Sword thought, gritting his teeth as he tried to maintain some dignity. *He's just doing his job. It's not like the old days when I could just walk in anywhere I wanted. But if he doesn't let go of my arm I'm going to—*

"Galen?"

Sword stumbled as he tried to turn to see who had called him. The man surprised him by stopping as well.

"Galen, what's going on?"

In a trim gray suit Sword had seen her wear on air, Kendall Marsh walked quickly through the warren of desks and chairs in the newsroom. He also saw a mixture of concern and amusement on her face. Wisely, he let her do all the talking.

By the time Marsh had managed to convince Lee Park that Sword was not a celebrity stalker, the business of the newsroom had come to a stop. A few of the reporters and writers recognized Sword from earlier glimpses of him—some from his appearances in papers and magazines, and some from the times he had visited Marsh here in her office.

"Sure everything's going to be all right?" Lee asked Marsh, reluctant to leave despite her explanations.

Marsh spoke each word slowly, as if correcting a pupil. "It's all right, Lee. Galen's an old friend."

The man picked up his videocassettes and tucked them securely under his arm. Then he took a last look at Sword. "Still never heard a ya, bud." He strode away.

Marsh led Sword through the newsroom to her office. It was different from the one Sword had visited in the past—

in the corner now, with two sets of windows looking over the busy streets of central Manhattan. Sword could just see the plaza of the Rockefeller Center across one street and twenty floors below.

Marsh sat on the side of her desk. The office was grander and larger than before, Sword noted, but it was just as cluttered as ever. He liked it that way, though. It made him feel comfortable.

Marsh smiled at him with a warmth that Sword hadn't seen or felt for a long time. "Now what the hell *are* you doing here, Galen?"

Sword held up his Zabar's bag. "Breakfast?"

Marsh lifted her eyes to the ceiling but her delighted smile remained. "It's nearly five."

Sword put the bag down on a stack of magazines topping an almost completely buried coffee table. "I don't think either one of us lives by the clock." The bagels were no longer warm, but as he took them from the bag, crinkling in their wax paper squares, they filled the office with a rich aroma. "Won't be the first time we've had breakfast this late." He held out a bagel to her. "Onion sesame with cream cheese, right?"

The smile faded from Marsh's face and she made no move to accept Sword's gift.

"What are you saying to me, Galen?"

Sword knew the real question she was asking but didn't want to acknowledge it. It would be so much simpler if they could just keep things uncomplicated.

"You don't like cream cheese anymore?" he asked lightly.

Marsh took the bagel to remove it from the playing field. She wanted no confusion, no double meanings. "Are you telling me that we're on again?"

"I thought that after yesterday . . ." Sword stopped. He should have expected this from her. But he wasn't ready for it. Not again. Not so quickly.

"Yesterday was yesterday," Marsh said plainly. "I'm talking here and now." She looked down at the bagel in her hands. "A man brings me breakfast, Galen, I have to ask myself why."

"Can't it just be breakfast?"

Marsh shook her head. "It's not that simple. We've been that route before, remember?"

"That was a long time ago. A lot has happened since."

Marsh pursed her lips as she considered his words. "Are you saying you've changed?"

Sword didn't have the strength for this conversation. He only wanted to talk with her, not plan their future. "Kennie, yesterday . . . yesterday you talked to me about making things happen. About making decisions even if I didn't know if they were right or wrong. I can always change my mind, you said. But the important thing was to *do* something, anything." He looked into her eyes, willing her to understand what he was trying to say before he made a complete ass of them both. "So I'm doing something. Whether it's right or wrong, I'm doing it. Can't that be enough? For now?"

Marsh tapped the bagel against her hand, lips still pursed. "For now?" she asked.

Sword gave up. He had no answer that could satisfy her.

She looked past him out the open door of her office. Sword glanced over his shoulder and saw two women waiting by the door, intense interest on their faces. One carried a file folder rippling with newspaper clippings. The other carried a cardboard box with a stuffed penguin and several quart cans of oil.

The woman with the penguin took advantage of what seemed to be a pause in Marsh's meeting with Sword. "We've got that stuff on the egg fraud story, Kennie. When do you want to go through it?"

Marsh got off her desk, checked her watch, then turned to Sword. "Meet me at the deli downstairs for a real breakfast in . . ."—she looked out the door and called out: "Consuela, how many penguins did he bring us?"

"Just one," the woman carrying the box answered. "But it's electric."

Marsh looked back at Sword. "Twenty minutes? Then I'll have at least an hour before I have to get into the studio." She handed the bagel back to Sword, letting her hand linger for just a moment, and then dropped her voice so the women outside her office couldn't hear. "That'll give us lots of time to talk. And if you're planning on breaking my heart again, Galen, . . ."

She walked out of her office, leaving her threat unspoken, and leaving Sword cursing himself because this was exactly what he had feared would be the result of his plan.

* * *

Forty minutes passed before Sword saw Marsh come out of the entrance to her station's building and head for the delicatessen across from Radio City. The sidewalks were clogged with office commuters heading home and Sword had to walk carefully to avoid pushing anyone out of the way.

He called out Marsh's name before he approached her, taking care not to startle her by taking her arm. That was never a good way to make contact on the streets of New York.

"Aren't we going to eat?" Marsh asked as Sword fell into step beside her.

"Let's talk out here first," Sword said. "We can grab a coffee over there."

In the Rockefeller Plaza, they found a marble planter ledge by some bedraggled petunias, still valiantly struggling to hold on against the past week's rain and the coming chill of winter. Leaving Marsh to hold their seats, Sword walked over to a pretzel wagon and bought two cardboard cups of coffee. He came back and placed them on the ledge between them. After carefully peeling back the plastic drinking tabs of their covers, he handed Marsh's coffee to her and held his up to sip at it. The vapor from it streamed away in a sudden breeze. Sword and Marsh both pulled their coat collars closed at the same time and smiled at each other. It was cool outside, but at least there was sunshine, the first the city had seen in a long time.

"So why aren't we indoors?" Marsh asked. Her deep pink lipstick left a half circle on the edge of her coffee cup.

"Because we're going to talk," Sword said. He smiled again as she studied him for some clue as to what he was really trying to do. "And for once, I'm going to talk first."

Marsh tapped her cup to Sword's in a toast. "I'd like that." She waited for him to begin.

Sword looked around them for a moment, making sure there were no potential eavesdroppers nearby. There weren't. Almost everyone in the plaza was on the move in one direction or another. The closest person sitting near Sword was a heavy-set black woman, apparently a courier because of the package she carried, who concentrated only on whatever was playing through the bright yellow headphones of her Walkman.

"You were right about the accident," Sword began, feeling safe. "Three years ago. The Testarossa. Something . . . happened."

Marsh nodded as if Sword had finally told her what she already had known. "A near-death experience, right? You died, then came back?" Her eyes were alive with intrigue.

"Something like that," Sword agreed. "But not exactly. It's . . . it's something I'm not comfortable going into right now." He saw the quick disappointment in her eyes, almost as if he had insulted her, so he reached out and put his hand on hers. To his coffee-warmed palm, her skin was ice cold. "With anyone," he said to lessen the blow. "But you were right about the effect it had on me. That's why I'm . . . doing what I've been doing the past three years."

"What exactly *are* you doing? You've never admitted anything, only told me I'm wrong every time I guess."

Sword smiled ruefully. "You've guessed it right from the beginning."

Marsh's eyes widened in victory. "I knew it. You *are* ghostbusting."

Sword cringed. "I hate that word, Kennie. What I'm doing is attempting to investigate and evaluate claims of paranormal activity—"

"Because you had a paranormal experience about the time you had your accident," Marsh finished for him.

Sword nodded, pleased that this part of it had gone so easily. He was happy to have Marsh believe whatever she wanted to believe, because the last thing he wanted to tell her now was the truth, for her own sake.

"Have you had any luck?" Marsh asked.

Sword shook his head. "I thought I'd been close a couple of times. But except for a dozen or so tricky cases where there just wasn't enough to go on, I've pretty well been able to discount everything." That state of affairs had been true for so long that Sword told the lie effortlessly.

"Did what happened at the museum have anything to do with one of your investigations?"

There was no way out of that one, Sword knew. "Yes," he said.

Marsh frowned in thought. "Some sort of psychic fraud related to the Society of St. Linus's fundraising?" she guessed.

Thank you, Sword thought in relief. "Something like that."

But Marsh wasn't satisfied with a half-answer. "Then why did it get so violent?"

Because the Society of St. Linus is composed of blood-thirsty shapeshifters preparing to go to war in the First World, Sword thought. "There was a lot of money involved," he said.

"This the story you were going to tell me about?"

Sword shook his head again. "I will, when I have names and dates. But there was something else I wanted to talk to you about."

Marsh's eyes flicked from his eyes to his mouth and back again, and Sword could tell she was looking for some sign of deception. "About us?" she asked. "Or about one of your . . . investigations?"

"One of my investigations."

Marsh looked away. "Jesus, Galen, then you really did just bring me breakfast. Nothing else. And you let me make a fool of—"

"No," Sword said forcefully and he gripped her hand hard in his. "Never. We're friends, Kennic. We'll always be friends."

She looked at him again. He felt her hand squeeze his back. "Then tell me what's going on here. Are we a reporter and her source? Are we old friends reminiscing? What are we doing here, Galen?"

We're trying to save my life, Sword thought. He tried to explain what he could tell her, safely. "You want to know what it is I've been doing since we . . . lost track of each other, and that's what I'm trying to tell you. If you can use it in your work, great, use it. But for now, it's just *me* telling *you* something about my life."

After a long moment, when he finally saw the resistance fade from her eyes, Sword felt the relief wash through him. Maybe she was going to be able to accept the way things were. The way they had to be. Without complications.

Marsh smiled sheepishly. "Sorry, Galen, You know how suspicious I get." She put down her coffee cup and held his hand in both of hers, squeezing tightly. "Occupational hazard, I guess. Too late to start this conversation again?"

"No," Sword said earnestly. "I'd like to think that . . . it's never too late to start again." Then he told her about the vampires, and every word was a lie.

THIRTEEN

T he hotel was newly renovated in the city's theater district. Twisted horns of glass and metal hung on the walls as flower vases and light fixtures. Throughout the austerely decorated building, legs of chairs and tables mimicked those vaguely menacing organic shapes in polished steel. But elsewhere in the hotel were hidden things, including one entire floor reserved for certain guests with special needs—among them the desire to spend their days in bedrooms with no outside windows that might admit the sun.

In one of those special rooms of the newly renovated hotel, accessible only by an elevator equipped to stop between the listed floors, Orion awoke.

It was hours before sunset, but he had had centuries in which to hone his reflexes and retrain his body's habits to escape the tyranny of the sun's arrivals and departures. Where once had lain an inanimate form with no detectable life signs, in the next moment lungs filled with an enormous intake of air as Orion ended his daily hibernation.

Instantly, he was alert. At his side, he pressed one finger against the button that activated his hibernaculum's passive sensors. Embedded in the lid inches above his face, a sleek panel of small LEDs flashed green. The motion and heat detectors installed in the pod's outer skin of brushed steel reported that no one was present in his room.

Orion pressed a second button. He heard the pod's safety measures disarm themselves so that the lid could be opened without triggering a release of dilation gas or the detonation of Semtex charges, which would pulverize any human within twenty feet and slow down most adepts.

When a second row of lights turned green, Orion pressed a third button and the lid puffed up on its pneumatic hinges. Instinctively, he inhaled again, tasting the air for a scent of anything that might wait for him beyond the capabilities of the pod's detectors.

There was nothing.

He had survived another day.

Orion sat up, then stepped from his pod to stand naked in the center of the hotel room. It was like most other rooms in the establishment, hidden or not. A fireplace decorated one pale gray wall. A precisely tailored rose velvet divan faced a lacquered gray cabinet which held a television set and small refrigerator. The room differed from others only in that its elegantly draped curtains covered blank wall, and that it had no bed—only a broad stone plinth designed to hold a variety of containers, from the wooden coffins of the romantics to the armored metal cylinders the Swiss built so well. For the more complex pods, an electric outlet for their battery rechargers was discretely hidden at the side of the plinth.

Orion knew that it was a modern development to have these completely equipped facilities so near the layer where the protected sanctuaries of the First World were close at hand, but he was thankful that he had not had to take chambers where any of Clan Tepesh might also have rested. Far better to enjoy the neutrality of the Second World, even if it did mean remaining in such close contact with humans.

The vampire stepped to the center of the room, unerringly turning to face the sun's position in the sky hidden beyond the shelter of the hotel, and began his waking routine. The muscles of his back and arms flexed into perfectly defined cords and planes as he pressed his hands together, palm to palm, centered above his chest. The pressure he exerted was enough to crush a human's skull or rip a shifter's molecularly compressed body in two. Yet Orion knew he was not strong enough. The hunger was building in him and his power lessened. Very soon, now, he knew he would have to feed, despite the risks of doing so in this city.

He continued to test his body, moving in an odd yet graceful amalgam of a dozen different disciplines of mind and body borrowed and adapted by him over the endless years of his life. How old he truly was he could not be sure. The most distant memories he claimed were hopelessly wound within the absorbed memories of those who had nourished him. The further back he sent his mind, the more diffuse his personality became until, filling himself with the sense-memories of a distant time of fire and flood and caves, of the hunt of the scaled ones, the taste of flesh from two different worlds bridged by the two-faced moon, he was no longer Orion alone. He was *all*.

The inner lids of his eyes slipped over his pupils with cauls of white and his feeding fangs extended in response to the seductive pull of those deepest memories. He knew there were mysteries there, still to be uncovered—or redis-covered—and he dared hope that Tantoo's gift of the charged memory crystal might bring back to him the clarity of his earliest years of life.

He was a vampire, an adept, immortal, immensely pow-erful, and yet like so many others he had known in all the worlds, Orion had no knowledge of his beginning. Nor, without that knowledge, could he look ahead and know what his ending might be.

Orion's exercise was over. It was his way of testing each part of him, a stocktaking which let him face each night with precise awareness of his condition and ability. He bowed his head and his soft brown hair slipped over his bare shoulders as he murmured his prayer to those who kept the clans. The final word he spoke was, "Isis."

With that invocation complete, Orion was at last prepared to face the night. And Galen Sword.

It was another sunny day in New York City, so Orion waited in the hotel lobby for the canyons of the city's build-ings to fill with shadows. The long and narrow lobby was softly lit, protected by a wall of darkly tinted glass from the eyes of those who passed on Forty-sixth Street. Except for the occasional presence of black-clad doortenders and the discrete name carved into stone above the main entrance, few would even know they passed a hotel.

The furniture scattered along the lobby's length was cloaked in barely colored fabric to form a collection of odd threatening shapes, some of which, Orion suspected, were bluebound halflings trapped in punishment chants.

Testing the air for the scent of magic, he chose a couch free of enchantment on which to wait and raised his hand to call for a steward. The staff of the hotel were all young and intent, and wore simple dark outfits with close-fitting tunic jackets whose high collars rose up to conceal their necks. For certain guests, it *was* a full-service hotel. Though

Orion preferred the passion of the hunt to the certainty of a routine business transaction.

Since the hotel could not offer any of the waters of the First World, Orion passed the time by reading the newspapers of the Second World, amazed, as always, by how much First World activity was contained within them without humans realizing what the true causes were of some events. The *Post* came closer than the *Times* in choosing to report First World incursions into the Second, but still its reporters told their stories without true awareness.

To Orion, it was almost humorously apparent that no headway had been made by the Council against the malevolent elf clans and their passion for the intricate and golden timekeeping devices that they constantly stole from humans. *The elvish are building their nests again and the humans still call it a rash of Rolex thefts,* Orion thought. How much more blind could humans be?

Less amused, he read the details of a murder in New Jersey which he knew had resulted from a focus shift in an illegal counters match. The victim had been found mutilated and the police, the story stated, had no leads. *Because a living Dark Embodiment leaves no forensic evidence in its brief hours of life,* Orion thought. He closed his eyes as he remembered those times when he himself had faced those living shadows, seeing them once again seep across walls and ceilings, dropping swiftly and silently through any crack that living light might also pass through. No unprepared human could withstand the touch of a Dark Embodiment, and Orion wondered at the audacity of the battling counters who had called forth such a spell in the Second World. He suspected the Seyshen might be behind the unspeakable action, though to what advantage hc couldn't guess.

With the sun still bright on the street, Orion at last turned to the sports sections. At least with baseball finished for the year, there were few indications that any of the other human contests were being subjected to the Light Clans' disdain for mathematics and the laws of averages. By treaty, they stayed away from football and basketball, but baseball had become their very own and Orion knew none in the First World who claimed any interest in the human sport, knowing how chaotic it had become because of outside interference.

Finally, the sun low but still evident, Orion was reduced

to reading the classifieds, effortlessly breaking the simple codes that enabled the listings to carry information back and forth among adepts who were otherwise out of contact.

Orion saw that the Seyshen were still recruiting humans to what they called their Second World church. A flurry of coded companionship ads from shifters seeking contact with whatever new leadership might have been formed eloquently told of the Clan Arkady's virtual disintegration after the disaster at their last Ceremony of the Change. Some elementals were even offering themselves as sex partners. Orion was astounded at their boldness.

It had been many years since Orion had last paid attention to the interplay between the First and Second Worlds and his reading of the situation today troubled him. There were far too many crossover incidents, too many chances being taken by adepts who seemed not to care if their activities were noticed. Altogether too much chaos and confusion and danger of revelation. *As if the legends of the elemental warrior in the First Clan rings were true,* Orion reflected somberly. Outside the streets were at last comfortably free of direct sunlight and he had been at rest too long.

Orion refolded the newspapers neatly and left them on the couch as he stepped out to the streets of the city, thinking no more of vague Softwind stories and the poetry of the rings. Superstition had no part in his life. He was a vampire adept and the only world he truly cared about was the real one. The First one. His own.

Orion had the cab driver let him off a few blocks from Sword's sanctuary. The walk would give him a chance to observe the field of confrontation in what remained of the daylight. He doubted that he would ever be called to action in this place, so far from the green boundaries of the layer, but he had not survived these many years without seeing the unforeseen become real. He was always prepared for those eventualities which were unlikely, as well as those which were imminent. To abandon either strategy would be a mistake.

The street of Sword's sanctuary was in shadow, and as Orion turned on to it, he tugged down the wide brim of his hat. Fifty feet past the garage entrance to Sword's building, a large truck was backed up to a loading dock. Orion listened carefully, tilting his head to angle an ear toward the vehicle, studying it carefully with his eyes as well, seeing the vibration of someone walking within it.

When Orion had first visited Sword four nights ago, he had decided that the sanctuary was most vulnerable through the common wall it shared with the building beside it. Hidden walls were always fair game for a fardoor, and no wizard was needed to set up a pattern that would extend through only a few feet of Second World brick and mortar.

Thus, Orion remained motionless on the streetcorner, focusing on the sense impressions that came from the truck, trying to determine if those that moved within it were human or adept.

Human, he decided, based on the muffled voices and the rhythm of bootshod footfalls as boxes were unloaded from the vehicle's trailer and carried inside. *Or at least human-form,* he added. He tasted the air but at this distance all he could scent was the truck itself. He walked on.

A few dozen feet from Sword's sanctuary, Orion was surprised to discover that the main garage door was open again. Sword *was* ignorant of what he faced in the First World. That night when they had talked within the sanctuary, Orion had been puzzled that anyone might take this Galen Sword to be the elemental Sword of tradition. In fact, Orion had almost concluded that it was most likely the Seyshen had lied to him about Sword's involvement in the disruption of the Arkady Ceremony of the Change. That is, until Sword himself had confirmed that he had faced shifters before. And the scent of something vaguely shifterish had hung heavily in the air of the Sword sanctuary.

Mostly as a test for Sword in that first meeting, Orion had given Sword some of the information Tantoo had shared with him in Softwind about the Tepesh plan to establish an enclave in New York. If Sword had now made the proper observations, then Orion was prepared to go the next step with him, perhaps even willing to provide some information about Sword's enemies that Sword might find invaluable.

But first, Sword must prove himself trustworthy and as . . . resourceful as the Seyshen's tales made him out to be. The only thing that bothered Orion now was that this Galen Sword was so young. Nothing at all like any of the stories he had heard.

The vampire paused by the entrance to the garage, though he had no need to. Sword himself had given the invitation to cross the threshold and enter, so the residual binding chant had been lifted and tradition upheld. But once again, Orion paused warily to listen and scent, to see what else he might learn.

There were voices in the garage. Two speakers. One he instantly recognized as Sword, the other a human female. Perhaps one of the "associates" Sword had said he worked with. Then again, perhaps not. The voices were arguing in such a way that Orion doubted the speakers could ever work together.

"Adrian asked me to," Sword said. Orion had no difficulty sensing the strain in his voice.

"He didn't tell you to take Martin with you," the female countered. "He just said to buy him some clothes of his own."

Orion built up a sense impression of the female from her voice. Young, he decided, early twenties. From the resonance of her words, he also knew she was slight though muscular. There was a strength in her that she might not be aware of, or which was not apparent when she argued with Sword. As Orion continued listening, he wondered who the Adrian was who could give orders to a Sword.

"So I bought him some clothes," Sword said. "What's the problem?"

"You took him out in public, Sword. You took a bloody shifter into Bloomingdale's for God's sake!"

Orion was shocked. A "bloody shifter?" Had there been another fight? And why did it need clothes? And why would Sword expose a shifter to humans? There were stores in the city that dealt with those of the First World, but he didn't recall that Bloomingdale's was among them. Could Sword be so cavalier about the covenants that existed?

Sword threw his words back at the female. "He's half-human."

A halfling? Orion thought, even more troubled. *Sword has dealings with a shadow dweller? And had to buy him* clothes?

The female made a sound as if lifting something heavy and for a moment Orion thought she might have struck Sword. There was that much animosity in her voice.

"That's not the bloody point, Sword. The point is he's half-shifter. The point is he doesn't know how to behave in public. The—"

"He was fine," Sword interrupted. Something heavy and metal clanged against concrete. "Hey! Watch it!"

"Sorry," the woman said and Orion could hear the lie in her voice. "I didn't see your feet there."

"Anyway, Martin behaved himself perfectly. I think some of the salesgirls even thought he was . . . cute."

"I don't believe you, Sword. Martin's just too different."

This time, Orion heard something metal clang against something else that was metal with regular pounding. Perhaps they were engaged in a ceremonial battle? But only the female appeared to be breathing hard.

"Believe me," Sword said. "When I took Martin to Times Square, he fit right in."

Clang! The sudden sound was enough to make Orion's sensitively focused ears spark with faint pain. He heard metal wheels roll along concrete and couldn't picture what they belonged to.

"Times Square?" the female shouted. "What the hell were you doing *there?"*

As Orion heard Sword's reply, he was certain Sword was about to strike the female with whatever weapons they were brandishing unseen. He wanted to know more about whatever ritual conflict they were involved in. *Perhaps,* he considered, *Sword and the female are mated.*

"Martin saw some things he wanted in the window of a shop. I took him in."

"What? You let him pick out his *own* clothes?"

"You tell me how we get him to wear them if they're not something he likes."

"I give up, Sword. I really give up."

Ah, Orion thought, *the conflict is over.* He stepped around the corner to enter the garage, eager to see what new human activity remained to be discovered there. It had been a long time since any Second Worlder had come up with something new.

"Good day, Mr. Sword." Orion stepped within the garage and waited for Sword's acknowledgment as he swiftly studied the bizarre device the female held in her hand. He recognized it as a Second World vehicle's muffler and tailpipe assembly only as Sword greeted him.

"Oh, Ryan, Mr. Ryan? Hello," Sword said, walking forward rapidly.

Orion saw something hidden in Sword's eyes at once, as

if he wanted to shield the female from him. The tall vampire glanced over Sword's shoulder as they shook hands, observing her. He had been correct about her age and build, if not about her activities with Sword. She wore oil-covered overalls and canvas gloves. A wheeled dolly was at her feet and behind her a black van with a large dent in its side was up on blocks. It seemed she was a mechanic. Orion was momentarily disconcerted that he had missed the obvious. He was beginning to suspect that there was little about this Sword that *was* obvious.

"I didn't expect you today," Sword said, shifting slightly as if still trying to block Orion's view of the female.

"You did not call the number I left with you. I grew concerned." Orion waited for Sword to continue, wondering why he was exhibiting such nervousness in the female's presence. Orion checked Sword's throat but saw no sign he had been taken by the Tepesh. Neither could he scent any of the spoor of a vampire's blood around him. But the scent of something shifterish still hung heavy in the garage. Perhaps from the halfling Sword and the female had been discussing. *But if they were discussing a halfling,* Orion reasoned to himself, *then surely they are involved in common pursuits within the First World.*

The complexities surrounding Galen Sword were so confusing that Orion was beginning to find them intriguing. There might be much more to this being than either he or the Seyshen had first suspected.

"Um, I don't really have anything to report right now," Sword said.

Orion opened his mouth to protest but saw Sword give his head a swift shake, then shift his eyes to the side to indicate the female. Orion closed his mouth, understanding the message.

But the mechanic must also have picked up the subtle signal in Sword's body language. She dropped the tailpipe and muffler to the floor of the garage with another loud crash, then stalked forward, removing the canvas glove from her right hand. Beneath the glove, her hand was wrapped in bandages and Orion wondered how she could still function.

"Melody Ko," the female said as Orion took her hand. He began to revise his assessment of her as he felt the spar-

kle of a Light enchantment beneath her bandages. Like
Sword, she too must have done battle in the First World.

"Ryan," the vampire said. *"Enchanté, mademoiselle."*

"Just Ko," the female said, frowning at Orion. She removed her other glove and the vampire saw it was also
wrapped in gauze and surgical tape. He savored the heady
fragrance of new skin growing beneath the bandages, of
barely healed cuts through flesh. His feeding fangs tickled
lightly against his tongue.

"I'm an associate of Sword's." She looked challengingly
at Sword and Orion could see the barely disguised dislike
still in her eyes. "We work for the same person." Orion
glanced at Sword as Sword shrugged. "What report were
you expecting from us?"

Interesting, Orion thought. He looked at Sword. "Then
you haven't . . ."

"No," Sword said. "As you requested."

Good, the vampire concluded, *then whatever else he is,
it appears this Galen Sword can be trusted.*

"Haven't what, Sword?" The female was becoming more
agitated.

Sword turned to Ko and held his hands up placatingly.
"Melody, this is something that goes a long time back.
It's . . . I haven't had a chance to bring it up with you and
Adrian."

Ko's eyes seared into Sword's. Orion followed Sword's
lead.

"Just Ko," he began, noting both her look of annoyance
and Sword's unexpected smirk, "I have been involved in
discussions of a . . . personal matter with Mr. Sword. A
matter which I asked him to keep confidential, even though
it might conflict with the conditions of his employment
here." Though Sword had never acted as if he were em-
ployed here. He had acted as if he ran the operation. *Ah,
well,* Orion thought, *humans.*

Before anyone could reply to Orion, the vampire's ears
picked up a soft electronic clicking that came from Sword.
Then Sword lifted his wrist close to his face, pressed a control stud on a flat black metal bracelet he wore, and said,
"Sword here."

Orion was impressed by the size of the communications
device. He wondered how powerful it was. It was even

smaller than the telephone the Seyshen had given him at the beach house.

A mechanical voice replied to Sword's acknowledgment. "Call for you. Should take this one."

Orion watched as Sword bit his lip, obviously not wanting to take any call at the moment but for some reason not able to refuse.

"I'll be right back," he said to Ko. "Ryan and I can explain everything then." Then Sword widened his eyes briefly at Orion as if to warn he really hadn't meant it.

Unfortunately, Ko had glimpsed enough of Sword's crude signal to Orion to understand it as well. She scowled as Sword ran quickly to an open metal stairway that led to the next level. Orion could hear the hum and crackle of complex electronic equipment in operation above him. He decided that might be a good place to start to deflect Ko's inevitable questions.

"The device Mr. Sword was wearing," he said, "must be quite intelligent. To be able to speak with an artificial voice, quite intelligent indeed."

Ko stared up at Orion. Her head was almost at the level of his chest. "That wasn't the device speaking. That was Adrian Forsyte. That's who we work for."

Orion was astounded. The device and its voice had been clearly mechanical in origin. There had been nothing of true life about it. Yet Ko said that she and Sword *worked* for it. *Was that what it was going to take for the legends to come true—not that humans could ever be able to best the First World, but that their technology and devices could?* Orion had never heard such an explanation posited by the apologists and the followers of the First Clan's rings before. But in the context of this modern age, it made a certain amount of sense.

"And how long have you worked for . . . it?" Orion asked respectfully. Since Tranquility, he suspected, when the true aspect of *leel* was revealed.

"It?" Ko answered. "Adrian Forsyte is a *him*. Dr. Adrian Forsyte. The physi—"

"That voice was made by a living human?" It was possible that Ko and Sword might not realize the true nature of their "employer," if all it had done was talk to them through such devices that would not reveal its actual nature.

"Dr. Forsyte has lost the ability to speak for himself,"

Ko said with a voice of ice. "He has to use a computerized speech synthesizer. I built it for him."

Orion felt disappointment that his exciting new theory of how the legends might come true was suddenly no longer viable. But the handful of words Ko had spoken had been enough for him to learn something else that was new. The female human loved this Adrian Forsyte. He could hear it in the complex wavers of her voice as she spoke the name and in the movement of her eyes and the subtle realignment of certain compounds of her scent.

Then what is her relationship with Sword? Orion wondered. *With so much anger and hostility between the two, there is another link between them, and if it is not love, then it must be . . .* Orion could not think what it might be. It was not blood, for they shared no common descent which he could see or sense. But they shared something of passion. Something unspoken that they somehow were not free to reveal even to themselves.

"How long have you known Sword?" Ko asked sharply.

Orion tried to come up with a safe answer. He could not be sure what Sword might already have said to protect the secret of their meeting. "I have known *of* him for quite a time, but only recently have we met."

"How recent is recent?"

Orion smiled charmingly. "I have some acquaintances who study the science of geology, and they would insist that 'recent' means anything within the past million years."

But Ko didn't return the smile. "Look, Ryan, I know a dodge when I hear one, all right? The thing for you to remember is that despite anything else that Sword might have told you in the past, right now he's part of a team. Whatever he's involved in, we're *all* involved in." She made two fists and rested her bandaged hands on her hips. "Now what were you expecting him to report about?"

"A private matter," Orion said simply. "Nothing that would involve a . . . team."

Ko continued to stare sternly up at him and Orion did not look away. He wondered if she knew he was lying, or if she just considered any acquaintance of Sword's to be a liar by association.

Before either could speak again, the metal stairway clanged as Sword returned. His scent had changed. Orion sensed sudden tension directed at both himself and Ko.

Ko caught the change in Sword's mood as well. *She must know him well to be able to tell such a thing with human senses alone,* Orion thought.

"Well?" Ko asked.

"I have to talk with Ryan for a few minutes." Sword gestured to the stairway. "Why don't we go upstairs and—"

"Who was that on the phone, Sword?" Ko wasn't willing to let it go.

"Nobody, Melody, just . . . look, I have to talk to Ryan. It's old business."

Orion was fascinated by this chance to observe Sword interacting with another human. Presumably, he had shown courage and remained collected when he had been present at the Ceremony of the Change, yet here his composure was obviously disturbed by an exchange with a mere coworker. Orion didn't understand the depths to Sword, or his motivation, but he found himself unexpectedly curious to know him better. Humans were seldom so complex that they actually interested him.

Ko strode in front of Sword to block his path to the stairway. Orion was amused by her singlemindedness. She turned and faced them both again.

"Listen, Sword, if you're holding out on us again, then the whole deal is off!"

Orion heard Sword's communication device come alive once more. He deduced a small panel on the bracelet was being made to vibrate to alert Sword to an incoming message. The sound was quiet enough that other humans might not notice it. This Sword was clever.

Sword brought the bracelet to his face again. He spoke with exasperation. "Yes, Adrian, what is it?"

Adrian's mechanical voice replied, "Marion E. Raycheba is on the phone again. She says if you hang up on her again, she will call the police."

The message meant nothing to Orion. He watched Ko for her reaction and saw that she seemed pleased.

"Okay, Sword, this sounds like it's going to be good. Who the hell is Marion E. Raycheba?"

Sword was obviously embarrassed. "Ah, she's Kennie's station manager."

"Kennie?" Ko asked. "As in Kendall Marsh? Your *old* girlfriend?"

"Yeah," Sword said. Orion heard the vibration of his bracelet again. Sword snapped his head around in the direction of the stairway. "*In a minute,* Adrian! Tell her I'm on my way!"

"So what's wrong with *Kennie?*" Ko asked sarcastically. "You stringing her along a—"

"She's missing!" Sword snapped at Ko. Then he paused to calm himself. "All right?" he asked, his voice more in control. "She didn't come in today. The station sent someone to her place and she's not there."

Orion studied Sword intently, using all his senses. Sword's physiological responses confirmed that Marsh *was* someone who was important to him, but still there was more to Sword's growing sense of alarm than mere emotional attachment to another human. Even though Orion couldn't sense what that was.

"Why are they calling you about it?" Ko asked.

Sword shook his head, not meeting her eyes. "I was . . . I think they think I was the last to see her."

"When?" Ko was apparently shocked by the idea.

"Yesterday, or the day before," Sword answered, his emotional distress increasing.

"Were you?"

"What?"

"The last to see her, Sword!"

"I don't know."

"*Were* you seeing her? *Again?*"

"Yes. No. I was . . . I was giving her a lead on a story."

Orion heard the vibration of the bracelet again and Sword's pulse rate jumped in response.

Ko folded her arms over her chest, becoming an immovable object in Sword's path. "What kind of story?" she demanded.

Sword exploded. "It was nothing to do with us, Melody!"

Ko responded with equal force. "Then who was it bloody well to do with, Galen?"

Sword's eyes flicked to Orion and the vampire immediately grasped the import of that revealing action.

So did Ko. She turned to look at Orion with renewed interest. "This guy?"

Orion ignored her and wouldn't give Sword a chance to

answer the female. "Who is this Kendall Marsh?" the vampire asked them.

Sword didn't answer.

"She's the news anchor on *LiveEye*," Ko said, alternately watching Sword, then Orion.

"*A reporter!*" Orion's voice rose alarmingly and both Ko and Sword tensed. "*You sent a human reporter into a Tepesh enclave?*"

As Saul Calder's had, the vampire's voice shook the metal of the van behind them with its focused intensity. Ko looked at him with widening eyes.

"Human?" she said. "Sword, I think you better—"

Suddenly a second metallic crash rang through the garage. Then another.

Orion looked past Sword and Ko as they jerked their heads to face the stairway where a brightly colored blur hit the metal stairs a final time, then leapt up through the air in a series of spins to land on two bare and inordinately hairy feet on the garage floor, all the while screaming with inhuman lungs, "*Uuuuuullllltimate Warrrrrriorrrrr!*"

Ko, Sword, and Orion became absolutely still and silent, stunned by the sudden appearance of this apparition.

Shifter, Orion thought rapidly as he assessed the strange being before him. *Or halfling. He must be the halfling they were discussing earlier. The one called Martin.*

Martin did indeed have the bestial nature of a shifter in him, as well as strictly human features. But whatever his true nature was, Orion could scarcely notice it beneath the outlandish clothing that he wore: billowing neon-yellow-and-green patterned pants pulled tight at the ankles, a red headband, and a sleeveless white sweatshirt with a garishly colored portrait of an angry looking human wearing long blond hair and a moustache and clenching a fist. Beneath the portrait were the words, "Hulk Hogan." Orion had seen nothing like it before.

The shifter halfling raised his burly arms above his head as if claiming victory in battle.

"Martin new clothes dress up pretty Hulkster no bare Martin," the halfling burbled excitedly. Orion wondered what tortures the poor creature had been subjected to in its brief life to reduce it to this behavior.

"Martin, I think you should go upstairs now." Sword spoke in a quiet but urgent tone.

The halfling's heavy brow creased beneath his headband. "Martin pretty?" he asked. Orion could sense there might be a fight if the answer were not positive.

"Yes, Martin," Ko said quickly, going to the creature. "Very nice. But please, you have to—"

And then the halfling's eyes met Orion's.

Martin's instant and instinctual howl of outrage and hatred exploded forth from him with the force of an elemental's storm.

Ko held both hands to her ears. "What the hell are you doing?" she shouted at Martin.

The halfling crouched, preparing for the attack. He pointed at Orion with a massive finger. *"Nightfeeder!"* he hissed.

Orion couldn't see an easy way out. He spread his arms, preparing for combat.

"Nightfeeder?" Ko repeated, wrinkling her face with a frown. She began to turn back to Sword. "What the hell is a night—"

Orion stretched his mouth wide as his fangs slid forward for battle.

"Oh," she said. And then the halfling attacked.

FOURTEEN

Sword moved without thought, throwing himself into Martin's trajectory to keep him from the vampire's grip.

But Martin's shifter reflexes would allow no interference. His arm lashed out and smashed Sword to the ground at his feet. Yet, as Martin prepared to leap again, Sword reached out through the pain of the blow and grabbed at Martin's legs.

The halfling growled and tugged one foot away. He raised his hand to strike Sword again.

"No, Martin! You can't!" Sword shouted. Blood ran from his mouth, his vision blurred, but he knew he could not allow Martin to face the creature. Beside him, Melody Ko dropped back from his field of vision.

During the entire exchange, the vampire who said his name was Ryan had not moved. He still stood ready for Martin's assault, body turned sideways, arms spread wide. "He's right, little halfling. Why even try?"

Martin didn't pause for an instant. He bashed Sword with the back of his hand, making him relinquish his grip. "Martin try!" the halfling snarled and leapt once more.

Still dazed, Sword pushed himself up in time to see Martin plucked from the air by Ryan's single blow. The halfling bounced away as if he had dropped in front of a speeding train, yet he managed to hook one hand into the fabric of the vampire's coat as he flew away.

The dark fabric tugged against the vampire, but he was unaffected by its pull. He remained fixed in place as the seams of the coat ripped around him, shreds of it trailing away with Martin's speeding form until the halfling crashed into the stack of empty light fixture crates from the previous day's shipment of new supplies.

Sword stood unsteadily, unfocused eyes looking where a handful of small objects from the vampire's black coat rolled and clattered across the garage floor. *At least Martin didn't hit the crates of demolition charges,* Sword thought.

He confronted the vampire. "Don't kill him! Martin doesn't understand what you are." Then he cried, "Melody, don't!"

But even as Sword shouted his warning, the vampire ducked and rolled as Ko swung her metal-former's hammer at his head, making contact only with his falling hat. Sword blinked once, trying to clear his eyes, and in that instant the vampire had moved behind Ko to grab her arm and force it against her back, immobilizing her.

Ryan ignored Martin where he lay on the floor, gasping to catch his breath. The vampire directed his attention to Sword. "I do not wish to harm any of—"

Ko slammed her heel down on Ryan's foot with crushing force. Ryan didn't flinch. Instead, he looked down at her and said, "Really, Ko, I believe you have missed the point of wh—"

Ko twisted forward and the vampire suddenly flew over her shoulder with a horrible crack. But before Sword could react, the vampire had moved in a blur and was on his feet again, a look of delight on his face. He smiled at Sword, then spun to Ko.

"Very good, Ko. It has been too long since . . . ah, but there has been a price, has there not?"

In front of Ryan, Ko's face had paled unnaturally and she clutched the arm he had grabbed. She slumped to her knees with a moan.

"Melody!" Sword stepped forward unsteadily.

Ryan wheeled. "No, Mr. Sword, no more. This is not a fair match. You have no chance at victory and I have no wish to fight. For now."

"Neither have I," Sword said thickly. He spat a mouthful of blood to the floor. "For now."

"Your associate's arm is shattered in two places. It must be quite painful."

Sword looked over at Martin as the halfling finally made it to his feet.

"What about him?"

Ryan smiled and moved his lips with an unusual twist. Sword stared in fascination as the vampire's fangs retracted behind his other teeth. "He is shifter enough. He will be fine. If he knows when to stop."

But Martin growled and crouched, ready for more.

"That's enough, Martin!" Sword told him. "Remember what we talked about in the car!"

"Shifter kill vampire!" Martin growled, beginning to circle Ryan.

"No, Martin! That's not the way we do things now." Ryan cautioned Sword. "If he attacks again, I cannot be responsible."

Sword kept speaking to Martin, who listened unwillingly. "Remember what I told you. There are many ways to fight. We have to fight a different way, now."

Ryan finally relaxed his guard as Sword stepped in front of Martin, effectively cutting off the halfling's direct line of attack. To the side, Ko was still transfixed in her kneeling position. Her almost colorless face was glistening with sweat.

"There are no 'different ways' to fight me, Mr. Sword. What you meant to say is that this fight has ended." The vampire bent to retrieve his hat and brush it off.

"That's not what I meant at all," Sword said as he brought his locater band to his lips. "I meant that there *are* different ways to fight." He pressed the call button. "Adrian, seal the garage and activate the new lights."

Ryan looked around quizzically as the heavy garage door began to shut. Sword wondered if the vampire would notice how much faster the door's operation was now than it was the first night he had visited Sword. And he wondered what the vampire might make of the intricate pattern formed by the overlapping panels of virtually unbreakable Kevlar II webbing that now lined the door's metal panels. Sword doubted there was anything in either world that could easily burst through those panels again.

The vampire's clear gaze returned to Sword. "You should stop this, Mr. Sword. You don't know what you risk."

"Nor do you," Sword said. Then he held his hand against his forehead to shield his eyes as upstairs in the main lab Forsyte triggered the newest of the Loft's defenses.

For a moment, Ryan acted surprised by the sudden blue-white radiance that filled the garage, glaring forth from a series of humming light fixtures newly mounted along the steel support beams above him.

Then Sword saw him realize exactly what had happened. The vampire took a step forward as if to challenge Sword.

But he had to turn his head to the floor. Then he snapped his arms around himself, shoving his hands inside his armpits to shield them from the blazing light.

Sword kept the locater band ready, waiting for Ryan to fully understand what he faced and how he could stop it. In the lab above, Sword knew that Forsyte would be watching everything through the Loft's multiple security cameras.

The vampire shivered, then brought his head up to stare savagely at Sword, fangs extended and dripping. He spread his arms wide, palms up, and looked directly into the ultraviolet bulbs that blazed down upon him.

"Iiiisis!" the vampire cried out chillingly and would not turn away from the light.

Now Sword felt the first tremor of fear. He had had no time to install a second level of defense. The ultraviolet *had* to work. There was no fallback position.

Ryan's arms fell to his side. He turned his head to find Sword. Slowly, he walked toward him, his eyes narrowed against the light, but not blinded by it.

Sword didn't retreat. As the vampire drew closer, Sword could see the red splotches that spread across the golden skin of his face. The light *was* working, Sword realized, only more slowly than he had hoped. Forsyte had said that it might take some trial and error to determine the precise wavelength of radiation that would prove most harmful to such creatures.

When he was close enough, the vampire reached out and caught hold of Sword's wrist. But Sword could tell that there was not enough strength in him to force Sword's arm to move.

"Turn them off." The vampire spoke with the dry choking voice of a man who had spent days in the desert. "We still have business to conduct."

Sword made no move to take his arm from Ryan's grip, though he had no doubt he could. "Then this fight is over?"

"For now," the vampire said.

So Sword did nothing. He could feel the vampire's shudder pass through his arm.

"Accept what I offer, Mr. Sword, or the only way you will survive is by never leaving this place again."

The vampire's lips were parched and cracked, his eyes rimmed with red. But Sword sensed truth in what he said. There was no need to look for more enemies. For now.

Sword pressed the talk button on his locater with his chin, then looked up to the closest ceiling-mounted video camera. "That's enough, Adrian. Shut them down."

One bank after another, the ultraviolet fixtures were extinguished above them. The vampire's hand fell from Sword's wrist. Sword went immediately to Ko. Martin was already beside her.

"Is it broken?" Sword asked as he knelt beside her and lightly touched her arm.

Ko winced. "What do you think?"

Martin had his arm around Ko and he moved to protect her from Sword. "Melody go wizard make better flowers sweet thing for after."

"We'll get her to the hospital, Martin. She'll be okay." Sword activated his locater band again as he felt it vibrate against his wrist. "What is it, Adrian?"

Forsyte's synthesized voice answered. "I have called for an ambulance. Best to hide evidence of fight. You have five minutes."

Sword nodded. "Martin, give me a hand?"

Martin rolled out his bottom lip in confusion. "Say what?" He moved his free arm behind his back as if to keep his hand from Sword's reach.

Sword caught Ko, in spite of herself, smiling weakly at Martin's misunderstanding of Sword's request. But before he could say anything else, he became aware of the vampire behind him.

"When did you know?" the vampire demanded.

Sword stood up. His ears still rang from Martin's blow. "Know what?" he asked.

"Who I was. What I was." The vampire's lips were almost healed now. The angry red splotches that had burned his face were just slight discolorations. Sword wasn't surprised or impressed. He had battled Saul Calder in this same garage. He found it odd how easily he was accepting each new experience which fell his way. Almost as if they weren't new at all.

"I knew when Martin did."

The vampire's expression clearly registered his disbelief. "You did not have those lights in place four nights ago when I was here."

"Four nights!" Ko sputtered. "Damn you, Sword, you've

done it again.'' She groaned as the force of her words made her broken arm move against her.

''It was the night that Ja'Nette went home,'' Sword protested. ''The night *before* we reached our agreement.''

Ko shook her head in frustration. ''You should have told us then, Sword. You still should have told us.''

''I didn't think anything would come of it. If you knew how many times I've been told that there are vampires in New York . . .''

''But you must have known *something!*'' Ko shut her eyes and bit her lip in sudden agony. When she spoke again, her voice was weaker. ''Bloody hell, Sword, you had the electricians here to put up those UVS the next day.''

''It seemed like a good idea to have it done at the same time we had the garage door reinforced,'' Sword said. And it was the truth as he had felt it. But he *was* troubled by the vampire's question: When *had* he known what Ryan was and what he was capable of? He seemed to have too much knowledge for it simply to have occurred to him at the instant of Martin's shriek of recognition. From an upper level, he heard the elevator motor start up. Forsyte would be coming soon.

''A good idea,'' Ko muttered. ''Right. Eight thousand dollars worth of lights for someone who didn't know he was dealing with vampires? No more stories, Sword.''

''I didn't know,'' Sword said firmly. ''I didn't think it was anything.''

Ko glared up at Sword. ''Is that why you sent *Kennie* off to check out his story? Because she wasn't going to find *anything?*''

The vampire's hand was on Sword's shoulder before he could answer Ko. ''What is she saying? *Did* you tell the human reporter what I told you?''

Sword nodded. How was he supposed to have known that Ryan hadn't been another crackpot? His mind reeled with all that must be done now. Ko to the hospital. Marsh's station manager threatening to call the police. And Marsh herself . . . what had he sent her into?

''And is it also true that she has disappeared?'' Ryan's grip tightened.

Sword nodded again. ''That's what her station manager says.''

"Do you know the trouble you have caused? What you might have set in motion?"

Ko came out with a whispery laugh. "Trouble? Sword? Tell me about it."

The elevator motor stopped and Sword heard the metal cage doors slide open.

"What's this?" the vampire said abruptly and stepped away from Sword. He stared in fascination as Forsyte's chair rolled forward on its twin treads to join the others. "Are you Adrian?" he asked in a tone that almost seemed to be of awe. "The one in charge?"

Forsyte's chair stopped in front of the vampire and Sword could see the intelligent eyes behind Forsyte's glasses inspect Ryan. What would the physicist think of a creature so powerful, so graceful, so seemingly full of life? Forsyte's tremulous finger tapped a single button on his keypad.

"Yes," the voder said.

"Then *you* must understand what has happened here."

Sword saw Forsyte glance at him and a rough, sudden frown appeared on the physicist's slack face.

"Yes," the voder said again.

The vampire nodded. "Then you also understand what you and your associates must do."

Forsyte blinked his eyes once, then laboriously punched in a long sequence on his keypad. From outside, Sword could hear the wail of an approaching siren. Forsyte hit the final key.

"We must do what you tell us to do," the voder said.

Sword opened his mouth to object but the vampire stopped him with a single look—a look of dismissal, of power, and, inexplicably, of fear.

"Yes," the vampire said. "You must now do precisely what I tell you. Or none of us will survive another night."

FIFTEEN

Except for the occasional hum and click from Forsyte's computers, the van was silent in the night.

In the back, the physicist monitored the motion detectors Martin had placed in the alleys that wound around and behind the BioproEx Community Blood Clinic. In the front of the van, the First World vampire and the First World exile waited, one with patience beyond time, the other unsettled by misgivings and self-recrimination.

Finally, the inaction became too much for Sword. He turned in the driver's seat of the parked van. "Call him again, Adrian."

But the vampire placed his hand on Sword's shoulder. "That would not be wise. I was able to hear the supposedly silent vibration of your communications device. So could others of my kind." The vampire looked back to where Forsyte's eyes glowed red with the reflection of the lasers in the thick black frames of his glasses. "Let the halfling remain where he is, in silence."

Forsyte's voder spoke for him. "Agreed."

Sword slumped back in his seat behind the wheel and then leaned forward to peer through the windshield of the van. Hours ago, after letting Martin off five blocks distant, Sword had parked the van on a forlorn street in Hell's Kitchen, lined with burned-out brownstones that were covered over with graffiti-streaked panels of plywood. Directly behind the van was a dented and twisted dumpster. Ahead, a line of equally dented and twisted cars and pickup trucks crowded together so that it appeared that not one could pull away from the curb without the others. At the end of the line of parked—or abandoned—vehicles, hidden in the shadows cast by the only two working streetlamps that served the street, the storefront entrance of the BioproEx clinic was dark.

Another block past the clinic, the World Plaza sky-scraper—a huge and modern monument to urban redevelopment—rose from the old neighborhood's stained and ramshackle buildings in spotlit postmodern tiers of marble and brick. From the ornate crystal-faceted cap on the top of its tallest tower, glowing shafts of radiance spread out over the city like the welcoming beacon of a lighthouse. But that welcome light did not reach the streets that huddled below.

Except for the passage of a single, slow-moving police cruiser most probably checking license plates for stolen vehicles, nothing had moved on the street for more than an hour.

"Are you *sure* that's the right place?" Sword asked. Each minute Kendall Marsh remained missing was another minute in which she could be lost forever. And this time, even Sword knew it *was* his fault everything had gone wrong.

"My sources were excellent," the vampire said succinctly. "And I examined this area myself the first day I arrived."

Sword regarded the vampire with skepticism. "Day?" he asked.

"The sun holds little terror for me, Mr. Sword. I can function adequately during daylight hours, despite what human legends would have you believe."

Sword had heard the usual tales of vampires trapped within their coffins from sunrise to sunset, but now he suddenly remembered another story he had heard in New Orleans, from the woman who had sold him 'Bub. Something about a vampire who had escaped a burning building by day.

"Ever been to New Orleans, Ryan?"

Though the vampire didn't move, it seemed his breathing stopped.

"My true name is Orion, Mr. Sword. My clan is Isis. You need know nothing more about me. For now."

Contact, Sword thought. He looked through the windshield seeing nothing move. "The UV lights in the garage stopped you pretty fast."

Sword heard Orion change position in the seat beside him. "I was not prepared for them. And I would caution you not to expect that I will be caught unprepared by them again. Do you understand me, Mr. Sword?"

Sword took a chance. "Seems the fire in New Orleans caught you unprepared, too. Maybe a lot of things—" He turned to look at the vampire and stopped as he felt the words dry up in his throat. He felt unable to look away from the vampire's steady gaze.

"You know a great deal of so very little," Orion hissed. "And so very little of such a great deal. But please do not behave as if you do not know what it is to enter into common cause with another clan. Remember that we work together in this, if you wish to see your Kendall again."

Sword then surprised even himself as he replied to the vampire's obvious threat with equal conviction. In the museum, Roth had called Sword a pawn, and whether that statement had been true at the time or not, Sword suddenly realized that in the past few weeks he had blindly accepted whatever he had been told about the First World. That wasn't the way to learn about it. He had to question. He had to probe. If there were rules that governed how adepts of Clan Isis and Clan Pendragon should act together, then he wanted them spelled out for him so he could have the choice of accepting or rejecting those conditions.

"This isn't just for Kendall," Sword said, shaking off the vampire's hypnotic pull with difficulty. "You came to *me,* remember? You need something from me just as badly as I need it from you. And my bottom line is that I can do what you're so afraid of—call in the police and the media."

"You wouldn't dare."

"What have I got to lose?" Sword asked. "I've already been exiled from the First World. I—"

"What?" Orion's gaze faltered. He seemed to be genuinely nonplussed by Sword's words.

"I'm an adept. I was born into Clan—"

"Yes, yes," Orion said irritably. "That much is known. Tell me about your expulsion." He leaned forward to listen to what Sword would say next.

Sword searched for some clue to the vampire's thoughts but could see nothing revealed in his dark and shadowed eyes. "There's not much to tell. From what little I've learned, I was five. I had no powers. A . . . wizard gave me a potion . . ." Sword looked down. "In fact, I remembered nothing of my First World life until three years ago. An accident brought back some of my memories. I've been trying to find out more about the First World ever since." He left out all mention of his brother Brin's healing intervention. Sometimes secrets held power, and Sword saw no reason to fully trust Orion.

"They *sent* you away . . . ?" Orion said.

"What about it?"

The vampire shook his head as if dismissing a mistaken thought. "No matter. There were legends, ancient legends of a warrior who . . . tradition claims might be a Sword of Pendragon. But this warrior is said to leave the First World of his freeborn choice. And that, Mr. Sword, would appear to rule you out." Orion smiled ruefully and settled back in his seat. He resumed his watch of the empty street.

"What else do the legends say?" Sword asked.

"Which one, Mr. Sword? There are so many, from the governing rings of the First Clan to the thousand tales told in the softwind tongues. And just as human legends of vampires are not true, so, too, do some of the First World legends rest more on the tale-teller's art than on any truth."

"A legend by definition has some basis in truth," Sword said. He knew that from his studies of ancient cultures. Since his final meeting with Marcus Askwith, he had known that there had been an unconscious reason why he had been drawn to archaeology as a way to fulfill his trust fund's condition that he obtain a university education and work in a field that would expand humanity's knowledge of itself. His college major had not come about just because his self-indulgence had prompted him to choose a series of courses that other students had assured him would be "soft." Even back then, even unknowing, he had been searching for the answers that he needed to return home. "The Second World legends of shifters say that silver is deadly to them, and I've seen that it is. And I've also seen that sunlight, ultraviolet radiation at least, can be harmful to vampires as well."

Orion tapped a finger against his lip in thought. "Yet I do not sleep in a wooden coffin among the soil of my homeland, Mr. Sword. I cast reflections, pass through running water, and though garlic can be irritating if properly prepared, it cannot prevent me from going where I choose."

Sword had a sudden memory return to him. "But when you came to the Loft that first night, you spoke to me from a distance and didn't step through the garage door until I had invited you in."

Orion gave Sword a mocking smile. "And was that enchantment at work, or First World respect for the master of the house?'' The smile vanished. ''If you ever decide to come after me with a wooden stake, Mr. Sword, take great care that you know exactly where to place it.''

The exile and the vampire locked eyes, but before either could speak, Forsyte's voder interrupted.

''Detector two is red.''

Automatically, Sword checked the pencil diagram on the pad of grid paper on his lap. Without Ko, he had been unable to program the pattern of the detectors into the company and Forsyte had been too busy monitoring them. Detector two was at the mouth of an alley that joined with the one that ran directly behind the clinic.

''Where's Martin?'' Sword asked Forsyte.

''Positioned by detector six,'' the voder replied.

Sword scanned quickly across the page. Detector six was half a block away from the van at the end of the direct alley. Sword marked Xs beside detectors one and six, then held the pad up for Orion. ''Could a vampire hear Martin over this distance?''

Orion hesitated, as if concerned that he might be giving up a clan secret. ''Only if the vampire were searching for him. Your halfling is not in danger. Yet.''

Sword turned back to Forsyte. ''Signal him, Adrian. Tell him to watch for someone coming out of the alley just beyond the back of the clinic.''

Forsyte clicked at his keypad.

Sword fidgeted as he waited to hear Martin's reply. ''Why wouldn't the vampires who set up this clinic use the passageways under the streets to move from place to place?'' he asked. The system he and Ko had found running beneath Central Park West had been vast and ancient, with most of the tunnels lit by floating facets of red crystal.

''Other clans run the other streets, Mr. Sword. If there are no treaties, then there is no passage. The Tepesh have always preferred to work alone.''

''How many clans are there?'' Sword asked abruptly. All Martin had been able to answer to that question was ''lots.''

But Orion didn't offer a better answer. His jaw tightened as he said, ''One more than there should be.''

''No response,'' Forsyte's voder said.

Sword groaned and closed his eyes. All he needed was for one thing to work out. Just *one* thing. ''Are you getting any bio-readings from him?''

"No."

Sword hit the steering wheel. "Damn him!"

"What is it?" Orion asked.

"Martin's taken off his clothes again." Sword slipped out of his chair and moved to the center of the van. "We don't have a locater band that can fit him so I pinned it to his sweatshirt. He *promised* he wouldn't take it off. He picked it out himself."

Forsyte's mechanical voice spoke again. "Detector three is red."

"Whoever it is has hit the main alley and turned toward the clinic," Sword explained hurriedly as he pushed his Mitsubishi transceiver into his ear and rapidly connected the thin wire that ran from it to the main unit strapped in place on his equipment vest. He handed a second transceiver set to Orion. "Wear this."

Orion held the device in his hand as if it might bite him. "Why?"

"So we can keep in touch with each other and Forsyte."

"Why?"

Sword stopped his preparations and stared at the vampire. "Are you related to Martin all of a sudden? We're going out there, that's why."

"We have not seen the indications we need to proceed," Orion said, trying to hand the transceiver set back to Sword.

Sword pushed the vampire's hand away. "Listen, the detectors are telling us that there's something moving through the alley along the back of the clinic. Martin was supposed to be up on the roofs to tell us what was on the move. But Martin isn't available. It's up to us. Now put on the transceiver."

"The halfling could already be dead."

Sword was stung by the possibility. He wanted to protest but he knew that what Orion suggested might be true. Perhaps Martin hadn't removed his clothes. Perhaps the locater band was still pinned to his sweatshirt. Perhaps there were no bio-readings because there was no life left within Martin to detect.

Swearing, Sword pulled a concealed panel from the floor of the van and reached for one of the cut-down Remingtons hidden behind it. Ko had trimmed their barrels and stocks herself. "How do vampires stand up to shotgun blasts?" he asked roughly, retrieving a box of shells.

Again Orion hesitated. "If you are close enough, it can slow us down. For a short time. But if you are that close to begin with, Mr. Sword, you will not have time to pull the trigger. I guarantee it."

Sword abruptly pumped two shells into the shotgun, then crouched behind Orion's seat. He had had enough of this game. "If I'm so damn useless, then why the hell did you bother coming to me in the first place?" he said.

Orion's head jerked back and Sword had a glimpse of ivory fangs appearing for just an instant in the vampire's mouth.

Orion inhaled audibly. "You disrupted Clan Arkady's Ceremony of the Change."

Sword was knocked off guard. "How'd you know about that?"

"The worlds are small, Mr. Sword, and bad news travels fast. Much is known about you." He held up his hand to stop Sword from interrupting. "What is important is that for almost forty cycles I have been preparing to fight a war. A war that would have torn the First World in two. Yet in one night, *you* were able to destroy Arkady's power and end that war before it could be fought. So I have been freed from my blood bond. Freed to fight my *own* war again." He gestured behind him, to the clinic. "The war with the Tepesh who made me the last of my clan."

Orion's hand snapped out and grabbed the collar strap of Sword's vest, pulling him closer. "The *last,* Mr. Sword. Unlike you, I have no clan to return to. But like those I once served, I have found a warrior to fight with me in my war—a warrior who could face the entire Clan Arkady." The vampire pushed Sword away, slamming him into the wall of the van. "And here my warrior is! A petulant human who tells lies to send a woman to her death. A powerless adept who has not even earned the respect of a halfling! Imagine my disgust, Mr. Sword, for having been tricked once by the Seyshen, and then again by *you!*"

To regain his feet, Sword smashed the Remington against the floor of the van with a jarring metallic crash. He could see Orion's eyes flicker at the noise. Perhaps, he thought with satisfaction, there were some disadvantages to having hypersensitive senses. He pulled himself upright as he questioned himself about what he thought he was doing by taking on a vampire, but the rest of him didn't care. The vampire was wrong and he was right. It was time someone besides himself knew that.

He spoke inches from Orion's face. "I'm getting sick of this whole damned conspiracy that's floating around me. *You* came to me! *You* lied to me! If those lies have put Kendall in danger, then you share the responsibility. And the fact is, whatever you've heard about me, Seyshen tales or not, *you* still need someone to *help* you go against the Tepesh." Sword had never seen a more murderous expression than the one now on Orion's face. He had witnessed the way the vampire had swatted Martin from the air. Whatever it took for Orion to lose his control, Sword knew that nothing could save him once that point had been reached. Not this close to him. Still he went on. "And what you've got is me!"

Orion's voice was flat and emotionless. "Do you know how near you are to death?"

Sword matched the vampire's tone exactly, his mind flawlessly alert in its flood of adrenaline. "At least if I die, *my* clan continues."

In the heightened silence of the van, Sword heard a brittle cracking noise and saw that Orion's hand had splintered the plastic arm of his seat.

"Have you no fear, human?" And the way Orion whispered the question left no doubt as to what he thought the answer should be.

But Sword just leaned closer to Orion, deliberately putting himself within reach of the vampire's fangs. "Not anymore, nightfeeder. I'm too pissed off to be frightened."

Orion's lips curled back and Sword saw twin ivory switchblades flash into place. But because Orion's attack was not instantaneous, Sword instinctively knew that it would not come at all.

For once, Sword had the unfamiliar and heady feeling that he had prevailed. And he knew that Orion could see that realization in his eyes.

Like morays withdrawing into their caves, Orion's fangs disappeared and he closed his mouth. "Before we go into battle together, Mr Sword, I think you should know that I believe you are insane."

"Is that part of the legend, too?" Sword asked recklessly as he reached down for his Remington. No tasers tonight.

No tranquilizer darts. Just shotgun shells and a knapsack full of blasting caps and demolition charges. Ko was going to miss a real party.

"As a matter of fact," the vampire said, "it is."

SIXTEEN

K o closed the door to the Loft's main entrance behind her, pressed the bandaged palm of her one good hand against it, and shut her eyes, tormenting herself with the promise of sleep.

But not yet, she told herself cruelly. *Not until I find out what finally happened. What the vampire told them to do.*

She wrenched her eyes open again, felt dizzy, and leaned against the door, overcome by the musty smell of damp plaster from the cast on her doubly broken arm. When she was sure of her balance once more, she reached out to the security control panel, punched in her code, and rearmed the Loft's alarm perimeter. According to its display screen, it had last been set at 20:27—just over four hours ago, and less than an hour after the ambulance had taken her away.

"Damn you again, Sword," Ko said fiercely as she made her way through the short hallway to the Loft's garage. Not only had Sword lied to them all again, he had exceeded himself this time by tricking that pea-brain television reporter he used to date into infiltrating an entire *nest* of First World vampires—not that it would be difficult to talk Kendall Marsh into doing anything, Ko thought. That was about the only reason she could see for the fool to have stayed involved with someone like Sword as long as she had—as far as Ko was concerned, Marsh didn't have the sense that nature gave planaria.

And then, worst of all, she herself had been forced out of the game plan because she had misjudged the angle of her pivot when she tossed the vampire over her shoulder, letting him keep his grip on her arm.

She had a phrase that summed up all her feelings and she spat it out to echo in the deserted garage.

Ko crossed the garage floor until she stood behind the damaged van she had been repairing earlier that evening.

She sighed heavily when she saw that the elevator cage was still on the garage level. That confirmed her suspicions that Forsyte had gone with the others. When she could only get the Loft's answering system in her calls from the hospital, she had hoped that Forsyte might have been running the operation from the main lab as he used to when she, Sword, and Ja'Nette went on their excursions. But it had been a foolish hope, Ko knew. Forsyte was determined to run the show, now. She knew he would never again be content to be left behind in the Loft. She wondered if that were the true reason why he had wanted to join up with Sword again. Not because of any longing for knowledge, and not because he ever really expected to find the adepts who had crippled him, but because he couldn't face being trapped in a chair in front of a computer screen for the rest of his life. Perhaps Forsyte didn't want to accept Sword any more than he wanted to face up to her declaration of love for him. Perhaps he just wanted some excitement in his life, knowing how little chance for it remained.

Ko turned away from the elevator cage to face the garage again. She knew she should rest. She knew she should return to her own apartment. But as was typical of her, she couldn't stand not knowing what was going on and she'd be damned if she left before Forsyte returned.

If he comes back, she thought and immediately regretted it.

She leaned back against the fender of the Checker cab parked next to the damaged van, preparing herself for the climb upstairs. She could make some coffee. Use some of the strong French roast she kept hidden from Sword because he wouldn't know the good stuff unless it had a label on it that said it cost five times more than anyone else would pay. Ko shut her eyes again. She wondered why she still let Sword bother her so much, especially now that Forsyte had a plan to keep him under control. *Fat lot of good that plan did.*

But still, that meeting where Forsyte had taken over Sword's operation had been a start.

It had also been an ending.

Forsyte, speaking to Ko with the slow and hesitant digitized sound samples of his voder, had acknowledged what she had confessed to him. Yes, he had known how she felt about him. Yes, he had known that since he had hired her as his lab assistant at MIT. And yes, at one time, if things had continued as they might have, there could have been a chance that he would have done more than acknowledge what she felt.

Ko remembered the humiliating tears that had streaked her face that afternoon, listening to the slow and deliberate clicks he made on his keypad, seeing the thin trickle of sweat that slipped down from his temple as he concentrated on creating echoes of his heart from the circuits of his computer. The pain of her arm now—just a warm pulse of chemically deadened nerves wrapped in plaster—had been nothing compared to the hurt she had felt then.

He couldn't love her, he had told her. He had coded in some trick of programming to emphasize that word: *couldn't*. As if it was beyond more than his body. As if it was beyond even the capability of his heart and of his soul.

But Ko didn't believe him. She couldn't accept what he said. Not after three years of hiding her feelings so deeply within her. And not just because she didn't want to listen to the harsh words he chose to drive her away from him, to make her no more than another worker in the cause. Sword's cause.

No, the reason why Ko would not believe the synthesized words of one of the world's great scientists was because that even as he spoke to her with his keypad and his computer, she could see the truth of what he really wanted to say in his eyes. Whatever the adepts had done to him, for whatever reason, they had not been able to get inside the man. His intellect and passion were unchanged and unaffected, and both shone forth from his eyes.

His words told her to go away, to leave him to the only fate his body had made him heir to. But his eyes asked her to understand the truth behind the shield of words he created.

And so, despite what he had said, despite what he would have her believe, Ko knew that Forsyte truly cared for her in return and was only trying to spare her further torment. His exquisitely prepared rejection of her was just a sign of the depth and strength of his feeling for her.

Now the only problem facing Ko was whether or not to show the same force of will in demonstrating her love for him—by doing what he demanded of her, giving him up forever, despite how each felt about the other.

To one who had thus far tackled the science of invisible

cats, shapechanging shifters, and teleporting fardoors, she thought wryly, it should be a simple problem. But for this one problem among all the others that she faced, she had no plan for where to begin or what to do.

Except, of course, to blame it all on that fool Sword.

Ko opened her eyes again, the world beyond her unchanged. She pushed herself away from the cab, deciding to take the elevator up to the next level. Her eyes glanced one last time across the garage, almost as if drawn to something that flickered just beyond the range of her vision.

In the center of the garage, she saw something sparkle on the floor and her first thought was of 'Bub reappearing. But the cat was supposed to be up in Martin's room and she doubted if even Sword would have given the animal full run of the Loft just before going off to fight vampires.

Ko blinked and looked more carefully at the floor of the garage. There was something small and metallic there. Something that did not belong.

She walked over, her sneakers squeaking against the concrete. It was a keychain. Two keys joined. She had a sudden recollection of something falling from the vampire's coat when Martin had snagged it and ripped it.

Keys, she thought. *I wonder what kind of car a vampire drives?* She thought of a hearse with tinted windows and knew that she needed either sleep or caffeine. She tried to bend over to pick up the keys, but her shoulder suddenly flared in pain.

To Ko, exhausted, drugged, distracted by her feelings and her situation, it was a diversion.

She looked around the garage and saw her small circular stepstool, useful for those times she had to lean into the open hood of one of Sword's cars. Except his Porsche, of course. He never let her touch that. Almost as if those sorts of things still mattered to him. She remembered the look on his face when she had shown him how she had removed the movement of his Rolex and transformed it into a galvanic skin response detector to use at the museum, as if a ten-dollar digital couldn't keep time just as well. Sometimes she wondered if Sword actually *had* turned his back on useless symbols of status and disposable income when he had moved to the Loft.

Ko walked over to the stepstool and began to push it back to the keychain with her foot. The stool rolled on spring-loaded wheels that withdrew whenever she stood on it, resting then on skidfree rubber pads. When it was beside the keychain, Ko put her free hand on the top of the stepstool, then knelt without bending over. By settling down on the backs of her calves, she could grab the keys.

They weren't for a car. She knew that as soon as she felt the weight of them in her hand. *Hotel keys,* she decided as she lifted them to eye-level. *What kind of hotel would admit vampires?* she wondered. Then she read the name stamped on the keys. *Oh, of course,* she thought, *that one would.*

She slid the keychain into the pocket of her overalls—no one in the emergency room had asked twice about how she had broken her arm when she had said she was working under her van and the jack gave way. Ko actually preferred her outfit with its sleeve cut off to accommodate the cast and sling. When she had a chance, she'd remove the other sleeve, too.

She was just about to push herself up to her feet when she saw something else glittering on the floor a few yards along.

What the hell? she thought and nudged the rolling stepstool along with her hand as she used it to move across the garage floor on her knees, too stiff to want to try to stand up and get back down again.

When she was close enough, she saw it was a small crystal, about half the size of the one that hung from 'Bub's collar. But 'Bub's crystal was clear. This one, presumably from the vampire's torn coat, had a yellow cast.

Ko knelt by the crystal but didn't touch it. Saul Calder had used a red crystal in his transformation and a different one to protect the kitchen door of his brownstone from intruders. *What had that one done to Martin?* Ko asked herself. *Coldblasted him,* she remembered. Until Sword had touched the glowing crystal and inexplicably extinguished its inner light and whatever power it had. "Like a bloody ground wire," she had told Sword in the Pit of the Change when she had realized that he could drain the power from the enormous, glowing red Crystal of the Change Arkady as well. And Roth and Morgana had known what Sword was capable of even before Ko had. As if they had always known what he could do.

Maybe that's why they tossed Sword out of the First World, Ko thought. *He's a walking power-failure.*

Ko pulled the keychain from her pocket and touched the yellow crystal with one of the keys, deciding she wouldn't be surprised if there was an arc of electricity. *No, not electricity,* she told herself. *Whatever's powering First World phenomena, it isn't electromagnetic. It can't be. Then again, what else is there?*

The key clinked against the crystal without sparking. She put the keychain down and tapped the crystal with one finger, the way she would lightly brush an unidentified wire to see if it were live. Not the sort of thing they put in the manuals but what the hell, it worked for low amps.

The crystal bounced an inch across the floor and she felt no more resistance from it than she would from a small pebble.

For a few moments, Ko considered her options. The reasonable thing she knew was to wait for the others to return. Martin was an almost endless trove of First World information—provided Ko could phrase a question in such a way that it made immediate and literal sense to him. Martin was not the type of . . . *well, person,* she decided, whom she could ask to tell her everything he knew. Such a recitation would last about thirty seconds and Martin would truthfully believe he had said all that was worth saying. Forsyte would also undoubtedly have some useful advice to provide about handling the crystal, and even Sword might dredge up something from his long lost First World childhood memories.

But then, she recalled, Saul Calder had derived his ability to shapeshift from his red crystal. What if this yellow crystal were part of the vampire's power? If she could keep Ryan from it, then perhaps that would give her a hold over him. She had no desire to face such a creature again without knowing that there were twice as many banks of UV lights in the ceiling.

That was the deciding factor—wanting an advantage over the vampire. Ko picked up the crystal.

Nothing happened.

So maybe it's a decoration, she thought as she hefted its insubstantial mass in her fingers. *Or a souvenir, or a used-up red crystal, or . . .*

She thought she saw something moving in a corner of the garage. Flickering like . . .

Bloody hell, she thought. *Now I've done it. As bad as*

Sword. She had nothing. No vest. No tasers. No Forsyte to call to for help.

Unconsciously, she gripped the yellow crystal more tightly in her fist, then pushed up against the stepstool. If she could just make it to the elevator—

—the elevator was gone.

Ko whirled around, panic rising. The whole elevator assembly had disappeared from the far wall of the garage. Most of the vehicles were gone as well. Instead of Sword's Porsche taking up two parking spaces by the work benches, she saw a beat-up old panel van with "PATTON'S ELECTRO-PLATING" painted across the side in dull blue letters.

Patton's? Sword bought this place from someone called Patton, didn't he? What's going on? What is this?'

It's called a waiting crystal, Melody.

Melody froze in the middle of the transformed garage, heart racing.

"Who said that?" she asked.

Usually, it can only give whatever its user can offer. And since you are not an elemental, alas, you can offer it nothing. But this waiting crystal is special, Melody. It already carries a charge.

"This is a bloody illusion," Ko shouted. But she noted that her voice did not echo as she had expected it would. She looked above her. The ceiling was lower than it had been a moment ago, made out of wood as it was before Sword's renovators had taken the place apart and—

Would an illusion alter the characteristics of sound waves?

"A good illusion would," Ko answered slowly, looking around for whoever spoke to her. And then she realized that whoever had spoken to her . . . his voice hadn't echoed at all.

It's not really my voice, Melody.

"Who are you?" she demanded. "Why are you doing this?"

You know who I am. And as for who is doing this . . . you are the one who holds the crystal.

All panic had left Ko, all feeling of exhaustion as well. Faced with a challenge, she could only respond with all that she had—everything.

Her closed fist didn't tremble as she brought it before her, slowly opening her fingers to look at the crystal. She could feel the stone growing warm to the touch and as her fingers opened, it blossomed with golden yellow sunlight like honey.

That's right, Melody. Look into the waiting crystal. Look into yourself . . .

Their names were Sonja and Heidi, and Ko disliked them from the first moment she even heard about them.

"Exchange students? So why aren't they in a class or something?"

Forsyte brushed a shock of long brown hair from his quicksilver eyes and laughed at her. It was like music. For a moment, standing in his office in the basement of the physics lab, Ko almost forgot what she was doing there. She only knew she wanted to hear him laugh again. To have him look at her with those remarkable gray eyes again, so open, so clear.

"They're doing their doctorates at the University of London," Forsyte explained to her. "No classes or courses for astronomy and physics. Just research. You might think about it for your own dissertation."

Fat chance, Ko thought. *I'm staying right here. With you.* She felt her cheeks warm with the embarrassment of even admitting that thought to herself. *Going to have to work to keep that kind of reaction under control,* she told herself. That's what her father would say. She was afraid that the instant Forsyte saw that she wasn't completely devoted to her *work* for him, that he would boot her out the door.

"That's a couple of years away yet, Dr. Forsyte."

Forsyte smiled again. "My name is Adrian. Please." He had made that request of her at least twice a day for the past two semesters and she still couldn't bring herself to dare attempt such dangerous familiarity.

"Anyway," Forsyte continued, swinging his long legs down from the top of his cluttered desk, "all I want you to do is show them the test bed you've got set up in the lab. Maybe try a run through if you've got the spare circuit breakers you ordered."

"Show them?" Ko asked. "Everything?" Didn't he realize what that experiment was going to be worth? The day it actually worked, at any rate.

Forsyte tapped his fingers on his desk. "I know what you're thinking, kid,"—he winked at her and that simple act made her catch her breath—"but I'm afraid that the bottom line is that this is an institute of higher learning. Sonja and Heidi believe that the tunneling process we're trying to create already exists in the reactions of supernovae. That's what they're working on. That's what we're working on. No sense in trying to retard the advance of science because of some grandiose dreams of patenting an instantaneous communications system."

Ko's cheeks reddened again. "I wasn't thinking that, Dr. Forsyte. I was just thinking that you've put so much work into this that it wouldn't be right if . . . well, if you gave anything away . . ."

Forsyte stared up at Ko for a few moments, then pushed himself off from his desk and rolled on his wheeled office chair over to his filing cabinet. The middle drawer was half-open because the files there appeared to be growing in disarray, preventing it from closing. The scientist pawed through the loose clippings and dog-eared file folders as Ko watched, silently wishing she could help bring some organization to the man's life.

Then Forsyte spun around on his creaking wooden chair to offer Ko a creased file folder. "Here's the correspondence on them. They're very above-board when it comes to describing how far along their research is."

As Ko took the file, she couldn't help noticing an oily and odiferous stain on its corner, and while listening to Forsyte's words she tried to understand how a physicist's correspondence file could get smeared with peanut butter.

"Don't think of it as a situation in which *we* might have to give something away . . . think of it as them being able to give something to *us.*" He pushed off against the file cabinet—which rocked unsettlingly—then rolled back to his desk. "Who knows, they might even save us a year or two of basic research. That should be worth something, hmm?"

Ko nodded in agreement, as she would to anything he said. No doubt she would understand what he was getting at once she had thought about it, but for now, all she could think of was the way he had kept saying "we" and "us." Almost as if he felt the same way she did. Almost as if they might have a future, together.

Ko disliked Sonja and Heidi even more when she finally met them—tall and white-blond with flawless skin and pale blue eyes. They could be sisters from some Aryan recruiting

poster, down to the heroic lines and angles of their faces.
But no, the women said, as if they had never been asked
the question before, they were not related, just friends. All
through the demonstrations in Forsyte's lab, Ko had glumly
wondered if Forsyte was unsophisticated enough to be
swayed by the women's surface qualities. Surely he'd realize
how shallow they were, doctorates in astronomy and physics
notwithstanding. But there had never been any question as
to what Ko would do, and she showed them everything that
Forsyte and she had devised.

But, as the demonstrations came to an end, she couldn't
shake the unsettling feeling that the two women had seen it
all before and actually knew more about transformable electron tunneling waveguides than she or Forsyte did.

"Then why are they here and wasting their time?" Forsyte asked Ko when she relayed her suspicions to him.
"Why aren't they publishing already?"

Ko and Forsyte were sitting in the corner of a students'
pub in the basement of the student union. Forsyte leaned
forward from his banquette seat, resting his arms on the
sticky table, idly picking the label from a beer bottle, deep
in thought. Ko sat carefully in her chair across from him,
hands in her lap, unwilling to even make contact with the
disgusting tabletop and whatever microbial cultures might
be growing on it.

She decided to lay it out for her instructor. Someone had
to remind him about the real world once in a while.

"What if they're spies or something?" Ko said earnestly,
keeping her voice as low as she could and still be heard
over the rap music pounding out from the ceiling-mounted
speakers.

"Melo*dy,*" Forsyte answered, indicating his complete rejection of the idea. "The cold war's long gone."

Ko knew that. "How about spies from the government?"

Forsyte looked up from his beer bottle. There was a little
pile of paper shreds at its side. Ko had seen his hands working on the lasing equipment they used in the lab and she
thought that using those skillful fingers to peel beer bottles
was wasteful. *"Our* government?" He seemed amazed at
the idea.

"Those two know a lot more about transformable tunneling than they admit. I've heard them talking when the
equipment's running. When they think I can't hear them.

They talk as if . . . well, as if they've already seen the process work."

Forsyte's eyes were wide. "Seriously?"

Ko nodded and had to look down at her lap.

Forsyte reached out across the table and touched her shoulder, making her head come up. "Come on, Melody. Is there more?" he asked.

His casual touch made her want to tell him everything, no matter how foolish it sounded even to her. She felt she had no defenses against him and she wondered why he didn't know that.

"Not just communications," she said.

"I don't understand."

Ko thought that unlikely. She was sure there was nothing that someone with Forsyte's intellect couldn't understand. Didn't he realize that that was why she was so drawn to him? He knew about everything except real life. And she knew too much about that. She had so much to offer him. To share with him.

"Objects," she said.

Forsyte kept his steady gaze on her, unblinking. She knew he could work it out from here.

"You mean, matter transmission?"

She nodded.

"Discrete, macro collections of matter? Other than electrons?"

"That's what they said." Ko knew how ridiculous it seemed, but that was what Sonja and Heidi had been talking about. She was sure of it. As if Forsyte's equipment for jumping electrons across twenty-foot gaps in zerotime was no more than a child's science fair exhibit.

Forsyte whistled noiselessly. "So you think we're being checked out, do you? And that they're trying to figure out how far we've come in duplicating whatever they've got going down in the Pentagon's basement."

"That's one possibility, Dr. Forsyte," Ko agreed. There were others, she knew, but they were ridiculous imaginings involving time travelers, unidentified aliens, and all types of other wish-fulfillment scenarios.

"Kind of hard to imagine that the Pentagon could get their hooks into the University of London," Forsyte commented.

"But this visit was set up by correspondence and fax,"

Ko reasoned aloud. She had worked it all out beforehand. "You never called anyone in London, did you? Never spoke to anyone other than the two of them?"

Forsyte shook his head. He took a long and thoughtful swallow from his beer bottle. "So what do you suggest we do, kid?"

Inwardly Ko cringed at his repeated use of the word *kid*. It made her sound so inexperienced. But she had thought the next part of it through as well. Maybe now he would see how capable she was. How mature. And how necessary she could be to him. "I think we need some help."

"Go to the newspapers?" Forsyte asked as if it was the most obvious answer in the world. " 'Sixty Minutes'?"

But Ko had gone beyond that. "They'd drop it if they were told that national security was at stake."

"Then who?" Forsyte asked, smiling at her as she saw he realized that she already had an answer for him. "The Blue Blaze Irregulars?"

Ko ignored his levity and leaned forward, looking serious. "There's this guy . . . he looks into bizarre things."

"Such as . . . ?"

Ko lowered her voice again. "Teleportation, for one."

"You're joking."

"Never," Ko said. *Absolutely never with you, Adrian,* she thought.

"Sure he's not a crackpot? Could easily be." Forsyte went back to picking at his beer label and Ko knew she was losing him.

"I don't think he is. I've read his letters in *The Skeptical Inquirer.* He's an archaeologist, I think. At least, he used to be. Now he sort of investigates bizarre claims of the paranormal."

Forsyte flattened his hands on the table and Ko cringed with distaste at what he might be exposing himself to. "It's a *science* lab we've got going, Melody. There's nothing paranormal about it." He looked away from her in amused dismissal and his long hair fell across one eye. "And you know I hate that word."

"But that's just it, Dr. Forsyte." Ko couldn't feel worse about the way Forsyte had looked at her if he had slapped her at the same time. *"We* know that transformable tunneling isn't paranormal, but that's the hook that would get this guy to come in and check this out."

Forsyte waved to some other students or faculty members who had just entered the pub. Ko didn't turn around to see who it was. She felt as if she was fighting for her reputation. And her future.

"So, how can . . . this guy help us?" Forsyte asked. It was almost an afterthought, as if he had already gone on to other matters that didn't involve her.

Ko spoke rapidly, willing Forsyte to pay attention. "He's not connected to anything, like a university or the media, so he might not be subject to the kind of pressures to stop his investigation that the government could bring to bear. And if he shows up here, then your Sonja and Heidi,"—she paused as she said their hateful names—"won't take him seriously for the same reason you don't take him seriously."

Forsyte shifted a few inches along the banquette.

Ko didn't stop. "He'll at least be able to give us a head-start, Dr. Forsyte. From what I've heard, he's good and he's thorough. He'll be able to find out if they *are* from the University of London. That might make it easier to go to the papers with a solid story if it turns out that the government *is* trying to shut down your work."

That got your attention, Ko thought in triumph as Forsyte suddenly looked at her again.

"So how much is this skeptical inquirer going to cost?"

"I don't think he charges," Ko said. "He's got his own foundation. That pays for everything."

Forsyte shook his head. "No one does stuff like that out of the goodness of his heart. If he has anything he wants you to sign, you be sure to read the fine print."

Ko was confused for a few seconds as she began to react indignantly to Forsyte's implied assessment of her ability to detect deceit. Then she realized what Forsyte was saying. "Then it's all right? I can call him?"

Forsyte shifted to the edge of the banquette, looking past Ko. "Yeah, sure, why not?" he said as he stood up. "What was his name?"

Ko turned in her seat, unsure about where Forsyte was going. "Uh, Sword," she said. "Gary Sword. Or something like that. He's in New York so I'll look him up and—"

"Sonja! Heidi! How good to see you." Forsyte had stood to welcome the exchange students to the table he shared with Ko.

Ko stood, too, more from habit than out of respect. She didn't like the unnatural brilliance of the women's hair and the casual elegance of the slacks and sweaters they wore. She watched Forsyte reach to them to take their hands in greeting and it was as if she watched her instructor stepping into a cage filled with ravenous lions.

"Please, sit down, join us," Forsyte said warmly, moving the table out to offer access to the banquette. He glanced at Ko. "Unfortunately, my assistant was just leaving. Has some calls to make." He winked at her as if he didn't see how flushed her face had become, as if he still didn't know how much danger he was in.

Sonja and Heidi slipped into the banquette, beckoning Forsyte to sit between them. Ko muttered something in leaving, hoped it wasn't as impolite as she wanted it to sound, then left, awkwardly stumbling into another table on her way out of the pub.

At the door, she turned back once to see that Forsyte was framed by the shimmering pale hair of the women. One rested her hand on his on the filthy table. *Why doesn't he get it?* Ko asked herself. *Why doesn't he understand?*

The yellow crystal was like molten metal in her hand at the doorway to the pub and the past.

Trapped by the exchange students whom Galen Sword would discover no one had ever heard of before, Adrian Forsyte had only sixteen days of normal life remaining.

And all Ko could do was watch.

All Ko could do was—

Look away, Melody. Look away from the crystal.

The honey gold light of the waiting crystal sputtered in Ko's outstretched hand, slowly dying.

They are not meant to be used that way, in the remembrance of that which disturbs us. There are better uses for them. Fonder recollections. Look away.

Ko pulled her eyes from the flickering crystal and stared out across the expanse of the empty garage. The electroplater's truck faded from her vision. The elevator cage and tower returned like a photographic image emerging in a tray of developer.

There was a figure standing before her. He took her hand in his and removed the crystal. The last of its light winked out at his touch. His hands were warm and smooth as they closed her hand again.

Ko tried to look at him, only three feet away, but it was like looking out onto a brilliantly lit beach from a dark cave. Colors smeared, details ran together. Yet he seemed so familiar. Had they come back so soon?

"Sword?" she asked.

There was no answer.

"Who? . . ."

You know who I am.

And with that her vision cleared, and she realized that she did know.

His eyes were like Sword's, there was no doubt about it. But he was younger, not more than twenty, with fine fair hair that fell across his forehead, and a look of concern which Sword would never have.

She had looked over her shoulder once and seen him in a doorway which led to other streets. She had looked over her shoulder as she walked out on Sword forever and seen him give a ring to Sword.

"Brin?" she said tentatively.

The young man bent to kiss Ko's hand as a flare of blue power grew from his fingers.

Ko felt something move deep within her broken arm. It wasn't unpleasant but it was . . .

Brin spoke for the first time, using his own lips and voice. "It will be all right, Melody."

Ko's arm was ablaze with blue power. She could feel bones shifting, growing . . .

"You and I, we have so much to talk about," Brin said. "And so much in common."

SEVENTEEN

Orion was the first to notice the messy bundle on the top of the van, but Sword was the one to recognize it.

"It's Martin's clothes."

Orion didn't understand the significance of Sword's concern and watched in silence as Sword pulled the pile from the van's roof.

"Here it is," Sword said as he found another of the black communication devices on the halfling's shirt. He stuck his head inside the van's open door and told Forsyte what he had found, dropping the clothes on the driver's seat.

Orion turned away and scented the night air, searching for his enemies. He found them. The air reeked of Tepesh and magic, and he knew he was close.

Sword shut the van door, waited till a mechanical click indicated the doors were locked—but not enchanted, Orion noted with disdain—then squeezed between the front of the van and the car it was parked behind to join Orion on the sidewalk. Sword wore a long black leather coat that hid his vest and the sling that held his shotgun at his side. If they were facing Second World mercenaries or First World children, Orion might have been impressed.

"Adrian wants to know how the clothes got there," Sword said, moving his shoulder to adjust his weapon's sling beneath his coat.

"Obviously, your halfling placed them there so they would not be lost," Orion said. "Surely there are more important matters to discuss than the habits of this brutish creature?"

Sword ran one hand over his short black hair, lifting it from his forehead. "You're supposed to have sensitive hearing, remember? How come you didn't hear Martin dropping his clothes right above your head?"

Orion had no answer but he refused to share that shortcoming with Sword. "Perhaps the halfling left his clothes while you were making so much noise."

The corner of Sword's mouth moved up in a half smile, letting Orion know that Sword didn't accept that answer. "Perhaps your ears aren't as sensitive as you say they are. Perhaps you really couldn't enter the Loft without my invitation. And perhaps a wooden stake would work just as well through—"

"Enough!" Orion interrupted. "Our fight is with Tepesh."

"For now," Sword said, then turned and walked off, away from the clinic.

Orion took three quick steps to intercept Sword. "The enclave is the other way."

"And you want us to march straight into it?"

Orion was angered and confused by the question. Did Sword know absolutely nothing about the nature of First World defenses? "Considering that will be the only entrance open to us, we have no choice, Mr. Sword."

"Martin will give us a choice. If we can find him."

Orion stared at Sword, still not understanding what he meant.

"Martin has a blue power," Sword explained impatiently. "He can open things. Anything."

"That pitiful creature . . . a *blue* power?"

Sword nodded quickly, again taking too much delight in a matter which disturbed Orion. "From his father, right? Blue powers are inherited from father to child, that's what Martin told us."

"True," Orion admitted. It did no harm to give Sword such information about the nature of adepts, considering that the halfling had already revealed this to him. "But if your halfling's father was mated to a shifter, then—"

"Martin's *father* was a shifter," Sword interrupted. "His mother was human."

That was even worse, as far as Orion was concerned. There were far too many variables at play around this Sword. "I know of few shifters who have blue powers. Blue powers belong to the elemental clans, to the stormbringers and cloudriders, occasionally folders and sirens, but—" He stopped suddenly, aware he had said more than he should. There was no way to be certain just how much Sword already knew which could give him power over vampires.

Orion saw no sense in adding to what knowledge he might already have.

But Sword had seemed not to notice that anything of import had been said. He was too anxious to act and Orion decided that that impulsiveness would probably be Sword's downfall.

"I've seen him use it," Sword said. "He's opened door locks, window latches, even the chain locks on the sacrificial stone in the Pit of the Change."

No, Orion told himself. That *couldn't* be true and he would not dignify Sword's falsehood with a question. No creature could lie upon the Lesser Heart of Clan Arkady and *survive,* let alone that such a creature should be the babbling beast that was Martin. Or, even more maddening, was there some strange power hidden within Sword still to detect?

"Look," Sword finally said in disgust, "if you want, you can stand here all night until they come looking for you. But I'm going to find Martin. He's going to be our way in." He began to stride away again.

Not knowing what else to do with Sword, Orion fell into step beside him. "But how will you know where to go?" he asked, almost as if he cared to know Sword's strategy.

"Martin was supposed to stay near detector six at the entrance to the alley that runs directly behind the clinic. That's the first place to look, just around the corner."

Orion kept pace with Sword and tasted the air. The stench of the Tepesh was falling off. At least they would not be walking into an ambush.

Side by side, Orion and Sword rounded a corner and started down another street much like the one they had just left. Though this time there was no glimmering new building to add an unreal backdrop to the rotting cityscape they passed through.

Orion scented the air again, trying to sense beneath the foul garbage that festered in the stone stairwells and over-turned garbage cans, and past the miasma of Second World vehicle exhaust fumes. Here and there, he thought he might have caught some subtle note of floral magic, but it was a large city and, as the newspapers had shown him, there were many cases of incursions and crossovers. It might very well be old magic he detected, from events not connected to Tepesh or himself.

Sword halted in front of a narrow alley opening, barely large enough for the passage of a single Second World vehicle. Orion stopped beside him, knowing that the alley was far too dark for Sword's human normal vision.

"Is Martin near?" Sword asked, apparently accepting Orion's greater ability.

"Yes," Orion said, wrinkling his nose. The halfling's bestial scent was everywhere.

Sword checked up and down the street, then swung his shotgun out from underneath his coat. "Anything else down there I should know about?"

Orion adjusted his vision, increasing its sensitivity until the alley was gray and glowing in the low ambient light of the city. The passageway between buildings was filthy, littered with indistinguishable lumps of refuse, lined with rusting fire escapes and dangling wires, random wreckage from a decaying city. But there was no movement within it and Orion could scent nothing in hiding.

The vampire shook his head, stepped into the alley, and was astounded to feel Sword's hand on him, pulling him back.

Orion twisted around in outrage and had to shut his eyes against the now painful light levels that came from the streetlamps. When he had adjusted his light sensitivity again, he saw that Sword had placed a finger against his ear transceiver and was speaking aloud.

"Adrian, we're going into the alley near detector six. Orion can identify Martin's scent but sees no activity in the alley." Sword paused. "Just a second." He dug into his coat pocket and pulled out the transceiver set he had tried to give to Orion in the van. "Will you just put this on? Adrian has a question for you."

Orion refused the transceiver again. "Your devices are clever, Mr. Sword, but there is no function and no honor in employing them within the First World."

Sword kept the transceiver extended. "We're doing this together or we're not doing it at all."

"Human technology belongs with the human world. It has no place in the affairs of the adept."

Sword's face became a mask of puzzlement. "Didn't you tell me you were preparing to fight for the Seyshen?" Orion nodded once. "And didn't they tell you what other weapons they were going to use against Arkady?"

Whatever Sword was about to say, Orion could already sense the truth of it and grew concerned. "What other weapons are there, Mr. Sword?"

"The Pit of the Change was in a cave." Sword spoke as if he were amazed that Orion didn't already have knowledge of what he said. "At dawn, just as the ceremony was under way, the Seyshen attacked."

At least that answered one question, Orion thought. "So that's how the halfling was freed from the sacrificial stone. By Seyshen warriors."

But Sword shook his head. "Martin freed himself while I kept the shifters away."

Impossible, Orion thought contemptuously.

"But the point is that the Seyshen did not attack alone," Sword continued.

"Another clan has joined with them?" Orion was astonished. He had been desperate. When he had agreed to serve the Seyshen, he had needed their support as much as they had needed his. But what other clan would descend willingly to the depths necessary to ally itself with Clan Seyshen? And why?

"No," Sword said slowly. "Not another clan. Humans."

"Never!"

"I saw them," Sword protested. "We all saw them. Human soldiers in uniforms and helmets. They carried automatic rifles. They arrived in Apache attack helicopters."

Orion felt the sidewalk shift beneath his feet, so great was his shock. What honor could remain in the real world if the covenants had been broken? How could the real world survive if the human world had now been swept up in its machinations?

Yet from the rhythm of his heart, the scent of his sweat, the undertones of his speech, Orion knew that Sword spoke only the truth. The Seyshen had broken the most important law of civilized behavior. No wonder the worlds were interconnected as never before. The long-brewing war between Arkady and Seyshen was not just another war between clans apart in council. It had gone far beyond that.

"What is it? What's wrong?" Sword asked. For the first time this night, there was no hostility in his words. His concern seemed genuine.

"You couldn't know," Orion said, overwhelmed by despair. He had only been away for less than forty cycles, yet the worlds had changed in ways unfathomable, just in that brief time. With rigid fingers, he reached out to take the obscene transceiver from Sword's outstretched hand, feeling the last vestiges of his own honor fall from him as he placed the small device into his ear. His feud with Tepesh now seemed distant and insignificant.

But he would see it through tonight. In the nights to follow, there might not be another opportunity to seek revenge for the destruction of only a single clan.

Orion gratefully saw that Sword was wise enough not to pursue his questioning. Instead, the exiled adept—perhaps the harbinger of all that had happened, all that was still to come—touched the transceiver in his own ear.

"Orion's on line," Sword said. "Go ahead, Adrian."

Orion stiffened at the unfamiliar closeness of Forsyte's mechanical voice. "Do you see any sign of whatever set off the first two detectors?"

Orion shook his head. Then he remembered that Forsyte could not see him. "No. There is nothing moving within the alley."

"Be careful," Forsyte transmitted. In spite of himself, Orion was bemused by the admonition. It had been centuries since anyone had said those words to him.

Orion glanced at Sword. "Now?" he asked, knowing that with Sword's answer a line would be crossed, to which they could never return.

Sword strode into the alley as if his eyes were the match of Orion's.

The vampire watched with true incomprehension. Each of his senses confirmed it. There was no fear in Galen Sword. Only resolve.

Twenty paces into the alley, the passageway widened to three times the width of its entranceway. Moving ahead into the larger space, Orion judged that even Sword would be able to see the most apparent divisions between darkness and the dim light. But Orion's ears were still superior, and it was the vampire who first heard the halfling's muted cries of anguish.

Before he alerted Sword, Orion motioned for him to remain still to better isolate the halfling's precise location. The whimperings were coming from a distance twenty feet ahead to the right, and about twelve feet above the alley's floor.

At that location, Orion saw a large, teardrop shape swaying back and forth on a thick cord. He pointed to it and watched as Sword squinted into the darkness, trying to make out what the vampire was showing him.

Orion beckoned Sword forward until the two of them were stopped beneath the halfling.

"Is that Martin?" Sword whispered, as he looked up at the shape twisting above their heads.

Orion held out his hand. "Have you a blade among your devices?"

Sword slipped his hand inside his coat and brought out a knife and a flat metal disk with sharpened points arranged in a starburst pattern.

"Ah," Orion said. *"Shiruken."*

He took the Japanese throwing weapon from Sword, then whispered to Martin, twelve feet above him. "Halfling! Prepare yourself!"

Orion had no doubt that Sword could hear the blubbering that came from the halfling now. Then he threw the *shiruken* with a snap of his wrist, cleanly slicing the cord that supported the net encasing Martin. The weapon sparked against the bricks, then ricocheted into the night.

Orion watched as Martin began to fall to the ground and, after only an instant, saw that the halfling was not flipping to land safely. Moving quickly enough that Sword would see him only as a blur, Orion caught the halfling and lowered him deftly to the ground.

But Martin did not acknowledge his rescuers.

Orion and Sword both knelt by Martin's quivering form and Orion opened his mouth to taste for the telltale odors of poisons. There was still nothing in the air except the same faint residual scent of magic, and the overwhelming fear of the halfling.

"Shh, Martin, shh," Sword said, trying to quiet him. "What's wrong? Are you hurt?"

Orion carefully split the webbing that held the halfling, noting that it was braided of simple Second World fiber. But Martin didn't attempt to sit up. He lay in a naked curled-up ball, hands covering his face, rhythmically sobbing like a frightened child.

Sword was worried. "Has he been exposed to something? Or enchanted somehow?"

"I have detected nothing." Orion watched the halfling

with detached interest. In the garage, even knowing that he could not win, the halfling had not hesitated to attack the vampire. Martin had shown no fear then. What could possibly inspire such behavior now?

Sword leaned in closer to pull the halfling's fingers away from his eyes. The large shifter hands were slippery with tears. "That's enough, Martin. You have to stop. Someone might hear you."

Martin's only response was to squeak and try to make himself even smaller. Orion stood and scanned the alley. Still no sign of others lurking nearby, but with the racket the halfling was making, that situation might not last much longer.

Orion looked down at Martin's quaking body and with his foot nudged the halfling's shoulder roughly enough to be sure he had the creature's attention. Sword got to his feet with some human oath, but he did not intervene. "Mr. Sword told me your father was a shifter. What would he say if he saw his son cowering like tagged prey?"

Martin's crying stopped for a moment as he drew a noisy gulp of air. "Mr. Sword said your father gifted you with a mighty blue power to open all that was closed. What would he say if he saw his son trapped in a web of glitterless rope?"

Orion bent closer to Martin as he heard the halfling's ragged breathing slow. "Your father would scoff at your weakness. Your father would say you had no blue power. That you were not his son." Orion stopped as Martin whimpered something. "What was that, you fatherless shadow dweller?"

"Don't say!" Martin coughed. "Not true don't say don't say!"

Sword cut in. "Martin, it's all right. I won't let him say it any more—"

I think not, Orion thought.

"—just tell me what happened to you. Why *didn't* you use your blue power to get out of the net?"

Martin whimpered again.

"What was that, Martin? I didn't hear you. Say it again."

The halfling pulled his hands away from his face and looked up at Sword with wide staring eyes. "She told Martin not go! She told she told!"

"Who told you not to go?" Sword asked.

The Tepesh Keeper I met in Softwind, Orion decided, thinking the mystery was solved.

But it wasn't. The next words Martin spoke were enough to give even Orion pause to reconsider his plans.

"Black hunter," the halfling wailed. Orion immediately stepped back and glanced around the alley. "Black hunter told Martin not go from net. Or black hunter take Martin." It was too much for him. He covered his eyes and began cringing again.

Sword stared at the vampire's expression. *"You're* frightened, too?"

"I am cautious," Orion said crisply, bridling at the suggestion that he might show fear like a common beast. "And I would advise the same response for yourself." He continued to scan the alley again, but slowly and methodically this time. No wonder he had scented what he thought had been old magic. No wonder he saw nothing move within shadows.

"What's so bad about a black hunter?" Sword asked. "Martin called me that once and I never frightened him the way he is now."

Not stopping his search of the alley, Orion laughed scornfully. *"You?* A black hunter? Hardly, Mr. Sword."

Sword didn't share Orion's amusement. "I want to know what a black hunter is. And I want to know now."

Orion swept out his hand to the night. "What do you *see* out there, Mr. Sword? What do you *hear?* What do you *scent?"*

Sword stared into the dark chasm before them. "Nothing," he said.

"Exactly. Nothing. There could be a dozen black hunters out there even now, within arm's reach if they chose to be, and not even *I* would know it."

Sword swung his shotgun around. "What kind of creature are they?"

"Adept, Mr. Sword. Gone rogue against their own kind. And how the worlds have fallen if now they work for one clan against a—"

Something moved in the alley.

"I saw that," Sword whispered. He pointed with the shotgun's stubby barrel. "Over there. Heard it, too."

"Then it wasn't a black hunter," Orion said.

Sword's head whipped to the side. "And there! Another."

Sword ducked down beside Martin again. Orion missed what he said to the halfling as Forsyte's mechanical voice exploded in his ear. "All detectors red. All detectors red."

Orion tore the buzzing speaker from his ear and threw it to the ground. "What does he mean about their color?" he demanded of Sword.

"Whatever's in the alley has got us surrounded," Sword said grimly. Orion could hear him tugging at the buckles and snaps of his equipment vest. "Let's go, Martin. Black hunter's gone. Won't be back. We've got vampires to deal with. Tepesh vampires."

Orion moved into a defensive crouch, tasting the air intently. Sword was wrong. There was no Tepesh scent in the alley. It was something else. Something almost familiar. Something that . . . reminded him of Softwind. Then Orion saw the low and glittering shapes slowly move into the center of the alley, ringing his position, their edged weapons held high and darkly gleaming, and he understood what he and Sword and Martin faced.

Just as Orion had had his sentinels to protect him when he served the Seyshen, so did the Tepesh have their own sentinels of a different clan. And with that realization, the assault began.

EIGHTEEN

Sword swung the barrel of his shotgun back and forth, not knowing what he was looking for or where to find it.

The dim light made it almost possible to see in this wider part of the alley, and what he could observe made him think of beetles, large and scuttling, with carapaces of deep and shining green.

But the creatures that scrabbled around him now were two-legged. He could see that much as one of them ran across his field of vision, stumpy feet scarcely touching the ground, as quick as a roach scurrying from sudden light. Sword saw then that the carapaces were actually armor—rounded bulbous plates of polished metal that covered the creatures' squat and oddly jointed bodies like segments of a fragmented armadillo. And each creature carried at least two weapons: one a short sword, the other long and twisted like a heat-distorted spear.

"What the hell are these things supposed to be?" Sword said as the creatures moved in to tighten their perimeter. There were eight of them that he could see clearly. The shadows could hold twenty more, at least.

"Close trolls," Orion answered as he tracked their maneuvers. "I saw them talking with the Tepesh in Softwind. But never did I think that they would sell themselves so—"

"I don't care about that. Will the shotgun work on them?"

Orion was spreading his arms wide as he had just before Martin tried to attack in the Loft. "Not against the living armor they wear. But against their flesh—perhaps."

A high-pitched staccato squeal ripped from the bricks of the alley buildings and a large round projectile thudded into Orion's chest, knocking him against the wall behind him.

Sword watched helplessly as a three-foot-tall Close troll raised its short blade and plunged it into Orion's chest. The creature chirped shrilly as the vampire writhed. It turned its green-helmeted head to Sword and he saw an ugly child's face with eyes that were four times the size of any human's, beautifully shaped and framed by long luxuriant lashes. Then the eyes bulged from the flattened skull as Orion's powerful hand grabbed the creature's thick neck and squeezed.

Sword turned away as he heard the liquid pop of the Close troll's death. Something hot and thick sprayed across his hand and he refused to think what it might be. Sword looked back at Orion, the Close troll crumpled at his feet, as he pulled the weapon from his body, trembling as he did so.

"Will you be—"

"Behind!" Orion shouted.

Sword whirled in time to see a second Close troll leaping for him and he fired his shotgun before he had even time to think.

The Close troll's head exploded in a fountain of black First World blood and the body tumbled to the ground. Sword looked down at it as he heard a moist clicking sound. The holes the shotgun blast had made in the troll's armor plates were healing themselves, like hundreds of small mouths closing.

"Pay attention!" Orion commanded, coming to Sword's side. Sword could hear him breathing hoarsely.

"Are you going to be okay?" Sword asked.

"It's been too long since I've fed." Orion's head moved from side to side as he followed the Close trolls' senseless patterns. "Their weapons are tipped and I can't—*another!*"

As Orion caught a third hurtling form, Sword ducked and then lunged forward to club the creature with the stock of his shotgun.

But Martin beat him to Orion's defense.

The halfling grabbed the Close troll by its feet and pulled and pivoted, swinging Orion's attacker against a solid brick wall. A troll sword suddenly appeared embedded in Martin's arm and he stumbled to one knee. Sword fired another round at a gathering of trolls and, as the echoing roar of the discharge faded, he heard the slurping sounds of their living armor plates making themselves whole again. He double-pumped and fired two more shells, then knelt by Martin's side.

Martin held the blood-dripping troll sword in his good hand, studying it intently.

"Your arm—" Sword began.

Martin waved the sword. "Not silver. Bloodrip go fast." Then he straightened his arm and drove the sword into the body of the Close troll he had smashed against the wall. The creature gave a brief chirp and lay still.

"Martin sorry Martin bad." The halfling looked up at Sword with eyes that were not apologetic. "Black hunter scare Martin bad bad bad."

Right, thought Sword. *We've still got one of those to deal with, too.* "That's okay, Martin. We'll be able to lick the Close trolls."

Martin looked dubious. "Trolls taste bad."

Sword didn't want to know about that. "Stay close to me and Orion. If they keep attacking in ones and twos, we'll be—"

As if Sword had given them a signal, the five remaining Close trolls hurled themselves at Sword, Martin, and Orion with hideous scratching shrieks.

Sword lowered his shotgun. Martin crouched. Orion spread his arms and—

—the nearest Close troll suddenly staggered, wavered back and forth for an instant, and then its head toppled off as if the creature were nothing more than a broken doll. Three streaming gouts of black blood pulsed from the exposed neck before the body followed its head to the ground.

The four remaining Close trolls stopped instantly, weapons held ready, large eyes looking suspiciously at their targets.

Sword glanced quickly at Orion from the corner of his eyes and saw the vampire looking at him just as doubtingly. They both looked at Martin, but he hadn't moved, either.

Then a second troll grunted and clutched at its armored chest as one shoulder and arm slid from its torso. More blood sprayed as the bisected creature twitched and chirped and sagged to the ground.

"What's happening to them?" Sword asked. He was certain it was nothing Orion was doing.

"Windblade," the vampire said ominously.

"What's that mean?"

"Black hunter."

Orion stepped back to the wall and pulled Martin and

Sword with him, pushing them flat against the bricks. "Say nothing!" he hissed threateningly. "Do nothing! Perhaps it is just the trolls she hunts."

From the Close trolls' reactions to the fate of their companions, it was obvious that they also understood the significance of a windblade. The three left standing chirped rapidly one last time, then began to flee in three different directions.

Began to flee.

None lasted longer than eight seconds.

Sword saw a silver flash of light like silent lightning streak down toward one running troll. The flash exploded behind the creature, spraying out like a sparkling spider's web to enmesh the troll with gleaming strands of fluid metal. The instant the web was sealed around the troll, the creature's piteous cry was cut off, though Sword could still see it kick and struggle against whatever held it.

Another troll chirped just as Sword saw a dark shape drop from the air before it. *Humanform,* Sword thought as he watched the indistinct black figure move its arm in a swift and powerful arc. The troll fell to its knees with a gasp. The figure brought its arm back down and the troll's head split in two. But Sword could not hear the whistle of a weapon cutting the air or the thud of its impact. He could not hear anything except the sound of the troll hitting the floor of the alley.

But before that sound had died, the figure once again moved through the air, and by the arc it made Sword guessed it swung from a rope too thin to be seen from his position.

The figure flipped once, as smoothly as Martin descending from a ceiling support, and landed behind the last remaining troll. Sword could not hear the sound the figure must have made as its feet hit the ground.

The troll kept running, its weapons flying to the side, abandoned, but the figure did not rush in pursuit. Instead, as the Close troll reached what could only be the back entrance to the BioproEx clinic and began to scrape wretchedly at the sealed door there, the figure lifted an arm in the troll's direction, and Sword saw the arm and figure jerk back as if responding to the recoil of a silent gun. Something long and black snaked out from the figure's hand and erupted around the cowering Close troll.

Must be some sort of catapult net. Would Ko ever like to

get her hands on that thing, Sword thought as he watched the figure pull on a taut black cord and haul the captured troll back to it.

Whatever type of net held the last Close troll, it was not like the silver web that had encased the first. Sword could still hear the last troll squeaking and snorting as it fought against its restraints. But its struggles were ignored by its captor. Without a wasted motion, the dark figure moved its arm to first one position, then another, as if firing the silent gun again against two facing walls. Then the figure twisted the cord from the troll's net around a second cord that suddenly appeared to be pulled taut between the walls the gun had fired at.

It's firing pitons or grappling hooks attached to climbing ropes, Sword decided. *But why can't I hear the cartridges fire?*

Sword leaned closer to Orion. ''Can you hear—''

Orion's hand squeezed painfully against Sword's shoulder and Sword decided it wasn't the proper time for questions. Unfortunately, Forsyte chose that moment to check in with the group.

''How far have you—''

Sword winced as he felt his transceiver yanked from his ear and the wire snap, cutting off Forsyte's synthesized voice in mid sentence. Orion silently handed the dead earphone back.

In the alley, the dark figure jerked on a single cord and the last troll bounced up, swinging in its net a few feet from the ground just as Orion and Sword had found Martin. Sword began to understand why Martin had been so terrified. The figure had killed or captured the trolls in a handful of seconds without making the slightest noise.

With the troll hanging in its net and presumably in no danger of escaping, the figure paused and began to move as if it adjusted the weapons or armor it wore. Then it placed one hand on its opposite shoulder, and to Sword it was as if the light in the alley had suddenly increased. The figure was no longer indistinguishable from shadow. And it was no longer just a figure. It was a woman.

Of course, Sword thought, *both Martin and Orion said 'she.' The black hunter.*

As well as Sword could judge from twenty feet away, the woman was tall and lithe and wore a tightfitting dark bodysuit that reminded him of Ko's preferred manner of dress—no excess to get in the way. Her red-gold hair looked substantial, but it was tied so it could only spill down her back— again, Sword thought, so it would not interfere with her activities. Over the bodysuit she wore a harness to which were clipped a variety of shapes, vaguely similar to the equipment vests Sword had devised and Ko had outfitted. He tried to lean forward to get a better look at her. But, despite the fact that the black hunter certainly resembled a Second World being, Orion still wouldn't relieve the restraining pressure on Sword's shoulder. Sword could only presume that some sort of danger still existed.

The woman turned away from her captive and walked back to the troll which had been snared with silver. Sword was surprised to hear her footsteps since he hadn't been able to hear her jumping from place to place a moment earlier. As she approached the silver net, he saw that a long, flat weapons sheath was strapped down one leg, stretching from hip to knee, and that a small sack hung at her waist on the opposite side of her harness belt.

The woman dropped to one knee by the silver net which Sword now saw had formed itself into a sphere only two feet across. Then she reached into the sack at her side, withdrew a glowing point of ruby light which Sword knew could only be a red crystal, and touched it to the sphere.

It settled like a deflating beach ball, and when the woman stood and lifted the limp silver web with her, the Close troll it had contained was gone. Sword shivered involuntarily.

The woman returned to the troll hanging in the ordinary net and quickly folded the silver web into a small packet which fit into a pouch on her harness. Then, in a movement that confused Sword until he saw the result, she pulled something from the sheath at her side, pushed her hand into the net to grasp the Close troll's head, and with a flash of silver cut through the net, the troll's armor, *and* the wailing troll, gutting the squirming creature as quickly and as smoothly as a butcher might slaughter a calf. Martin held his hands over his mouth to keep from squealing.

Small dark glistening shapes slipped out of the Close troll's body and plopped to the ground at the woman's feet. Sword felt his throat tighten and his stomach threaten to revolt. It had been such a calculated, callous action. To kill in battle was one thing, Sword had come to know, *but to hack apart a helpless creature without passion* . . . He shook his head in irritation. Where had such thoughts come from? What did he know about killing in the passion of battle?

Now the woman stood beneath the troll's body and forced her hand into the empty cavity of its gut. Sword heard the sound of what she did and wished for her to invoke silence again. She reached into the creature with a second hand. He saw her body move as if she cut or chopped at something hidden within.

Then whatever she searched for was free. She brought her hands out and Sword saw that though they dripped with gore, they also held something that seemed to shine with its own pale light. Whatever it was, the woman slipped it into her sack, then wiped her hands against her legs, and slowly moved her eyes around the entire alley, passing over the shadowed wall where Orion kept Sword and Martin hidden . . . as if she saw nothing.

She looked back at the Close troll's body and Sword felt his heart begin to beat again. Just as she had the ability to make her appearance obscure and to mask all noise she made, he wondered if she were able to induce fear in those around her by some First World technique. Though, if she had such abilities, then how could she not have seen the three of them?

The woman knelt again and thrust her hand into the quivering pile of organs that lay beneath the troll. When she stood again, she held something wet in her hands. Sword felt sickened. What did she intend to do with her gruesome trophy?

Then the woman turned and walked straight for Sword. The closer she came, the more her dark bodysuit seemed to take on the coloration of the bricks and debris in the alley.

Orion's hand became like steel against Sword's shoulder. Martin lost his valiant struggle and moaned in terror. And Sword felt each thudding of his heart, each bristle of hair that rose erect on his arms and neck, and the shudder of his lungs as his breath caught and would not come again.

For as the black hunter approached him with a dripping offering plucked from the chest of a troll, Sword *recognized* her.

The woman stopped within arm's reach of the three and there was no doubt in Sword's mind. Not as she acknowledged him with a nod of her head, not as she tossed whatever organ she held to land wetly at Sword's feet, and not as she smiled terribly at him and said his name.

"Little Galen."

That was all. That was enough.

She was the woman who had appeared atop a crumbling wall at Delphi, cloak billowing in the wild wind of a storm approaching, rifle held at her hip, ready to fire again. And between Sword and her, lying on the ancient marble, a werewolf had lain dying, Sword's first chance at breaking through the barriers into the hidden world, lost to this woman's silver bullet.

As that shifter had died, he, too, had called out Sword's name, and Sword had seen the shock of recognition in the woman's eyes.

Now it was his turn, but she began to turn away to leave.

"Wait!" Sword called after her, straining against both Orion's grip on his shoulder and Martin's arms now wrapped around his legs. "Who are you?"

The black hunter paused in midstride. Her golden eyes gave up nothing. "I thought you had remembered everything," she said with disdain.

Sword shook his head, the only part of him his companions would allow him to move. "Not *everything*. Only *some* things. Please, tell me . . ." He broke one hand away from Orion and held it out to her. ". . . tell me more."

The woman lifted her head as if to see Sword more clearly, as if to hear his words more carefully.

Sword spoke in a rush, not knowing how long this opportunity would remain. "I know you were at Delphi. You killed the shifter I had trapped."

Martin howled.

"I believe it was the other way around," the woman said.

Sword waved his hand, erasing her words. "I don't care. I don't care. But the shifter *recognized* me! *You* recognized my name at least. *How* do you know me? *Why?* From where and when?"

The woman looked truly puzzled by Sword's questions. She opened her mouth to speak. But then she turned her head as if there had been a sudden noise. Sword heard nothing.

The woman raised her fist to Sword and he knew enough to see it as a First World greeting. "This is not the time," she said. "This is not the place." She glanced down the alley in the direction of the clinic. She looked directly into Orion's eyes. "You have matters of your own world to attend to."

"Wait! Don't go!" Sword cried. Orion made no sound. He had turned his head away.

The woman touched her fist to her shoulder and for an instant Sword saw a pattern worked with metallic thread emblazoned on the fabric of her body suit. It flared silver white as she touched it, leaving a black afterimage in Sword's eyes. An afterimage of the entwined dragon and sword engraved on his mother's ring. The symbol of his clan—Pendragon.

And when the flare of light had passed, the woman was gone, replaced by a dark figure, without detail, indistinct as if seen through distant mist.

Sword wouldn't give up. "Then tell me what *will* be the right time. Tell me where the right place is."

The figure remained motionless. The woman's voice could be heard as if from blocks away.

"Softwind," she said, and then the dark figure turned and walked silently away until it stood by the dangling net. Instantly, the net, the troll, the black cords that stretched from one wall to another were traced with dancing arcs of silver light. This time when the light faded, the objects it had engulfed were gone as well.

Holding a silhouetted object that extended like a narrow pipe, the figure pointed from one troll's body to another. Each flared with silver and vanished with the return of night until there was nothing left of the battle except the offering at Sword's feet.

The figure placed the pipelike object back against her leg and ran for a fire escape and leapt up for it, swinging effortlessly around a bar of rusted metal, so that even in the darkness Sword could see it sag beneath her weight. Yet it made no noise.

The figure vanished above them and only when the silent shaking of the metal ladders and balconies had ceased did Orion and Martin relinquish their grips.

The vampire cleared his throat. "You have dangerous acquaintances, Mr. Sword."

Martin sniffed suspiciously at the steaming organ the black hunter had left for Sword. "Troll liver. Bad bad bad."

"To a shifter perhaps," Orion agreed. "But the black hunter does you a great honor, Mr. Sword."

Sword grimaced as he saw Martin take an experimental lick at the offering when he thought no one was watching. "What kind of honor is that?"

"The liver is the center of the warrior's fighting spirit, Mr. Sword." Sword thought he detected something odd in Orion's voice. Perhaps the vampire had *also* recognized the woman. "The liver portion is always given to the hunt master."

Sword pulled Martin away from the liver. "That's enough, Martin." He looked at Orion, seeing no trace of the wound the first troll's attack had made. "I'm not the hunt master. I don't even know what that is."

"The black hunter knew who you were," Orion said in a neutral tone. "But why did she call you *'Little* Galen?' "

"My mother called me that," Sword said, and then he remembered. "And Roth did, too."

"Tomas Roth, the regent to Pendragon?"

"Yeah," Sword said, "that's him."

"What was your father's name, Mr. Sword?"

Sword was surprised by the question. Roth had asked him that as well. "I . . . I don't know. Why?"

Orion raised a hand in dismissal. "No matter. The black hunter was correct. This is not the time."

Sword stepped within inches of Orion. "I'm getting sick and tired of you people telling me that."

"For now, you have no choice." Orion pointed toward the clinic's back entrance. Streaks of blue and red light splashed across the walls in rhythmic patterns. "There *are* matters of your own world to attend to."

"What now . . . ?" Sword said as he looked down the alley, then tensed as he saw the signatures of blue powers and red crystals combined. But he relaxed as he saw it wasn't what he had feared. It was only a car with flashing bubble lights on top, and not the right color for a police car, either.

"It's just a private guard company," Sword said with relief. "That last troll must have set off an alarm when it banged on the door."

The car rolled to a stop by the clinic's back entrance. A flashlight beam shot out of one window to examine the door.

"See?" Sword said. "We can wait till they're gone." He

began working at his transceiver wire to see if he could reconnect it and get back in touch with Forsyte.

Then one of the guards stepped out of the car and began playing his flashlight across the rest of the alley. Sword blinked as it came to rest on the transceiver equipment.

"You there!" a human voice bellowed. "In the corner! I want to see hands!"

Past the glare of the flashlight, Sword saw the guard draw a revolver from a holster. On the other side of the car, a second guard stepped out carrying a full-barrelled shotgun.

"Here's your chance to show me how well vampires stand up to those things," Sword said.

"As long as we get closer," Orion said. Then the vampire placed his hands over his head and began walking toward the guard's car as the guards shouted at them to come forward.

"This should be good," Sword said to Martin as the two of them followed Orion. Sword didn't feel concerned. After Close trolls and a black hunter, he didn't think a pair of minimum-wage security guards were going to give them much to worry about.

Well, more than a pair, then, Sword thought as he saw the second guard open the back door of the car.

Martin stopped beside him. Orion stopped in front him.

"I said, come forward!" the guard with the flashlight yelled. Then she turned the flashlight back on what was coming out of the back seat. "Because you sure as hell aren't getting away!"

Two glowing eyes reflected the flashlight back at Sword like a pair of highway markers.

Martin had the word for it.

"Shifter," he growled.

NINETEEN

At last, Orion thought. The Tepesh had wisely placed two defensive arcs around their enclave—Close trolls to guard against intruders from the First World, and shifters to guard against those from the Second. However, the unexpected appearance of the black hunter had prevented the trolls from fulfilling their duty, and now the hapless Second World sentinels were going to face an enemy they could not possibly withstand.

Orion felt his fangs slip into place with pleasure. He had been among humans for too long. He had remained too hungry for too long. He ignored the human guards who flanked the car. They would be no more substantial than spider strands as he moved to his true prey—the shifter who even now Orion could sense was not prepared to battle a vampire.

Orion began to stride forward, one foot after another, faster with each movement, using all his adept skill. He sought the shifter's glowing eyes. He sought the contact of . . .

The vampire imprinted.

The shifter howled.

A bullet tore into Orion's chest but it was only soft metal that was unable to expand against the power of his tissues and bone. His body expelled the spent slug, no more consequential than an insect's sting, even as another hit his arm to no avail.

Orion ran now, all senses pushed to maximum sensitivity. He saw the second guard fire his shotgun. He saw the bee-swarm flight of the pellet cloud that emerged from its twin barrels, trailing lazy bursts of fire and smoke. He ran faster and the pellets missed him.

Orion reached the first guard and crushed her face with

one blow before the other human could even know that his partner had fired.

Then the vampire placed one hand on the hood of the car and propelled himself over it, streaking for the second guard with the shotgun who still looked along his barrel, searching for the target he had seen in the instant before he had pulled his trigger.

The second guard's eyes might have seen a shadow leap at him from the side. His nerves might have acted, the signal might well have been on the way to his brain and his consciousness as Orion struck with the force of a First World typhoon. But the signal found no living brain when it arrived. The guard was dead by Orion's hand before his legs even gave way.

Human blood steamed from the dank floor of the alley, the clouds of vapor it produced in the chill autumn night caught by the car's headlights, the fallen flashlight, the sweep of the emergency lights. With his magnified and overlapping senses, Orion saw the scent of that blood. He heard it. It coated his body with its warmth, offering him life and survival forever.

But he rejected it without thought and could no more partake of it than he could the food of humans.

The vampire had imprinted and released the bloodlust and now only one nourisher could satisfy his thirst.

Orion looked within the shifter, hearing its enormous heart pulsate, tasting its scent and its breath. Tasting its life.

His prey's name was Wick—a true Right wolf in shifter-form, female, biped, seven feet tall, with an monstrous barrel chest thickly coated with glossy gray fur.

Wick now stood atop the car's roof, the metal buckling beneath her clawed hind feet. She raked her gleaming white claws at the vampire, reflexes accelerated to almost match his own.

Almost, Orion thought, already feeding on victory. This was no skilled shifter warrior he fought. There would be no fighting eyes to contend with. Wick was scarcely four changes old, less than thirty Second World years. What could an adept learn of fighting vampires in that brief time?

The answer was: *nothing.*

Before the shotgun had fallen from the second guard's hands, Orion had punched his fist through the windshield of the car and found the thin metal post that separated it from the door frame. Now as Wick crouched to swipe at his exposed face, Orion reached in and pulled the metal post free, ripping it in two and stealing enough support from the car's roof that it collapsed under Wick's mass in an explosion of glass as all windows on the car blew out.

Wick lost her footing and tried desperately to save herself as she fell off balance. One hind foot managed to rake across Orion's shoulder, slashing his shirt and flesh but leaving her foot within his reach.

Orion took Wick's ankle in his hand. She lashed out with it, throwing him against the clinic's back door as she scrambled to regain her stance on the sloped roof of the car. Her claws raised thin ribbons of paint as they tore at the metal, digging in for resistance.

Orion was in no hurry. He knew she couldn't escape. He threw himself forward to his knees, reached beneath the side of the car and pushed himself to his feet to heave the car into the air so that it rolled over once before it hit the opposite alley wall with Wick beneath it.

He smiled coldly as he heard her cry of surprise and outrage. He felt pity that she had been told she would only be fighting humans. He scented the volatile notes of free gasoline. He tasted the heat of the engine. Death and destruction. He raised his hands to embrace it as he had for centuries, for millennia, for uncounted ages. For with death and destruction came his salvation and his refuge.

Wick pushed the car from her and it rolled and sparked against a brick wall. Wick roared at her opponent.

Orion spread his arms for her.

The car erupted in a thunderous explosion that was intensified by the close overhanging buildings and, as flames licked at them both, Orion flew at her.

Wick's jaws strained open. Her long muzzle reared up. Her claws reached forward. And Orion passed through her inadequate and unskilled posture and had her magnificent head in his hands and his teeth in her throat before she had even time to call out to Tarl David that she would join him soon.

Orion's fangs slid home, past fur and shifter flesh, effortlessly finding the wellspring of life eternal.

Dimly in the throes of that consummation, Orion was aware of his companions, unmoving, stunned by what he was capable of when the bloodlust reigned.

Good, Orion thought. *Now Sword will know. Now Sword will know whom he dared challenge. What he dared challenge.* Then there was no more room in Orion's being for conscious and coherent thought.

The vampire drank.

The vampire was *transformed.*

TWENTY

Galen Sword stared at the carnage in the alley, and despite all he had witnessed in the past two weeks, from the Ceremony of the Change Arkady to the defeat of the Close trolls, his mouth was open in disbelief.

From the moment the shifter had unexpectedly appeared with the human security guards to the last shudder it gave beneath Orion's fangs, fewer than fifteen seconds had passed.

In the brief instant Sword had actually been able to see Orion, the vampire had been a blurred image, a film run too fast for human eyes to follow.

And now, it was over. The gunshots, the deaths of the two guards, the demolition of their car, and its final explosion. The security vehicle blazed on its side, bathing the grim and filthy passageway with warm and out-of-place orange light. The flickering shadows the flames created made the rusty fire escapes and malodorous piles of refuse seem to dance back and forth in jerky counterpoint to the crackle of the fire. They made Orion appear to shift shape himself as he bent over the werewolf, which had now sunk to its knees.

Sword slowly walked closer to the vampire, shotgun bouncing in his hand, fascinated, repelled, and wondering why Orion had let any of them live when he was attacked in the Loft's garage. Saul Calder's shifterform had been large and grotesque and powerful, but it had been a harmless forest creature compared to the blinding speed and ferociousness of Orion as he had charged this new shifter.

And I taunted him, Sword thought in amazement. *I yelled at him. I grabbed his arm. I put myself within range of his fangs on purpose . . . and I am still alive.*

He felt Martin tug on his coat sleeve. "What is it?"

Martin rocked from foot to foot. "No closer. Nightfeeder hungry."

"I can see that, Martin, I can—"

It wasn't a trick of the shadows. Orion *was* shifting shape. He was *becoming* what he consumed.

"Oh great . . .," Sword said.

The werewolf flopped to the ground as if not a bone remained in its body. Orion loomed over it, head bowed, wet strings of coagulating blood hanging from his mouth, and with each deep and rasping breath he took, his chest expanded and did not shrink.

Orion's black silk shirt was pulled taut by the expansion, actually tearing where the werewolf had slashed the shoulder. His brown hair was now as light as the coat of the werewolf at his feet. Sword saw long white claws extending from his blood-drenched hands, saw the glimmer of more gray hair fluttering down over his bare forearms. Sword estimated that Orion's height had increased by a full foot.

Orion looked up with a sudden snarl. Sword's hand tightened on the stock of his shotgun, knowing it would be useless. He had seen Orion move *faster* than the guard's shotgun blast.

Now the vampire's face was distorting—a muzzle formed from an outthrust nose and upper teeth and fangs that were twice the size they had been before. The eyes were no longer Orion's eyes. They were shifter now. Phosphorescent green and reflective.

The shifting vampire looked at Martin and pointed a long and growing talon at him.

"Martin . . .," Orion breathed in an oddly soft and light voice. "Where have you been?"

Sword was surprised by Martin's response. The halfling didn't make his typical oooing sound of dismay. He didn't try to run. Instead he held his ground and answered back. "Away. Martin away."

Orion blinked his shifter eyes, and despite the muzzle, Sword saw a frown. "Your room is empty . . . your . . . John and Brenda, they won't say what happened. Not since the change."

"No bad happened," Martin said. There was a soothing quality to his voice that Sword had never heard before. "No bad."

"So worried about you," Orion said, still using his other

voice. "We used to play, remember, Martin? Do you remember the runs and the nights and the—" The vampire doubled over, wrapping both arms around his midsection with a deep moan of pain.

Martin edged closer. "Runs good. Nights good. No bad happened."

Suddenly Sword knew what was happening. *That's not Orion talking. He's not only taken the shape of his prey. He's taken its mind.*

"Martin," Sword whispered, stepping up to be with the halfling. "Who are you talking with? Who's . . . in him?"

Martin looked at Sword, tears in his eyes. "Wick," he said. "Wick good Martin. Wick good *Arkadych* enclave."

Orion wheezed and brought up a fist-sized clump of something dark and shapeless to splatter on the ground. He raised his head again and there was even less of Orion in his face.

"Martin," the vampire gasped. "Why did they take you to the ceremony? What happened to the Victor?"

Martin edged forward with small steps, hand extended in a loose fist.

"And the enclave must close," Orion said faintly. "John says we must be in common cause with Clan Tepesh if we're ever to see our Victor Morgana again." He strained to extend his hand—his paw—matching Martin's salute.

"But I'm afraid to go into the alley, Martin. I'm afraid. I'm afraid."

Martin lightly brushed his knuckles against the outstretched hand. "No afraid. Wick no afraid."

"The Close trolls are gone, Martin. Everyone's gone. The Victor's coming back, John says."

Sword realized he was seeing Martin's friend die within the body of the vampire. She was speaking the random and confused thoughts of a disassociating mind. No matter what the Arkady keepers said, their Victor Morgana could never return. Sword had left her and her consort, Roth, in the Pit of the Change, rushing for a fardoor that Sword had collapsed. Ten feet behind the two, a black wave of Seyshen had been coming for them. Sword doubted that either had lasted more than two seconds.

Martin stood close to the shifted vampire, hand still touching Orion's.

"Will we play again, Martin? Will we run?"

Sword could barely hear Martin's voice over the roar of the burning car. "Martin play with Wick. Martin run."

Orion took his hand from the halfling's, then caressed Martin's upturned face. "Poor precious *Myrch'ntin*. If only you knew. If only they'd tell you . . ."

"Martin play! Martin play Wick! *Es sool ta! Es sool ta Wi'kelta!*"

Orion nodded his shifter head, then stepped back heavily. "I have to fight now, Martin. I think I smell a nightfeeder in the alley and the Close trolls are all gone . . . all gone . . ." The vampire closed his eyes. His body trembled, half-Orion, half-Wick, but when he opened his eyes again, the green shifter irises were gone forever. In a low voice that once more sounded like his own, Orion said, "It is over."

Martin clawed at his own bare chest and howled. He pulled his fingers over his face leaving trails of his own blood. Then he stumbled away from Orion to hide behind Sword.

The vampire moved away from the still-smoldering car to stand next to Sword, who held his ground. The vampire was already losing height and girth. He began another series of deep breaths and this time with each exhalation his chest shrank closer to its normal, human muscular configuration. "Remember what I told you about your Second World legends?" he asked Sword.

"In the garage, why did you let us live?" Sword asked him in return.

Orion closed his eyes and wiped at his face, which was still taking shape. "It was not time to hunt. To release the bloodlust is to feed. And you would hardly make a worthwhile meal, Mr. Sword."

Sword watched in continued fascination as the gray color faded from Orion's long brown hair. "How long does the victim stay with you like that?"

"The *prey*, Mr. Sword. The prey." Orion's hands were his own again and he used them to pull small strings of red from his teeth, moving his fangs up and down in his mouth experimentally. It was repulsive to see but Sword couldn't turn away. "The prey stays with me forever."

"All of them?" *What must that be like,* Sword thought, *to contain so many dying souls in confusion?* And even as his mind was unable to comprehend the scale of the nightmare, some dim memory surfaced in response to the sight of the bloodcovered nightfeeder, the sparking embers, the smell of recent death and . . . a trace of someone else describing to him exactly what it *was* like to hold so many souls and the necessity of it. But he had been a child then . . . just a child . . . Little Galen . . .

Visions of a living gargoyle rose up in Sword's mind just as a familiar noise grew in volume nearby, and he lost hold of the fragile tendril into his past.

The noise approached from the same direction that the security guards' car had come and Orion turned quickly to face it. Reluctantly, Martin stood upright at Sword's side. "Too much fight," he said so only Sword could hear him. "Too much bad fight."

Sword put his hand on Martin's shoulder and the halfling was too tired to pull away as he usually did. "Not this time, Martin. I know that sound."

Past the gently dying radiance of the car's flames, a gleaming black Harley-Davidson Heritage Softail rolled down the alley, slowing to stop in front of Orion.

Its driver was Melody Ko.

Ko killed the Harley's motor and slid to the side of the seat to brace herself with her foot. As soon as she slipped off her glossy black helmet, she could smell the pungent odors of burning tires and plastic. She decided Brin had been right. Whatever mess Sword had stirred up now *was* going to take a lot of explaining.

Sword was the first to come up to her. Behind him, Martin was naked—big surprise—and Orion looked as if . . . Ko squinted at him. He looked somehow different in the firelight. More filled out.

"I thought your arm was broken," Sword said.

Ko frowned. "Why, hello, Sword. Good to see you, too."

Sword apparently didn't get her sarcasm and reached for the arm Orion had snapped in two places. Ko firmly bent it at the elbow to pull it away from him. She knew she didn't have to say anything. There was only one explanation for what had happened and it was already in his eyes.

"Brin." He said it like it was an invocation to a god. "He came to the hospital for you like he came for me."

"Wrong again, Sword." Ko responded to Sword's unspoken question. "He was at the Loft."

"Why?" Sword asked urgently. "Did he say anything? Did he tell you anything?"

Ko watched Sword's expression carefully. "He said you were in trouble. He said he himself couldn't intervene. So he healed my arm." She flexed her arm in front of him, moving it easily. "And he told *me* to help you." She didn't take her eyes from him. "Looks like you could use it, too."

"That's it? Nothing more?"

"He said you have to fight, Sword. Oh yeah, and he wanted to make sure you were still wearing your mother's ring."

Sword lifted his fist and the heavy gold clan ring gleamed in the fire's fading light.

"I told him you never took it off," Ko added.

Sword nodded his head as he stared at the deeply etched sword and dragon symbol on the ring. "Thanks."

Right, Ko thought with satisfaction. *You've accepted everything I said, just as Brin said you'd do.* She allowed herself a smile and noted that Sword obviously misinterpreted it as a signal that she was back on board. *Whatever it takes, Sword. Just as long as we get through this night. And then, are there ever going to be some changes.*

"Did Brin say anything about the blood clinic?" Sword suddenly asked.

Ko kicked the Harley's stand into position and dismounted. She tugged down on her equipment vest and saw Sword take a quick inventory of everything she'd attached to it, including five demolition charges.

"Brin told us to shut it down," she said. *At least that much is the truth,* she thought.

"Well, we're already started out here." Sword waved to indicate the destruction around them.

Ko looked around as well: a flaming car that would have brought the police in five minutes in any other part of town; two bodies in security guard uniforms; and a long mound of white powder slowly blowing away in the night breeze. Shifter dust, she realized. *Good.*

Ko jerked her thumb back at the clinic's back door. "Anyone in there?"

Sword shook his head. "One of the trolls tried to get in but . . . it didn't make it."

Ko lifted one eyebrow. "One of the *trolls?*"

"It's a long story."

"Right. You can tell me all about it later. Where's Adrian?"

Sword looked shocked. He reached toward his ear, but Ko saw there was nothing in it.

Ko snorted and pulled up her own transceiver earpiece from her vest. "We're supposed to be a team, remember? You can't keep forgetting about everyone who isn't here." She inserted the earpiece and thumbed the switch on the main unit strapped near her shoulder.

"Ko here. Are you on line, Adrian?"

"Damnation," the voder transmitted. Ko blinked. It was a new one on her.

"Bit of trouble in the alley, Adrian. All clear now."

"Why you? What about arm?"

"I'm fine," Ko said tersely. Hell's Kitchen or not, someone was going to be by to check out the burning car sooner rather than later. "Wasn't as bad as we thought. We're going to crash the blood clinic now."

"Detectors by clinic red. All others green."

Ko looked up to see that Martin and Orion had joined Sword. "We're all together in front of the clinic's back door, Adrian. There's a car on fire back here, so the police might be by real soon. We'll close the clinic door behind us so with luck they won't think to check it out. Sound good to you?"

"Yes," the voder said. Then added, "This time, stay out of Central Park."

Ko laughed, ignoring Sword's puzzled reaction.

"You sure you're okay?" Sword asked. Ko realized the reason for his concern. It seemed to have been a long time since she had laughed that way.

But she flexed her arm again. "Must be the blue power." *It just might be,* she thought. She hadn't felt this well in years. Except for the throbbing pain in her left little toe. That had been a surprise. But as Brin had explained it, the blue power didn't heal by taking injury away, it healed by collecting it and putting it all somewhere inconsequential. "After all," he had told her in the Loft, "I'm not a magician. I'm an elemental." She had laughed then, too, even though she felt she hadn't understood what Brin had really meant.

Moments later, Ko, Orion, Sword, and Martin gathered around the BioproEx clinic's backdoor. Orion touched the frame of it and Ko watched as his mouth opened slightly. "There is no magic here," he said. She could see dark stains around his mouth and on his neck. She wondered how the shifter had died.

Martin was next to approach the door. He cupped his hands over the door handle and wiggled it gently. Then a fast spark of blue light flared from his palms and the door handle clicked. Martin tried pushing the door open, but it didn't move. Another flash of blue light jumped silently from his hands to run around the door frame, collecting at hidden locks at the door's top, bottom, and sides. There was the sound of three heavy bolts forced aside, and then the door swung open at Martin's touch.

Once more, Orion stepped forward. He checked the air again. "Clear," he said, and they stepped into the enclave of Clan Tepesh.

TWENTY-ONE

For the neighborhood it was in and the look of it outside, Sword thought the BioproEx clinic was surprisingly clean and well maintained on the inside. At least, for what he could see. All but the overhead emergency lighting was out.

The back door to the blood clinic had opened into a narrow corridor, lined with tall stacks of white cardboard boxes labelled with the names and logos of several drug companies and medical supply houses. Between two columns of boxes was a single stack of green plastic containers with screenlike openings on their sides through which Sword could see single pint glass bottles marked as sterile saline solutions. He wondered how much it cost for vampires to hide their tracks in the city. He wondered where vampires obtained the money to pay for it all. Behind him, he heard the back door shut again.

"Who organizes all this?" Sword asked Orion, waving at all the supplies in the back room. "Who places the orders? Processes the invoices? Makes the payments?"

As he spoke, Orion checked the room out carefully in the light from the wall-mounted battery fixtures. "Keepers, Mr. Sword. Each clan employs them to help run the Second World enclaves." He pointed to the ceiling by the door that led from the storage room. "There is a discoloration in the plaster there, a roughness. I suspect a hidden wire." He looked at Ko. "Is that significant?"

Ko nodded and took a small black box from her vest. "Martin, give me a boost."

Martin bent down, wrapped his arms around Ko's knees, then lifted her so she could run the black box over the section of the wall Orion had indicated. Sword saw a red light flicker on the device.

"It's live," Ko said. "The door is alarmed. I'll bypass."

Martin lowered her to the floor again and Ko snapped open a small case with shiny silver implements. Sword left her to her work.

"Who are the keepers?" Sword asked Orion as they waited for Ko. "Humans? Vampires? Other adepts?"

"Whatever is best, Mr. Sword. Different strategies are useful at different times, in different places. For the enclave the Tepesh are attempting to establish here, it would be wise to have a mix. For color and legitimacy they would need human doctors. For affairs that must be handled in daylight hours, they might choose adepts who are apart from their own clans. And, for those negotiations that belong to the First World—vampires."

"Complicated," Sword observed. "What happens when the system breaks down and humans realize what's going on?"

Orion looked enigmatic. "Occasionally such things do happen. But then, how many humans believe in vampires?" He smiled and Sword found the bloodstains around his mouth disconcerting. "We have had many years to refine our strategies and techniques. And most important of all, Mr. Sword, vampires *do* believe in humans. Knowledge of one's enemies makes one safer, would you not agree?"

"Got it," Ko suddenly said.

Sword looked over to the door she worked by and saw two long loops of wire dangling from the frame.

"This explains why the first door wasn't wired," Ko continued. She pointed to what appeared to be a blocked-off air conditioner opening over the back door. "Whoever set up security wasn't all that interested in keeping anyone out of this backroom. The idea behind this wiring is to let in whoever is determined enough to break in. And then, when this door is opened,"—she patted the door with the by-passed alarm—"there's a mechanism up in that air conditioner outlet that would slam shut the back door and seal it with those hidden bolts."

"So whoever was in this storage room would be trapped," Sword said.

Ko began to put away her burglar's tools. "A regular Roach Motel, Sword. And no evidence to have to turn over to the police."

"As I said, Mr. Sword, we have had many years to refine our strategies." Orion smiled again at Sword.

Ko stepped back from the door. "Okay, Martin. It's all yours."

Martin touched the deceptively simple doorknob and a blue spark leapt from his hand to the metal door plate. Then he opened the door.

Sword heard a loud hum from the mechanism over the backdoor.

"That's all right," Ko said. "The system thinks it's caught someone but I redirected the wire that controls the bolts so they won't close. We're home free."

Sword stepped through the storage room door, shotgun held ready. "I wouldn't exactly call this home, Melody."

Ko shrugged as Sword passed by. "I thought that's what you were looking for."

The next section of the clinic was a corridor lined with inexpensive wood panelling. Several other doors similar to the storage room door were spaced evenly along both walls. More emergency-light fixtures glowed at both ends of the corridor.

Sword waited for Orion to join him. "What now?"

The vampire tasted the air. "Tepesh," he said, then pointed to the right. "There is an updraft from that side."

"An updraft?" Sword asked.

"This structure is not large enough to contain an entire enclave. There must be something more beneath it."

Sword looked over to catch Ko's eye, but saw no shared commiseration in her. "Twice as good the second time," she said briskly, then followed Orion down the corridor.

Except for the sinister trap set in the storage room—Sword wondered how many would-be burglars had simply disappeared after making an easier than expected after-hours entrance into the BioproEx blood clinic—nothing else seemed out of place in the rest of the facility.

They found two washrooms, four offices apparently dedicated to paperwork and file storage, and a large room with six neat cots outfitted with blood pressure wall gauges and rocker trays where blood bags could be gently moved back and forth, mixing the donated blood with anticoagulants—*if vampires like the taste of anticoagulants,* Sword thought queasily.

Another large room held a long folding table laid out with cookie tins and two plastic bags of paper cups. Public health posters decorated the walls.

"This all seems so normal," Sword said as they looked into the final room.

"If it appeared to be anything other than what it is supposed to be, then surely it would be a failure." Orion pointed to a section of wood-panelled wall between a large refrigerator and a card table covered with health brochures. "There," he said.

Ko and Sword both examined the wall but could find nothing, so Ko asked Martin to join them. Though Sword could see that Martin's uneasiness was coming back the longer they stayed in the clinic, Ko was able to keep the halfling calm enough to place his hand on the wall in several places.

At the fourth spot Martin touched, his blue power glimmered and the wall popped forward by a few inches.

"Thank you, Martin," Ko said. Then she held a finger to her transceiver. "Adrian, we've found a disguised entranceway in the clinic. It's in . . . I guess you'd call it a lounge. By the refrigerator."

Sword knew why she gave Forsyte that information. It was in case they didn't come back and Forsyte had to convince others—perhaps the police—to go after them.

Ko nodded once as she heard Forsyte's reply. Then she spoke to him again. "You got any activity out there?" After a moment she nodded again and looked at Sword. "Adrian thinks something's up. Three police cars have driven past the clinic in the last five minutes. But none of them has stopped."

"Could we have triggered a silent alarm?" Sword asked.

"Not one which would alert the police," Orion said. "The private security guards who were with the shifter would be the only ones to respond to any signal. Any other response would be too risky."

"Maybe it's the burning car," Sword suggested to Ko.

"Any fire sirens out there, Adrian?" she asked. Then, "He says he hasn't heard anything."

Sword knew what he wanted to do next but he also remembered the new arrangement and he knew he liked having Ko back and working with him again. He wondered if her meeting with Brin was responsible for her new attitude. So Sword went along with what he had agreed to. "Ask Adrian if we should proceed."

Ko repeated the question for Forsyte and smiled, though

Sword didn't find her expression to be altogether friendly. "He says yes."

At her words, Orion and Martin carefully eased the open section of wall forward until it came loose on the right and could be swung open like a wide door. Through the opening, Sword could see another emergency-light fixture shining down on a narrow wooden staircase constructed of new, unfinished lumber.

The staircase led down.

Martin carefully edged his head over the stairwell and Sword saw him sniff, then shake his head. "Lots nightfeeders. Lots shifters. But not now. Before. Maybe later. Not now."

Orion stepped through the opening and tasted the air himself. "The halfling is correct. Vampires *and* shifters. Together."

"Is that unusual?" Sword asked. "After all, this place was being guarded by a shifter." He turned to Ko and added, "That's part of the long story, too."

Orion nodded thoughtfully as he ran his hand along the staircase's wooden railing. "For one enclave to hire a shifter through intermediaries to serve as a Second World sentinel is quite common. But for the number of vampires and shifters whose scents intermingle below to be in such proximity, together, that is *most* unusual."

Ko rested her hand on one of the black-wrapped demolition charges on her vest. It was about half the size of a paperback book and she had told Sword it could punch a hole through five feet of brick wall. "Maybe we should just shut it down here," she suggested.

Sword was startled. "Kennie's probably down there, Melody."

Ko ignored him and looked up at Orion. "How many shifters and vampires do you figure are down there?"

Orion closed his eyes in concentration. "Perhaps fifteen to twenty shifters have passed this way in the last night. Twice as many Tepesh as well."

Ko turned back to Sword. "Forty-five to sixty adepts, Sword." She gave him the same odd smile she had worn before. "Sure you're up to it?"

Sword felt cut by her words. "How can you even ask that question?" He pushed past Ko, stepped onto the wooden stairs, and without looking back, began his descent.

Sword deduced that the lower passageway to which the newlybuilt stairway led was close to thirty feet below street level. The stairs had turned at two rough wooden landings, each one lit by the same type of battery-powered emergency lamp.

The passageway itself was smaller than the ones that had led him and Ko to the fardoor that had opened into the Pit of the Change, and this one was dry and smelled of fresh paint. More emergency lights studded the bare concrete ceiling every ten feet, following a neatly installed electrical conduit. There was still no sign of crystal illumination.

Martin was the first to join Sword at the bottom of the stairs. No one else was behind him.

"The others?" Sword asked sourly. He wouldn't be surprised if Ko and Orion had decided not to join him below. But he was surprised to see Martin come down alone.

"Melody nightfeeder put wall back. No one know from other side. Easy to hide," Martin said. He wrinkled his nose. "Many bad nightfeeder stink bad. Dead people, too."

Sword heard footsteps on the stairs and Ko's voice. She was talking to Forsyte, making sure that her transceiver could continue to transmit from below ground.

"He's still reading us," she said as she reached the floor of the passageway. Then she gave Forsyte a description of what she saw—the construction and the length of the corridor, the number of lights, and the stench.

"Any idea what that is?" Sword asked Orion.

"Human corpses," Orion answered as if commenting on the weather. His attention was focused on the closer end of the passageway where it appeared to dead-end against a blank wall.

"Corpses?" Sword said. "I thought the idea behind the blood clinic was so the Tepesh could take blood without killing their . . . prey."

Orion walked toward the blank wall. "Accidents happen, Mr. Sword. Especially to those society won't miss. And in this city, there are thousands of them." He placed his hand against the wall. "Here, this way."

"But there are doors in the other direction," Sword said. He had seen the indentations of their frames in the freshly painted white walls of the passageway leading the opposite way.

"They'd just be processing rooms," Orion said, bending closer to the wall to scrutinize it closely.

Sword joined the vampire at the blank wall. "What kind of . . . processing?"

Orion stopped his examination of the wall and turned to Sword. "If you'd really care to know, Mr. Sword, please feel free to look. But if you're interested in *living* humans, then several have passed through this wall in the past two hours."

"Kennie?" Sword looked quickly for the telltale flicker of a fardoor perimeter.

"At least one female," Orion confirmed. "Though since I have never met your Kendall, I cannot know if it is she I detect."

Sword knocked on the wall and it sounded solid. "I can't find the fardoor in it."

"Perhaps that is because there is no fardoor to be found." Orion called back to Martin. "Halfling, we have need of your blue power once more."

But Martin refused to touch the blank wall. "Crystal in wall. Martin touch, Martin coldblasted."

Orion's lips tightened. "Feedback. That's not good."

Ko stepped up to the wall. "Feedback? Are you saying that crystal power acts like electricity in a circuit?"

"Both are fundamental forces of nature, Ko. Why would it not?" Orion stretched up to tap his fingers along a top corner of the wall. Sword heard the crack of thin plaster and saw a familiar red glow spill across the concrete ceiling.

"Is that it, Martin?" Sword asked.

Martin folded his arms across his chest and nodded.

"Give me a boost, then?"

Martin shook his head so Sword made the same request of Orion.

"Why? You will not be useful to us coldblasted."

"Don't worry, I won't be. Just let me get a look at it."

Orion shrugged, then joined his hands to serve as a step for Sword. Sword jumped up and peered into the small pocket in the wall containing the red crystal. It was irregularly shaped, about the size of a large marble. "I've got it," Sword said.

"No! Don't!" Orion protested.

Bit it was too late. Sword already held the crystal in his

hand and its light was no longer visible. He hopped down and showed the dull gemstone to Orion.

"How . . . ?" the vampire began. "That is at least a five whole."

Sword placed the powerless crystal in his coat pocket. "I sap them. That's how we got away from the Arkady shifters. I threatened to touch their Crystal of the Change."

Orion stared at Sword with an open mouth and then burst into deep, appreciative laughter. "And did you touch it?" Sword shook his head. "Then what became of it?"

"Last I saw, it was about to fall into the hands . . . or whatever . . . of the Seyshen."

Orion nodded. "That could certainly explain why the remnants of Arkady now work with the Tepesh. It will not be an easy task to barter with the Seyshen for the return of the Arkady Crystal. Action might well be required, and against the Seyshen, a cabal of vampires and shifters *might* have some chance of success." He tapped his fist against the wall again and this time, without its protective crystal, it sounded hollow and insubstantial. "This enclave could be what you would call a training encampment, where vampire and shifter learn to battle Seyshen."

Orion turned his back to the wall. "And if that is the case, we must turn back now. If there are sixty warriors in training beyond this wall, not even I will be able to withstand them without preparation.

At once, Martin straightened up from his crouch, prepared to leave. Ko began to unfasten a demolition charge from her vest. But Sword ignored them, and Orion. He swung his shotgun up and smashed its stock against the wall.

It was made of plaster less than a quarter-inch thick and exploded into a shower of small fragments and dry dust. An almost identical extension to the present passageway stretched off into the distance beyond. It was deserted.

"What do you know," Sword said as he peered through the opening he had made, brushing the white powder from his sleeves. "There's nobody home."

TWENTY-TWO

Forsyte knew his heart was pounding because he could hear its pulse in his ears. But he could feel no tremor in his chest, and no flutter in his stomach. Just as he was apart from the other members of the team, he was apart from his own body.

Focus, he commanded himself. *Watch the detector status lights. Check the van alarm system again. It's been less than a minute since they stepped through the false wall and continued along the passageway.* But no matter what he told himself, his heart still thundered through his eardrums.

The twenty minutes in which he had lost contact with Sword in the alley had been nervewracking, but nothing that he hadn't encountered before in his three years of monitoring Sword's and Ko's excursions. Because they had often had to take up positions in which they couldn't risk being overheard, he had been driven to design the team's first version of the locater bands which Ko had subsequently miniaturized so they could actually be worn. He hoped she would have some spare moments in the next few days to finish assembling a complete set of replacement bands. But most of all, he hoped that Ko would find some spare moments in the next few seconds to get back in contact with him and tell him what was going on.

Over the hammering of his heart, Forsyte slowly became aware of another rumbling noise from outside the van. He saw the windshield smear with light from a pair of headlights as a vehicle drove along the street. He blinked three times and tapped his chair's joystick to the left and the central screen on the control console he sat before came to life with an image from the miniature video camera mounted at the back of the van's roof. He tapped a key on his pad and the camera's signal was reprocessed for light enhancement. On the screen, Forsyte could now see that the passing vehicle was another police car. That made four police passes so far and Forsyte couldn't understand why it was taking them so long to find the burning car that Ko had said was in the alley. Surely even New York cops would have to notice *something* as they drove past the alley's entrance. But apparently they hadn't yet. Which made Forsyte immediately think that perhaps the police were not *seeing* the alley's entrance as they drove past.

That could explain it, he thought. *People facing onto the alley see the fire. They report it to the police. The police come to investigate but the alley has been . . . masked somehow. The police can't see it but the reports keep coming in. They know something is wrong but have no way to discover what it is.*

Maybe there are more reasons than most people think for why the police force seems so ineffectual against some types of activity. Forsyte began to consider a series of experiments to demonstrate how pervasive First World influence might be in affairs of the Second World. Unfortunately, he could not come up with a falsifiable protocol. If any such experiments showed that the First World had absolutely *no* influence on the Second World, then it could mean that either the adepts had no power *or* that their power was so great they had influenced the experiments. Forsyte's mouth twitched up into a small grin. *Now that's an interesting problem,* he thought.

The signal acquisition light flashed on the control console and Forsyte quickly pushed down on the center keypad button in front of the joystick, then blinked twice, alerting his chair's computer to switch its control functions from the van's monitoring system to the radio link. Ko's voice instantly came out of the console speaker.

"We've come to another dead end, Adrian. All we've got here is a second wooden staircase. Fresh wood, rough construction heading up, just like before." For a few moments, Forsyte heard a background noise he couldn't identify. "Ah, apparently not just like before," Ko added. "Martin just pointed out that this set of stairs has *lots* more scrapes and scratches on the treads. He's calling them claw marks and Orion agrees."

Well, at least that means they didn't walk around in a circle and end up at the same staircase they started from, Forsyte thought. His finger jabbed at the keys, assembling the phrases he had already programmed into them for the excursion.

"How far did you go?" his voder asked. "What direction?"

"Same direction as before," Ko answered. Her signal was still strong. "This passageway is a straightline run-on from the first one. Sword estimates we've gone about two hundred to two hundred and twenty yards."

Forsyte closed his eyes and pictured the map he had memorized of the area. He created a mental image of a grid to represent yards and laid it over the map. Then he mentally counted off the squares from the clinic's location. Two hundred to two hundred and twenty squares took them out from under the row of buildings the clinic was in, under the street, and almost into the middle of the next block. Forsyte opened his eyes in surprise and tapped at his keypad.

"You're under the World Plaza complex," he transmitted. "How far up does the new staircase go?"

He heard Ko repeat his question, then say, "Orion's checking now." A few seconds passed. "At least a hundred feet. Through an open shaft. Any idea where that will put us?"

Forsyte thought it out. One hundred feet less the thirty they already were below street level would put them at plus seventy. That could be either tower of the complex. He'd have to be able to do better than that.

"Can't estimate precise location," he transmitted. "Will get plans."

"Should we wait or proceed?" Forsyte had heard enough of what had been said between Sword and Ko to know what the situation was this night.

He assembled the sentence and pressed the send key. "Not up to me this time."

Ko took her time replying. "Understood." The acquisition light went out.

Forsyte didn't waste time agonizing over what his associates would do. *Associates*, he laughed to himself. *A powerless adept, a bloodsucking monster, a human/werewolf hybrid, and an eccentric, single-minded genius who wants to share her life with me. A regular Clowns 'R' Us.* He blinked and tapped the code sequence that would link the van's computer with the Loft's Cray-Hitachi II. The faster he could get the information to them, the better chance they would have to plan a quick escape. He knew for a certainty that Sword would never consent to stalling at the bottom of the stairwell waiting for Forsyte to get back to them. They were probably already up to street level and climbing fast.

Forsyte waited impatiently as he heard the roof mechanism slide open so the mini-microwave dish could be deployed. Its own microprocessor took its present coordinates from the van's navigational computer, scanned the visible sky to lock in a signal path to the most accessible relay station, then sent out a coded signal to the multi-band antennae that bristled from the roof of the Loft.

In less than ten seconds, the Loft's mainframe acknowledged the signal, sent back a coded reply to verify the sending source, and then waited for instructions.

Forsyte pushed a button that would initiate a request to access the New York City Fire Department's Large Building Plan Database. The Loft's computer promptly dialed a central emergency number and logged on to the state's emergency preparedness computer network, providing a name, number, and password—which Forsyte had prepared more than a year earlier—and that would make the network recognize its requests as coming from a precinct in midtown Manhattan.

Forsyte was online in less than a minute. He typed in the address for the World Plaza complex and a menu of blueprint options came up. He chose an elevation study first to compare the heights of the various component towers. The network began downloading the graphic data to the Loft's mainframe, which immediately uploaded it over the microwave link to the van.

On Forsyte's screen, a side elevation of the project slowly grew, line by line. While that process continued, he switched his controls over to the radio voice link and contacted Ko again.

"Blueprints downloading. What is the revised estimate on the height of the stairwell?"

Ko was out of breath when she answered. Sword had obviously been making them run up the stairs.

"Switched from rough wood to metal and terrazzo about five levels ago," Ko panted. "We're definitely inside a legitimate structure now. But there are no exit signs, no fire extinguishers, and nonstandard railings.

"Understood," Forsyte transmitted. The lack of those

seemingly inconsequential features meant that whatever part of the World Plaza building Ko and the others traveled through, it had never been inspected or approved by the city of New York. They were in what could only be a hidden passageway somehow secretly built into the center of a major new construction project. "What is the height?" he had his machines ask again.

"Light is dim, so it's hard to say." Forsyte could hear the thudding of Ko's feet as she ran. "Orion says at least another hundred feet higher in addition to the hundred we've already come up."

Forsyte watched the display screen where the drawing of the complex was almost complete. Only one tower—the main one—continued to grow. The height of the other parts of the structure were too short to allow for a two-hundred-foot interior drop.

"You are in the main tower," Forsyte transmitted. He read the technical description at the bottom of the screen. "Sixty-five floors total." The top of the tower began to fill in. It was a decorative, multi-faceted glass pyramid sloping up from all four sides to a point. The glass cap appeared to sit above the elevator equipment and not much else. "Looks like there could be some dead space up top," he added. "How far up will you go?"

"We're following Orion's and Martin's noses now. Both say vampires and shifters brought humans up this way quite recently." Ko sounded winded but determined.

"I will download all floorplans for the upper floors. Contact me when you are ready to leave the stairwell." Forsyte waited a moment to see if there would be a reply, then transferred control back to the computer link, selected "Floorplans," from the network menu, and requested all floors above level thirty-five. Then, just before he gave the "enter" command, he also selected a separate file which would show the central tower's main structural supports. If there were an interior passageway hidden within it, he might as well see if there were room for others. He transmitted his request and once again began to wait.

Four minutes later, the entire floorplan file had downloaded and the structural file came up. Forsyte blinked and tapped the codes that would allow him to study the floorplan while the second file was retrieved in the background.

Office plan after office plan flashed by his eyes and he

quickly saw the pattern to the tower's layout. He guessed that the hidden stairway Ko and the others took was attached to the side of one of four main concrete support pillars that ran up through the structure. The pillars seemed to have too large a cross-section according to the technical specs provided. Forsyte could easily visualize how a small column could support the structural load from within what was essentially a hollow concrete tube, which also held a secret stairwell. In that case, he realized, there could be three other stairwells hidden within the three other supports in the building. He reminded himself to run checks of additional sets of blueprints for other buildings. There was no telling what other rooms and installations he might uncover that also had been surreptitiously built within major construction projects so complex that no one person could keep track of everything that went into them.

Forsyte was impatient again as he waited for the structural file to finish loading. If he could examine it in relation to the floorplans, he was sure he could deduce the most likely spot in which the hidden stairwell might make contact with the rest of the tower's interior. He doubted few other physicists had been in the position of finding a Cray-Hitachi to be too slow.

But even as he watched the graphic display that showed how much of the file was left to download, the transfer rate slowed even more. *Bad static.* Forsyte thought. *The error-checking procedures are requiring data to be retransmitted to compensate.*

The data transfer stopped.

Forsyte sent a reset command and another five blocks of the file were transmitted. But nothing else happened.

Hearing his heartbeat speed up again, Forsyte transmitted a status request. Ten seconds later—an eternity for a supercomputer—the status report came back. The mainframe was overloaded.

Impossible. Forsyte thought angrily. *I could model the Big Bang in that thing and it wouldn't overload. Besides, it's still under manufacturer's warranty.* He sent an additional reset command but nothing came back.

Not even adepts would be able to break my security procedures on that machine. Forsyte told himself. *It has to be a bad microwave uplink.* There was another strategy to try. Slower, but more reliable.

Blinking and tapping furiously, he called the mainframe from the van's cellular phone. *Only 9600 baud if I'm lucky,* he thought, *but at least I'll be able to get the rest of the—*

The line was out of service.

The only place Forsyte could feel a chill was across his scalp, and he felt one there now. Desperate, but not able to move or command his devices any faster, he rerouted the van's cellular phone to an emergency cellular connection in the Loft that was independent of any outside power source. That call went through.

He channeled his electronic signals from that phone to the rest of the Loft's communications system, finally getting back in touch with the mainframe. And it *was* overloaded. The reason was printed on the console's display screen—the Loft's security system had been breached.

Shifters, Forsyte thought. *They tracked Sword down and invaded the Loft at the same time Sword was tracking them down.* The physicist lifted his finger from the key pad, his mind conceiving of and discarding possible strategies at a blistering pace. There were additional demolition charges still in the garage, Forsyte knew. And though he had never attempted it, it should be possible for him to take control of one of his spare wheelchairs from here, transmitting motion controls to have it go to the charges and—he had a vision of the Loft erupting into an enormous fireball. Much of their work would be lost forever, but perhaps their lives could be saved. Especially if the shifters thought that Sword and his team were in the Loft when it was destroyed.

Forsyte went back to his controls, his decision made. Sword was wealthy. He could construct a new base. But first, Forsyte knew he must confirm the enemy's identity. He transmitted the commands that would patch him through to whatever still functioned of the Loft's security system. If any of the hidden surveillance cameras were still operational and he could direct their signals back to the microwave uplink for realtime reception . . . Forsyte solved the complex programming problem in seconds. In the stress and the heat of the conflict, he felt alive. He forgot his body's infirmities and soared with the power of his intellect alone.

The two smaller display screens flanking the main computer screen on the console flickered with black and white video images. Forsyte blinked rectification commands and the images steadied, then solidified. He would be able to see what manner of beast had invaded the Loft in his absence. His mouth twitched in fierce anticipation. He was ready for war.

One of the invaders passed by a camera hidden above the garage door, where it could monitor half of the interior space. Forsyte had the camera track the shape until it stopped, then commanded it to zoom in until the invader's face could be clearly seen.

In his surprise, Forsyte tried to speak, and all that came out was a dry and strangled croak. The invader was not a shifter, not a vampire.

It was Sword's doctor—Leah Bernstein.

What the hell is she *doing in the Loft?* Forsyte gurgled, still in shock. Then another figure moved on screen and faced the doctor. Forsyte had the camera zoom back to include both figures and again he recognized the intruder.

Detective Trank? It was the police officer that Sword had met during the investigation of Marcus Askwith's death. They still kept in contact with each other. They had worked together in some matters, but still Forsyte had no explanation for what he was seeing.

The detective and the doctor were conducting an intense conversation and Forsyte cursed the cameras for not having audio pickups as well.

He sent more commands to the security system, misblinking and mistapping a dozen times in his haste and agitation. Finally, a second camera in the garage came online. It was directed at the van Ko had spent the past three days repairing. Forsyte could see it rock back and forth as if something were moving in it.

He made the camera pull back until the van's open rear doors came into view. Inside, there was something moving through the van—two uniformed police officers. One emerged as Forsyte brought the camera into focus. It looked as if she had found a rag. Forsyte could see that she wore plastic gloves.

They're looking for evidence, Forsyte realized. *But what kind? And why?*

The officer with the bundled-up rag stepped from the back of the van and Forsyte could see her mouth open as she called out. On the center screen, both Trank and Bernstein turned together. The officer walked over to them, crossing from one camera's view to the other. She stood in front of them, doing something to the rag until it unrolled before them and Forsyte saw exactly what they were searching for and why.

The police officer had found Ja'Nette Conroy's torn and bloodied nylon jacket. And having found that, Forsyte knew, now they would have no choice but to search for and find the dead girl's guardian—Galen Sword.

TWENTY-THREE

The echoes of their footsteps as they jogged up through the tower came closer and closer together, which meant they were finally coming to the end of the staircase. Sword felt relief, even though it meant his confrontation with a combined force of shifters and vampires was also that much closer. But the truth was that the straps of his equipment vest had rubbed his shoulders raw through his black cotton T-shirt and his long leather coat was too heavy for the physical effort he was putting out. He didn't want to take it off, though. If its thickness could give him an extra eighth-of-an-inch protection against whatever claws and fangs he might face in the next few minutes, then wearing it on this mad hike would have been worth it.

Obviously Ko was thinking the same thing because she also had refused to part with the leather jacket she had worn when she had arrived in the alley on the Harley. Sword actually found it odd to see her preparing to go into action without her arms bare, her equipment at the ready, and all extraneous trappings eliminated so nothing could slow her down. But Ko was different tonight—*or this morning,* Sword corrected himself, remembering how late it must be. Her encounter with Brin must have affected her as profoundly as his own had three years ago. He wondered if she had had hidden memories as well. He wondered what more Brin might have said to her. He wondered if they would both survive what was ahead so he could question her again.

Overhead, at least four levels above him, Sword heard Martin and Orion slam to a halt. Then he and Ko were upon them in seconds. Neither halfling nor vampire seemed touched by the long upward rush, but both Sword and Ko had to rest their knees on the tops of the last risers. Sword leaned heavily on the stock of his shotgun. Ko lay an arm across the curiously thin and poorly supported metal railing.

"Where now?" Sword said between deep breaths.

"Home," Martin said and began to move down the stairs past Sword.

But Orion dropped a firm hand on Martin's shoulder. "I think not, little halfling."

"Why home, Martin?" Sword asked.

Martin's only answer was to duck his head and point up to the last landing of the staircase. It was encased by three walls and a roof of solid concrete. There was no door. Not even a hint of where a door might be.

When Martin was sitting reluctantly but obediently on the top step, Orion tapped his palm against the three walls he could reach. Each sounded solid. But Sword had heard that before.

"There's got to be a crystal around somewhere, giving strength to one of them."

But Orion shook his head. "If there were a door to be opened, then Martin would know it. It is part of his gift."

"Is that true?" Sword asked the halfling. "If there were a hidden door here, *would* you be able to know where it was?"

Martin nodded unhappily. "But Martin see nothing here. Go home, okay?"

"How about the human scent?" Sword asked, looking at the vampire. "Is that still around."

"Yes. They came this way. Shifters and vampires and their prey."

Sword sat down on the steps. "Melody? Any suggestions?"

She pointed at the fourth wall that rose up opposite the stairs from the second to last landing. It was unreachable from the topmost landing. "If I were going to hide a door, that's where I'd put it. Shifters and vampires could make the jump, but humans couldn't."

Sword patted Martin's foot. "What about it, Martin? Could there be a door in that wall?"

Martin shook his head. Then he folded his hands in his lap and was still.

Sword looked back to Orion. "So how would a vampire take human prey through a concrete wall?"

Sword and Orion answered the question at the same time. "Fardoor."

Then Sword added, "I don't get it. Why go to all the time and trouble of building secret passageways and hidden enclaves, when fardoors can get you from place to place with no trouble? I mean, all the adepts could live underground at the south pole and still go shopping in New York everyday."

Orion kept looking around the walls and ceiling that enclosed the top of the stairwell. "A fardoor is an expensive proposition, Mr. Sword. Wizards are needed to align the portals. Crystals are needed to power them. The greater distance that is covered or the greater area a portal encompasses, the more crystals are needed. Only a few of the clans can afford the stones on a regular basis, and even then they are used mostly for ritual visits to sacred sites."

Sword pounded the wall beside him, being careful not to scrape his mother's ring. "Still seems like it would be a hell of a way to have an army launch a sneak attack. Why bother training warriors at the top of a skyscraper? They could just step through a wall and come out in the bedroom of the Seyshen's leader while he's sleeping."

Orion folded his arms imperiously. "First, Mr. Sword, a fardoor can not be established until portals have been cast at both ends. Second, the Victor of Clan Seyshen is female. And third, Seyshen do not sleep."

Ko stretched her legs on the stairs like a runner limbering up. "Orion, a question. How long does it take a fardoor to become established? Once both portals have been cast?"

Orion gestured with empty hands, indicating there was no absolute answer.

"Is it related to the distance that the fardoors cross?" Ko persisted.

At that, Orion nodded. "The farther apart the portals, the longer it takes for the fardoor to be linked."

Ko smiled and Sword asked her why.

"There's a science to it all, Sword. I bet I could write equations to quantify the relationship between the crystal power the fardoors use in relation to their reach and their area. And I bet it would behave according to the three laws of thermodynamics, too. Despite what anything we've seen looks like, there's a pattern to it all. There's cause and effect, logical relationships."

"You didn't see the Close trolls," Sword said. "Or their living armor."

"I don't have to. None of this is magic or supernatural. It's just a technology that's using a force of nature that humans have never noticed before."

Sword rubbed gingerly under his vest straps. "That's all well and good, Melody, but it still leaves us sitting at the top of the World Plaza trying to figure out how the other adepts got any farther." He glanced up again, studying the featureless concrete ceiling as Orion had. " 'Cause there just doesn't seem anywhere farther to go . . ."

Sword stood up and turned on the stairs. If fardoors were too expensive and none of this was magic, then there *had* to be a simple way out of this blind alley. And the simplest way that Sword could think of was there *still* must be somewhere farther to go.

He slipped a *shiruken* from his vest. "Heads up," he said, then flipped the serrated disk straight up at the ceiling.

It passed through the concrete and, after an appropriate time delay in which it would have made it to the top of its trajectory and fallen back to the height of the ceiling again, it reappeared on its way down.

Orion's arm snapped out and plucked the weapon from the air. "Well done," he said.

Martin and Ko stood up to look again at the ceiling above them. "Why didn't Martin know about this?" Ko asked distrustfully.

"Not door. Not sealed," Martin said. He crouched to jump up to the edge of the wall.

"No, Martin! Don't!" Sword said. "There could be spikes or blades of some sort on the tops of the walls. There might be only one place safe to climb." He stepped up to the landing. "Orion, can you lift me through enough to see what we're facing out there?"

"No need," the vampire said, then jumped up with a graceful spin so that he passed through the ceiling up to his shoulders.

He landed with all the noise of a leaf falling. "The space beyond is large, unlit. Splinter wire, full of glitter, lines all walls. But there"—he pointed to a spot on the narrowest wall—"is an opening." He held out his hand. "Give me your rope."

Sword pulled the coil of black nylon cord from his vest

and passed it over. Orion went over to the spot he had indicated, then leapt up the wall as quickly as if he had fallen toward the illusory ceiling. An end of the rope dangled down a few seconds later, being lowered to arm's reach.

"Better tell Adrian what we're up to," Sword said to Ko.

Guiltily, she put her hand to her transceiver. "Adrian, we've reached the top of the stairway. Orion's gone the next stage and he says the ceiling opens into a large unlit space. Any idea what we're facing?"

Ko fell silent but Sword could tell from her expression that she was waiting for Forsyte to reply.

"Ko here, Adrian. Are you on line?"

Sword saw some tension leave her face as she responded to Forsyte's voice. But it didn't last. Whatever he was saying to her made her face darken.

"Sword . . . Adrian says the police are at the Loft."

"What?"

"He's watching them on the surveillance pickups. Trank's there. And Dr. Bernstein."

Sword needed to hear nothing else to know what had happened. "Ja'Nette," he said. "It's because of Ja'Nette, isn't it?"

Ko scowled, still concentrating on Forsyte's transmission. "They found her jacket."

Sword tightened his shotgun sling so it would stay closer to his chest when he climbed the wall.

Ko watched him as if she didn't understand what he was doing. "Sword! Didn't you hear me? I said the police have Ja'Nette's jacket. The one she was wearing when—"

Sword pointed at the rope. "I'll deal with that *later,* Melody. Right now we can't risk any distractions."

"Distractions?" Ko slapped her arms at her side. "Sword, this is about Ja'Nette. She was—"

"Ja'Nette's dead!" Sword said it loud enough that Martin whimpered. "And it's my fault. I admit it. I accept it. I'm the one who has to live with that. But the only thing I can do about it now is to climb that goddamned rope and find Kennie so that what happened to Ja'Nette won't happen again!"

Ko shook her head. "You'll never make it, Sword."

"I didn't think I'd make it the first time in the pit," he said bluntly. "As far as I'm concerned, it's all borrowed time from here on in."

Sword grabbed the rope in his fist, spun it around his forearm, then tugged on it. *"Orion!"* he called. "I'm ready."

He jerked his head back to stare at Ko. "Are you?"

With a sudden yank, Sword rose to the next level.

TWENTY-FOUR

The toes of Ko's sneakers scraped against the wall of the landing as Orion pulled her through the projected image of the false ceiling. At least Ko presumed it was projected. She had checked after Sword and Martin had gone through and, unlike the Lights which had surrounded her near the pond in Central Park, she was only able to see the ceiling when her eyes were open. Ergo, photons were coming from it, which meant electromagnetic energy was being expended in the process of being transferred from a projecting source to the air above her.

It was a good theory. Except it failed miserably to account for the feeling she had of intersecting a cold and wet membrane as she passed through the plane of the illusion.

Damn them all, Ko thought as Orion swung her down from the wall and to the floor on the other side. *Damn First World crystals and fardoors and transformations of living flesh without regard for the conservation of mass and energy. Damn Galen Sword for what he was and what he is and what his brother says he must become.*

And damn us all for killing Ja'Nette.

In spite of what Sword had just said, Ko knew she shared in that as well.

Orion landed lightly beside her in the gloom of this new section of the tower. There were no light sources from any world in the cavernous space they were in, but Ko saw a sparkling display of refracted light coming from various clear vantage spots in the area around her. It took her a disorienting amount of time to realize she was looking at the lights of Manhattan as they filtered through the multi-paned crystal pyramid that capped the World Plaza tower. She hadn't realized that there were so many other tall buildings so close to this one.

Sword apparently recognized the distorted view as well

and thought of something that Ko hadn't considered. He checked his watch and held it out for Orion.

"I know," the vampire said. "Better than you with your movements and singing crystals. The sun will rise in less than an hour. It will be time enough."

"Are you sure?" Sword asked.

Orion nodded and pointed to a pale and looming almost cubic shape that seemed to take up more than half the volume of the crystal pyramid they were in. "They're in there," he said. "All of them."

In a sweeping movement, Sword swung his long coat back and his shotgun forward and walked toward the shape that dwarfed them all.

Ko hung back even as Orion and Martin fell into step beside him unquestioningly.

Why? Ko asked herself. *Orion can crush Sword like Sword smashed the plaster wall in the tunnel. And Martin doesn't trust or understand him. So why are they following him?*

She fell into step behind the three of them, automatically running one hand over her vest to ensure that all her materiel was still in place. *Maybe it has something to do with what happened in the alley,* she reasoned, remembering the powdered remains of the shifter she had seen there and Sword's cryptic remarks about something called Close trolls. *Maybe they saw something there or did something there or . . .* She decided she really didn't care what had happened to Sword anymore. All she had to know now was what Brin had told her. It was enough. And it had been exactly what she had expected.

She caught up to the others as they circled the immense blocky shape that filled the space within the glass pyramid. It towered at least thirty feet above them with walls more than seventy feet long, once again formed of pale gray concrete. Ko could still see the imprint of the plywood sheets that had been used to make the forms.

The concrete structure was heavily textured with a random pattern of indentations and alcoves through which she supposed wiring conduits might have been intended to run. But the block or shape or whatever it was seemed unfinished. It was even hoisted up on six wide columns like stilts instead of resting directly on the concrete floor.

Sword squatted down by one of the stilts, balancing himself with his shotgun. The stilt was cylindrical, at least eight feet in circumference, but only five feet high. As were the others, it was set in another five feet from the outer edge of the block. Sword seemed to be concentrating on what the stilt was resting on and he called Ko over.

As she peered under the block, Sword shone a small palm light at the base of the column. "Does this look familiar?"

Ko saw that the column was resting on what appeared to be a bulging blue plastic bag contained in a large vat set into the floor.

"Are they all like that?" Ko asked. She knew what it was but this structure was far too massive for that kind of application.

Sword shot the beam from his palm light under the block, hitting three other stilts. Taut blue plastic glinted back from each base.

"It's floating on them, isn't it?" Sword asked.

Ko had to agree. "It's pressure equalization of some kind. But I've never seen an oil bag system work with anything this big."

"What if it's hollow?"

Ko stood up again. "It would *have* to be if Orion says everyone's inside it, wouldn't it?" Chief among Sword's many faults was his penchant for stating the obvious. "But still, this block's made of concrete. Hollow or not it should be heavy enough to pop those bags like party balloons."

Orion broke in. "What purpose do they serve?"

"Two that I know of," Sword said. "In tall buildings like this, it's common to have massive counterweights near the top that can be controlled by computer to move back and forth against any swaying caused by wind or earth tremors. Keeps the tower from oscillating. The counterweights can be huge blocks of concrete floating on an oil bed or otherwise rendered frictionless."

"This *is* a tall building," Orion observed. "For a Second World construction."

Ko wanted to find out more about that offhand remark. What were First World constructions like? She started to ask Orion to explain his comment, but the vampire spoke first.

"What is the other use?"

"Safe rooms," Sword answered. "But they're usually much smaller than this, and they're installed in embassies or government buildings. They're essentially a room within a room, specifically constructed to prevent vibration from getting out of them—especially sound. They're used for conducting secret meetings, or for sending and receiving restricted communications. Usually they're also shielded so spillover radiation from the communications equipment can't get out.''

Orion was not impressed. ''The things you humans must resort to, all because you killed your wizards so early on.''

Ko held out her hand to interrupt. She *had* to break in on that one.

But Sword wouldn't let her. ''So why would First World adepts be needing this type of technology?'' he asked Orion. ''Someplace stable, soundproof, maybe shielded from radiation? Could vampires work here in the daytime?''

Orion reached out to touch the enormous block. ''A properly trained vampire can work anywhere throughout the daylight hours, provided sunlight is avoided. Nothing so elaborate and ungainly is required.''

Martin tugged on Sword's sleeve.

''What is it, Martin?'' Sword said. He had almost forgotten the halfling's presence, Martin had been so quiet.

''Find out what inside. Go inside.''

''*Is* there a entrance?''

Martin pointed down the length of the shape and began to lope away.

Sword glanced at Ko, then he and Orion jogged after the halfling. Ko followed again, and as she ran past the glass walls she noticed that in the east, the dark sky was becoming deep blue with the dawn. She decided that the angle of the glass panes must have created the illusion of the nearby buildings she had seen earlier, but this wasn't the time to calculate that angle. *If we can just last another hour without a total screw-up, then we can go home,* Ko told herself. *Just as long as Sword doesn't do anything so stupid as to make the Second World aware of the First.*

Martin led them to an offset square of darker concrete, about four feet on each side, jutting out a few inches from the side of the block and level with its bottom surface.

''No crystals?'' Sword asked Martin.

Martin shook his head.

''Magic?'' Sword asked Orion.

''Just the spoor of Tepesh,'' the vampire replied.

Sword looked closely at Martin. "Are you *sure* you want to go in?"

Martin nodded and looked to the brightening sky. "Almost morning. Martin fine now."

"All yours, Martin," Sword and Orion stepped back as Martin pulled out the edge of the offset concrete square so that it slowly swung out like a perfectly balanced door. There had been no flash of blue light from his hands.

"What happened to your blue power?" Sword asked with concern.

Martin shrugged. "Door not locked."

Orion jumped easily to crouch within the four-foot-square opening. He disappeared inside and then Ko saw his hand emerge and motion the others to follow. Sword went next and Martin made Ko precede him so the halfling could be last and swing the doorway closed again. But before she entered the new passage, she transmitted a brief report to Forsyte who informed her the police were now searching each room in the Loft.

The cramped horizontal tunnel they moved through was more like a large ventilation shaft than a passageway. Ko was thankful that Orion was there to pull them up any long ascents if the tunnel should become vertical. Whatever Brin had done to heal her arm had also relieved her of her exhaustion. But that had been hours ago and, as if she had taken a stimulant that was wearing off, Ko felt a new onslaught of weariness now overtake her. And her little toe felt as if it were sitting in molten metal.

Fortunately, when the tunnel did angle straight up, there was a built-in ladder on one wall; a narrow ladder with thin rungs spaced too closely together to make sense, Ko thought. Until Orion explained it.

"This is a wizards' entrance," the vampire said as he tilted his head back to examine the ladder in the soft red light that spilled down the twenty-foot shaft.

"Is it unusual for wizard clans to work with shifters and vampires?" Sword asked.

"There is only one clan of wizards, Mr. Sword. Large, but only one. And they make themselves available to all."

"Even Seyshen?"

Orion turned away. "They have no choice in the matter." He began to climb before Sword could speak again.

Sword had Martin follow Orion, though he didn't explain

his reasoning. Then he stood away from the ladder. "You or me next?"

Ko didn't move. She had been trying to contact Forsyte again, but Sword's observation had been correct. The concrete block was opaque to radio and Forsyte had not replied. "Does it matter who goes next?"

Sword glanced up the shaft. "Not really. If those two can't handle whatever's up there, I doubt there's much hope for either of us."

"Maybe you should have saved Martin for anything that might come at us from behind." Sending the two most powerful members of the team ahead had been a mistake as far as Ko was concerned.

"Maybe," Sword said. "But I saw no sign of any guards the whole way up here, almost as if something important is going on." He put a hand on one of the small rungs. "My guess is that every adept connected to this enclave is already somewhere up there. Good enough reason for Orion and Martin to have gone first?"

Ko said nothing. If Sword was looking for support from her tonight, after what Brin had told her, then Sword was going to be disappointed.

"Let me put it another way, Melody. Sometimes you just have to make a decision." Sword had a strange look in his eye as he spoke, as if the words reminded him of something someone else might have said to him. He put his other hand on the rung. "And I just made one."

Sulkily, Ko followed Sword up the ladder until they emerged into a narrow, low-ceilinged room that was illuminated by the same sort of floating crystal she had seen in the passageways leading to the Pit of the Change. Sword reached out and lightly brushed his fingers against one facet about half the size of an old-style record album. Its light flickered as Sword made contact.

Standing with Martin at the side of the entrance to the shaft, Orion observed Sword's action and frowned. "I have never heard of such an effect on red crystals. It smacks of wizardry but for what reason or purpose I cannot say."

Hearing Orion speak like that frustrated Ko anew. There were so many new questions she wanted ask him now—clarify this, more details about that, define and describe, names and dates and reasons and secrets . . . and until this excursion was over, she knew Sword would never give her a chance.

That's odd, she thought suddenly. *Brin must have the same knowledge Orion has about the First World, yet I never thought to ask him . . . anything. Must have been the medication for my arm,* she decided. *I wasn't thinking clearly. That must have been it.*

While Ko stood in thought in the red-lit room, Orion, Martin, and Sword moved ahead to explore it. Sword and the vampire had to stoop over to avoid the low ceiling. Ko and Martin did not. All about them were small tables and chairs—apparently plastic children's furniture. Against one wall was a messy stack of empty take-out pizza boxes and plastic orange-juice bottles, and copies of *Byte* and *National Geographic* strewn everywhere. Most of the magazines seemed to have several pages partially ripped out and folded over. As she moved through the room to join the others, Ko was tempted to see if there were a pattern to the pages that had been marked in that way.

But Sword was more interested in what lay beyond the small doorway at the end of the long room. He crept through it, holding a hand up behind him to call for silence. Then Ko heard him swear.

Moving quietly, she came up behind him and looked past his shoulder. The space beyond the doorway was a seating gallery of sorts, like a glassed-in observation balcony, with two rows of small chairs stretching out from both sides of the doorway. *But what are you supposed to see?* Ko asked herself, pushing up on her toes—despite the sudden flare-up of pain in her left little one—trying to see past Sword.

Then she saw what Sword saw and she swore, too.

The chairs faced a wall of floor-to-ceiling glass windows that angled in from top to bottom so that whatever audience was intended to sit in the gallery would have an unobstructed view of the room that lay twenty feet below.

Ko estimated that that lower room took up three-quarters of the volume of the bizarre concrete shell they were in—it was at least fifty feet on each wall. And that innermost room was at least as complex as anything she had seen at the Jet Propulsion Laboratory or the Johnson Space Center—with bank after bank of computer equipment and monitoring consoles arranged in tiered and concentric half-circles facing away from the balcony overlooking them. Each installation, filled with flashing lights and flickering video displays, was angled at the far wall—a large white surface on which cryptic lines and geometric shapes had been drawn in an incomprehensible pattern. Each element of the diagram—which is what Ko assumed it was—had been labelled in a cursive scrawl which reminded her of the inscription she had seen in Saul Calder's clan ring.

But more strange than finding such sophisticated electronics in this unlikely location, and much more frightening, was that for all the high-tech equipment installed in the room beneath her, there was not a single person within it.

But the room *was* full of intent workers.

It was just that none of them was human.

TWENTY-FIVE

"It's mission control," Sword whispered. "But for what?"

None of those with him could offer an answer. The scene was too surreal, too badly mixed between the Second World and the First.

As he and the others crouched down by lower ledges of the viewing windows, staying hidden, Sword saw a series of computer memory components standing against one wall of the control room far below. Even from this distance, he could recognize the familiar IBM logo on their front panels. But they were being attended by wizened creatures barely three feet tall who wore powder-blue smocks and brilliantly white beards that reached past their waists. Beyond them, at least ten shifters stood with arms or wings or other manipulatory organs folded behind their backs, as if waiting for something.

Sword saw a technician wearing a large headset with earphones and a thick microphone suspended before her lips. But the headset had been cut apart and reassembled with extra metal brackets because the technician was a shifter-form creature with a baboonlike snout and whose ears swept back in leathery fans of constantly rippling flesh.

At another console, something typed feverishly with three appendages. At yet another console a diminutive wizard and a towering vampire looked first at a complex, multi-colored graph on a computer screen and then to whatever strange tricks of light filtered through the clear orb of crystal the wizard held in his hand, as if comparing data from two different sources.

A row of vampires against the large white wall wore headsets, taking instructions for the intricate lines and polygons they drew on it with slender paint brushes that dripped with something red. In the extreme left section of the room, Sword saw two shifterforms whose wrinkled gray shapes and gaping triangular mouths made him think of bats crossed with apes. The creatures argued over the remains of a small bird, gutted on the drawing surface of what appeared to be a Hewlett Packard graphic plotter reconfigured to operate with shining scalpels instead of pens. Beside them, a saffron-skinned vampire in a long chainmail shift used the end of a pencil to examine the bird's organs. At her side, another wizard took notes on a handheld computer, awkwardly balanced on one short arm.

Sword heard a roaring in his ears. He felt dizzy. The overwhelming wrongness of what he saw threatened to make him throw up his hands and pound at the glass windows and shout out a warning to all those below who didn't see the danger of what they did. So close to the power of the First World, his memory jumped as violently and as vividly as it had beneath Brin's touch. He was a child again, back at the old school, Seth sitting crosslegged nearby on the chanted grass, anxious to play, cycles before the change that forever set him apart from his elemental friend.

Galen sat on the rough lap of the gargoyle. He held one long and stony claw in his little fist, watching the dry lips move as the whispery voice of ancient rock Gave The Lesson.

Instead of the best of both worlds, the gargoyle said, *what if the worst of both were combined? Can you imagine what that would be like, Little Galen? Can you imagine?*

And Little Galen hadn't a clue. Little Galen couldn't translocate a feather or fill a waiting crystal with even the smallest spark of elemental light.

But now, so many cycles afterward, Galen Sword *could* see what might happen. He *did* know the terror and the atrocities that could arise if the greatest of humanity's arts were combined with the greatest of the adepts' by beings who cared only for advantage, for power, for victory.

It was all there before him in a room full of microchips and glowing crystals.

What the gargoyle had said had come to pass.

Can you imagine, Little Galen?

He didn't have to.

The worlds had conspired to show him what the worst could be. The only question that remained was, could the *best* be achieved?

Within himself, as if hearing soft songs through the leaves of the deep forest, Sword thought he sensed the beginning of an answer.

Ko knelt rigidly between Sword and Orion, peering over a window's bottom ledge, shock turning her body to ice.

She didn't care about the perversion of science and superstition she saw before her. She had no use or emotion for the presence of creatures that offended every tenet of biochemistry and evolution. In the entire room filled with monsters and machines, all she cared about were the two adepts, almost human normal, who sat together at a desk to the side, whispering to one another as they watched a computer screen and the white wall where the unfathomable diagram took shape.

The adepts were both female, with flawless pale skin and long, unnaturally luminous hair. Ko recognized them. Ko hated them. She knew their names.

After three long years, she had found the adepts who had destroyed Adrian Forsyte's life.

"Down there, Sword. Those two women. At the small desk."

Beside her in the dark gallery, Sword looked in the direction she indicated. She heard him inhale sharply. "The exchange students?"

"Sonja and Heidi." Ko spat out their names. "We're not leaving here without them. For Adrian's sake."

"We can try to take them," Sword said. "But we'll have to get them away from the shifters and the Tepesh."

Ko placed her hand to her transceiver and called Forsyte's name, but the concrete structure they were in was just as shielded on this level as it had been in the tunnel.

"We won't *try*, Sword. We bloody well have to do it."

Sword nodded automatically as if watching something no one else could see.

But she didn't care. It made no difference to her what Sword saw now. Even Brin's warning had no importance. It was time for Ko to do what even Sword agreed she must.

Ko made her decision. Just as Sword's search was beginning, Ko's would at last come to an end. The adepts would be hers.

Orion could taste fear and apprehension in the small balcony he shared with the others. And he could taste their anticipation as both Sword and Ko independently seemed to arrive at some inner conclusion. The halfling, however, remained a constantly changing impression of conflicting emotions, though Orion sensed that Martin shared some unadmitted bond with Sword and Ko which would, in the end, outweigh any transitory panic the halfling might feel now.

In contrast to the others, Orion felt no fear or apprehension, or even anticipation. His greatest desire and his greatest fear were both before him in the incomprehensible cabal of wizardry and technology spread out beneath the viewing gallery. Because, as he had set out to be from the moment he learned that the Seyshen had abandoned him, Orion was at last within reach of Manes Hel, Victor of Clan Tepesh.

The architect of the betrayal of Clan Isis was engrossed in her augury of a treaty fowl. Orion had recognized her tunic of woven metal and the harshly sculpted lines of her face, shaped by the consumption of uncountable souls. Ten thousand years of age, the softwind said, and for half that time Manes Hel had led the Tepesh. She had *been* the Tepesh.

Until this night, Orion thought, *when Isis will be avenged.*

Now the only obstacle Orion faced was how to challenge the Tepesh Victor. In the room below, Orion had also recognized the savage keeper he had confronted in Softwind and more than half of the other forty Tepesh who worked there. He had no doubt that Manes Hel would fall before him. Though as yet, he had no idea how to meet her in single combat when so many others of her clan were in attendance on her.

But, unlike Martin who was prey to his uncertainties, Orion felt no conflict at his dilemma. He would face it as he had always faced such matters.

With the patience of time itself. And the knowledge that he would survive.

"Any idea where they'd keep humans?" Sword's voice betrayed his anxiety. Kendall Marsh and the other prey had to be found before any action could be taken against the adepts. Sword didn't know exactly what action *could* be taken, but the fact that whatever was happening in the control room below seemed vital to both Clan Arkady and Clan Tepesh was reason enough for him to know that it should be stopped.

Orion appeared distracted as he answered. Perhaps he

wasn't used to thinking of the safety and well-being of humans. "There will be a storage pen nearby. Somewhere in this structure. So they can be close at hand when . . . needed."

"Storage pen. Needed." Sword rested a hand on one of the demolition charges he carried. If he could get down to the next level and find the human captives, then he would be able to lob some explosives into the control room. Somewhere on the outside of the concrete shell, there had to be another entrance that would lead to the rooms below.

Sword turned to Ko, ready to outline his plan.

But Ko ignored him. She peered down through the angled window, and pointed to something. "It's her. Kendall."

Sword stared intently over the window ledge, but saw only four humans in the all-too-familiar tattered and colorless clothes of New York's homeless. Perhaps beaten, perhaps drugged, they stumbled in a single file, as two shifters pushed them past the diagram wall and over to the far right corner of the room. But Sword couldn't see Marsh in the sorry line.

"Where is she?"

Ko pointed more emphatically. "Over *there*, Sword. Third one in line."

Sword felt his chest tighten as he finally picked out Marsh and understood what she had done—gone undercover. He had told her about a clinic that bought blood and plasma yet had no customers to whom it sold anything, hinting that it might be the front for a cult of self-styled blood drinkers. Now, in hindsight, he knew that instead of observing the clinic and questioning those who went to it, Marsh must have decided to infiltrate it as a blood donor from the desperate neighborhood in which it operated. He doubted she had been identified by the vampires as a reporter—Sword was certain they would have left her alone in that case. But, of course, she'd been healthy, so she had been chosen. And as Orion had said, the disgrace of the Second World was that there were so many of its people who could be stolen at will from its streets with few others noticing or caring. Sword wondered how long the Tepesh had been operating in just that fashion, feeding on the abandoned and lost in Sword's adopted world.

In the far right corner of the room below, vampires prodded the four humans into a listless group. Then the

chainmail-clad female vampire left her study of the mutilated bird and moved over to their corner. She stood in front
of the humans, lifting one's head by the chin as if judging
livestock. Marsh was the next in line, but the vampire didn't
wait.

With a reflexive action as blindingly fast as Orion's had
been in the fight with the shifter, the female vampire
snapped her head forward like a striking cobra and bit the
neck of the first human.

Sword saw the wretched man stagger back and open his
mouth in a cry that could not be heard in the balcony. But
the glass in the viewing window rattled with the strength of
it.

"Goddamn them," Ko said.

"No," Sword countered. "Blow the bastards up."

"We can't set off anything in there, Sword. Not while the
humans are in the room." She turned away, unable to watch.

Sword dropped down below the window ledge and leaned
against the small rise of wall. "Not *in* there, Melody. We'll
set off the charges on the outside of the structure. In the far
left corner. Concentrate everything we have there and the
humans should be far enough away."

Ko slipped down to match Sword's position, but she
wasn't convinced by his plan. "All that'll do is blow a hole
in this rock. Big deal."

"It is," Sword protested. "First of all, the structure's
been put together as if structural integrity and lack of vibration is essential. Even minor damage will ruin that for
them. And second of all, look at the time." He held out his
wrist for her so she could see his watch. "Twenty minutes
to dawn. If we time it right, the sun will burst in at the same
time the wall goes down."

Orion tapped an index finger against his lips. "It will be
good to see the sun again," the vampire said.

TWENTY-SIX

"**S**o I plant the charges and blow out the wall at dawn," Ko said, sounding unconvinced. "Then what?"

Sword looked over at Orion. The vampire's fangs were visible but he quickly withdrew them when he saw Sword watching him.

"Can we go through these windows?" Sword asked, pointing to the glass before them. "You and Martin jump. I'll use the rope. Grab Kendall and the other humans—"

Ko spoke sharply. "I want those adepts, Sword."

Sword glanced at Martin. "And Martin rounds up the two adepts who got Adrian." He met each of the others' eyes. "Can we do it?"

One by one, they agreed.

Ko got to her knees and told Sword to give her all the charges he was carrying. She checked her watch. "When do you want it to go?"

"Can't risk them moving the humans around down there," Sword said. "Can you rig some kind of detonator that you can bring back up here so we can see what's happening?"

"Can't use radio," Ko said. Her eyes went out of focus for a moment. "But I can leave a radio detonator outside the block and run a wire down to it. Okay. Done."

Sword reached over and slapped Martin's arm. "You go with her. Just in case."

The halfling pounded his fist against his chest. "Martin keeper. Melody safe."

Sword handed the last of his explosive charges to Ko. "Try to position the charges so the glass from the tower's roof will fall in on the structure and not out to the street below." Ko nodded. "And if anything goes wrong," Sword added, "get out of here the most public way you can. We'll meet back at . . . I guess the Loft isn't safe anymore."

Ko jerked her head at Orion. "We'll meet at his hotel. I know which one it is. See if he'll tell you." She crept away from the gallery window, then got to her feet at the doorway to the narrow anteroom with the shaft. She looked back. "Let's go, Martin. We're going to help Adrian."

Martin grunted something Sword didn't understand and took off through the door, bounding ahead of Ko.

Orion returned to watching the control room through the viewing windows. "Your associates are working well with you this night, Mr. Sword."

Sword nodded. "Guess there's a first time for everything." He checked the control room again. Marsh was still standing in the far right corner. But only two other humans stood with her. The body of the fourth human lay on the floor like so much discarded rubbish. His skin was ashen.

"Will that one become a vampire, now?"

Orion leaned his forehead against the window and sighed. "Really, Mr. Sword, your Second World legends are so tedious. Vampires are a natural race. We are born, not made. If the Victor had wished, she might have left that prey enough life to be as a *golem* for her clan. But such trickery is not needed in these times."

Sword was surprised to find himself feeling embarrassed by his question. "Just checking," he said. And then he made a strangled choking noise as in the left far corner of the control room the flickering outline of a fardoor formed and he recognized who was stepping through it.

Dmitri.

Orion leaned closer. "Is that the Ronin from Softwind? The skull?"

"Yes," Sword said in a cold voice. It *was* Dmitri. It could be nothing else. From the way the dead white skin pulled over the fleshless, hideously swollen skull, from the way the bony fingers clutched at the ornate silver crucifix that hung on his chest, from the blue tunic and pants that fluttered on his seven-foot-tall frame, the way the awful eyes swirled with glowing silver specks in pockets of translucent azure liquid, this was the creature who had killed Marcus Askwith and had tried to kill Sword.

"I heard he was dead," Orion said.

"He was worse than dead," Sword explained. "I threw him into a one-sided fardoor.

"Perhaps you did not throw him hard enough, Mr. Sword."

Dmitri stalked through the room with long insectlike strides until he was at the side of the Victor of Tepesh. A wizard hurried to join them, climbing up onto a chair and then onto the top of a computer display to be at their eye level.

The Victor, Dmitri, and the small wizard bent their heads together for a brief conversation, then the wizard turned to the room, clapped his hands, and called out an order. Except for a few groups of shifters and vampires waiting at the sides of the room, the other adepts hurried to what appeared to be preassigned stations. Dmitri wrapped both hands around his crucifix and Sword could see the creature's thin feral lips pull back over cracked and gumless teeth in what could only be a smile.

As the electric lights in the room dimmed to half-level, Sword saw a brilliant flare of red burst out from the top of the central console closest to the screen.

Two wizards hopped up on chairs and held wand-shaped devices over the console, taking readouts from small calculator-type instruments in their hands. Together, they both turned and nodded at the wizard with Dmitri and the Tepesh Victor. The Victor and the wizard began another discussion. The wizard appeared to pull a small yellow flower from the air and Dmitri shook his head vigorously.

With all adepts in the control room keeping their attention fixed on the wizard and the Victor, Sword risked moving to the far end of the gallery to look down into the console from which the red light poured.

Ten red crystals were aligned within it, all gigantic, two almost the size of the Crystal of the Change Arkady.

Orion crouched beside Sword. "What we are looking at is beyond a fortune. Those crystals are so large, so powerful . . . a dozen clans would be bankrupted by the expenditure of any two such crystals."

What could be worth that? Sword thought uneasily. He had no answer.

"Another fardoor opens," Orion observed.

It was the same one Dmitri had entered through. This time, though, four small shifters with faces reminiscent of wolverines waddled through carrying a glowing blue humanoid form on a stretcher made of hide and wood.

"What's that?" Sword asked as the shifters dropped the glowing body in front of the console with the crystals, then began to lift it to balance on its feet. Sword studied the outline of the shape as it rose, posed stiffly as a statue. "Is it a shifter of some sort?"

Orion was noncommittal. "Perhaps. Whatever it is, it's coldblasted."

"Is *that* what that means?"

"Conscious but incapable," Orion said. "A curse to be feared, that can last for centuries. Though those who endure it so long seldom survive with their intellect intact."

Frozen for centuries while remaining conscious, Sword thought. He felt himself shiver at the horror of it. "But what are they doing to it now?"

Shifters and wizards alike swarmed around the cold-blasted form. The body was upright and two wizards stood on chairs at either side, hammering metal spikes through the body's forearms.

"Can it *feel* that?" Sword grimaced in dismay.

"The coldblasted feel *everything,*" Orion answered.

When the spikes had penetrated both arms, a second pair of wizards attached thick red and black cables to both ends of each spike with copper-colored alligator clips.

"Those are car-battery booster cables!" Sword said.

"As you have been learning, there is much overlap in the technology of the worlds, Mr. Sword."

The other ends of each set of cables were connected to a gray metal junction box that sat on the floor near the crystal console. A single thick cable stretched from the junction box to the console, where it disappeared inside a cabinet cover.

As Sword watched mesmerized, Dmitri approached the coldblasted figure and scraped his talons along its back. Sword felt a twinge, remembering the touch of those claws in his own mind.

"Ko and Martin are returning," Orion suddenly said. "They are not in a great hurry."

Sword looked over his shoulder toward the doorway, but no one was there.

"They are at the bottom of the shaft," Orion said without turning from the window. "It will be a short time before they arrive here. But look below. There is a counter to lift the spell of living ice."

Sword looked down on the control room and saw a fat, brown-skinned man with a short stripe of black hair that stretched from his forehead to beneath the back of the collar of his white suit. The man stood before the blue glowing form of the coldblasted shifter and took a handful of red crystals from his jacket pocket. Then he looked nervously around, tugged on his shirt collar with a finger, and chose a single crystal with his free hand.

Sword blinked. The counter had *three* arms—one on the left and two on the right.

The counter began to move his mouth in a chant and the crystal he held began to glow. Then, as it continued to increase in brilliance in the dimly lit room, Sword saw that the blue glow around the shifter began to diminish.

As Ko and Martin returned to the balcony, the red crystal winked off like a light bulb burning out. The counter began picking through his handful of crystals, obviously looking for the next one to use.

Martin squatted down beside Sword, Ko beside Orion. She held a radio transmitter in her hand from which trailed a thin black wire.

"Everything's set," Ko reported with satisfaction. "Charges are in place. This will fire them." She held up the transmitter. "And Adrian's ready to open the van doors when he hears our running feet. Sky's pretty bright out there, too. Not much longer." She looked down at the control room for the first time. "What the hell is going on down there now?"

Sword was surprised when Martin laughed. "Coldblasted shifter. Big surprise wake up with Tepesh." He laughed again, making a sound like a barking dog.

"The guy with three arms is a counter," Sword explained for Ko. "He's using his red crystals to take away the glow around the frozen shifter. See it?"

Ko frowned. "I see it, Sword. I just don't understand it."

"That shifter has been connected to the greatest treasure in red crystals I have ever seen," Orion said.

"Oh, yeah?" Ko pushed herself closer to the glass to see more clearly. "In series or in parallel?"

"Melody," Sword said. "Give it a rest."

In the control room, as the counter extinguished another red crystal, there remained little of the shifter's blue glow. As the counter picked out the smallest crystal he had, Sword saw that the coat on the frozen shifter was magnificent, almost metallic silver in color. And the creature's snout was solid and impressive. *Too bad it's a murderous, flesh-eating shifter that deserves to die,* Sword thought.

The last red crystal flared out and the final residue of blue faded from the shifter's body. Sword saw the shifter start to move its arms and legs very slowly, blinking large green eyes in confusion.

Beside Sword, Martin stood up against the window until his whole body was pressed against it and his hands began hitting the glass harder and harder.

Both Sword and Orion reached up at the same instant to grab Martin and pull him down.

"What do you think you're doing!" Sword said. "They'll see you down there. Do you want to be like that coldblasted shifter?"

Martin's mouth hung open. "Already am," the halfling said in an anguished voice. "Coldblasted shifter *Astar.*" Then Sword understood Martin's reaction. He had heard that name many times.

The shifter wired into the wizards' machine was Martin's father.

TWENTY-SEVEN

Sword knew his own strength alone was not enough to keep Martin down and quiet, but he had to try. He clamped his hands on Martin's shoulders, doing his best to keep the frantic halfling still.

"What happened to your father, Martin? Why was he chanted?"

Martin tapped the backs of his hands to his forehead. "Don't know don't know. Martin bad. Do bad things. Martin taken far away. Astar chanted. Bad Martin. Bad Martin."

"No," Sword said urgently, "that's wrong, Martin. You aren't bad. You aren't."

"Martin bad. Lose father. Martin good, father still be with Martin." The halfling took his hands away from his head and placed them on Sword's wrists. "Martin want father. Martin want father back now." He began to squeeze.

"Don't, Martin." Sword kept his voice even, not wanting to alarm the halfling more. "We can get your father back when we rescue the humans and take the adepts. You're good, Martin. We'll help you."

Sword felt the pressure on his wrists increase. He heard the bones beneath his skin begin to grind against each other. "Together, Martin, I promise."

The halfling looked deep into Sword's eyes, as if using unnamed senses to probe for the slightest hint of falsehood or equivocation.

Sword held Martin's gaze. He did not turn away. Nor would he ever turn away again.

"I want my father back, too, Martin."

The pressure eased.

"Galen Sword help Martin. Martin help Galen Sword."

Sword held out his fist in the salute of the First World, loosely bound to give Martin a choice of response.

And the halfling chose to brush his knuckles against Sword's with his own hand opened flat.

Galen Sword was his leader now and Martin would follow. The covenant they made was not spoken in words and so could not be broken.

Sword turned from Martin to Orion. "Any theories why Astar is hooked up to that machine down there?"

Orion hesitated over his words, having trouble thinking in a Second World frame of reference. He held out empty hands. "I cannot say, Mr. Sword. The shifter . . . Astar . . . he would have the blue power he passed on to his son. But it would only be for the opening of things that are closed. Red crystals can do it just as well. Sometimes better."

"But why so many crystals?" Sword asked the question they had all wrestled with. "What are they trying to open that needs that much substance? That much glitter?"

He felt Ko staring at him as he used the First World terms as if they were native to his vocabulary. *Well, once they must have been,* Sword thought. *And they will be again.*

"There's *got* to be an answer. *What* are they trying to open?"

Then all expression drained from Ko's face. "No," she whispered as she looked down into the control room. "They can't do that, too . . . they *can't* . . ."

Sword, Martin, and Orion turned back to the windows to find what Ko saw.

Sword saw it, too, and Sword understood.

They were coming back.

Crimson arcs of energy danced from the fortune in First World red crystals installed in the console. Astar clenched his fists and howled as jagged bolts of blue power crackled from his hands to the metal spikes in his forearms and along the cables to merge with the crystals' fire.

Only the computer screens and monitors added more light to the control room. The floor shook, the glass rattled, and on the white wall, intricately inscribed, completely smooth, even in the strobing flashes of the unchained elemental energies that had no name in the human world, Sword saw the perimeter of another fardoor take shape.

It grew across the wall like a water stain spreading, shifting quickly to match the lines and shapes of the red-painted diagrams it traced.

It grew beyond the confines of any room. It grew to a size that Sword had only witnessed once before—the size of a cave mouth hidden deep in the caverns of the Arkady Pit of the Change.

"No," Ko whispered as the fardoor solidified and the first images of what lay beyond became clearer. "They just can't . . ."

Then the fardoor was perfect.

The crystals had carved out the path with their energy. Astar's living blue power had opened the impenetrable barrier that was found at the end of that path. And the monstrous consolidation of First and Second World arts had fused to create a fardoor that had reached through space—

—*and time.*

Past the fardoor's perimeter, Sword saw Tomas Roth and Morgana LaVey exactly as they had been two weeks earlier when he had collapsed the fardoor that led back to New York and had trapped them in a cave before a rushing wave of invincible Seyshen warriors.

They had been and still were seconds from death—a death Sword had thought inescapable. Yet there they were, Roth's face slashed and bloodied by Seth's parting blow, Morgana's naked body fixed halfway through her transformation from humanform to something ancient and scaled. Her eyes were reptilian slits. A sinuous forked tongue snaked from her open mouth.

Then Morgana saw the fardoor as it opened again—to her as if only a second had passed since Sword had collapsed it. All around were the shifters of the clan she led and they saw their escape, too.

But just behind came the unstoppable black tide of massed Seyshen.

Morgana silently screamed her commands to her warriors, pointing at the Seyshen, the light from the fardoor glinting on the yellow scales that rippled across her stomach.

The shifters were warriors. For their Victor, they turned their backs on freedom and prepared to face the enemy.

Morgana took her consort's arm as he stumbled, blinded by his own blood. She retreated from the fardoor to retrieve the Crystal of the Change Arkady where it had fallen after Martin had thrown it at them to force them back, just two weeks ago.

Ko turned urgently to Sword. "You can't let them back, Sword! They're dead! The Seyshen killed them! If they come back, they'll only start the war all over again."

Orion stood beside Sword now. "She's right, Mr. Sword. To permit the Victor of Arkady to return is to risk the threat of a final conflict between both the worlds. You've seen what just the remnants of Arkady could do when joined with Clan Tepesh. Imagine if both clans were at their full strength. You must stop them."

"How?" Sword asked. He had no weapon which could stand against what was assembled in the control room.

But Ko held up the detonator.

"This way!" she said triumphantly. "When the wall goes, the perimeter will be disrupted." She pressed a switch on the detonator, then moved abruptly to the window to watch her handiwork.

Without thought, Sword leapt at her, pushing her into Orion, and snatched the detonator from her hand. She had armed it, but not fired it.

Ko erupted in fury. "What are you doing, Sword! Do you *want* them to come back again after what they did before?"

Sword stepped back, out of Ko's reach, detonator held high and out of the way. "Of course I don't! But look down there. Remember where you placed the explosives."

Beyond the fardoor, Morgana had picked up the Crystal of the Change from the cave floor and was struggling with it, inching toward survival.

Sword appealed to Ko. "If we fire the charges now, we'll kill Astar!"

Martin jumped from foot to foot. An enormous bolt of red energy hit the high ceiling of the control room and dislodged a handful of concrete with a roar.

Ko turned to Martin. "Your father's a powerful shifter, Martin. Astar can survive an explosion. But if Morgana and Roth come back, they'll hunt you down and kill you! They'll kill all of us! Tell Sword to push the button while he has the chance!"

Another flash of red blasted through a gallery window, spraying them all with glass.

Beyond the fardoor, Morgana and Roth were two steps from passing through to the control room.

The detonator was heavy in Sword's hand.

Morgana and Roth had tried to kill him. And Ko was right. They would try again.

He put his thumb on the fire button. He looked at Martin.

"Martin," he said over the roar and the rumble of the elements unleashed below. "I . . . *won't!*"

"Sword!" Ko shouted.

Orion stepped forward. "Don't be a—"

Sword swung his shotgun up and held it on the vampire. He said two words.

"I promised."

Martin scurried to Sword's side and crouched there, growling at Ko and Orion.

In the control room, the thunder of the elements was replaced by howls and screams and the applause of padded and furred hands.

Roth and Morgana had passed through the fardoor.

They *were* back.

TWENTY-EIGHT

"You asshole!" Ko roared. "This isn't just another one of your classic screw-ups, Sword. This is a real war you've started here! You know how many people are gong to die because of you?"

Sword didn't take his eyes off Orion. Alone, Sword knew he wouldn't have a prayer of making the vampire stand off. But with Martin beside him to give even a split second of interference, he knew he could pull the trigger of his shotgun before Orion could reach him. Ko was another matter. He didn't understand what she was talking about.

"How is a war between Arkady and the Scyshen going to end up killing *people,* Melody? What are you talking about?"

She made her hands into fists and clenched them at her sides. "You *never* understand, Sword. You never understand *anything.*"

She took a step toward him and he instinctively twitched the shotgun in her direction.

"You'd shoot me?" She closed her eyes for a good two seconds. "You'd risk a First and Second World war to save a *shifter,* but you'd shoot *me?*" She held her hands out, almost speechless. "You're truly insane, Sword. You're—"

Orion placed his hand on her shoulder and began to step away from the window.

"I believe there is a better chance of not being detected if we—"

Ko spun around and punched Orion in the chest. He looked down in surprise but made no move to defend himself. "Really, Ko, I—"

"NO!" Ko yelled. She spun back the other way, trying to break out of his grip. "Let go of me, now! I've had it with—"

Orion let go.

Ko obviously hadn't expected such quick compliance and she lurched backward.

Orion reached out to catch her extended arm.

She took his hand in hers.

But it was too late.

Ko's elbow swung back against the window behind her and kept on going, sending shards of glass out into the control room and onto the adepts below.

"Remarkable," Orion said. "After all this time, a mistake."

TWENTY-NINE

Sword resisted a sudden impulse to go and push Ko the rest of the way through the window. Instead, he dropped to his knees and risked a quick look below.

The reaction to their presence was immediate.

Sword could see a phalanx of shifters forming around Morgana and Roth and the Crystal of the Change Arkady. A large bearlike shifterform was now carrying the foot-wide, spherical working crystal set in an ornate stand of Lights' finest gold, which depicted the kneeling figures of the clan's First Four. Other shifters wrapped glittering scaled robes around their Victor and her consort. Roth himself was pressing his hands to his face and Sword could glimpse the familiar glow of a blue power at work. When he took his hands away, though his face was still covered with blood, the gashes Seth had left were completely healed.

Something thudded into the wall just below the window Sword looked through but he couldn't see what. An instant later there was a sudden explosion.

"Splitters," Orion announced, now standing with Ko against the gallery's back wall. "Working crystals set to explode."

The window in front of Sword shattered and fell on him as a second splitter found its target. It hit the back wall and bounced back toward Sword. He saw it was an object shaped like two black rubber balls half-melted together. One sphere had a small red crystal embedded in it. The crystal was growing brighter and brighter so Sword simply reached out and touched his finger against it.

The crystal faded.

"So much for splitters," Sword said.

After five similar weapons had been thrown into the gallery and Sword had sapped each one, the first attack ended.

Sword stuck his head up for an instant and what he saw made him call Martin over.

"Look over the side, quickly," Sword told the halfling. Martin did. "Martin bad again?" he asked, forlorn.

By the console, Sword had seen that Astar had been cold-blasted once more, the metal spikes still piercing his arms. Sword had also seen a steady movement of shifters and vampires escaping into the smaller fardoor through which Astar had been brought. The ten large red crystals had already been taken to safety.

"Galen Sword help Martin father?" Martin asked. It was clear he didn't think it was possible.

Sword called over to Orion and Ko. "Will the coldblasting let Astar survive the explosion if I fire it now?"

"He will not fragment," Orion said, "but he will experience the force of the blast."

Ko seemed to have regained her control and spoke in an expressionless voice. She didn't bother to look at Sword. "It doesn't matter anymore. If any adepts got outside the block and are coming after us through the wizard's entrance, then they've ripped out the detonator's wire by now."

"But what if they're avoiding the sun or people coming to work?" Sword said. "What if they're all trying to get out through the fardoor?"

"It's too late, Sword. You've screwed up for the last time."

Angrily, Sword rose in the window again, preparing to start a diversion that would allow him to drop down and move Astar before—

"Martin! Up here! Look!"

Martin stood up beside Sword and followed his pointing hand.

Astar was being carried back through the fardoor on his stretcher.

Sword and Martin ducked down. "At least he'll be safe, Martin. At least we know what's happened to him."

"Next time?" Martin asked.

Sword nodded as he gestured sharply for the others to cover their ears. Then he jumped up in the window, held the detonator over his head, and yelled, "*Pendraaagonn!*"

Each adept remaining in the control room stared up at him and from a dozen, from twenty, from more than half of them came another cry.

"*Sword!*"

Morgana and Roth pushed through the protective ranks of their shifters. "Kill him!" Roth shouted.

But Morgana pulled her consort back to her. She hissed in Sword's direction but gave no command of her own for attack. Instead, she called out to her shifters to run for the fardoor and they did so, pushing the other adepts out of their way.

It was a stampede in Dante's inferno and to Sword it was perfect. Roth and Morgana were rushing straight toward the spot where Ko had planted the charges.

He waited the two seconds it took for them to reach the correct point just in front of the fardoor, and then he pressed the button.

The fardoor became the mouth of Hell.

THIRTY

Orion felt the shockwave of the explosion pass through the floor and throw Ko against him. He had no way of judging the strength of the charges but he thought that it seemed large enough to destroy the entire building the control room was built atop.

After a few seconds, though, when he had not detected the beginning of the long fall through floor after floor, he opened his eyes and allowed the muscles of his inner ear to tighten again, restoring his hearing.

He heard moans from the control room below and the sounds brought him deep pleasure. He saw rich golden light shine brightly through a cloud of dust that billowed inside the control room and the balcony. He smelled city air, full of the promise of morning and dawn.

He stepped to the now glass-free window frame to see with his own eyes what his other senses told him. Sword and Ko had done it. The east wall and corner of the Tepesh structure were missing, replaced by a mound of gray concrete rubble. He could see through to what was left of the surrounding glass walls of the World Plaza pyramid.

Orion held his hands out to the death and destruction beneath him. He could smell fresh blood. It made him feel young again.

With one quick glance to see that Sword and Ko and Martin had not been damaged by the blast, Orion dropped through the window frame to land on a clear spot of the control room's floor twenty feet below, behind a bank of machines with screens that fluttered with static and human gibberish.

Slowly, like a connoisseur taking in the bouquet of a fine wine, Orion tilted his head back and sampled the air. He sifted past the blood, past the explosive's trace by-products, seeking the one scent which would tell him his hunt was over.

It was there, still in the air.

He scented the presence of the Victor of Tepesh and his fangs emerged for battle.

Kendall Marsh and the other human prey appeared to be unscathed in the far right corner, so Sword knew he had achieved his most important goal. But the rubble was too deep by the wall that had held the small fardoor and he couldn't be sure that Morgana and Roth had been caught in the blast. He glanced over the edge of the balcony and saw that Orion had made it to the control room level and for a moment wondered if he could find the same way down.

Then he remembered what Orion was, and went to Ko who was standing in silence as she looked at the damage—and asked for her rope.

He could see the resentment in Ko's eyes, worse than it had ever been. "What about the adepts?" she asked. She didn't have to say anything more. There had been close to one hundred of them in that room. But Ko only wanted to know about two.

"They're still down there," he said, gesturing to the desk he had seen Sonja and Heidi huddled beneath. Bullets and knives might not work against most adepts, but they all seemed to share a healthy respect for large pieces of falling concrete. "You'll have to hurry. There could be other fardoors, other hidden stairways to the tower."

Ko took her rope to the edge of the balcony, tied a reef knot around two window frames, yanked on it, then stepped over the edge and rappelled twenty feet to the ground without saying a word.

When she had unhooked the rope from the climber's clip on her belt, Sword took the same route down.

By the time Sword hit the ground, Orion was out of sight and Ko was heading directly for the adepts' hiding place. He considered offering his help, but he knew she wouldn't take it. Not for what she wanted to do now. It was personal. It was for Forsyte.

Sword waved the rope back and forth and called up to the balcony. "Come on, Martin! Down here!"

Martin stuck his head out the balcony window above Sword. "Big noise," he said.

"Look what it did." Sword pointed his thumb over his shoulder at the ruin of the wall.

Martin looked, then rolled forward from the window, caught the rope in his feet, and slid down at a speed not very different from freefall.

"Find father now?" he asked.

"First we'll get Kennie. Then we'll get some rest. And then we'll start looking for your father." Sword began to walk over to the protected corner where he had last seen Marsh.

And we'll talk to the police about Ja'Nette, Sword thought. *And to Ko about where she got all her strange ideas about a war between the clans turning into a war between the First and Second Worlds.* He was intensely curious to find out *everything* that Brin might have told her.

Marsh and the two men with her were still alive, though unconscious. Carefully, Sword lifted Marsh's head in his arms and said her name over and over again while Martin looked on. Her hair was caked with concrete dust and her dark face was pale with it. She seemed to be trying to rouse herself but whenever her eyelids fluttered, Sword could only see the whites of her rolled-up eyes.

"That Galen Sword friend?" Martin asked.

"That's right," Sword said as he arranged Marsh into what he hoped would be a more comfortable condition and began to check the other two humans beside her.

"Too bad," Martin said.

"I know," Sword agreed. The other humans who had been Tepesh prey were also out cold though breathing evenly. "But I hope she'll get better soon."

"Never get better," Martin said.

Sword didn't need to hear that kind of talk right now. "What do you mean?"

But Martin didn't answer. He simply remained sitting nearby, and pointed at the side of his neck.

With a cold chill of fear moving through him, Sword went back to Marsh and gently pulled away the filthy sweater jacket that she wore tucked up around her neck.

"Golem," Martin said sadly. "Galen Sword friend *golem."*

Sword didn't have to know what the word meant. There were twin punctures on Marsh's neck. That was as bad as it could get.

And then, fifty feet away, Melody Ko screamed.

* * *

In the first glimmer of dawn, now only minutes away, Ko saw the barest shadow of movement among the debris that lay behind the desk where Sonja and Heidi had been working. She moved quickly and silently to block any escape route the adepts might try.

She had nylon restraints on her vest. She had a taser and a gas pistol with a clip of three tranquilizer darts. And if it came down to it, she had saved one last demolition charge. Sonja and Heidi would have to tell her exactly what they had done to Forsyte that night in the lab, or they would suffer a worse fate themselves.

There was no morning breeze and the dust from the explosion still hung unmoving in the air. From outside the structure, Ko could hear the occasional faint tinkle of glass as, she assumed, damaged panes fell from the support scaffolding of the glass pyramid. The hard part of what she planned to do next was going to be getting her captives back down the tower to the van without running into the police and the fire department. She considered using the hidden stairway, which was presumably how the other shifters and vampires and adepts had escaped so quickly.

Ko stopped behind the console closest to the desk and prepared the gas pistol. She couldn't see Sword, which was probably just as well because he could be counted on to do something which would give her away. She couldn't see Orion or Martin either.

Fine with me, Ko thought as she slipped the safety off the pistol. *I'll do it all on my own. Turns out that's the best way, anyway.*

She stood up, slipped the first dart into place, then charged the desk.

Sonja and Heidi were still there and Ko felt like whooping with joy. Her sneakers skidded over a pile of rubble, but she maintained her balance and kept the pistol trained on the two adepts as she waved them out from their hiding spot.

They stood calmly, raising their hands high at Ko's command. *So long ago it seems,* Ko thought, *but they haven't changed at all.* She wondered how old they were. She remembered the age of the shifters—virtual immortality—and what she felt made her want to kill them.

"Surprised to see me?" she challenged, surprised herself

that their capture had been so easy. *Why did they wait so long?* she thought. *Why didn't they run off with the others?*

Sonja shook her head and her metallic blond hair made a slow waving motion. It didn't seem dulled by the layer of dust covering most everything else now. Ko looked at Heidi's hair. It was free of dust, too.

"Not really," Sonja said calmly in answer to Ko's question. "It took you long enough."

Ko's finger twitched on the pistol's trigger. If she had to tranquilize them and could carry only one away, then she'd take Sonja.

Ko asked the question that had been in her every day for three years. "What did you do to Adrian Forsyte?"

"Who?" Heidi asked. She glanced out through the blasted open wall. Sunrise was only seconds away.

"Dr. Adrian Forsyte," Ko said. "The physicist at MIT who—"

"Oh, him," Sonja exclaimed. "He was okay, wasn't he?"

"With the glasses?" Heidi asked. "And the, ahem, . . ." She gave her partner an exaggerated wink and they both giggled.

Ko knew what they were trying to do and she refused to go along, but it made her even angrier just the same. Just the very same. She stepped forward to give them a taste of the kind of payback they could expect if they didn't restore Forsyte to the way he was before they destroyed him.

But before Ko could make a move, the sun rose and she found out what they had been waiting for.

As if they were two puppets run by the same controls, both adepts held their arms out in front of them, hands at waist level, palms down.

"Don't try anything," Ko warned. But even then she knew she had waited too long.

The adepts rolled their eyes back in their heads, twisted their heads on their necks, and began vibrating in perfect unison. Their platinum hair shook away from their bodies, becoming fuller, lighter, taking on the icy sheen of metal in the new sunlight.

Like they're hooked up to a Van de Graaf generator, Ko thought. That's what their hair looked like, now suspended around their heads in a spherical shape, held aloft and apart by the crackling of a static charge.

Ko stepped back, not understanding where that voltage was coming from.

Their clothing began to crackle and also lifted away from their bodies.

"No! Stop it . . .," Ko said, but even she couldn't hear her voice over the sound they made.

Then both adepts closed their eyes, and the moment their lids met they rose from the ground and flew at Ko crackling and snapping and humming like high-tension wires in a rainstorm.

Ko fired her pistol wildly as she screamed, unprepared for the sudden loss of such an important dream. She fell back on the rubble, feeling rough edges dig into her. She fired twice more but the adepts wheeled and circled through the control room, then rushed out through the open wall like foam on an ocean wave and vanished in the shafts of the light they had waited for.

Sword arrived on the run, but when he saw what had happened he stood beside Ko and watched the adepts whirl away. Martin crouched beside him.

"Flyers," Martin breathed. He began to wave to their small figures, and then stopped, as if caught repeating a childish habit.

"Melody, I'm sorry," Sword said. "But at least we know they're still around."

Ko got to her feet stiffly, refusing Sword's offer to help. She clipped her pistol back to her vest.

"Where's Orion?" she asked without looking at Sword.

"Sun's up," Sword said. "Probably long gone. And we should get going, too."

"What a waste," Ko said bitterly. "What a bloody bloody waste." She slipped again on the rubble as she walked away from Sword, heading for the easy way out of the structure.

She was halfway there when the first vampire dropped in front of her and lunged.

THIRTY-ONE

The sun rose and this time it was not Orion's enemy.

His enemy was the Tepesh and he could scent their presence everywhere within the shadows of the rubble and the ruined wall. But those who burrowed frantically to hide from the slightest glancing ray of sunlight were of no concern to him. He scorned them as weaklings who could not master their adept bodies' simplest power—the power of control.

Let the sunlight take them, Orion thought disdainfully as he prowled the shattered slabs of fallen concrete. *And let it take those who sought the shelter of the fardoor and the hidden passages in this tower.*

But there were those among the Tepesh who did not fear the sun. Who knew control. Who had not fled.

Orion's senses told him that three Tepesh remained among the destruction he had brought to their enterprise with Clan Arkady. And Orion knew that there was only one purpose to their continued presence.

He smiled as he stalked his killing ground. His fangs ached to feel the pressure of succumbing flesh. He was the reason the three Tepesh remained, and he would not disappoint them.

As he waited patiently in a protected corner for one of his foes to make the first error, Orion heard a cry from a section of the ruined concrete shell where its outer walls still held. It was Ko, but the sound she made was no response to danger. It was anguish for some great loss.

Orion heard two sets of running footfalls and knew that Sword and the halfling were rushing to Ko's position. Though he had never cared much for humans and their confusing ways, Orion was oddly gratified that these three had survived the night with him. There was a refreshing fire of purpose in Ko and Martin, and many mysteries still to fathom in Sword.

A breakneck fluttering sound crackled through the air above him and Orion saw two fliers sweep through the sky and to safety, charged by the dawn's first light. He presumed they were what had prompted Ko's cry. She had seen so little of the real inhabitants of existence.

Orion brought his senses back to bear on his immediate surroundings and knew at once that his had been the first mistake. Even as that thought formed in his mind, he felt the wrenching impact of two heavy booted feet strike his back to throw him forward against a layer of fist-sized rocks.

As he fell onto the rubble, his hands grasped at handfuls of stones, so when he hit the ground and rolled to the side he was able to hurl projectiles with numbing speed at the Tepesh who scrambled to his feet behind him.

Orion didn't even have to see his attacker. His hearing was acute enough to guide his hand, and the first rock punctured his attacker's skull.

By the time Orion regained his feet, the Tepesh male was writhing on the ground, his bootshod feet kicking wildly, his hands flailing in hapless, random motion.

Orion considered his fallen adversary and recognized him as one of the two male attendants who had accompanied the belligerent keeper in Softwind. The injury to the brain was severe, even by vampire standards and, Orion calculated, at least ten minutes would pass before the young Tepesh could fight or even move again.

Orion bent over his victim to ensure that those ten minutes would become eternity, and in less than a minute, he had detached the head and tossed it beyond reach of the body's jerking arms and legs.

The vampire had been young. With his somatic integrity breeched, the first signs of rot were immediate but subdued. It would take fully half an hour before he became dust. Orion quickened the process by throwing the still-twitching body into a patch of sunlight.

Two Tepesh remained, and the scent of the Victor grew closer.

Orion pretended indifference and stood in a shadow by the rapidly decomposing body of the Tepesh attendant, slowly passing his hand back and forth through the golden sunlight that made a lustrous wall of rippling shafts in the dust that still filled the air. He had seen humans make the same motion with their hands over lit candles and now he understood the attraction of something so beguiling and so harmful.

He heard footsteps behind him, adept soft and vampire careful. He continued to stare into the sunlight streaming past him, thinking of nothing but the scene his senses created for him.

The scene was perfect. Orion spun as the second attacker was in mid-leap. He thrust out both hands to deflect the angle of the attack and flipped the Tepesh high through the air.

Chainmail sparkled in the sunlight and Orion bellowed with the bloodlust finally upon him. Manes Hel—in metal shift and spiked battle mask—had tried her best and she had failed. Now it was Orion's turn.

But as he ran through the veil of glowing dust to the central area of the ruined control room where he had thrown her, he saw that he had neglected to account for others taking part in his fight.

Manes Hel had landed nimbly in front of Melody Ko and before Orion could warn Ko, the Tepesh Victor struck.

In the second it took Orion to reach striking range, the Victor held Ko as living hostage to ward off attack. The human's arm was twisted behind her back. The Victor's claws embraced the human's throat.

Orion hesitated, which was all that was needed to show the Victor that the human *did* mean something to him. Orion could see no sign of expression behind the protective Tepesh battle mask of metal and leather, but he saw her grip tighten on Ko's neck.

Then Sword and Martin arrived and, as Orion had, they paused.

Sword raised his shotgun. "Melody, you all right?"

Ko's voice was strangled but intelligible. "What do you think, Sword? I'm getting to like this happening to me?"

Sword glanced at Orion and the vampire was curious to see that there was no sign of desperation in Sword, nor any apparent willingness to negotiate for Ko's release. There was actually the barest flicker of a smile on his lips.

"Just remember what happened last time," Sword said evenly. "We don't want to overwork Brin."

Is that a code? Orion thought incredulously. *Don't they know that Manes Hel will eviscerate Ko with one—*

Ko slammed down her heel on the Victor's foot.

The Victor blinked in surprise and looked down at Ko as if pleased by her victim's pitiful attempt to resist. In that split second of inattention, Ko twisted forward and the vampire flew over her shoulder.

Orion heard no crack of bone. Ko had obviously learned her lesson. And then he was on the Tepesh Victor and slicing through chainmail with claws and fangs and—

—this close to her, his senses were deceived no longer.

He ripped the battle mask from her face and threw it a hundred feet away with a furious snap of his wrist.

This was not Manes Hel he fought. It was the Tepesh keeper who had faced him in Softwind.

He howled with outrage and the keeper struck savagely at him, forcing him from her and giving her time to gain her feet again.

Orion rolled to his back and jumped to his feet from a full horizontal position. He now stood in a pool of shadow from the dawn. Five feet away, the keeper stood in the same. But between them the sunlight streamed through the dust-filled air like a river of molten rock.

"Your Victor has no honor!" Orion cried to provoke her. "To hide behind the clothes of others. To dishonor her own clan's battlemask is shameful!"

The keeper laughed at Orion, baring her fangs. "I hid behind the mask, *Isis*. My Victor hides from nothing. It is you who bring shame to the memory of your clan by being so easily fooled."

Orion heard Sword pump shells into his shotgun.

"No, Mr. Sword, this is *my* fight. For *my* clan."

Orion did not take his eyes from the keeper, but at the edge of his peripheral vision, he saw Sword lower his weapon.

"That's right, Mr. Sword," the keeper mocked. "This is his *last* battle. For a clan pulled by the moon!"

Orion spread his arms wide. "Do you fight as a warrior or as a novice with insults?"

The keeper lunged forward but balked at the closeness of the sunlight.

"What do you fear, shameless traitor?" Orion taunted.

The keeper snarled hideously. Her fangs dripped in anticipation of feeding. But she did not advance into the light.

"What do you fear, betrayer of your kind?"

The keeper punched her fist into the shaft of morning light, then snapped it back again.

"What . . . do . . . you . . . fear?"

"Nothing!" the keeper shrieked, and as one, the vampires leapt from the darkness and met in the light of the sun.

THIRTY-TWO

S word saw them as dark silhouettes against the crimson disk of the rising sun, their shadows long and ragged across the debris of the control room. And unmoving.

It was as if they had been frozen by the brilliance of the sun, trapped forever within its heat and its fire by the epic passion of their struggle.

Looking closely, he could see the faint tremble of Orion's densely muscled arms as his hands pressed against the equal pressure of the Tepesh keeper's. She trembled, too, each muscle locked in place, refusing to yield.

The sun blazed down on them.

"Can we stop them?" Ko asked, her voice dropped low as if in respect for the magnitude of the conflict she witnessed.

This was not one adept against another, Sword knew, nor even one clan against one clan. This was a battle of honor against expediency, of loyalty against opportunity, of the bright lines of the future against the dark patterns of the past.

"Perhaps we could stop it," Sword answered truthfully. "But we can never stop their fight."

He took Martin's hand and nodded his head at Ko to tell her they should move to the side, away from any chance of involvement.

The sun rose higher and the city woke, and still the vampires remained locked in combat. Sword would hear a sudden grunt, a foot slide, the slap of flesh meeting flesh in a new grip, a new battle.

From the sidelines he could see the toll the fight was taking. On the half of Orion's face that was turned to the sun was the scorched red of raw meat and the skin of his forearm cracked and oozed a clear liquid. But whatever the damage inflicted on Orion, the carnage that was the body of the Tepesh keeper was much worse.

Her perfect skin had blistered in a hundred perfect squares where the sun pierced the pattern of her chainmail shift. Angry fissures on her reddened face ran with blood, mixing with the blood that dripped from her swollen lips where her own fangs had punched through her flesh.

There was life-giving shadow behind each. But neither would yield. The battle would be fought. The battle would be won. One way, or another.

There was another slip and flurry of movement as the vampires sought new purchase and better leverage. Then Orion pulled his arms back, as if yielding the fight, only to hurl himself at the keeper again so that his hands met on either side of her head.

Instantly, the keeper matched his grip.

"Crush," Martin chanted. "Nightfeeders crush crush crush."

But Martin was wrong. Sword saw that Orion was not attempting to squeeze life from the skull of the keeper, he was forcing her head to turn, to face directly into the sun.

Sword could hear the Tepesh keeper's inarticulate cry of agony as the untouched portions of her face came into the light. He saw her hands tremble at the sides of Orion's head as she forced him to turn the same way.

Orion turned.

The keeper almost lost her grip in surprise. Orion turned his full face to the sun and bared his fangs at it and thundered the name of his clan.

"Iiisiiis!"

Sword and Ko and Martin heard that name echo from the few panels of glass that still glinted in the morning sun above.

Sword felt that name reach out across the city and make the buildings shake.

Sword saw that name roar out from the sky and make the sun itself waver in its strength and its beauty.

The keeper opened her mouth. The first sounds of "Tepesh" formed on her bloodied lips, and then as quickly as the streaming shafts of light bored through her, the final breath left her body in a sigh and her head twisted full circle beneath Orion's hands to face behind her with a dull crunch. She deflated like a balloon and her skin shrivelled inward and her shift settled gently on a simple swirl of fine gray dust, caught by the sun and by the gentle morning breeze and by the outstretched empty hand of Orion.

Sword had never seen such power. He had never dreamed of such conflicts. But he realized that what he had witnessed was accepted and true to the First World.

This is the way I must fight now, Sword thought. *With the heart of Orion. With the soul of my clan.*

He watched the vampire stand alone in the sunlight, making no move to leave it. Instead he held his hand to the sun and slowly let the dust of the keeper stream from his fingers to join the other dust of destruction and be lost forever to all the worlds.

Sword watched the vampire, not understanding how he could withstand the sun, not knowing what the effort was costing.

Until the final grain of gray fell from the vampire's hand, and in a hoarse whisper, sadder than any Sword had heard before, Orion spoke a final word to the rising wind.

"Isis."

The wind took that name as it had the dust, and when there was silence again, Sword stepped forward to guide Orion back to the shadows that were his home.

THIRTY-THREE

Safe within shadows, Orion leaned against the wall that disguised the hidden stairway which had brought them to the roof. The damage the sun had caused him only moments ago was almost healed, but Sword could see there was harsher damage still inside, deep in the vampire's soul. It had been a hollow victory.

"It was supposed to have been the Victor," Orion said.

Sword held out his fist to the vampire and Orion met it as an equal. "Next time," Sword said. Then he paused and said, "Or the next."

"Spoken with the patience of a vampire, Mr. Sword."

Sword glanced away to where the morning sky showed through the shattered glass pyramid. Even on the roof of the building, he could hear the sirens from the fire trucks below. There would only be minutes left now.

"Come with me, Mr. Sword."

Sword looked at Martin and Ko beside him. Martin waited expectantly for Sword's decision. Ko didn't seem to care either way. She was too busy examining a small shard of glass from one of the pyramid's broken panes.

Sword shook his head. "I can't. Not now."

Orion frowned. He waved his hand dismissively toward the sky and the sounds of the city. "That is not your world out there."

"I know," Sword said.

"And still you return?"

"When I leave, it will be because I choose to leave. Because I know where I'm going, not because I have to run away."

Orion nodded. "Those legends of the warrior we discussed . . . they say he will leave his world of his freeborn choice . . . but they do not say which world that is." He looked at Sword for a moment, then glanced at the smooth wall beside him.

Sword stepped back so Orion would have room to scale the wall.

"What else do the legends say?" Sword asked.

Orion smiled and this time there were no fangs to be seen. "I am a vampire, Mr. Sword. I do not believe in legends."

He bowed formally to Ko and to Martin, then turned to the smooth wall and leapt up it as quickly as if it had been a ladder. He was gone.

Sword began to walk back to check on Marsh in what was left of the control room when he saw Ko looking at him with bitterness. "There're going to be police waiting for us downstairs. Probably going to arrest us for murdering Ja'Nette."

"I know," Sword said.

"And you're not worried?"

Sword shook his head. "Not anymore, Melody. Not after today." He nodded at Martin and the halfling came over to stand at his side.

But Ko didn't move. "What was so bloody special about today, Sword?"

Sword looked at the ruins of the massive concrete structure. "Look at it, Melody. We stopped them. We—"

"Stopped them? Sword. Roth and Morgana are back. They can—"

"They can what? Their clan is dispersed. They have no crystals." He waved at the enormous wreck before them. "This facility is exposed and useless to them. The blood clinic is closed. The street people are safe again." He put his hand on Martin's shoulder. "Admit it, Melody. It wasn't clean, it wasn't exactly what we wanted, but this time we won."

"Won? Won what?"

Sword shrugged. "Call it a battle. We went up against two First World clans and we won."

Ko folded her arms tightly against herself. "So we won a battle. What do we do now?"

Sword finally smiled. Of all the possible questions she might have asked, that was the one that he could answer.

"Now, we start to fight the war."

ABOUT THE AUTHORS

Judith and Garfield Reeves-Stevens have also written two bestselling Star Trek novels, *Memory Prime* and *Prime Directive*, both of which are based on the original television series, and *Shifter* and *Black Hunter*, the first and third volumes in *The Chronicles of Galen Sword*. On his own, Garfield ('the Tom Clancy of horror' – Stephen King) is the author of the horror/thriller novels *Bloodshift*, *Dreamland*, *Children of the Shroud*, *Nighteyes* and *Dark Matter*.

**Exploring New Realms
in Science Fiction/Fantasy Adventure**

Calling all fantasy fans!

Join the

FANTASY FAN CLUB

for exciting news and fabulous competitions.

For further information write to:

FANTASY FAN CLUB

Penguin Books Ltd.,
Bath Road, Harmondsworth,
Middlesex UB7 0DA

Open only to residents of the UK
and Republic of Ireland